Eagle Bennett

Eagle Bennett

Changers

Cover art by
Sadie "Salty Buns" Caraway

"The Sun rises and sets and time changes" From Tam's Story

Eagle Bennett

Eagle Bennett

Sales of this book without a front cover may be unauthorized. If this book is coverless, it may have been reported to the publisher as "unsold or destroyed" and neither the author nor the publisher may have received payment for it.

Copyright © 2016
All Rights Reserved. Unauthorized reproduction, in any manner, is prohibited.

ISBN: 978-1-48358-942-8

Eagle Bennett

I would like to thank the women in my life that made this book possible:

My grandmother, who introduced me to the fantasy genre and opened up a whole new world for me.

My mother, who encouraged all my dreams my whole life.

Most importantly, my wife of nearly 22 years, who supported encouraged, read and edited all of my early attempts and through it all has always loved me.

Special thanks to my friends, and early readers, Emily and Julia, thanks for the enthusiastic encouragement!

Eagle Bennett

Chapter 1 Kena

Kena shivered and wrapped her arms tightly around her bare shoulders. If she moved any closer to the dying fire she would be in the fire. A big part of her wouldn't mind letting the fire consume her to join the bodies that were all ready ash in its flames. It was still early winter but the snow had all ready started falling, warning of a bad winter in the future. Kena let a tear drop from her face onto the ground. She didn't need the warning the snow brought, she knew it was going to be a horrible winter. The fire that gave her warmth contained the last of her sister and mother. They had died of a fever, a fever that hit quickly and hard. Her sister had survived a week her mother no more than two days.

Kena ignored another tear dropping from her reddish brown eyes tracing a line down her face to drop onto the ground below. There was no one to see her cry so it was safe to do so. If her father saw her tears he would beat her again, but he was not here. The sun was still an hour maybe more before rising and her father, noticing the fever in two of his sons had loaded the wagon and ran for the nearest healer. Kena seethed with anger, completely overriding her grief. She shouldn't be surprised after all, she was a traveler. Travelers counted their women no better than property, a commodity to be bartered and traded, easily replaced when their usefulness ran its course. Now sons, sons were important, important enough to forget all about a daughter, leaving her to die at the funeral pyre of her mother and sister.

Kena glanced behind her at the wagons of her clan, she could just begin to see shadows of movement as the women of the clan began to rise and rekindle fires so breakfast could be cooked before the clan set out for the day. She turned her attention back to the fire and let her mind wander to what she was supposed to do now and how she was going to manage to stay alive. She had no idea how long her father would be gone and the clan would not wait for his return. It was essential they make the trip south before the snow got too deep or they would be trapped in the north where there was no work, which meant no food except for hunting, and winter hunting was problematic at best. No, the clan, with or without her father and brothers, would leave as soon as their fast was broken and the horses hitched. She knew better than to expect help from any of the others in the clan. Oh, they were all related to her through her father in one form or another, but she was female after all and not deserving of assistance from the clan. If her father cared so little for her to take her with him, then the clan would also care so little.

As if her thoughts had awakened it, the sun began to rise in the east casting orange and red light down onto the ground all around her as noises from the camp behind warned her it too, was awake. Kena still hadn't moved when she felt and heard a presence behind her. She didn't need to look up to know it was Leandal. Leandal was her father's half brother and wealthiest clan member due to his eight sons. The clan spent three seasons a year traveling from farm to farm and village to village, trading work for money and goods. The proceeds of that work were divided amongst the clan with each male who had reached the full working age of twelve receiving a full share. Partial shares were given to any male six to twelve. Females received no share, even though they worked right alongside the males doing the exact same work.

Eagle Bennett

Leandal forced her thoughts back to the present. "Where is Kevil, girl? His wagon is missing." he grunted at her. Leandal was small for a traveler male but that did not make him any less intimidating.

Kena struggled to her feet. A female never sat when addressing a male superior. It was a task made hard by the cold, the stiffness of her legs, and the torn and seeping flesh on her back from her most recent whipping at the hands of her father and his belt. Leandal reached out and steadied her. Kena was careful to keep her eyes respectfully down as she answered, "My brother, Jayred, and the baby both showed signs of fever. My father took them in search of a healer." She fought back her anger she didn't think she would survive another beating.

"And left you to die here alone? Kevil is shortsighted as usual. Well, I won't be leaving you here to die, girl, as others may have. My wife can use an extra pair of hands, you can help her to earn your keep. Come on, girl, there is work to do before we can go."

Kena was surprised she had expected to be left behind to survive or die as fate decided, but she covered her surprise and quickly fell in behind Leandal, following him to his own small fire. Six of Leandal's sons were up and dressed and accepting small packets of food from the woman Kena knew was Leandal's wife. Kena was stunned when he spoke to his wife in a kind fashion, not barking or growling orders at her. That was the only way her father or her brothers spoke to women.

Eagle Bennett

"Carla? Seems my idiot brother has left the only thing he owns of real value to die here so he can save his sons from the fever." Carla looked up at her husband, and to Kena's surprise, made eye contact though she didn't speak. "Didn't think you would mind some help and I'm sure we can spare the food."

Carla smiled down at her as she nodded to her husband. "I welcome the company as well." She replied as she handed her husband the same packet of food she had been giving the boys. She handed Kena the same packet as well. When Kena hesitated taking it, Carla smiled, "Go ahead child, you'll have not eaten yesterday. You'll need your strength and I always make a little extra, the boys are always hungry." Kena was shocked not only to be fed, but to be given the same food as the men. Her father and brothers got the best of everything, she and her sister whatever was left when they were done.

Kena accepted the packet with a nod of thanks and sat down near the fire to eat, wincing just a little as she banged a fresh bruise. Inside the cloth wrapped packet was a peeled boiled egg, a hunk of cheese, and a biscuit, still warm. Carla must have risen well before the sun to have baked biscuits this early. Kena had barely taken a bite of the cheese when the final two sons arrived, leading four horses saddled and ready to ride. They each took small sacks from their mother with a word of thanks and growled at two of the other boys who quickly shoved what was left of their breakfast into their mouths, grabbed small sacks themselves, and followed their brothers', mounting their horses.

Eagle Bennett

Leandal nodded at his son's. "It'll just be the four of you riding scout this morning. Kevil's boys are sick. I will have Mokul or Denkin send a couple of sons out as soon as we are ready to leave. I'm sure they will catch you up quickly, and they can use the experience even if they are a bit young for the responsibility."

The boys nodded at their father, but before they could leave their mother spoke up, "Keep your eyes out for game, we have plenty of dried food but the cold larder is nearly empty and you all get mighty testy when you have to live on smoked meats or go without."

Kena carefully kept her expression neutral, but she was shocked. Women did not speak to men this way and women certainly did not give men directions. She waited for the explosion from the boys and the inevitable beating that would come with that explosion.

All the boys smiled at her before the oldest responded. "Of course, Mother, you can count on us. Certainly wouldn't want you to have to put up with nine grumpy men." He turned his horse and trotted him out of the camp before breaking him into a fast gallop followed quickly by his brothers. Kena knew that hunter scouts were sent out before the wagons. It was their job to make sure the way was clear. It was also their responsibility to find tonight's campsite. Certainly not a hard job since the clan and many other clans had traveled these routes for generations. They would also hunt along the route bringing in fresh meat to the clan to be distributed by share to each of the families. Kevil's clan was not the largest of the traveling clans, but with eight families, it was by no means the smallest.

Eagle Bennett

As soon as the boys turned to leave Leandal turned his attention to his wife pulling her away from the fire and having a whispered conversation that ended in a kiss before he headed to take care of one chore or another. Kena acted like she had not noticed the exchange concentrating on her food, eating it quickly. The remaining four boys ate as quickly as her, then got busy hitching the horses to the wagons. Leandal's family drove four wagons, the most in this clan, one for each son that had reached eighteen and would be looking for a wife at the spring gathering of the clans. If they were lucky enough to strike a deal with a girl's father they would take their wagon and become the male head of their own family. Kena's oldest brother would soon be getting his own wagon his eighteenth birthday having passed late summer. Kevson couldn't wait to take a wife, Leanson, Alsel, and Tryp, Leandal's oldest sons, had elected to build their wealth for a few years before taking on a family. It seemed to Kena that was the smarter way to go. Having their own wealth would allow them to have more choice of wives.

Carla motioned to Kena who quickly rose and went to her. "Ah, child, one look in your eyes and I can tell how little sleep you have had these past days. There will be little rest for you when your father and brothers rejoin the clan. You will be responsible for everything a full grown woman would have to do. Neither I nor Leandal think Kevil will return for a few days, so this morning it will be safe enough for you to sleep and this afternoon I will begin teaching you things your own mother would not have as yet had time to teach you." Carla turned her attention to Leandal's instruction for his younger sons.

"Timbult, you will work with Cash, driving the second wagon. He still isn't as good as he needs to be and that leaves you, Marlin, to drive the third, and Dax, the trail wagon."

Carla turned back to Kena. "Good, you will sleep in the back of the second wagon. Timbult is the smoothest of drivers, when we stop for the noon meal you can safely transfer to the first where I will be working." Kena glanced at Leandal. Girls were to walk alongside the wagons unless they had work that had to be done inside one. Girls never slept in a wagon they slept under it if they were lucky. If a family had many boys the girls found beds where ever they could. "Don't worry child, Leandal doesn't subscribe to your father and some of the other more strict males' belief about women. He will have no problem with you getting some rest. If you don't, you will sicken too. He may act gruff to maintain appearance but he is kind hearted. He would never want you to suffer if he could prevent it and he can prevent it at least while your father is away. So go get some sleep and I will see you at noon meal." Kena followed her instruction and was surprised when Timbult or maybe it was Cash actually assisted her into the wagon before raising and stowing the steps. Clearly Leandal taught his sons his beliefs.

She found what was clearly an unused bed and fell into it, kicking her shoes off. She had planned to stay awake and think about everything that had happened but the softness of the bed, the first bed she had ever slept in, made that impossible. She didn't even awaken when the wagon lurched into motion.

Kena startled awake when the wagon stopped. She quickly rolled out of bed and out the door nearly falling as the steps had not been lowered yet. Cash smiled at her as she jumped out without use of the stairs and headed for the lead wagon to help with the noon meal. Leandal had lowered the stairs and Kena hurried in before he could be mad that she had been idle all morning. Carla was making up little packets of food again. These included two slices of carved poultry, a slice of cheese, two rolls, and a red fruit. Kena quickly went to work, not needing instructions.

"Good morning child or really good afternoon. Thanks for the help. We'll make up two packets each for the younger boys. They're growing and always hungry. The packets stow easily enough for an afternoon snack."

Kena nodded. They were done before Leandal had finished with the horses and peeked his head in the wagon looking for his food. Carla tossed him his meal and he disappeared with a smile of thanks. One by one the boys came in and were handed the same packet as their father, only they took two each, and disappeared back to their own mid-day chores. Kena helped Carla clean everything up before the two of them sat down to a quick bite of their own. The poultry had been nicely spiced and seemed to melt in her mouth. She had never had meat that tasted so good. The meat she usually got was tough and tasteless. She usually skipped it as inedible, preferring to gather her own edibles in the evening while she gathered wood.

"It's slow roasted that's why it isn't tough. I will teach you how to do it, but the spices I use are expensive and Kevil will never waste money on them." Carla told her noticing her enjoyment of the meal. "Well child let's get to work, you have a lot to learn and I have no idea how long I will have to teach you." Carla rose and put a companionable hand on Kena's back causing her to wince. "What is it child?" Carla asked as she pulled Kena's tunic up to see her welt covered back, still seeping blood. "My goodness child, no need to ask who, but why did Kevil do this?"

Kena hung her head in shame. "I was whipped for crying for being beaten and beaten for crying for my mother."

"Oh child I am so sorry. Let me treat those welts. I have a balm that will help ease the pain and prevent infection. Take that tunic off so I can get at them. I'll be as gentle as I can but it's going to hurt." Carla talked the entire time she was working keeping Kena's mind of the pain. "It amazes me that two men raised by the same father can be so different. Leandal would never beat one of the boys. Oh I know boys are too valuable to take a risk like that with, but Leandal wouldn't beat a daughter if we had been gifted one. Anyway child for your own sake you must learn to keep all your feelings locked inside. To the world you show a blank face. I know it's going to be hard. My father was very like Kevil, quick with his fist, faster with his belt. Like you I have my own set of scars, but like me you can survive if you're careful. Just remember all your thoughts and feelings must be kept inside hidden from the world, it is the only way you can protect yourself. " Kena said nothing but listened to everything and took every word to heart.

Kena trailed behind the lead wagon walking beside Carla. It had been nearly a week since Kena's father and brothers had left, longer than even Leandal had figured. The clan had simply moved on more than willing it seemed to follow the more even tempered Leandal. As the days went by, Kena feared Kevil and her brothers were dead and Leandal would reverse himself and abandon her. Surprisingly it was Leandal's oldest son, Leanson, who put her mind at ease on that score.

"Father always wanted a daughter. Perhaps he will still get one, mother is still young enough, but he would still welcome you as his. I guarantee he will find you a better husband than Kevil will and neither he nor any of us would ever abuse you as your family has."

Kena learned everything she could from Carla who was patient and willing. Kena was sure she could at least keep her father and brothers happy and perhaps avoid a beating for inadequacy. Kena remembered how many times her mother had appeared with black eyes and bruises. Carla had warned her that Kevil was quick with his fist and judgmental. The best way to survive was to be out of his sight and never draw his attention. A noise from the back of the wagon train brought Kena's thoughts up short. Kena knew it was the sound of a wagon coming on fast. Kena nearly cried, she had honestly hoped they were dead and she would be able to stay with Carla and Leandal.

Carla turned to Kena putting a hand on her shoulder. "Remember Kena, become as invisible as possible, control your feelings, never let them show, and do not make him angry. If you need anything you are always welcome at our fire. Leandal and the boys will do what they can for you."

Kena nodded and as her father's wagon passed her Kena obediently jogged to her place trailing behind her

Eagle Bennett

father's wagon walking alone head down and mouth shut concentrating on keeping every thought and feeling controlled and hidden.

Chapter 2 Sami

Sami concentrated hard on the log in front of her. Scraping the bark off and cutting the notches was hard and if she wasn't careful it could lead to missing fingers. She and her brother Ty were improving the shelter they used when they were hunting. Ty was out trying to secure them some fresh meat for dinner. She had drawn cooking duties for the first night of their trip. Her parents had allowed them a full week this time deciding they were old enough and capable enough now to be on their own for a little while. Sami glanced over at the fire place. It was the first improvement they had made turning their childhood fort into a hunting lodge. She and Ty had traded work for the brick and mortar and in the process gained the knowledge they needed to build the fireplace they wanted. The pot of water was boiling away just like she wanted. Ty was better with a sling than a bow so was more likely to bring home a bird for dinner. By having the water boiling before he got home she could get to plucking that much faster. Ty had been gone about an hour and should be back anytime if his hunt was at all lucky. Sami turned her attention back to the long log she was working on. The main reason for this trip was about working on the hut not on hunting and she needed to get this done. The only way they could safely hunt in the winter was to have a warm secure shelter near where they needed to hunt.

Sami found the scraping and cutting relaxing, and she was just starting to build a rhythm when she heard Ty

Eagle Bennett
call for her as he jogged up the path. She quickly
dropped what she was doing to go meet him. She knew
how lucky she was to have a brother like Ty. He was
her best friend and the only person she could share all
her secrets with.

Ty burst in the door holding two geese by their webbed
feet. "Had good luck at the little pond, a whole flock of
geese heading south had just landed to rest. Got two
before they spooked." He was justifiably proud.
"Head shots so I didn't bruise the meat."

Sami smiled at her brother, "Ty that's great. We'll spit
one for dinner and I will boil the other up for soup
tomorrow. We won't have to take time away from
building to hunt. Here I'll get them cleaned and cooked
you take over working on the logs."

"Sure, you cook today and tomorrow and I will take the
next two days. After two days of goose I'll be ready
for some red meat. With the early chill in the air all the
animals are moving about getting ready for winter.
Shouldn't be too hard to keep us fed." Ty ,

Ty had finished all three of the logs they needed for the
corners of the new room by the time the goose was
cooked. Sami fried up some tubers and onions while
she turned the spit and added some edible greens tossed
in a sweet nut oil to complete the meal. Ty, like their
father, was actually the better cook, but she did okay
with simple hearty fare. They sat on the floor to eat
since the only furniture in the hut was their beds. They
had talked about adding some more homey touches, but
they just hadn't had the time to build what they wanted.

Eagle Bennett

"You're cooking improves big sister, you may be able to attract a husband yet." Ty teased. Sami tossed a piece of onion at her brother. He knew full well she had no interest in men. "Speaking of that, I saw you admiring the potter's new apprentice. I have to admit she is sort of pleasing to the eye."

Sami and her brother had similar taste in women, "No, I don't think anyone could deny that, but I think she is more your type than mine. She's a little too much of a princess for me. I like my girls to, I don't know, not be afraid to get their hands dirty."

Ty smiled knowingly at his sister, they both wanted the same thing, a relationship like their parents had, a full partnership. Their parents owned a fabric shop in the village center. Customers came from miles around for the fabrics they made. "Sami when are you going to admit to mom and dad that you're not interested in getting married?"

"Ty, Dad has been talking about grandchildren since we were old enough to know where children came from. I just can't seem to bring myself to disappoint him. I've tried like a million times, but I just can't seem to do it besides avoiding the conversation all together is much easier."

"You know he won't care, nor will mom. They just want us to be happy. It's why they encourage these little jaunts of ours and why they don't want us to work in the shop. What are you going to do when dad starts parading eligible boys in front of you? At sixteen you're nearly of age."

"Easy," Sami joked rising to clean up dinner, "deflect, disappear and look to my baby brother to protect me."

Ty joined her helping with the clean up, "I can do that." He told her with a smile and a quick hug knowing he would do anything for her even stand between her and any beaus his father found. Even standing between her and their parents if need be.

The snow was falling in earnest as Sami and Ty rode home. It had been a fruitful and fun week. They had finished the additional room on the hut, got the entire hut sealed against winter, laid in emergency food supplies, and even found some time to hunt. They were returning home with enough meat to last the family several weeks. They herded the sheep in from the far field saving their father the chore. The goats had already made their way to shelter, but the sheep weren't smart enough to come in from the cold on their own. The goat, sheep and two horses were the only animals they had on their little farm. They kept the livestock for their wool. It was cheaper to raise the animals than buy the raw wool to weave for the shop. They also had a large garden where they grew several kinds of fibrous plants. Between their father's ability to spin and mothers ability to weave the shop was kept well stocked.

Ty took the horses to the stable while Sami took their provender to the cellar. Neither of their parents were home from the shop yet, but that wasn't surprising. The first snow always brought more business as the villagers looked to make cloaks, scarves and gloves before the bitter cold of winter.

Eagle Bennett

By the time their parents returned from the shop, Sami and Ty had refilled the water cisterns in the kitchen and bath, prepared dinner, eaten and cleaned up leaving plates for both parents near the heat of the kitchen fire and were relaxing by the fireplace.

It was their mother who joined them first, "Welcome home! Hope your trip was fruitful. Thanks for taking care of the chores tonight, your father and I are exhausted. The shop was brutally busy."

"Ty cooked so the food should actually taste good." Sami told her mother as she moved behind her so she could rub her shoulders. "We can help in the shop till things calm down if you want."

"Ahh, Sami that feels great. Your father and I will take the help, but only until it slows down. We want you two to enjoy being young, not slaving in the shop. You only have, at most, a few more years left to be young."

It was Ty who answered. "But it's our family's shop, we should help more. We should be learning more about the business."

Their father entered the room carrying the two plates, handing one to his wife. "Why? Just because your mother and I have a craft we love and are good at doesn't mean our children will have the same talent and loves. I can't hit the broad side of a barn with an arrow or get the stone to fly out of a sling, yet you two keep the family fed. Can you honestly tell me you would be happy sitting inside all day, every day, spinning or weaving? Your mom and I appreciate both of your dedication to the family and while we will accept your help in the short term, in the long term we want you to find your own way and your own loves. As long as you are happy we will be happy."

Ty and Sami both knew when not to push their father and wisely changed the subject to their little hut and the great hunting the area around it provided, but they carefully failed to mention where it was located wanting to keep the hut the one place that was just theirs.

Sami watched the snow falling through her window. She should be asleep but she couldn't seem to convince her head of that. Winter had come early, hard and fast this year. Hunting had been nearly impossible and she and Ty were going stir crazy. It was a problem she knew many kids her age wished they had. Sami had gone with her father on a trip to Fringle last summer. It was the first time she had encountered slaves. Some of the slaves she saw working in the fields couldn't have been older than 12. Her father had told her children younger than that worked in the house. Her father was disgusted the king would allow such things. On the other hand, why should they be surprised by the king's actions? The kings concerns centered on his wants and enjoyment and didn't extend to the condition of his people. The king was an evil man who truly enjoyed inflicting cruelties onto others and reveled in his power over the people. Ty and Sami had once thought to become soldiers, but the thought of swearing loyalty to such a man sickened them both.

She rolled over to face away from the window trying hard to shut her mind down. If the snow would just let up a little she and Ty could take a hunting trip to the hut, or even possibly take a load of fabric into the surrounding villages in trade, anything to get out of this house. Ty was as stir crazy as she was. He had spent hours trying to dig out an area big enough so they could at least get in some bow and arrow practice. It was no use the snow was falling too hard and he was forced to concede. It was so bad her parents hadn't even been able to go into the shop. It was a lost cause her mind was running at full gallop and she knew enough to surrender when you were fighting a losing battle. She threw on yesterday's clothes and wandered to the kitchen to heat water for tea and maybe to throw some breakfast together. She had just got the fire lit in the little stove when her father came into the kitchen startling her.

"Good morning Sami, I know you're an early riser but this is a tad early even for you." Her father teased as he opened the tea jar. He had heard her in the kitchen and decided to take the opportunity to broach a subject he and his wife had just been discussing. Tobias knew his daughter was the key, Ty went where his sister led. So he just needed to get Sami to like the plan.

"Couldn't sleep. You?"

Her father turned his young handsome face to her. Even after nearly twenty years of marriage he still maintained his youthful looks. Both Ty and Sami resembled their father, light hair round youthful face. Sami had inherited her mother's green eyes while Ty had dark brown eyes with flecks of red that were as expressive as his face. "Me neither," he answered as he scooped tea into the pot and grabbed a couple of rolls left from dinner and the pot of honey putting them on the table. "Being snowed in here is starting to drive me a little bit crazy. I find my hands itching for something to do."

Sami added some slices of red fruit to her father's gleanings on the table and sat down. "I think that was my problem. I feel a little trapped when I have to stay inside so much."

"I understand. You and your brother both need to be active to be happy." Tobias nearly choked when Sami gave him exactly the opening he needed, "Maybe next summer you should take an apprenticeship with the rangers. Most people would find it a hard and miserable life, but I think it would appeal to you. If it doesn't, you can always come home."

Sami had never considered joining the rangers. Unlike the army, the rangers were not associated or loyal to the king. They had been formed long before the monarchy, even before this land was one country. Legends said the rangers were formed to protect people from the ancient beasts that roamed the world, but like most legends it was a little unbelievable. Now they were the protectors of the land. Their numbers had dwindled as, like her father said, it was not an easy life with little or no glory to gain, but it would suit her and Ty both. Rangers lived on horseback never staying in one place for any length of time. Hunting and gathering for your day to day food as they patrolled the wilderness for poachers and trespassers. She liked the idea. She couldn't actually think of anything she would like more, "Do you think they would take me?" She asked her father as she spread honey on a roll.

"I don't see why not. You ride well enough and you're a dead shot with your bow. You're smart, resourceful, and very able to take care of yourself. So I think they would be happy to take you on, probably your brother too. He'll be sixteen in a few months making him old enough for an apprenticeship as well."

Sami warmed to the idea, especially if Ty would be with her. "Could we afford the horses we would need? Rangers have to join with two each?"

"Yes, I think we can swing it. I have some credit with a couple local breeders. Sami, it would also give you more opportunity to find someone you might like. The rangers travel the entire country. You might find the kind of person you're looking for." Tobias tried to carefully phrase the last statement. He and his wife were fully aware that Sami had no interest in men at all and it really didn't matter. There were some cultures that would look down on such things, the traveler clans for one, but then the traveler clans had a backward view of women in general. He and his wife wanted nothing more than Sami to be happy, if that was with a woman for a partner, then so be it. It was hard to convince Sami of that though, when she wouldn't admit it to him or his wife. For some reason Sami had convinced herself that her parents wanted her to settle down and marry young, which couldn't be farther from the truth, but nothing had been able to sway Sami from that belief, not even out right telling her. Sami, like most sixteen year olds, heard what she wanted to hear not necessarily what was said, but her good qualities more than made up for this one little foible of youth.

"Yeah maybe," Sami answered and was saved from any more uncomfortable conversation by her mother's entrance. "Good morning mom," she said rising to kiss her mother on the cheek. "I think since the snow is too heavy to go out I might go lay back down." Sami made a hasty retreat.

"Sorry," Gwyn whispered to her husband as he took her into a hug. "I didn't mean to break up your conversation."

"You didn't. Sami was going to bolt one way or another you just gave her the opportunity she was looking for. I was pushing, I should have known better."

"Tobias she will tell us when she is ready. Right now she has convinced herself you will be disappointed in her if she allows herself to be who she is. It's not like she isn't sharing with Ty. As long as she has someone to confide in she'll be fine and we should let her be. You know full and well Ty would never let anything or anyone hurt his sister, not that she needs any ones protection, including ours. She is a fully capable of taking care of herself."

"I know." Tobias paused as he considered his wife's words. "She did seem open to joining the rangers. I agree with you it could be the perfect fit for both of them. I don't however think she will go if Ty doesn't." Tobias poured his wife a cup of tea. "The two of them are thick as thieves."

"Having them both leave at the same time will be hard, but knowing they're together will help. They are close and that's why you don't have to worry about Sami. I know you just want her to have support, but she does have it. Ty would do anything for his sister and her for Ty." Gwyn moved over next to her husband and put her hand on his shoulder. She was desperate to make him understand. It was always hard for a man to realize his little girl was a woman and no longer needed her daddy. "Don't worry, they will be fine." Gwyn leaned in close and kissed her husband's neck. "Doesn't look like the snow is letting up anytime soon, I guess were stuck here again." Her words said one thing her tone and actions said another as she took her husband's hand leading him back to bed where she had every intention of making him forget about the problem of their children at least for a little while.

Chapter 3 Kena

Kena found herself once again, thankfully, alone at her family's fire. She was lost in the intricacy of the dancing flames. It had not been an easy winter. She never seemed to do anything right. No matter how hard she tried her father and brothers found fault in everything she did. Kena could only imagine how hard it would have been had the baby survived the fever or without Carla's continued help and training. The very first day her father had returned he had dropped two squirrels at her feet. "Clean and cook 'em." was all he said as he swaggered off. If it hadn't been for Carla's training she would have no idea how to do that. Carla knew her father would not consider her a girl anymore expecting her to do all the work his wife had done as well as everything she and her sister were responsible for. Carla couldn't help with the work load, but she could teach her the easiest and fastest ways to get it all done.

Well, somehow, Kena had survived the winter by never speaking and keeping her head down. She had even heard her father telling one of the other men that he thought she must have had the fever and it addled her brains, but she did the work and there were men who would have her preferring a dumb mute to a woman who could offer an opinion. Kena had ignored the comment, knowing full well her mind was whole and planning her escape.

She had learned quickly of her father's plan to trade her for a new wife rather than waste hard earned goods. By traveler clan law Kena was too young for marriage and would remain so for another two years. She had barely reached her sixteenth birthday, but there were men who would ignore the law. Leandal had argued against the idea, but had been ignored by her father. It was Cash who had made a point of warning her of the plan being heartily disgusted by the whole thing. Kena had no intention of willingly becoming the child bride of some old man. Ever since she had been plotting and planning her escape. By clan law she was not a slave. She had the right to leave the clan at any time, but as a female she owned nothing but the clothes on her back. If she had left the clan at the start of winter she would have starved, so instead she had planned and learned. She had learned from Leandal and his sons how to build fish traps, how to make a bow and how to fletch arrows. They had shown her the basics on using them as well. Cash had taught her how to use the stars to navigate, and Tryp had shown her the basics of building a shelter. Carla made sure she had some basic healing knowledge as well as sewing, cooking, cleaning and a million other homey things. They had even taught her to twine rope out of the strong vines that grew along the roadside and use it to make traps. Kena was sure she knew enough to keep herself alive now.

Eagle Bennett

She had secreted away two knives, a ball of twine, a couple of small candles, a canteen with a slow leak, and a few pieces of dried meat and vegetables. Now she just needed an opportunity to disappear. She could simply announce her plan in front of all and walk away, but then she could not take anything with her. However if she disappeared they would think she was killed by some predator or another and she could take her carefully stolen hoard with her.

A noise from a campfire on the other side of camp caught her attention and she looked up. She carefully did not look over at the fire if it happened to be a fire her father or brothers were at she would be beat for looking. She diverted her gaze to the cliff face the wagons were camped against. It was only then she noticed what looked like a small cave. They had camped here many times and she didn't remember a cave. Of course it looked small the entrance no bigger than a person and certainly not big enough to provide shelter for the clan. It could also be no more than a shadow, but Kena had to get a closer look, this could just be what she was looking for. Rising, she wandered outside the circle of wagons picking up loose wood. She looked to anyone who might notice her as if she was simply gathering more food for the fire. She carefully planned her wandering to leave her near that shadow that could be a cave. She was surprised to find it was indeed a cave, it felt a little too good be true, but she wasn't inclined to refuse the gift.

Kena looked into it as much as she could without drawing attention to herself. It was pitch black but it seemed deep enough to hide in until the clan departed. Kena forced herself to relax she meandered away from the cave back to her fire where she stacked up the gathered wood. She ducked behind the curtains under the wagon to her sleeping area and grabbed her old warm cloak. It was chilly out and no one would think anything of that. She shouldered the small bag full of her carefully gathered hoard placing it in the small of her back then put her cloak on concealing it. She crawled out and wandered back out of the circle of wagons. She again began gathering more wood slowly making her way back to the small cave. Along the way she stopped to pick up a long straight stick. When she got to the cave she didn't hesitate she just walked in until she was swallowed by the dark there she stopped giving her eyes time to adjust. She dropped the wood and using some of her twine she bound up a small bunch of it. Kena grabbed her long stick and using it to feel her way she carefully moved deeper into the cave.

Kena felt like she had been walking for hours and it may have been it was hard to tell in the darkness. Her progress was slow as she carefully felt her way deeper into the cave. Until she was sure she was deep enough that a fire wouldn't be spotted she didn't dare stop. Suddenly her stick hit something hard. She reached out her hand and felt the stone wall at the end of the cave. She felt around and found emptiness to the right and adjusted her measured steps in that direction. She moved several feet down the right hand corridor then stopped. She could stay here and wait until the clan gave up looking for her and moved on, but something inside her warned her to continue moving deeper into the cave that safety could be found there. She couldn't however keep going like this she needed light. She reached into her pack and pulled out the flint and a knife. She peeled off bark and mixed it with the twine she had used to bind the wood and with a couple of careful swipes she soon had a small fire going on the sandy floor. Kena carefully placed a few of her sticks onto the fire to keep it going then stuck the end of her long stick into it until it caught. It was a crude torch but it would work saving her candles. Holding the torch she extinguished the fire stood up and looked around. The cave was more tunnel than cave and seemed to go deep into the mountain. Well she certainly would be less likely to be discovered the deeper she went. No one would think she would have the courage to travel deep into a dark cave and few would think she was smart enough to make a torch. She grabbed up her pack and the remaining wood and quickly moved deeper into the cave tunnel.

The cave was truly more like a tunnel, other than the one turn it continued straight with no bends or turns. The tunnel itself was large enough for a horse, but certainly not large enough for a wagon. It would however make very good shelter as well as a place to hide for her. The clans didn't come this way often in fact most of the clans avoided this valley. Strange things happened here and many attributed the events to ghosts or demons. Kevil had never believed such things and as far as Kena knew nothing odd had ever happened to her clan, well not her clan anymore. She had made her choice for good or bad, at least it was her choice and not one made for her. Kena tripped a little on the uneven ground and forcefully pulled her attention back to what she was doing, the last thing she needed was a broken leg. Paying better attention to where she put her feet she continued to move deeper into the tunnel that inner voice pushing her on.

Kena couldn't tell how long she had been walking. In the darkness of the tunnel time seemed to stop. Her torch had barely burned however so it couldn't be as long as she felt. She was sure she had to be deep inside the mountain. She stopped and moistened her lips with her tongue. The only sound she could hear was the trickle of water. She was shocked straight ahead of her was a light, bright and golden. It made no sense, yes she had been walking deep into the tunnel but there is no way she could have traversed the entirety of the mountain. The light could not be coming from the sun or the moon. Every part of her being said run away, but that strange inner voice told her no that here was safety. Here she could shelter and live without fear. Kena didn't know why she listened to that inner voice but with hesitant steps she moved toward the light and into an enormous open cavern and in the center of the cavern was a huge beast. Kena stood transfixed, she had walked right into his trap and now she was nothing more than its dinner.

Kevil was angry when he walked out of his wagon to find a cold reception. Where was that useless girl? Why hadn't she started the fire and gotten breakfast ready? That was her job was she incapable now of doing even the simplest things. With a growl he roused his youngest son, Jayred "Go wake your sister tell her make breakfast and for her laziness she can do without food for the day."

The boy hurried to do as he was asked while Kevil stirred the hot coals of last night's fire into life and added wood till he had a pleasant little fire. He turned at the sound of someone coming up behind him prepared to chastise his lazy stupid daughter only to find his son alone. "I'm sorry father she's not there. "

Kevil's anger boiled over "What do you mean she's not there? Where could she have gone? Wake your brother, search the camp." The boys were quick to do as they were bid. Kevil's bellowing had awakened the rest of the camp and many of the men were assembling near his site hoping for an explanation. Kevil ignored them for the moment and paced around his own wagon looking for any sign of the girl or missing items. By the time Kevil had established nothing but the girl was missing his sons had returned.

"She is nowhere in the camp father and none of the other women have seen her since last night. Several saw her gathering wood just outside of camp."

Kevil nodded perhaps she had simply fallen and hurt herself. "Go search the woods for her." The boys hurried to follow their orders and Kevil for the first time acknowledged the gathering of the clan's men. "All of you, Kena is missing. I want you to send your sons into the woods to look for her." The men dispersed to do as they were directed only Leandal remained.

"How much time will we waste looking for a simple girl?" Leandal asked rather bravely considering Kevil's mood. He knew Kena wasn't just missing. All winter, Kena had spent all her free time at his family's fire, partly to learn from Carla, but Leandal also knew it was to learn other things and he and his sons were all too willing to oblige her. It was one of the few things they had been able to do for her, and he was now sure she could survive on her own. Every time he saw her this winter she had new bruises, and her back was a criss-cross of scars and new welts. Worse yet the man Kevil planned to trade her to was possibly worse than Kevil, an evil man made bitter by his inability to father sons. His wives died young; used, abused, and discarded.

"As long as we need to, she is promised in trade for me a new wife." Kevil all but growled as he rounded on his half brother.

Leandal nodded in respect, but did not leave off, "Of course, but if she is not hurt and has chosen to leave you have no right to force her back unless she has stolen from you. Is anything missing?"

It took everything in Kevil not to beat his half brother to a bloody pulp for stating what he al eady knew. If Leandal weren't his brother or the wealthiest most respected clan member he may have done just that, instead he answered his question, "NO nothing is missing, if she left, she left with no more than the clothes on her back as is allowed."

Leandal knew he had won the argument, "Then…"

"Then," Kevil cut him off "if she is not found hurt somewhere quickly we will move on and I will find some other way to buy a wife."

Leandal nodded and backed away from his fuming brother hiding the smile and hurrying to share the news that Kena had indeed escaped with his family and to make sure his sons didn't look too hard.

Chapter 4 Sami

Sami was thrilled beyond measure to see the sun. She and Ty were riding the fence line of their property looking for any damage the deep winter snows may have caused. The lambing season was fast approaching and holes in the fence would be dangerous. After the long winter it felt good to be out riding in the warm spring sun. Piles of snow still dotted the landscape while the early flowers were starting to bloom. Sami took a deep breath relishing the fresh air.

Ty looked over at his sister and smiled, he felt the same way. It felt so good to be out of the trap their little house had become all winter. "If it all plays out right, next winter we may miss the warm little trap and soft beds. You know the rangers work all year. We'll be camping out even in the winter."

The thought sent an unexpected chill down Sami's spine. Ever since her father had suggested it and she had shared the idea with Ty it was all either of them could think or talk about. Her father had sent messages to contacts he had and a group of four rangers had appeared on their doorstep in between blizzards. Both she and Ty had been asked some pretty pointed and personal questions then asked to prove their abilities with their bows but by the time the group left they had both been offered apprenticeships. Ranger Oak had been thrilled to be able to take Sami under her wing and her partner Egan had been more than willing to take Ty making it possible for the siblings to stay together. They promised to return in early summer and to be ready to go. Her parents had already made arrangements to buy the horses they would need as well as obtaining other essential items.

"Come back to me big sister, I seem to have lost you to your thoughts." Ty called over to her. "We need to get this done. Who do you think is going to do this when were gone?"

Sami was confused by the question, "Do what, ride the fence?"

"No dummy, take care of the livestock and the farm. We've been doing it since what you were six and I was five. Do you think mom and dad will have time when we are gone?"

"Dad said they're thinking of selling the sheep since they need the most care and just keeping the goats. It's the goat's wool everyone wants anyway and it takes and experienced spinner to make it into thread strong enough to use. I'm glad father showed me how, but I won't miss doing it that's for sure. Anyway with just the goats he should have time. He's a good deal more worried about the garden without us here to keep it weeded and watered all summer. Worse he hasn't been able to find a local supplier of most of the plants. We don't do a huge business in the threads and ropes he makes from them but the village and travelers will miss it all the same."

"I hadn't thought of the garden, maybe he could hire a local child to take care of it. I'm sure he could find one to work for fabric, yarn and threads for their family. I'll suggest it at dinner tonight."

It was a good idea and Sami told him so, "Well, that's the last of the outer fence and we know the inner fence is fine so we are done. I'll race you home." Sami looked over to see the competitive light in her brothers dark brown eyes and knew he was up for the challenge, "On go, one, two, three… go!"

Eagle Bennett

They were surprised to find both parents home when they returned. Closing the shop this early usually meant trouble for someone. They hurried through the care of the horses and ran to the house.

"Father, why are you home?" They were calling in unison as they entered the house.

"Relax, I received a message from Oak, she and Egan will be here to retrieve the two of you by the end of the week. It seems they need to move on sooner than they had planned and may not have time to come back for you so you must go now or not at all."

Sami looked at her brother and knew he was feeling the same mix of nerves and excitement she was.

"So your mother and I decided since the weather is so nice we would have one last family outing in the morning. I was thinking a picnic maybe out by the lake. We haven't been in a while. So we came home early to get everything ready. We'll take the cart, hope you didn't wear the horses out too much."

"They'll be fine," Ty answered warming to the idea. "It's a great idea."

The whole family was up before the light. Ty and Sami had the horses hitched and ready by the time it was light enough to leave. They all climbed into the cart for the long ride to the lake. The time flew by as Tobias regaled them with stories of the ancients. They spent the entire day fishing, playing tag, hide and track, and a myriad of other games. The weather was uncommonly warm, but no one thought anything about it. It was nearly dark by the time they all piled back into the cart for the return trip home. The events of the day along with the warmth of the evening combined to send both Ty and Sami to sleep early into the trip home.

Tobias urged the horses to greater speed trying desperately to get the tired beasts to add speed. The weather had turned and a storm was brewing up behind them. Tobias knew it was going to be bad, and they needed to get home before it hit. He could hear the wind howling behind him and lightning lit up the sky in front of him. Thunder roared across the sky as fat rain drops began hitting the road all around him. They were almost home they just needed another few minutes. It was minutes he wasn't going to get. Lightning struck just to the right of the road and the horses spooked. They broke into a hard gallop off the road to the left. Tobias tried everything he could to get them to stop or turn, but their fear was far too great. The reigns broke just before the hitch shattered. The cart flew into the air and rolled and that was the last thing he remembered.

Sami woke face down in mud. She remembered waking to the sound of thunder and her father yelling before being launched into the air. She had no idea how long she was out cold, all she knew was that she had to find her family. It wasn't hard to locate the wreckage and her father. He was unconscious and trapped half under the cart. She called for Ty and her mother but got no answer. She tried to look but it was so dark and the rain so heavy it was nearly impossible. She turned her attention to the cart that had come to a rest completely upside down. Part of her knew, just knew where they were going to find Ty and her mother, but she refused to think about that right now. She knew for sure her father was still alive and she needed to get the cart off him. Her efforts were in vain, she just didn't have the strength or leverage to get it to roll. She needed help. Thankfully the village wasn't far, Sami tried one last time to wake her father, but when she failed she took off running as fast as she ever had to the village and help.

The whole village turned out to assist. Her parents were very popular. When they were finally able to flip the cart off of Tobias they made the unfortunate discovery both Ty and her mother had died crushed under the cart. Sami was relatively unhurt only because she had been thrown free from the wagon. Her father had been badly injured. His hands were broken and mangled from fighting the reigns and he had broken ribs that were pressing on his lungs making it hard to breath. Getting Tobias somewhere warm and dry and into the hands of the healers had to take priority over the bodies of the dead.

Sami seemed to be living in a daze. Warm coats and blankets were thrust at her from every angle and she accepted one at random. She stared at the mangled bodies of her mother and brother barely aware of anything else going on around her. She may have known intellectually that they were dead but to see and actually know was almost too much to bear. She heard the wagon her father was in slowly start moving back towards the village and the healer and part of her realized she should be with him, but she couldn't bring herself to leave. Most of the people who had come to help were starting to leave only a handful of men and one wagon stayed behind. Sami watched as they respectfully removed each of the mangled bodies from the muddy field, wrapped it in a blanket, and placed it in the wagon. It was the big smith that guided her to the seat of the wagon making sure she was safely settled before he gently put his horses on the road back to the village.

Chapter 5 Tamaloc

Kena had walked right into the beasts trap. She stared frozen in terror where she stood. Well at least it would be a quick death as she was devoured, she thought as she sized up the beast in front of her. Calling it huge seemed to diminish it somehow. It was more than huge. Its muzzle was as large as the draft horses that pulled the wagons and full of large white teeth. She forced herself to look away from the teeth and saw the silver green eyes that were as round as she was tall. The eyes were set in a head that was as black as night itself. Its body was covered in dark black scales that turned to gray green on its belly and wing tips. It had a long black scaled tail that ended in two sharp looking spikes. The tail wrapped around its prone body and twitched occasionally grabbing Kena's attention. She nearly died from fright before she could be eaten when the beast spoke to her.

"I will not harm you child of the ancients. You are safe here, far safer than you have ever been in your life. I would not eat you even if I had the strength left to do so. You have nothing to fear from me."

Kena forced her breathing to return to normal and tried to slow her beating heart. She looked more closely at the beast and realized its black scales were dull with age and weakness. Its eyes were cloudy with pain. Its neck trembled with the effort to even have its head raised to look at her. Kena didn't know or understand why, but she felt profoundly sorry for this beast. "Please sir," Kena replied, "please lay your head back down. I apologize for my rudeness in barging into your chamber. I was looking for a safe place to hide from my kin and stumbled upon this place." The beast seemed to laugh. It was a guttural sound more like thunder, but Kena was sure somehow it was meant as laughter.

"I will do so if you will come closer so I can see you with out my head raised. I promise I will not hurt you." Some how Kena believed him and as he laid his head back down on his fore arms she moved so she was sitting in front of his long muzzle. "Thank you," It replied. "It was getting very hard for me."

Kena couldn't help her curiosity. It had always gotten her in trouble as a child, girl children were not meant to be curious that was reserved for boys. Girls were meant to follow orders. "I'm sorry sir, but will you tell me please what are you?"

"I do not mind telling you child, in fact I am glad you are willing to talk to me and ask me questions, I am afraid in my current state of weakness you are more of a threat to me than I am to you. I am a dragon one of the ancients of this world."

"Ancient? What is an ancient?" Kena again asked interrupting even though she was afraid of being again in trouble for asking questions.

"You never need worry about asking questions here child. I welcome the opportunity to answer your curiosity, how else can you learn?" Again he laughed and Kena found herself answering that laugh, "Ancients ruled this world before the pests came."

"How did you know I was thinking asking questions could be bad?" Kena asked, concerned.

"I am reading your thoughts. I am sorry child it is bad manners to do so, but I am afraid of you."

"Afraid of me? Dragon you could swallow me with out chewing how am I threat to you?"

"As weak as I am, you could easily kill me with a knife from your pack. But I think perhaps I am more afraid for you. You have never been truly loved, and while you have always had food and drink you have never had that which feeds the soul, and for that I am truly sorry. Your life has been hard yet your heart remains kind and good, your nature considerate and accepting. By reading your thoughts I am able to know what to say to comfort you to help you relax to make you feel safe. You are safe here Kena, I hope you believe it."

Kena wasn't sure if she believed it or not. "So all ancients can read thoughts?"

"No little one, just the ancients that possess that gift; Dragons, Gryphons, Gryphels, Tiguras, and Pegasi. When necessary we can also plant thoughts and memories into the mind as well."

Kena stared at the dragon, not sure what to make of this. "It was you, that inner voice telling me to go deeper, to come here?" She asked as the realization hit her.

"Yes, actually it was the gryphon, but it is of no matter."

"But why, if not to eat me?" Kena rightly wanted to know, but perhaps she shouldn't have reminded it that it was hungry.

"Because little one, you are a child of the ancients and this cavern and all its secrets are yours by blood right."

Kena stared at the Dragon, my blood right? How could anything be her blood right? Women had no rights to anything. Their husbands owned everything. Women lived only at the whim and benevolence of their husbands or fathers. "How can that be? I am female, I own nothing, I am nothing."

The dragon rumbled in laughter once again, it felt good to laugh again. It felt good to have someone to talk to again. "In the traveling clans, women own nothing and have few or no rights, that is not the way of others, even of the pests. It certainly is not the way of the ancients, child. Female or male makes no difference to a dragon. In Phoenix and the Tiskin races the females are larger and stronger then the males. Female Tiguras are as large and fully meaner and no male Gryphon or Gryphel would ever have the courage to anger a female of their race, not if they value their manhood."

Kena was shocked by this, "How is that possible? Women are smaller, weaker, meeker. Females lack the innate intelligence to survive on their own without the guiding hand of man. "

"You quote your sire, but like a great many things, he is wrong. You are as smart and capable as any of your kind, and be careful saying females are meeker here you may have an unwelcome surprise." The dragon answered again with a rumbling laugh. "Look around child, do any of them look weaker or meeker than the others?"

For the first time Kena took her eyes off the dragon and saw to her surprise paintings on all the walls. But they were more than paintings for they moved and made sounds. She jumped back right into the dragons head. She gathered herself quickly though everything in her wanted to run she stayed planted where she was. "I'm sorry for bumping into you dragon."

The dragon interrupted her with a snort. "You know, I do have a name and if you wished you would be welcome to call me by that name. It's Tamaloc, or just simply Tam."

Kena smiled. Of course he had a name, and how rude of her not to have asked it earlier. "I am sorry, Tamaloc, for not discovering your name earlier. I must confess that all this is a little startling for me, and I seem to have forgotten my manners. Did those paintings just move and make noise?"

"They are not paintings Kena, they are living murals and part of a long story that this night you have become part of. Would you like to hear it?"

"Yes, I believe I should if I am to have a role in it." Kena replied once again sitting down only this time closer to Tam. She was surprised that after only a few moments she had no fear of him.

Eagle Bennett

"Well then relax and listen for this story begins many years ago. So many years ago that we the ancients have become no more than legends and fables to your kind. So many years that the actual truth of the story lives only here in this cavern, which is precisely where our story begins."

Kena startled when in her mind's eye she could clearly see all the paintings alive and sitting around the cavern she now sat until she realized it wasn't real, merely a thought planted by Tam to bring the story to life.

"We, the ancient races, lived here with out the presence of man and were happy. We had squabbles and arguments but it was the job of the council to see the disagreements settled in an equitable manner. For the most part problems both minor and major were easily settled by the council. Then the pests came. They were no more than a good meal to most of us and something to be ignored by the rest, after all they were like ants to us; swarming, building, stinging, annoying. But we were short sighted. There were a few of our kind that were indeed prey to these new beings. Fairies, with there small stature and good natures, had no defense against the viciousness of these beings that called themselves people, to us forever pests. Pests captured them and used them for there magic and destroyed them. Whole forests of fairies were going missing. The fairies closest allies the Gryphons demanded the council rise up against this new threat. 'We, the ancient races who were bigger and stronger, it is our duty to protect the others.' Gryphons by their very natures are overly dramatic." Tam told her that last line in a sort of aside whispered to her alone. Kena barely heard him caught up as she was in the telling. The pictures in her head helped the story come alive and even though she didn't know what half the characters in the story were she was still enjoying the picture narrative. She nodded and Tam continued. "Many if not most of the council were ready to do as the Gryphons wanted. Small arguments broke out and all was ready to fall apart as those who didn't want a war were attacked by those who did. It was the phoenix who put a stop to the fighting. 'If it is a war you want then a war we shall have, but do not think it will be easy. The pests are indeed small and weak, possessing little or no magic, but they are numerous and reproduce much faster than we can. They will overwhelm us with their numbers. I agree we must help the Fairies, but an all out war may not be the way to do this. I have personally counseled the fairies to hide and they have indeed gone into hiding which is why they are not represented here today. I and my race will as always support the decision of this council. If it is war you want then war you will have and I pray there is enough of my race to save you all.' With that the council room fell quiet. The phoenix were a race gifted with great wisdom due to the fire that was part of them, and deserved to be listened to and the words of their representative carefully considered. The Gryphons were disgusted. 'She sweet talks to us and Fairies die. We, their closest allies, have not seen a one in days.' It was the dragon who had a reply to that. 'Could that not be because as the phoenix says they have gone into hiding?' It was the pictures that told the story now. The creature she had identified as the Gryphon spread its wings in anger. "'My race will do what is right with or without the support of the council.' and stormed off. While the others stared after him the phoenix lowered her head. 'The end begins, I can feel it in my heart.' With that she spread her great wings and flew out of the chamber." Tam stopped and looked down at Kena.

Eagle Bennett

"That is how the war began. The Gryphons, good to their word, did strike back at the pests and just as the Phoenix predicted, the sheer numbers the pests had over them made things go very badly. As more Gryphons died, other races joined the fight. Soon all of the races were involved and all were hunted. The land was scattered with bones and bodies of all, pests and ancients alike. I am not sure why the war ended, most think it is because there were no more to fight, and some think it is because we tired of death. I think both are right. Either way the fighting stopped, but we were still hunted. We, the Ancients of the world and rightful rulers, were forced to live in hiding on our own world. The Phoenix had been right. Many years passed with us in hiding and some things began to change. Oh we were still hunted by the pests, but some of us discovered that not all of the pests, these people, were bad. Some we even came to love and of course with love came children, but our numbers kept falling from being hunted. A final council meeting was called here at the council chamber. It was the Phoenix who had called for the meeting. 'My warning went unheeded and our deaths have been the payment. I come with another warning within a generation we will all be extinct. We will follow the Fairies into the darkness living only in the legends of the pests who have eliminated us and stole our world. Already my race grows extinct, I know of only three more Phoenix that have yet to return to the fire.' The council room grew quiet for a long while before anyone spoke. Once again it was the Dragon who answered the Phoenix. 'Is there nothing we can do? I do not believe you would have called us here if there was no hope for our survival.' The Phoenix looked around at her peers, 'I know this is not what you want to hear, but no, in legends is the only way our races will live. There is no hope and nothing that can be done. Eventually the pests will root out the last of our hiding places and kill us, or we will simply die without having children either way our demise, as we are, is certain.' She paused there meeting everyone's eyes. 'We will however survive in the children of the pests that share our blood. Unfortunately if we do not take some precautions those children will never know that they are special.' The dragon held is head high 'Then you do have a plan.' The Phoenix looked him dead in the eye when she answered. 'I have learned of a way, but the way will not be easy. By combining our magics, we can place a representative of all of the surviving races permanently on the wall of this chamber. Call it a living mural. The murals can not be killed since they are already dead, but they will have consciousness and memory. The murals will be able to communicate and use their gifts and in time our children will come to this place. We will be able to advise them help them care for them in a way we could never do dead.' The Gryphon nodded as he answered 'I can find no fault in your plan, though I will need time to think on it, but how do we make sure the pests do not find this place and destroy it?' The Phoenix nodded as she answered, 'We can use magic to keep it hidden and we will seal a guardian in with us. A guardian who is not a mural, but a living representative able to protect this cavern, and help the children when they come.' There was an uproar among the ancients, 'Who? Which of us will be chosen to live.' The Phoenix spread her wings and screeched into the melee. 'There is only one choice, the guardian must be a Dragon. Only Dragons have the life span required and even at that, the guardian will have to go into a hibernation to survive as long as will be needed for many of our generations will pass before one of our children comes to this place.' A Dragon was chosen to guard the living murals, but he was not best pleased to be chosen. He was young and rash, wisdom had not yet come to him. He was not afraid to die at the hands of the pests in fact he took much pleasure in killing them. He was even less pleased when he found he was to wait here in this chamber for generations waiting for a pest to show up, but he was the youngest of the grown dragons so he was forced into servitude. Inside this chamber all was peaceful, but outside what the Phoenix said would happen did indeed happen. The ancient races were hunted and killed. Their very existence becoming no more than legend, the evil in stories told to scare the young."

"The sun rises and sets and time changes, over the years the guardian gained wisdom. He listened to the living murals each chosen to represent their race because of their wisdom, but more importantly they were chosen because they had loved a pest and had a pest love them. The guardian learned how loving and caring some of these beings could be and he came to care for the children who were to come, children who would share the blood and the gifts of his kind. But as time passed and he grew older and weaker he began to doubt he would ever see the day that ancient blood returned to this chamber. Yet here I am and here you are child of the ancients. I fear death is near, but I have seen the return of ancient blood to this chamber and I will die satisfied."

Kena sat staring at Tam. She was thankful that Tam seemed patient enough to wait until she could gather her thoughts. The story was a bit hard to believe, but here was the proof sitting in front of her and moving all around her. So it must be true. She tried to remember some of the fables her mother had told her, but her brain seemed covered in fog. The only thing she could think of over and over was, but which ancient. If indeed the story was true and she was a child of the ancients what ancient did she share blood with. Well there was only one way to find out, "Tam, who, I mean which one...."

"Only you and they know," Tam answered. "Go to the murals child. You will know."

Kena seemed to be walking toward the murals before her mind even made the thought to do so. As she approached the closest picture she sized up the being she saw there. It looked like nothing more than a large tiger complete with orange and black stripes and large white teeth, until she approached and it spread its wings.

"That is a Tigura, they are strong fighters with an even stronger gift of mind speech. Do you feel any draw to him?"

Kena never looked back simply shook her head and moved on to the next mural. She easily recognized the next mural as a Dragon since it looked just like Tam, only red instead of black and smaller. Kena shook her head at Tam before he could ask, no she felt no kinship with this mural or Tam. The next mural she recognized from the story. It had a head, chest and front legs like a golden eagle, but the rest of its body seemed to be that of a lion, when it spread its wings they were feathered like an eagles as well.

"That is a Gryphon, next to it you will find a Gryphel. Gryphon and Gryphels are very closely related. I am sure you feel no link to either of them. You are way to calm and your nature is more to think first fight last. Gryphons are always ready for a fight."

Kena Sized up the mural next to the Gryphon and indeed they did seem to be almost mirror images of each other. The Gryphel had the head, chest and front feet of a lion and the back legs and body of an eagle. When it spread its wings they were fury more like a bats wings than a birds, but she again felt no attraction to it at all. She needed no help identifying the next murals. They were both legends to the traveling clans. The first was a Unicorn the second was a Pegasus. The Pegasi was the mark of all traveling clans and it was a painted feature on all of their wagons. Legend said the Pegasi were the traveler's protector and if something ever befell them it would swoop out of the sky to fight for them. Nobody really believed that legend, but still she was sure here must be the ancient whose blood she shared. But no as she by passed the Unicorn and approached the Pegasus it stomped it's front foot and shook it's head. She could here it making noises, and she could clearly understand it was telling her no.

"I'm sorry you feel no attraction to the Pegasus or the Unicorn. Pegasi have limited mind speech and the ability to create water out of air and the Unicorn can jump from place to place in seconds, both very useful gifts."

Kena was shocked, what other ancient could she, a traveler, be, but she moved on. The next mural looked like, well, a dog standing on two legs. It certainly had a muzzle and face of a dog, and even though it had man type hands they were furry. It was dirt brown with black splotches here and there. It grunted as she approached and raised an ax like weapon to her.

"That, my dear, is a Dokal. They are the only ancients with hands and are master builders and crafters, which are where their gifts lie, in the building and crafting of things. It was the Dokal that built this cavern. As much as I would like it, I do not think you have Dokal blood." Kena shook her head in a negative and moved on once again to another picture. She was beginning to lose heart. She looked ahead and found only two murals left. The last mural was the smallest mural. The being portrayed couldn't be much larger than a medium sized dog. It resembled the sleek form of a wild cat, but its head was more squirrel-like, with small round ears. She was curious what it was, but it was the next mural that had grabbed her attention. In front of her was the most beautiful bird she had ever seen. It was huge for a bird, easily man sized. It was covered in red, yellow and orange feathers, with bright red eyes.

As Kena approached the mural made a sweet trilling noise that to anyone else would have sounded like no more than just that a trill, but Kena understood the words perfectly. *Come granddaughter, come to me where you will be loved and cared for in a way you have never known.* Kena could do nothing but follow those directions, as she made her way to the mural.

Tam chuckled and ever so lightly she heard him say "Ha Phoenix, I knew it." but Kena had eyes only for the Phoenix. As she got closer the great bird spread her wings and burst into flames or rather the flames became the bird, then the feathers were back. Kena reached out and touched the wall it felt warm and the warm seemed to spread through her warming her completely. She felt safe and secure, like the world outside no longer existed. She felt loved and cared for, wrapped in the warmth of her grandmother's fire.

Dear granddaughter, you have not had an easy life and you know not what love really is, but fear not for you are here now and I have and will always love you. Kena sat on the soft sand next to this beautiful being, unable to take her eyes off of the mural. *Sleep child, I will be here to watch over you. Tomorrow you begin a new life and I will be here to help you every step of the way.* As Kena followed the directions she heard Tam whisper "I will be here as well as long as I am able, little one", but before she could comprehend those words she was asleep.

Chapter 6 Caleb and Seth

Caleb woke miserable. As was his usual state, every muscle hurt. He couldn't remember a day without pain in one form or another, but that was the life of a slave. Caleb carefully rolled over so as not to disturb his little brother Seth or any of the other slaves that slept in a pile to share in the heat their combined bodies gave. He groaned inwardly when he saw the light just starting to come in. He roused Seth, "Seth wake up you have to get to the kitchens before the sun comes up and they realize you're not where you're supposed to be." Seth groaned but quickly and gently extricated himself from the pile of slaves. The kitchen slaves were not to associate with the yard slaves. They had very different duties and schedules, but Caleb was Seth's only family and really only friend. Caleb watched as his brother made it to the door with out a sound and slipped out. He would be where he was supposed to be by the time he was expected to be there. Caleb groaned. Seth was always in trouble in the kitchen. He wasn't big enough for the jobs they assigned him to do and he was stubborn and smart, and not inclined to hide it, a bad combination in any slave. Seth was also sickly, suffering from a lung disease that stole his breath. Caleb sighed, as much as he would like to he would not be able to get back to sleep even if he did have a few more hours before he with the rest of the slaves would be roused. Yard slaves worked from two hours after dawn to two hours after sunset. This made for long hot summer days working in the fields. Winter days may be shorter, but the misery was multiplied by the cold since no slave was given more clothing than was absolutely necessary. Caleb had learned when he was small enough to be working in the kitchens that it was more expensive to buy clothing than slaves, so if the cold killed a slave or two the overseers just bought more. Caleb had never seen his actual owners. The owners owned many of these plantations and seldom visited them, or at least never visited this one. It was up to the overseers to make sure the plantation was profitable and as long as they were turning a profit they were allowed free reign to do whatever they wanted.

Caleb rolled to his back and, finding no handy body to prop his head up on, he folded his arms behind his head. It was sickly warm in the barn right now and he would love to move closer to the one window, but dared not. Not that he was afraid of waking anyone, he was more afraid that an overseer would see him at the window and since he was awake he would find some unpleasantness for him to do. He had made that mistake before and would never make it again. Some of the overseers were more sadistic than others. This plantation had six overseers and their families. Each one had their place in the hierarchy, with Devlin as the head overseer. Devlin was brutal and mean, but thankfully seldom dirtied his hands in the yard or fields so Caleb saw very little of him. Seth however saw an awful lot of him. Devlin could come up with punishment that no person should ever have to endure. He also preferred young boys and girls to sleeping with his own wife, so all the kitchen slaves kept as far away from Devlin as possible. Thankfully it was to the house overseer, Mardra, that kitchen slaves reported to. She was the only female overseer on the plantation, but her heart was as black as her male counterparts. She was not married and had no children. She enjoyed starving her slaves then making them cook and serve fabulous meals. That in itself was torture, but when a slave would then succumb to temptation and steal food she would have the slave whipped and locked in a closet with nothing but water for days or weeks. Caleb remembered the closet well. He had seen it many times when he served in the kitchen. All slaves too young or small to serve in the yard were assigned to the kitchens. Really there were only two places slaves were assigned, the kitchens or the yard. Since all aspects of the plantation were run by slaves, there were of course specialized slaves but they reported to either the kitchen overseer or one of the yard overseers. As bad as Devlin and Mardra were they were no match for three of the four yard overseers. Bleck, Kemp, and Coler were the worst beings ever born on this world. They were brothers born into a noble family but cast out after they raped and murdered their own sister. They had actually been the cause of more than just their sister's demise, but it wasn't until they dared to harm another of noble blood that their father took notice. Caleb had seen too much of the brother's work to know the story probably understated what the brothers were capable of. No woman was safe anywhere on the plantation from them. They would take her right from the field rape her in front of her fellow slaves then send her back to work. Occasionally they still killed slaves, but since Devlin had started taking the price of a new slave out of there wages they had mostly stopped that. Of all the overseers, only Pax was fair and somewhat kind. He never used the whip, and seldom called for punishment. Pax was the evening overseer. It was his job to make sure the yard slaves had finished all the chores and jobs that needed done and everyone was in the barn. He checked on the slaves that worked in the blacksmith, stables, mill and all the other places slaves were required to make the plantation work. The special slaves slept in their respected areas and not with the yard slaves and was the main reason all yard slaves wanted to be moved to one of the other locations.

Caleb himself was hoping to be moved to the stable. He had overheard the other stable boys talking about stealing grain from the horses and making a sort of rough flat bread. Bread was a treat the slaves never got. Caleb had only tasted it by stealing it when he worked in the kitchens. Seth was not as good at stealing as he was and Caleb had strictly forbidden him from doing so. Seth was weak and sickly and time in the closet would kill him. Sneaking away to sleep with the yard slaves would get him time in the closet too, but Pax just turned a blind eye when he saw Seth, and Bleck and Kemp, the morning overseers, never bothered to appear till after the slaves were fed. If you could call what the slaves were given to eat food. Morning was watered down porridge and dinner was always some sort of broth that may or may not have anything else in it. The pigs were given better food then the slaves. In the summer, sometimes a slave with quick hands could sneak a bite of whatever food they were picking or working with that day, and Caleb was very good at sneaking. Caleb was also very good at hiding in plain site. It was only when he had to defend Seth that he was ever noticed. An unnoticed slave was a living slave.

There were times he wondered if it wouldn't be better to stop helping Seth, but Seth was his brother. It was with desperation that his family had let the Tax Collector from the King take the two youngest sons for payment of taxes the family could not afford to pay. Caleb hated his family for doing so. Why send him and Seth, and not his two older brothers', full grown and able to take care of themselves. After all he was only twelve and Seth a mere eight when they had been taken. He had learned the next year his sister had been taken and died in a brothel and the following year the Kings Tax Collector took the whole farm killing his father and oldest brother and selling his mother and last free brother into slavery. Kemp took great pleasure in informing slaves of their relations demise so it was with a joy almost exquisite that he told Caleb about his brother being whipped to death for daring to hit an overseer. As far as Caleb knew his mother still lived and if Kemp knew of her death then he would have told him, but Caleb had told Seth that she was dead. Until that point Seth still had hope that they would be saved by their parents, now he knew they were stuck with the life they had unless Caleb could find a way to escape. Escaping was risky. They would find no help from the free, for knowingly helping a slave would send the helper into slavery. The slave himself would be killed and his body hung until it was no more than bones as a warning for all to see. No, if he were to escape, it would have to be into the woods and keep running until they couldn't find him. Then he and Seth could live there until they could convince others they were free.

Eagle Bennett

If they could prove up enough land somewhere so they could pay taxes they would be allowed to keep the land. Caleb forced his mind away from his escape plan. He couldn't leave Seth, and Seth was too sickly to run very far very fast. Only a few steps of running and he couldn't breathe. Seth may be twelve but he was a small twelve and Caleb may be strong and well built for his sixteen years, but he couldn't carry Seth far or fast. No, if he was to escape he would have to wait until Seth was bigger, if he survived that long. Somewhere in these thoughts Caleb drifted off into a dream of freedom.

Seth quickly and quietly made his way across the yard to the latrine. Caleb was always worried he was going to get caught, but he was smarter than that. It wasn't like he wasn't allowed to go to the bathroom in the middle of the night. If he was caught he would just tell them he was going to or coming back from the latrine. Seth made a quick look around before he ducked into the outhouse.

Seth finished his business quickly and made his way back to the kitchens and his morning duties. He wished Caleb would quit worrying so much. Yes he had gotten into a few scrapes, but nothing he couldn't handle. He wasn't a child anymore. He didn't need a protector anymore, no matter what Caleb thought. If Caleb knew half of the stuff he did and got away with he would kill him. He hadn't gone hungry in years stealing food was easy when you knew when to do it. The key was to take bites when he was delivering the food to the table not after. It was hard to see a missing bite from a plate piled high, but a nearly empty plate it was easy to spot.

Eagle Bennett

Seth stealthily moved across the kitchen courtyard. He had cultivated a relationship with Mardra. She was the reason he had not be moved to the fields yet. Caleb thought it was because he was still to weak for the rigors of the fields, but the fact was Mardra liked and trusted him. She often sent him on errands and favored him with special freedoms and treats.

Seth smiled as he ducked into the kitchen. By the time the cook arrived he was hard at work filling the cisterns with fresh water, making sure to get plenty for himself while he did. He even had a small flask he had stolen from Devlin that he kept full of water in an inside hip pocket he had sewn himself. Devlin had assumed his wife had taken it. The fact was Seth had lots of useful little things secreted away in a hidden spot near the latrine. Needle and thread, rope and twine, small stubs of candles, the blade of a broken knife, he had even been able to pocket some small coins. In truth if Caleb would just relax a little Seth could make his life a lot better too.

Chapter 7 Sami

"No Father absolutely not, I will not go with Ranger Oak. I'm sorry but that dream died along with Ty."

Tobias shook his head at his daughter. He had to make Sami understand. Perhaps he was rushing things it had only been a few weeks since the accident and they were both still a little lost. Tobias knew he just didn't have the time to give his daughter grieve. He had been able to quickly sell the farm, livestock and all, and move to a house in the village. When he was recovered enough to reopen the shop he would buy the raw wool from the family that purchased the farm. His biggest fear concerned Sami, if, no when, he died he didn't want her to keep the shop open. He wanted her to pursue her own life not try to keep his life going. He was searching for someone to buy the shop, but he had to build up a little more savings. Now if he could just convince Sami to leave with Oak. "Sami, Oak is leaving in the morning. She has delayed her departure as long as she could. This is your only chance. If you don't go with her now, you will never be a ranger."

"Father, you're not listening. I will not become a ranger anymore." Sami was frustrated, she had to make her father understand. "I'm sorry. I don't mean to be disrespectful, but please try and understand being rangers had become Ty and my dream. It was all we could think about all we could talk about it. It was our dream, Ty's and mine together, but Ty is dead. Becoming a ranger now would only serve to remind me of what I lost. Every day of my life I would be forced to remember I lost my best friend, the friend I was supposed to have and work with forever was taken from me. I don't think my heart can take it. Father I can accept Ty is gone. I can go on living for both of us, but I can't do that. I couldn't take the knife to my heart every day of my life. I have to find my own way now. I have to find my own way, my own dreams, and my own life without Ty."

Tobias fought back the tears. He did understand. He had lost his best friend too. His wife was a big part of the reason he had so quickly sold the farm. There were just too many memories to live with there in their little home. He knew how close his children had been and he would give anything to change places and have it be Ty standing here arguing with Sami. He shook his head in frustration. "I get it. I do understand, but Sami

I don't want you focusing all your energy on the shop like you're doing now. You need to find your own loves whatever that or they may be."

"I will Father, someday I will, but right now at this moment I need to be here with you. I need to help you. I may not be as good as you are but I can spin. You can't anymore. I can run the loom too. Sure I can only make the simpler designs but at least we could keep the shop open and our income coming in. I promise someday I will find whatever it is that I am to do, but please understand right now I need to do this."

Tobias had to agree she was right. His hands were permanently crippled he would never be able to run the loom or the spinning wheel again. He had some savings and the sale of the farm gave him some ready cash, but it wasn't enough survive on let alone make sure Sami was taken care of. He needed to keep the shop open and functioning for at least a few more months. Part of him wished Sami was different. There were several young men that would be good matches for Sami and would treat her right. Part of him wanted to encourage Sami to settle for the simple life he and his wife had been so happy in, but he knew that Sami would be miserable. Tobias knew if he asked she would do just that, settle with a man she could never love and work the shop until she was old and crippled like him, but it would be a living hell for her. She hadn't admitted it but he knew part of her already wished she had died with Ty. Honestly part of Sami did die with Ty, how could he ask her to give up more. How could he ask her to live a life she would hate just to make him happy? In his heart he knew Sami was destined for something great. He had no idea what that could be, but he refused to allow her to languish in this little village instead of realizing her true potential. "You're right, we need the income from the shop and you're all I have, but Sami I don't want you to give up your life. The shop's not right for you. You need freedom, fresh air and open spaces. You need to be able to ride and hunt. I have no choice but to accept your help for now, but it's only temporary."

Sami was pretty sure she knew what her father was thinking and part of her wished she could give him what he wanted. Perhaps settling with a husband wouldn't be so bad. If it would help her father she would do it, but part of her knew there was something more out there for her than this village and the shop. Part of her knew she was meant for something important she just hadn't figured out what that was yet. She had never considered a life without Ty. Every discussion, every hope, every plan they had ever made for their future, had always included each other. Now Ty was gone and she had to figure out a future without him and she had no idea how to do that. She knew Ty would not want her to give up on her dreams, but she just didn't know what her dreams were anymore. All she knew for sure was she had no interest in ever being a ranger without Ty. One thing was certain whatever her future held right now she had to help her father. Sami swallowed her tears. She just had to concentrate on work and helping her father.

Tobias watched his daughter as her eyes unfocused and he knew she was thinking of Ty. She was doing that more and more often lately, losing her focus usually right in the middle of a conversation. He had been concerned enough to take the problem to the healer, but she assured him it was just part of the grieving process. Sami and Ty had been as close as twins, maybe even closer. They had never tolerated being separated growing from crying and temper tantrums as toddlers to flat refusal as young adults. Perhaps he and his wife had made a mistake encouraging the sibling's closeness, but it was too late for regrets now. The fact was part of Sami's heart died when Ty died and the events of that night and the following weeks had kept her from truly grieving for him. To make matters worse Sami refused to let her father see her upset, he had yet to see her cry. He had heard it late at night when she thought he was sleeping. That worried him too, Sami didn't sleep. Oh an hour or two here and there, but never longer. She spent most of her nights pacing around the house like a caged animal. Tobias sighed, he had to face it, that's what she felt like. Whether she would admit it to him or not she did feel like a caged animal. She was wild and she needed to run free to be truly content. Between shock, grief, and restlessness Sami was on the verge of imploding. Unfortunately, he had to have her help; he had no choice, yet.

Sami heard her father sigh and it snapped her out of her thoughts. "So, are we done with this argument?"

"Parts of it yes, the entirety no, but for now I am willing to let sleeping dogs lie if you are?" Tobias took the opportunity to hug his daughter. There was so much he wanted to say but the hug seemed to say it best right now.

Chapter 8 Kena

It had been several weeks since Kena had escaped her family and discovered Tamaloc and the ancient murals. It had not been an easy time, but she could not remember ever being so happy. Tam was back in fine health since she had been able to bring him plenty of food and water. That seemed to be all he needed to regain his strength. Now he even flew again leaving the mountain at night to hunt on his own, always staying to uninhabited land so as not to be seen by anyone. Kena had learned how to hunt as well, but she had her best luck with the fish traps she had made. Kena had also been lucky enough to stumble upon a clay pit and with Tam's help she was able to make and fire bowls, pots, plates, anything she needed even a water trough for Tam. Clean clear water trickled just outside the chamber opening, Kena simply needed to place a clay bucket under it to gather it. She made sure to dump it several times a day into the trough so it was always full. It was much easier than carrying bucket after bucket of water from the pond or river. Kena had also gotten very good at skinning, cleaning and, with Tam's help, drying the skins of what she was able to hunt and now had many skins and furs ready to use. She still lacked any way to make thread so she was unable to really make anything useful out of them, but she carefully stored them so if she ever got the opportunity she could trade for the supplies she needed.

Each day was much like the last here. Though there was no one pushing her awake she still rose very early, usually before the sun. She would dump the water bucket and stir up the fire. Then she would make her way in the slight early dawn light to the pond where she would empty her fish trap, clean the fish using the unwanted portions to bait her other traps, then grabbing some of the many herbs and edible plants that grew around the pond she would return to the chamber to make breakfast. Tam preferred his fish whole and raw so she always gave him the lions share and carefully grilled hers over the fire. She always watched it closely since she hated burned fish and if she burned it, it was eat it blackened or go hungry and she still wasn't sure which was worse. After breakfast she would work with the clay making a few things that she needed or wanted. She found the act of molding soothing, allowing her to think and relax while she worked. Once they were molded to her liking she would take them over to a far corner of the chamber. Any of the murals that may have wandered over to that portion of the chamber would make a hasty retreat as Tam lumbered over and fired the clay. Tam's flame was hotter than any flame she could hope to reproduce. The clay was dried after only a few moments of Dragon fire, but Kena was careful to let it sit and cool. Her afternoons were filled by checking her traps and hunting. If she was lucky enough to get anything she would skin and gut the animal as far away from the cave entry as possible. The first time she had gotten an animal she had taken it back to the chamber to skin it. That had proven a big mistake since the cave and chamber were hidden from people, not bugs, and bugs had come aplenty to feed on the remains of the skinning. She had to leave the chamber while Tam fired the entire place to get rid of them. Well, that was a mistake she wouldn't make again. If she had a particularly good day she would take whole beasts back to Tam, who preferred to eat things fur, head, horns and all, but if her hunting and trapping hadn't been good Tam could and would hunt. Kena hated when he did so though, she was always afraid he would be seen and killed. In the evenings as soon as Kena had eaten she would make her way to her bed. She had made a nice soft wallow in the sand and covered it with a large soft fur right next to where her grandmother, the Phoenix, liked to be. She would lie down and cover herself with another fur. She had never had such a comfortable bed, but the best part was her grandmother would talk to her. Her grandmother and Tam were teaching her much and Kena soaked up any and all learning like a sponge.

This morning came like any other and as soon as she had dumped the water bucket she made her way to the pond for the fish trap. It was fuller than normal and Kena had a hard time lifting it out of the water. "Well, at least Tam will get his fill this morning." Kena said to no one in particular smiling to herself.

"Who's Tam? The man you ran off with?" said an angry voice from behind her, a voice she had hoped never to hear again. "I told Father you weren't dead. You cost me a wife, and now you're going back with me so I can trade you for one." Her brother grabbed her and started dragging her away toward the main road. "No!" Kena wanted to scream, but she was stiff with fear. Without her even realizing what she was doing she swung the fish trap that she could barely lift and hit her brother in the head with it. Then without dropping the heavy trap she ran back to the cave her brother in hot pursuit. She was able to out distance him and made it to the cave before he caught her. He tried to follow her into the cave but some unseen force intervened knocking him out cold. Kena stood staring at him, not even breathless she was in better shape than she thought unless… In her mind she called to Tam, *Do you know what just happened?* She asked thinking it only in her mind knowing Tam would hear her.

Yes we all know. Tam answered.

Is he dead? she asked watching the still form in front of her.

Eagle Bennett

No simply knocked out cold by the force of mind control. Not something we like doing, but necessary since he had every intention of killing you when he caught you. Tam answered, anger coloring his mind tone.

He will when he wakes up you know. He will not leave this place until he finds me and kills me now. She answered, very afraid. She felt the soothing trill of her grandmother even though mind talking was not something the Phoenix could do. Kena couldn't really talk to Tam she let her thoughts form and Tam grabbed them then put his thoughts back in her mind. Tam had been quick to warn her that this was not the Phoenix gift and she would only be able to do so with an ancient who did have the gift, so Tam must be echoing the trill to her to calm her.

Fear not as soon as he entered the cave he put himself within our power. The Gryphel has planted a memory of you running from him and falling from the cliff, the Gryphon has planted a false sight in his head whenever he looks over that cliff he will see your body. You need simply pull him from the cave entrance and he will never remember that the cave is here. You are safe.

Kena stared at her brother. How was she to move him? He was much larger than she was. Yes she had built strength since she had started living in the cave, but surely not that much.

Call on the part of you that is Phoenix, like you did when he grabbed you. The Phoenix part of you is more than strong enough.

Eagle Bennett

Kena looked down at the filled fish trap she still held like it was nothing more than a feather. She dropped the cage shocked but she believed in Tam too much to doubt him now. She grabbed her brother's feet with perhaps a tad too much strength since she nearly flung him over the cliff instead of dragging him next to it. In a sort of shock she slipped back into the cave, but only just inside the entrance. From here she could watch what her brother did safely. She could see him, but the protections on the cave kept him from seeing her. She sat down hard on the floor of the cave and watched. She didn't have long to wait. As soon as she was safe the Gryphon and the Gryphel released his mind and he began to wake. Her brother stood up and looked right at her. She could see the glassy, dazed look in his eyes as he turned and looked over the cliff. "Too bad little sister. Well, I guess I can report you are truly dead this time. I know father will think of another way to get me a wife, this was just the quickest, easiest and cheapest." He turned then and began jogging down the road back the way he had come.

Kena rose slowly from where she sat. There were so many thoughts jumbling her mind that she couldn't seem to focus on one.

Come little one, return to me and I will help you understand, Tam spoke to her in her mind and she felt surrounded by love and reassurance.

Kena grabbed up the fish trap, turned and without really thinking followed Tam's directions. She could find her way through the cave in complete darkness now and in full run if she needed. Now she moved slowly and with care. She hesitated just a moment before entering the chamber where Tam and the living murals waited.

Eagle Bennett

Come little one, in here you have love, acceptance, and support. We would never hurt you as your kin has done and would have done. We can help you settle your troubled thoughts. We can keep you safe. We can be the family you deserve.

Kena knew Tam's words were true. Was it the fact that she truly had escaped her family that was causing such confusion, or was it some of the other surprises of the morning? Kena sighed and stepped into the chamber. The black bulk that was Tam waited for her and as soon as she was in the chamber he reached out and gathered her to him. He held her there close to him. Kena was not afraid by the claws that grabbed her, she knew Tam would never hurt her. She accepted the comfort he offered, buried her face in his soft chest scales and for the first time in her young life cried with abandon with no fear of repercussions.

Kena had no idea how long she stood in Tams embrace, crying, but eventually the tears stopped and she pulled away from Tam. "Thank you Tam, I'm not sure what happened this morning, but I feel better now and there are fish that you might as well eat. I don't think I should go back out today and I think you should stay in for a few nights just to make sure no one is around. So, you'd better eat what I have. I'm not hungry anyway." Kena went to where she had dropped the trap and fed all of the fish to Tam who gulped them all down whole. "That should keep you satisfied till morning. If my stomach settles enough so I can eat. I have plenty of vegetables and fruit safely stored." She was about to look for something that needed done when Tam stopped her.

Eagle Bennett

"Kena, little one, it is time you learned more of your abilities. We cannot keep you safe outside the cave and you cannot stay here forever."

"No, I have to eat and so do you, and the only way that gets done is for me to leave the safety of the cavern." She smiled at him and began to sit.

"No little one, go to her," Tam told her stopping Kena, "It is for her to teach you not I."

Kena's stomach lurched again. She knew who Tam had meant by her, and she turned to face where the living mural of the phoenix stared back at her. She had assumed a rather striking pose and Kena was a little afraid of what was going to happen, but she went to the picture anyway. She heard the trill that she understood completely.

Come granddaughter, you are Phoenix, it is time you learned how to become what you are.

Kena walked to the picture and touched the cave wall. The wall should have been cold to the touch, but it wasn't, in fact it was so hot it should have burned Kena's fingers but it didn't. The warmth spread from her fingers through the rest of her body filling her with reassurance and confidence.

The heat, the fire, it is part of who we are granddaughter. It is the fire within the emotional fire that you must touch, must harness to realize your true power. Search within yourself granddaughter, reach within find the fire.

Kena closed her eyes and tried to find the inner fire, but it was not that easy. She started to open her eyes but the Phoenix stopped her.

Do not give up so easily granddaughter, look again child, reach deep. Your emotions have been controlled for too long, let them out child, it is in them you will find the fire. It is always so. Love and hate, anger and joy, pain and pleasure.

Kena reached again into herself. Love, joy, pleasure these were emotions she had only recently discovered and they did not burn in her, but the others…. Oh she knew hate, anger and pain, in fact her whole life had been filled with these emotions. She could almost taste the hate she felt for her brothers and father. She felt the burning, it was so hot in the pit of her stomach. It felt like her middle was on fire and it was spreading up and down her entire body. She opened her eyes to see that she was on fire. She threw her arm over her face in an instinctive defensive maneuver only to see it too was ablaze, covered in flames. The pain was unbearable and Kena knew her death was only moments away. She turned tear stained eyes to her grandmother in a plea for help only to realize that the pain was subsiding. She glanced down at her arm that wasn't an arm anymore, but a wing. A wing covered in red, orange and brown feathers. Her feet had become large three clawed razor sharp talons. It was only then she realized she was looking down a beak. She tried to concentrate on the beak only to feel her eyes cross, making her dizzy so she stopped but not before she was able to see the deadly sharp curved point at the end of the beak. She looked to her grandmother, "What happened? What am I?" She called to her ancestor.

Eagle Bennett

You have become what you are, what you were born to be granddaughter. You are a Phoenix.

Kena took one more long look at her body. The feathers were rather magnificently colored. Her belly was a light orange, almost white, becoming gradually darker higher and lower on her chest and torso. The leading edge of her wings was reddish brown with the trailing edge true red. Her feathers went clear to her claws and they were the same color as her wings. She did indeed resemble a flame, or maybe the flame, the flame of a Phoenix. "I don't mean to be rude grandmother, but I am not at all sure that I wish to be a Phoenix."

You don't need to remain in this form granddaughter. You may change back and forth at will now that you know how, and it need not be so painful again. Now that you have claimed that part of your blood the flame will not hurt, no flame can hurt you. Phoenix were born in flame and belong to the fire. It is just one of our gifts.

"Does that mean I have more gifts?" Kena asked forgetting her predicament for the moment as her curiosity took over.

Of course we possess many gifts, but I think mastering this gift is enough for you for now. I will teach you more as you are ready. For now perhaps you would be more comfortable as your old self? Kena nodded in response. *Reach back into yourself the way you did before and think of changing back.*

Kena did what she was told and repeated the process. This time the pain was minimal; instead of burning she felt only strain like she was stretching a cramping muscle. When she opened her eyes and looked at her hand the wings were gone and her plain fleshy self was back.

You may call up the Phoenix part of you at will and I would suggest you do so. It will be necessary to become familiar with your new form. Kena looked doubtful at her grandmother and she must have read her expression. *Child, in the form of the Phoenix you will be much safer. We are certainly not indestructible, but we are much stronger and faster. A Phoenix can call up fire at will, even consuming her whole body in it without harm. When we are fire, nothing can harm us, not arrows or swords. Our weakness lies in our feathers, but we also cannot remain fire all the time. It cannot hurt us but it will consume us. We can be become lost in the fire forever, however when danger threatens it will protect us. And we can fly.*

Kena still looked doubtful, but she knew she would do what she was asked. Neither Tam nor her grandmother would force her like her family would, but she also wouldn't do anything that would upset them either. She was new to this love and caring thing but she was starting to get it. The last thing she wanted to do was disappoint either her grandmother or Tam. "Okay, you win. I'll fit practicing in sometime, not sure when, but sometime."

She heard Tam chuckle and she turned to see what it was he found so funny, "Little one, it is time for me to take up more responsibility around here. You have helped me become well again. I am as strong as I have ever been. There is no reason I can't fetch food for us at night. We have a steady supply of water and all the other necessary items of survival thanks to you. You took care of me now it is time for me to take care of you, then you can spend as much time as you need learning what you need to learn, and little one, you have much to learn and not much time to learn it." Kena shook her head but there was no arguing with Tam.

Chapter 9 Caleb and Seth

Caleb groaned to himself as he straightened his back. He had been pulling weeds in the fields and he was sore and tired. Summer had come early this year and he was hot, tired, and dirty. While the slaves had the opposite problem in the winter, now they had to somehow keep cool. At night they slept as far apart as possible and Seth could no longer slip in at night without waking someone. Caleb had ordered him to stay in with the kitchen slaves. Caleb was just as glad not to have to worry about him anymore, but now the only time he got to see him was when Seth brought water to the field slaves. He missed seeing his brother more than he thought he would. Seth was still young enough not to have lost hope and Caleb was surprised by how much he needed that hope to fuel him. He had long ago lost all his hope, but he refused to take Seth's away and in so doing kept just a spark of hope alive in himself. Caleb saw Coler making his way towards him and quickly went back to pulling weeds before he got to him. This time Coler wasn't after him, he stopped a few rows over to harass one of the young girls that had recently been added to their number. In Caleb's opinion she was too small to be out here, but nobody was asking him his opinion.

The girl was saved some unwanted attention by the arrival of the kitchen slaves with the water. Coler had to join his brothers in overseeing the distribution of the water. The slaves were only given a few swallows, whatever they could hold in their cupped hands. The overseers were there to make certain no one tried to get extra or return for seconds.

Four slaves brought buckets of water and ladles to each field where there were slaves. The slaves would line up in one of the lines. As soon as they reached the buckets they would cup their hands and a ladle of water would be scooped into them. The quicker they drank the water the more they got before it dripped out of their hands. This suited the overseers well, because the quicker they drank the quicker they got back to work. Caleb always chose Seth's line. He couldn't talk to him of course but he could get a look at him. There were more bruises on his face and arms today. It was common for slaves to be bruised and battered, but Seth seemed to be a favorite target of Mardra. Today both of Seth's eyes were black with a large bruise on his cheek. Caleb was relieved to see that other than the bruises he seemed fine. Seth ladled the water into Caleb's hands with a slight smile, and Caleb quickly moved on sucking the water quickly down. He rubbed his damp hands on his head and neck to cool himself down a little and jogged back to his place where he immediately began working again. Coler just nodded at him as he passed.

Seth scanned Caleb for injuries as he ladled water into his hands. He seemed fine as good as he could be as a slave. He noticed Caleb's interest in his bruises. He would have loved to tell him he got them breaking up a fight between slaves and not from one of the overseers.

In fact his quick action had earned him extra rations from Mardra. All he could do was flash a smile and hope Caleb interpreted correctly. He knew he wouldn't, Caleb thought he was an idiot child.

Seth watched his brother work out of the corner of his eye as he continued to give water to the slaves. Caleb was always talking about escaping but he never did anything about it, claiming he was waiting for him to get bigger and stronger, but he was stronger, Caleb just didn't want to see it. He hadn't had a breathing attack in two years. Well, Caleb could wait, but he wasn't. He had managed to gather a decent stash of stuff and enough money to buy more supplies if they needed it. It was all conveniently located near the latrine, so leaving in the middle of the night would be easiest. He had worked hard at earning Mardra's trust and he had a certain amount of freedom when his duties allowed. If he were to disappear after the evening meal, no one would look for him until he didn't show up in the morning, plenty of time to get far away. He would have been gone before now if it wasn't for Caleb. As angry as his brother made him, he still couldn't leave him behind. After all, he was still his brother.

By the time the nightly ration of food was brought to the slaves shed Caleb was nearly asleep. He had managed to secure himself a spot by the one window and had no plans to give up this prime sleeping location. Besides, the slop they were fed at night wasn't worth getting up for, so he just closed his eyes, one of the other slaves would be happy to have his portion. Caleb was surprised then to feel his shoulder shaken and even more surprised when he opened his eyes to see Pax sitting there.

"I wanted to make sure you got your share tonight lad, for once it's edible. This heat has made it so no one in the house wants to eat and I convinced them to give the leftovers to the slaves." Caleb sat up like a bolt. "Don't be scared lad, I won't hurt you. Here." Pax shoved bread and meat at him and cup of liquid that was colored so he it couldn't be water. Pax noticed his eyes looking at the cup. "Its juice, I know you haven't seen anything like it here before, but I snuck some out of the kitchens, enough for everybody. I have to sneak the cups back in, but it's worth it, at least to me. I used to be a slave, I know what it's like for all of you. I do what I can. The reason I came over though is to warn you. The heat has made the brothers want out of the field during the day, so they are switching with me. They will make sure the slaves get where they are going in the morning. During the heat of the afternoons I will take over then they will take back over at night. So if your brother is still sleeping in here you better warn him off. I didn't mind, but they will." Caleb nodded surprised by this unexpected kindness. "I'll see you after first water tomorrow. Drink up so I can take the cup." Caleb followed the order and gulped down the sweet liquid and handed the cup back to Pax. "Prime location, I can see why you didn't want to leave it," Pax commented as he rose and walked away.

Caleb watched Pax for a second digesting what he had just told him. It was bad news for the women, that was for sure. He had a feeling no one in the shed was going to be getting many good nights' sleep. However, Pax on the afternoon shift meant a little easier going in the heat of the day. Pax never drove them as hard as the others. Of course if he did really used to be a slave, well, that could explain it. He had been told once that a slave could earn his freedom but he didn't believe it.

Eagle Bennett

He noticed the others staring at him and he looked down at the uneaten food. He quickly took a bite of the meat and found that Pax hadn't been lying about it being good. It had been a long time since he had tasted meat that wasn't rancid and he savored the taste. He bit into the bread and was surprised by it as well. It was heavy bread, full of seeds and little pieces of dried fruit. Caleb was careful to eat slowly he didn't want to get sick from eating such good food after years of having little. He turned his back on the rest and faced the wall so he could eat and think in peace. As soon as he had finished eating he laid back down flat on his back and folded his arms behind his head. His stomach was full for the first time since he had been taken from the farm and as much as he wanted to stay awake to think, the heat and full belly worked like magic, and he was asleep before he could form a thought.

Chapter 10 Kena

"Very good Kena, you are truly a master of your shape. You are neither pest nor ancient, you are something different, you are a Changer, the first of a new race." Tam yelled out to her as she landed on the sandy floor.

Kena quickly changed back into herself and smiled at her mentor. "Thank you, it certainly is easier to hunt when you are doing it from the sky."

"Have I not told you this? Is any of that for me or will I be hunting for myself come dark?" Tam asked all but drooling over the small dear Kena had brought with her. Kena could hunt by daylight since she looked enough like any other bird of prey no one would notice. Of course she was the wrong color and about four times the size, but from the ground it was hard to notice these differences. Tam however could never disguise his size and shape so he was restricted to night flying. At night in the sky Tam was all but invisible. Even if someone was out and about they may hear him as he was anything but a silent flyer, but they would never see him or realize what he was.

"Of course it is all for you. I have my own." Kena answered as she took a few chuncks of meat out of a fur bag she wore so it hung on her back. It was one of the odd things about changing, anything you had on you at the time of changing changed with you so when she changed back she was always fully clothed. This proved to be a good thing when she needed to change back outside the cave to dress down meat or pick plants. The bag however she had designed to not change with her. It was made so when she was a Phoenix she could slip the straps over her wings and the pack would sit quite well on her back between her wings. She stacked up some of the wood she and Tam kept on hand for a fire whenever it was need. At least now she no longer needed Tam to start the fire, she had perfect control over the fire she could call. Kena carefully extended her hand over the wood and thought just a little about the anger she felt for her brother and watched as her arm burst into flames. She was so used to the slight pain of the burning that it was inconsequential to her now. She dipped her burning arm/wing into the pile and waited for the dry wood to take. It didn't take long and she removed her arm. A quick thought sent her arm back to what it should be, but now she had a happy fire going right in front of her. She could actually do this partial change with any of her limbs and head if she wanted to and she smiled at her control. It had taken many hard painful hours of work to get the control she had. She grabbed up a stick and sitting in front of her little fire plunged the meat into the fire. When she was the phoenix she actually craved raw meat but she always resisted that instinct.

Tam watched her closely. Kena was very comfortable with herself now. It was time to spring another gift on her and it was time for her quests to begin. "You do very well with your changing now little one." Tam replied drawing her attention from the flames.

Kena had always been fascinated by fire, only now she knew it was because fire was part of her and it was completely natural for her to yearn for the flames. In fact it would have been against her nature to fear fire like most pests. "Thank you Tam," Kena replied, but she could tell by his tone that he was not finished. "So, what is it Tam? I know you too well, what is it I need to do for you now?"

Tam laughed, if there was anyone else in the chamber they would have run screaming, but Kena knew it for what it was a chuckle no more. "You do know me little one, better perhaps then any flesh being. Yes there is something I need, but more for you than for me." Kena sized up his look and knew whatever it was might be for her, but it was not something she was going to appreciate. "Kena, it is time for you to learn another of your gifts. One that will help you greatly succeed at something you must do."

Kena had always done what Tam and her Grandmother had asked and she knew in her heart she would do anything for them, but she was certainly not going to do something without asking lots of questions. "Well, I think you should start with what gift I am to learn and what I am to do before I agree to do anything." Tam

Eagle Bennett chuckled again at her tone and the look on her face. He lumbered over and flopped down next to her. His eye, an eye that was bigger than she was, was an arms length away from her. "The gift is empathy. It is the magic of the Phoenix. The quest is you must find more of your kind, more of this new race, more Changers, and bring them here to be trained as you have."

Kena sat silent for a moment. She had learned of empathy, her grandmother had seen to that, but her grandmother had never even hinted that it was something Kena could do. As far as looking for others she had been thinking that was to come. It was luck or fate that had brought her here, but she knew the other ancients wished for their grandchildren to come here too. The only way for that to happen was for someone, her, to go and get them. If she and they waited for fate to bring another here it could easily be generations before it happened again. "Okay, I understand the second part, but how will empathy help me to succeed?"

It was her grandmother who answered her from the other side of the chamber. *You must first understand what empathy is, child, before you can understand how it can help you. I am afraid time may be short for you to learn so you may not learn the way I wish you could. Tam will be no help in this training. Only I can help since the Phoenix is the only ancient with this gift. Emotions are the living's inner fire. It is through our inner fire we possess this gift. Empathy can be an active gift. Empathy can be controlled and projected, it can even be a weapon if it is trained properly. You will be able to feel what others are feeling unless you or they are shielded against it. Most importantly you can*

Eagle Bennett

use your empathy to find the others. It can be used like a map to lead you to where others like you are.

Kena looked at her grandmother. She was always thoughtful before she answered and this was no different. She carefully weighed what she had just heard. She was not surprised. Nothing surprised her anymore, not after wandering into a cave and finding a dragon and living paintings. She understood the basics of empathy. She did try to always consider others in her thoughts and decisions. She never wanted to hurt anyone. She knew if she had to make a choice she would allow herself to be hurt before she knowingly hurt another. Her grandmother had explained before that was empathy. She didn't feel herself very wise, certainly not like her grandmother. Her people believed that only the aged could be truly wise. Her grandmother had laughed when she had heard that. She had insisted she knew many aged beings in her life and they were no wiser than the young. The difference was they had no reason to keep their opinions to themselves anymore and they felt since they had already lived their lives they knew everything. Why was she hesitating? She knew she was going to do it, there was nothing she wouldn't do if Tam or her grandmother had asked it of her. Perhaps this was the sign of her wisdom. Either way, whether she wanted to or no, she wasn't in a position to not do it. "Ok Grandmother, Tam, I would be happy to learn what you feel I must, but please can we start after I eat?" Tam chuckled again a throaty growl like sound. "Of course little one, eat, it is always better to learn on a full stomach."

Kena stood before her grandmother waiting for her to begin her training. Tam was in the far corner of chamber. He would be no help and he may prove to be a distraction so he had taken himself as far away as he could.

If you are ready, Granddaughter? Kena nodded, as ready as she would ever be. *The first thing you must learn is to shield properly since the very first day you walked into this chamber, I or Tam, or one of the others have kept a shield on you as well as making sure we ourselves were well shielded so as not to leak our emotions on you, but now it becomes imperative that you learn to do this yourself. You cannot leave this area and not be able to shield. We can only do so if you are near us and the world is an emotional place as you well know. So first we teach you to shield both yourself and others.*

Kena nodded again there was no need to answer her grandmother she was aware that Kena was giving her her undivided attention. *First, yourself. It is important that any shield you cast either on yourself or on another is grounded to a source of energy. If you do not do this then the shield will draw its energy from you and deplete you. For a Phoenix the easiest source of energy is fire which is why I had you leave the little fire going. Once you learn how you will not need a living fire to harness its energy but it's easier while you learn to have one nearby. So in your mind think of a rope running from the fire to you. The rope is not on fire and it will not burn.*

Now Kena understood why the Gryphel was near at hand since a picture popped into her head of what her grandmother meant. She adjusted the picture in her own mind to one she could more easily visualize. *Good. Now think of a window encircling you. Now Shape it in your mind to encompass you. Make it a circle and think it all the way around you top and bottom as well as sides. There can be no gaps. Think of emotions as fluid like water. If you do not seal all of the cracks in the container it will leak. In this instance you will do more than need water more often, you could in fact drive yourself insane.*

Those words snapped Kena's concentration. "How, Grandmother? I can control my emotions, even you commented on how much control I have."

Of course child, but you cannot control the emotions of others. With that thought Kena was hammered by feelings she knew were not her own. Feelings of loneliness and longing, feelings of loss and grief, it was like a weight being dropped on her from all sides. The force of the emotions pushed in on her as she fell to the sandy floor. Tears sprang to her eyes as she curled into a protective fetal position. As quickly as it began it stopped. Kena lay where she had fallen for a few seconds before she rose to face her grandmother again. "That was the emotions of the others, wasn't it?"

Yes Granddaughter, imagine what it will be like when you are around pests. If you cannot shield you can never leave this area where we can shield for you and if you cannot leave all of these will never know the joy I feel.

Kena thought about their longing. No she had to do this. She had to find the others like her and the sooner the better. Hope was something everyone needed and deserved. She had lived without it for too long to take it away from any one.

Eagle Bennett

Again you show wisdom. Wisdom that is true to our fiery nature. Try again, start with the fire rope and remake your glass encasement. Kena did as she was asked and this time she concentrated hard on making sure the glass in her mind sealed edge to edge. *Think it strong as stone, even as it is clear.* Kena did and was not surprised when in her mind a brick flew at her newly formed glass wall. The glass shattered in her mind. She quickly rebuilt it and thought it stronger just as another brick came into the picture this time it chipped but didn't shatter the encasement. *How can you stop the brick from damaging your shield child?* Kena thought for a moment and pictured her wall strong but flexible and bouncy. This time the brick did no damage as it bounced harmlessly off. Instantly her walls were attacked by many bricks coming from every direction. She quickly thought the solution at all her walls all the way around and brick after brick bounced harmlessly away. *Good granddaughter, you learn quickly. Now you must learn to make this a part of your very being. Even when you sleep this must be a part of you. To do that you must anchor it to you without anchoring its energy source to you. Move your fire cord from the little fire now.* Kena did and instantly felt a weight on her. A weight like carrying a rabbit in her hand or on her back it was not a weight that cost her much to carry a small way, but if she had to carry it for a long way her arm would quickly become tired. She now understood what having a shield not connected to a power source could cost her. *You must find an internal energy source that does not drain you as it feeds your shields. If your shields are not mobile then they are useless. Think child, can you figure this out for yourself or should I show you.* Her grandmother had used this training technique before. And Kena had no intention of needing her grandmothers help. In fact it was an easy problem to solve. She had learned when she had learned to change that emotions were a powerful force in and of themselves. It was emotions she used to fuel the fire that caused her change. All of her gifts touched on emotions. Why couldn't she anchor her shield to the thing that actually fueled fire? It should make the shields stronger than fire would as it was a more powerful energy. As her grandmother had warned the thought became the deed and the cord seemed to sink in to the picture that she had in her mind made into her core strength, the place where all emotions started. She immediately felt the weight lifted and knew she had done what she needed to do. She was not surprised by the bricks that began pelting her again, and while the first were able to chip at her again she quickly repaired the damage and thought them strong and bouncy again so the remaining bricks did no harm. As soon as the bricks stopped, water plummeted down on top of her and when she looked down she was floating on water as well but inside her shields she stayed dry and safe. Quickly the water stopped and she opened her eyes. As soon as she did she was flattened once again by the emotions of the others. She quickly closed her eyes and erected her shields again. *Think them there even when you do not see them.* Her grandmother sent to her and Kena followed her instructions and opened her eyes. *Well done, Granddaughter. Be prepared; we will send our emotions at you often. You must maintain your shields at all times. They are well anchored into a source that will never run out of energy as long as you live. You can always layer your shields like panes of glass stacked together to keep out the cold. A many layered shield is strong and durable. One last thing, remember Kena for the Phoenix emotions are fire, if you ever lose control of one, you lose control of the other, it is imperative for all you love to never lose control.* Kena nodded in understanding. *Now we teach you to sense the emotions of others and project those feelings if needed.*

By the time she was done being taught everything her grandmother felt she should know she was exhausted. Night had fallen and Tam had went and returned from his evening hunt so it was late indeed. She curled up into her bed and was asleep before she could think twice. She was rudely awakened many times during the night by emotional assault and she learned quickly to maintain her shield even in her sleep layering many levels on top of the others so if one broke or disappeared there were always other layers in place. When she awoke in the morning she was more than ready for the hits aimed at her. Her grandmother was very pleased and chirped her pleasure.

You have done well granddaughter, and are nearly ready to begin your quest. There is just one more thing you need to do. First though, Tam has brought you some breakfast, he was even able to bring you some berries, but I do not think you will be able to harvest from the tree again.

Kena glanced over to where Tam sat, looking very smug. She had to quickly stifle a laugh since Tam had indeed gotten her some berries in fact he had brought her the entire bush roots and all clutched in his claw. He also had some roasted meat there for her as well. She dragged herself over to Tam and her breakfast, grateful that she did not need to catch her own, at least not this morning. She ate quickly and returned to her grandmother.

Eagle Bennett
You have done well child. You have learned quickly and are nearly ready. There is just one more thing that I must teach you before you can go. You must learn to find those that are like you, those who share blood with the ancients. It is simple, since their blood will call to you, you have only to learn to listen. Kena thought about that. How could she listen for blood? She was certainly willing to try, but how? *I can tell you child, but only you can do it. We the ancients can tell those that are if they come to us, but we cannot actively search for them. They must come to us, which is why we need you child.*

Kena understood completely and after feeling what the others were feeling she knew how important it was. They had waited for generations for someone to come and had all but lost hope that they ever would. It had only been her grandmother's insistence that it would happen that had kept them going. They had waited long enough. "Tell me what you can grandmother, I will work the rest out for myself by strength of will if I must.

The Phoenix nodded. *It is similar to sensing, only instead of sensing emotions you are looking for a feeling of sameness. I think you will know it when you feel it.*

"Okay Grandmother, I think I have an idea what you are saying and I would like to try it. If it works I should feel that feeling with you and the others. I am going to lower my shields a little, please no bricks or waterfalls?" She heard noises from all the ancient living murals and while she couldn't understand there tongue she knew they were laughing, but she was not offended. They had only done what they had to do to teach her what she had to know. She did and felt for that sameness and instantly felt what her grandmother had meant. She did indeed feel called by that sameness. It felt safe and secure. The strongest pull was from Tam which made sense since he still had blood in his veins. Without telling anyone, she carefully reached outside the chamber and sought the same feeling from any other beings in her range. She had discovered last night she did indeed have a large range. She was mildly surprised to find a call from one not far away at all. Then she did something her grandmother and the others did not know she could do, she linked her empathy to the call so she was not only able to feel where the being was, but also what the being was feeling. She gasped as she felt pain and exhaustion, hatred and fear. She quickly put her shields back up before the beings very strong emotions overwhelmed her. Kena felt her grandmother and Tam surround her with shields as well.

You should not have done that child. You could have been consumed by the others emotions, or worse, lost control.

"I know grandmother, but I kind of had to. Just because I have found another does not mean I can convince them to come here. You must admit it does seem a pretty farfetched story. If the being was happy or content with their life I do not think I would be able to convince them and there would be no reason to waste my time with them. If that was the case I would have searched for another, someone more like myself willing to try anything to not live like I was. I think we are fortunate in that this is such a person. I am afraid from what I felt he is a slave. My people have worked beside slaves before and I know that feeling too well.

While they will indeed be more than willing to abandon their life it may not be easy to get them away." Kena felt the disappointment even through her shields and quickly moved to reassure everyone even while she added a layer to her shields. "Don't worry I didn't say I wasn't going to, only that it would be hard. I can't imagine any overseers have had to deal with a fire creating bird before. I am stronger and faster than any full grown man. I will succeed in my task, have no fear. I only meant it wasn't going to be easy, but then what in life is easy? I need the day to rest and the night to sleep in peace, but in the morning I will leave. Tam, will you smoke me some meat tonight? I will need it so I do not have to hunt while I figure a way to help the slave escape. I will take water with me as well. I can carry my little pack I do not think anyone from the ground will notice it, after all if they do not notice an orange and red bird that is as big as a full grown man they are hardly going to notice that same bird is wearing a back pack." This enlisted a laugh from everyone. Kena had learned quickly when she started flying that the pests, as the ancients called them, only saw what they expected to see unless the truth was shoved into their face. Now I want nothing more than to stretch my wings, a little then rest. The morning will be soon enough." And with that she quickly changed and sprang into the air reveling in the freedom flight gave her.

Chapter 11 Caleb and Seth

Kena felt the warm thermal under her wings and used it to soar higher. Tam had taught her how to fly using the thermals to save energy whenever she could and she was grateful, not just for making flying easier, but for making it more fun. It was hard to reach this height without the help of the thermals and the higher she flew the better she felt. She loved the feeling of the wind in her feathers as she flew high and fast. Her pack was resting lightly on her back. She had never actually carried this much weight in an extended flight before, but she found she was having no difficulties. Her grandmother had told her that eventually she would have the ability to carry the weight of a full grown man for many miles without tiring, but she was not anywhere near that yet. A man would feel much like the pack to a Dragon or even a Gryphon, for as big as she was as a Phoenix, she was nowhere near the size of even a Gryphon. The paintings on the walls were deceptive, Tam had told her. On the wall the Gryphon looked only slightly bigger than her grandmother, but in reality Gryphons and Gryphels were much larger. In full growth they reached the size of her travel wagons. Of course the dragons were the largest of the ancients. Tam was the size of some of the smaller manors they had worked at. Her grandmother had groaned when Tam bragged about the size of dragons. "Size is a gift the Dragons hold, but their gifts are by no means as beneficial as ours." Tam had agreed as had all the others. Kena wasn't sure what gift was so beneficial, and when she asked about it her grandmother had told her it was a gift she could not teach, it was gift she would understand on her own but not until it was needed. Kena drew her mind away from those thoughts and opened her shields just a little to locate the being she was looking for. He wasn't far away at all by flight and as she peered ahead she could just make out a farming plantation. It was still a good distance away. Her eyes when she was a Phoenix were much better than when she was a pest. She adjusted her flight angle to descend slowly. She needed to find a tree near enough to see but far enough away not to be seen. As she approached the plantation, she tilted her wings so she could circle the entirety of the farm, taking careful notice of all the buildings and fields. She also noted what fields the slaves were working in and quickly ascertained which of these slaves her target was. She was lucky the fields the slaves were working in were the ones closest to a wooded area with rather large trees. Kena picked a tree with reddish brown foliage to better hide in. Her color would be like a beacon in one of the larger green pine trees. As she back winged to land she never took her eyes off of the boy she knew she was here to rescue. As she sized him up she slipped her wing out of one of the straps on her pack and shrugged her other wing so the pack fell down to hang on her chest. Using a beak that could shred a cow's hide with no effort at all she unbuttoned the fastening and reached in to take a strip of smoked meat out. She reached up with her right talon and took it out of her beak. Leaned over and tore a piece of it. It certainly was handy having a dragon around he could smoke meat in minutes, a task that would take, under normal circumstances, hours or days to do. She absent mindedly munched on the smoked meat while she watched the boy. He was probably her age or maybe a little older. It was hard to tell by looking since he may be small for his age. It was easy to tell his condition since in this heat he wore only the bare minimum of clothing. He was well muscled, but highly underfed. His dark hair was shorn short, and his dark complexion may be the fault of dirt, sun, or both. He wasn't what Kena would consider handsome, but he certainly would have no problem finding a wife.

Kena continued to study him as he worked. She was surprised when he looked up. She followed his gaze and saw four young boys headed toward the field carrying jugs of water. Kena was surprised by his expression and the emotions she was picking up from him. His regard was for one of the boys in particular and it wasn't hard to see even through the grime the familial resemblance. Kena reached with her gift and found the pull of sameness from the younger boy as well. Her mission just became harder.

She watched the rest of the day and made careful note of where the pests went as night came on. As soon as it was full dark and the plantation was quiet, Kena took to her wings. Smoked meat was filling enough but it lacked the flavor of fresh. Besides, hunting would take her mind of her problem of getting not one but two away from the plantation. She circled the dense woods that surrounded the plantation looking for a target. Her search would be a short one as she spotted a young and dumb tree hare sitting in the clear on a high limb. It was a mistake it would not get a chance to repeat as she dove, back winging just in time to strike, killing the tree hare instantly and soaring back into the night sky.

Kena returned to her perch on the outskirts of the plantation, her stomach full and her eyes heavy. Morning would come soon enough. She still had no clue how she was going to get her targets safely off the plantation. She shrugged her shoulders and settled her wings. Perhaps a thought would come in the morning, right now she needed sleep.

Chapter 12 Sami

The summer heat made the shop feel like a furnace, and working in it was miserable. Sami watched out the window as she spun the latest batch of wool into threads. Her father was dying the thread as fast as she could manage to spin it. Her father was particularly driven to get as much thread, yarn and rope spun and braided as possible, as quickly as possible. They had plenty of fabric in store but little of the threads and yarns it took to weave the fabric. Sami spent all of her time from early morning until late at night spinning all the different kinds of wool into yarns. When she wasn't spinning she was braiding. Sami looked down at her sore hands. The raw wool rubbed her hands raw and made them ache. The only small mercy, her father could at least handle the dye runs even with his crippled hands.

He had improved over the last few months since the accident, at least physically. She often heard him crying at night, but by morning he would be back to his old self. He was never interested in talking about any of it. Which was fine with Sami, she didn't want to talk about it either, not with anyone. She loved her father and they had a good relationship, but she had never shared her inner most feelings with him. Ty was the only one she had ever talked to. Since Ty died she kept all that to herself just like her father did. For good or bad, they had settled into a quiet routine of avoidance and work.

Sami heard the rear door of the shop open. There was a small fenced garden space behind the shop that they used to do the dyeing. The smell was overwhelming otherwise.

"Sami, got that batch ready for me yet?" Tobias called from the back of the shop. "I've got the last batch drying and I'm ready for the next."

Eagle Bennett

Sami's eyes started watering, even doing the dyeing outside the smell still leached in every time the door was open. It clung to her father's clothes as well. Like spinning, she hated the smell of the dyeing, but she had made him teach her. He was still adamant that she was not going to spend her life attached to this shop, but she knew she was. The only other choice was to marry and she would rather have watery eyes and raw hands the rest of her life than be with a man that way. She had tried. She had accepted many invitations from most of the young men her father approved of, but as nice as most were she felt no connection, no draw to them at all. As hard as she tried, she just couldn't change who she was. Ty had understood, but she still hadn't been able to tell her father. Part of her was sure he would understand, but the other part was just as sure he wouldn't and both parts knew he would be disappointed. How could she do that to him after everything else? How could she take that dream away from him after everything else he had lost?

"Sami, did you hear me? Come back to the real world daughter, there is work that needs done."

Sami pulled her thoughts back to the here and now. "Sorry Father, I guess I was wool gathering a little. What did you say?"

"I asked if the next batch is done?"

"Nearly, just a few more minutes." Sami answered picking up her pace on the wheel.

"Good. As soon as that batch is done, I would like you to quit for the day. Before you argue I only have enough dye left for this last batch and I don't want to mix more tonight."

"I should do one more batch…"

"I said no arguing. Why don't you take a walk or something? I'll meet you at home after I finish and close up the shop. Don't cook either, I'll do that when I get home."

Sami nodded, grateful he didn't add a jibe about her cooking. She cooked well enough but nowhere near as good as her father did or Ty had. It was no more than a moment before she was finished and headed out the door of the shop. She had no interest in taking a walk. Sami knew that if she wandered outside the village she would just keep going and never come back. She would head to her and Ty's little hut. Sami had no doubt she was a good enough hunter to survive, and she would be in the place she and Ty had been the happiest. As much as that appealed to her, she couldn't leave her father alone, so instead she turned toward the little house she and her father shared now.

It was a nice house, a little bigger than their farm house providing plenty of space to avoid her father when he got talkative. Sami didn't hesitate, she ran up the stairs to her little room and fell into her bed. She rolled away from the sun light streaming in the window. Her mood was dark and she didn't want to see the light. As she lay there staring at the wall she let her thoughts run where they wanted and invariably they landed on Ty. She knew most siblings weren't as close as she and Ty were, but most siblings had other friends. Ty had not only been her brother but her only friend. They were so much alike, she and her brother. It helped they were a little less than a year apart in age. They literally grew up together. Sami could not remember a time when Ty had not been by her side until the accident. They had grown up wanting the same things in life and admiring the same women. The last thought brought a smile to her face as she remembered some of their conversations over the women they found attractive.

Sami rolled to her back stacking the pillows up a little behind her. She was glad she was beginning to be able to remember Ty without the massive overwhelming grief. Her grief for her mother had been as intense but she didn't have that overwhelming sense of loneliness when she remembered her mother. When she thought of Ty she felt like a huge gaping hole opened up in her heart and nothing she would ever do would close that hole. As hard as she tried part of her wished she had been crushed under the cart with him.

Sami grimaced. She had to start thinking about other things. She loved Ty and her mother, but they were gone and she had to go on living. Her choices there were stark and she knew she had to get her mind around settling. She had to accept she had to take care of her father. As long as he needed her help she had no choice but to work in the shop to keep them alive. Sami knew she would, she may hate it but she would never leave her father to fend for himself. However she would not, could not marry. She would rather live alone the rest of her life than do that. As dark and angry as her thoughts were they didn't stop her eyes from getting heavy in the warmth and comfort of her bed. She didn't intend to but somewhere in the middle of her thoughts she drifted off to dreams of a better time and a better place.

Eagle Bennett
Chapter 13 Caleb, Seth and Kena

Kena was awakened by the sound of the slaves returning to work. She was growing bored and desperate after several days of watching the same routine play out in front of her. She kept one eye on her target and the other on the overseers. There were three this morning. She could tell without any help from her gift these men were scum. She watched as they tormented a young girl and she fought the urge to call fire to return a little torment. Kena forced her mind away from the overseers and back to her target.

Kena was about to take a break and stretch her wings when she felt the approach of her second target. Once again he and three other young boys had water jugs. They were accompanied by the overseer Kena recognized from yesterday. Kena shifted her gaze to the older target and watched as he stood stretched and made his way to the water line. Kena missed how it happened but one minute everything was fine, the next the young boy was on the ground surrounded by wet earth and shattered jug.

Caleb went white with fear for Seth. The urn had just shattered, but Seth was sure to be blamed. He looked over at Coler, who was already striding, whip in hand, with purpose towards Seth. Caleb started forward then hesitated, the whipping would probably kill Seth, but would getting himself killed instead be any better? Did he owe his brother that, did he owe anyone that?

Kena felt the intention of the overseer clearly. He was going to whip the boy to death and he was going to enjoy it. She rose on her perch and spread her wings, plan or no, she was not going to let this boy be killed.

She looked to the older boy, surprised and a little disappointed he hesitated, but glad when he did finally make his move.

Caleb shook his head. Yes, he had to protect Seth. He was at his brother's side before Coler and his whip. "It was an accident, sir, please don't!" Caleb begged.

"Out of the way slave, the boy has earned his punishment."

"Then I'll take the punishment instead, please." Caleb pleaded.

"Caleb no! I'll be fine." Seth countered, but Caleb ignored him.

"Oh, I think I will punish you both," Coler raised the whip and Caleb covered his brother protectively waiting for the searing pain of the whip on his bare back.

Pax grabbed Coler's hand stopping the whip. "Stop Coler, you forget once the water arrives, I am in charge until the slaves return to the shed. I get to punish the offenders not you."

"Are you sure you want to do this Pax?" Pax glared back at Coler. "Fine, I know where you sleep boy, I'll see you tonight."

Caleb continued to hold Seth down, waiting to see what Pax was going to do. "Slaves get your drink and get back to work." Pax watched making sure the slaves did as they were told before turning back to Caleb and his brother. "I only prolonged the inevitable," He warned

Eagle Bennett
has he squatted down next to the brothers. "I would suggest if you want to live to be gone before tonight." He whispered, then in a louder voice. "Fine, take him to the medico, but you'll be working twice as hard when you get back."

Caleb had no idea why Pax was helping them, and he really didn't care. He pulled Seth to his feet and supported him like he was injured and moved off toward the medico building. "Seth act hurt until we get out of sight. We have to make a run for it now. We need to get as far away from here before anyone but Pax knows we are gone."

Seth nodded and leaned heavily on his brother. "I have supplies hidden in…"

Caleb disregarded his brother, "As soon as we are around the end of the building run for the cover of the woods."

Seth knew when he was wasting his breath, so he nodded and as soon as he could he broke into his fastest run a few seconds before Caleb, pushing for the cover of the dense woods.

Kena watched the whole thing unfold, amazed by her luck. When the brothers started off she jumped into the air following their movements. They needed a distraction and she was uniquely qualified to give them one. She landed on the roof of the stable relieved by what she found. If the stable roof had been of good solid slate construction her job would have been harder, instead it was easy burning thatch. A quick thought and her talons were fire that quickly spread to the thatch underneath her claws. She skipped down the length of the building spreading the fire quickly as she went. When she reached the end of the building she turned to see what she had done and lost herself in the flames. *Flame will never burn you. Fire will never hurt you. You were born in flame and of fire so it will never cause you harm, but fire will always call to you. You will find yourself never wanting to leave the exquisite joy fire can mean to you and only you. Be careful or fire will consume you.* Kena heard her grandmothers words of warning come back to her in her mind and for the first time truly understood her warning. It would be so easy, so peaceful just to stay here cared for by that which gave her life. Kena shuddered, surprised at herself, she had a job to do and a life to lead. Kena stared at the fire for one last moment, silently promising *someday I will return to you but not yet.* The fire seemed to groan in response burning hotter and brighter as she turned her back to the pull of the flames.

She was relieved to see brave stable boys leading the scared horses to safety, but she wasn't done yet. She glided from building to building letting fire run free not even trying to control its hunger or its rage. Finally she jumped to the roof of the big house. It had a slate roof, but fire was too angry and hungry to be stopped. Kena leapt into the air circling making sure the destruction was complete and total. Assured the brothers wouldn't be followed for a while, she winged in the direction she had seen them run.

Caleb kept Seth running as fast as they could manage in the thick underbrush. He wasn't even sure where they were going they just had to get as far away as they could. "Stop Caleb look, the plantation it's on fire!" Seth called stopping his brother in his tracks.

Eagle Bennett

Caleb turned, amazed by what he was seeing. He stared for just a second. "Come on Seth I can't believe our luck this buys us time but we've got to keep moving." Seth hurried to catch up.

Caleb had no idea how long they had been running or how far they had gone. Seth was tiring. His pace had slowed to barely a crawl. The slower Seth went, the angrier he became. Seth was slowing him down too much. He should have left him behind. Caleb regretted the thought as soon as he had it. "Let's stop and rest a moment Seth." Caleb sat down on an overturned tree where Seth joined him.

Seth glanced up at the sun and knew they had been running for at least two hours. The going was anything but easy. He kept tripping and getting tangled in the thick underbrush. When he had looked back he realized they were leaving a path anyone could follow and had slowed down to try and do less damage to the fauna as they passed trying to cover their escape a little. He knew one thing; they needed to find ground not so densely covered in underbrush and trees. They could move faster and leave less of a trail. "What are we going to do now Caleb? Where are we going go?"

"I don't know!" Caleb snapped back at his brother. "It wasn't like this was planned. Maybe we should just sit quietly while you catch your breath." He growled.

Seth dropped his eyes to the ground, when Caleb got in these moods it was best to avoid talking to him. Sometimes his brother scared him, even before they were sold to the slavers. Sometimes Caleb was just mean. Mother had said it was just part of growing up and he would grow out of it, but Seth had failed to see any sign of that so far. In Seth's mind, perhaps even worse was his brother's ability to only see what he wanted to see. It was so frustrating, but there was absolutely nothing he could do about it. Seth ground his teeth in anger all but biting his tongue to prevent an angry retort. There were so many things he would have liked to tell his older brother, but he knew it was a waste of time. He didn't need to catch his breath and he didn't need a protector, but nothing he said was going to get through to Caleb. "Let's go." was all Seth could manage.

Kena flew as low as she could over the woods looking for signs of the brothers passing. Disappointingly she found their trail easily. As she followed she realized they had unwittingly gotten turned around and were now headed back towards the plantation. When they had headed this direction she had hoped they might find their own way to the mural's cavern without her having to show herself, but that hope was dashed with the signs of the trail. She landed a few yards in front of them, changed, and quickly stepped forward to stop them. "Stop, you're headed back the wrong direction."

Caleb jumped back, bumping into Seth when the girl came out of thin air in front of them. "What? Get out of our way, we're not going back! Don't make me hurt you."

"And I'm not going to try and make you go back. I'm trying to help. You've gotten turned around you're headed back the way you came." When the older boy looked angry and disbelieving she pointed at a small clearing through the top of the trees, "Look, that's smoke from the fire at the plantation. You need to turn

Eagle Bennett

around. Keep the smoke at your back and keep walking you'll find a river. I'll meet you there as soon as I cover your tracks a little if I can. You left a trail a child could follow."

Caleb felt his anger rise. Who was this girl to tell him he had screwed up? He didn't care that she was right, but who could move through this stuff without leaving a trail? And why was she helping them anyway. He wanted to argue but she had already left melting back into the dense brush without leaving a trail. When he turned to look for Seth he found he had taken the strange girls advice and was already making good time away from him, leaving him little option but to follow. He growled as he followed his brother.

Seth needed little more proof than the smoke from the plantation fire. He didn't care who or why this stranger was helping them, clearly she was. He didn't bother waiting to hear Caleb's argument, he turned and headed back the way they had come as quickly as he could. If Caleb chose to ignore the strangers warning and instead get himself killed that was up to him.

Kena did what she could with the brother's trail, but there just wasn't much she could do. They had beaten down to much of the growth. She changed and circled back to the plantation to see if they were being followed. She was comforted to see that as yet no one had been sent after the pair. She circled twice more watching the plantation burn, and then turned back to the river to meet the brothers.

They had beaten her there, but by the look of things not by much. Kena landed just out of sight changed again and approached the pair. "Glad I caught you. I haven't seen any one following yet, but I'm sure they will as soon as they realize you're missing. The fire is a stroke of luck, but they will notice your absence eventually. We still have several hours of daylight we should keep moving. If we follow the river it will be easier to hide your trail, as well as providing plenty of fresh water. There's a water fall a day's walk we will have to go around but other than that it's an easy walk."

Caleb rounded on her. "Who put you in charge? Maybe we decided to head the other way down the river. Why should we go up the river?"

"Caleb she's just trying to help." Seth tried to interrupt, but Caleb pulled him away refusing to listen.

Kena smiled. What else could she do? "I wouldn't, the other direction heads into populated areas."

Seth tried one more time to get his brother to listen "Please, Caleb?"

Caleb looked at Seth. "Fine, for now we'll follow the river."

Kena sighed, one obstacle crossed, now if she could just get them to the cavern or even near enough that the murals could help…

By night fall they had covered more ground they Kena thought was possible. She felt quite safe stopping for the night. "This is as good of a place to stop for the night as any. It will be dark soon and we really need to have a fire started by then. There are some predators in these woods large enough to be a threat to us. Would you mind gathering wood while I get the fire started?" Kena asked the brothers.

Seth was enthusiastically willing, but Caleb was sullen. "You know how to start a fire without a flint or anything."

"I was a traveler. I've been able to start a fire, flint or no, since I could walk, but I have a flint in my pack." She answered. She didn't have a flint, she didn't exactly need one. It was an oversight she would not make again in future quests. Caleb glared, but followed Seth into the near forest in search of wood. Kena made a fire ring with river rocks she found near their chosen camp site and filled it with small twigs and dried leaves. She could have started a fire on wood as wet as the river without kindling, but she could feel Caleb watching her so she needed to put on a show. She grabbed up two rocks and while knocking them together she called fire to drop down on the kindling. She watched it ordering it into a cheery flame just as Caleb dropped an arm load of wood next to her. She chose a few and dropped them into the fire and watched as they caught. "I'm going to go see if I can catch us some dinner. I have some smoked meat with me, but not enough for all of us. Do you mind keeping the fire going?"

Caleb nodded and Kena didn't wait for him to argue. She disappeared into the thickest brush she could find. As soon as she was sure she was out of sight she changed and finding the nearest clearing flew out over the woods. She was hunting, but she also wanted to double check for any one following. She found no one else in the woods, and drifted back to fly along the river where she could safely dive on her prey when she found some. The thickness of the woods made hunting problematic for her unless a stupid tree hare or squirrel showed themselves on the top branches. If nothing else she could grab a fish or two. Her luck was still with her when she found a family of hogs making their way to the river for a drink. She could easily take one of the adults, but she wasn't sure how she would explain that to Caleb, so she took one of the piglets. It was easily big enough to feed the three of them.

Caleb watched her disappear. He still didn't know if he could trust her, but she didn't seem to be a threat and if she was indeed a traveler it would explain her ability in the woods. It was easy to figure out why she was alone. Women in traveling clans were little more than slaves, she was probably a runaway herself. He checked the fire and dropped another couple logs on it before he went to the river and dipped a hand in to get a drink. He watched as Seth brought in more wood and dropped it on the pile before joining him.

Seth reached into an inside pocket of his pants and pulled out a small flask, downed the contents then joined his brother at the river. "Caleb, why are you being so mean to her? She's helping us and I think we need her help." Seth asked while he refilled his flask from the cold clear river water.

"Where did you get that flask?" Caleb asked accusingly.

"I stole it, of course, from Devlin. He never figured it out, he thought his wife had taken it to stop his drinking. I had lots of stolen supplies if we had been able to plan this… Never mind." Seth added when he noticed Caleb was completely ignoring him. "Caleb, why are you being so mean to her? She's helping us and I think we need her help."

"Maybe we do, but why is she helping? You're too trusting, no one helps just to help, especially slaves."

"And you trust no one, not even me." Seth countered before he turned his back on his brother and returned to the fire.

By the time Kena made her way back to camp with the skinned and gutted piglet Seth was already asleep and Caleb looked like he was lost to the world. She skewered the meat on a stick and shoved it in the fire. Caleb watched her but said nothing. Kena kept an eye on him out of the corner of her eye waiting. She didn't have long to wait.

"So, why are you helping us?" Caleb asked with no preamble and no courtesy practically growling the words out.

Kena understood his attitude, but she was getting really sick of it. "I'm Kena by the way. I know you're Caleb, but would you mind sharing your brother's name?"

"Seth, now answer the question."

"Because I hate slavery. I would have helped anyone I found escaping. Any other questions?" Kena regretted her tone immediately and softened her tone before she continued. "I mean, we have a little bit of a wait before the meat is cooked so we have some time to kill. It was too dark for me to find any edible plants, but we should be able to find some while we travel tomorrow."

"So you helped us escape, why are you still helping?"

"I can stop. If you want, in the morning I can disappear and leave you on your own. Can you hunt? How long before you starve? Can you make fire? Can you do any of the hundred little things needed to survive out here? You don't like me? Fine, is that a reason to kill yourself, or worse your brother, rather than accept help from me?"

Caleb wanted to dispute her logic, but he really couldn't. She was right, without help they would probably die, or worse, get caught. As much as he hated Kena's attitude he could tolerate it until they were safe. "You're right, I don't like it and I'm not sure if I like you but we need help. Where are we going? I mean you seem to have a plan?"

Kena was surprised by the question. She thought she had hidden her agenda well. "I do know a place, a cave really well hidden where you could hide. The river runs quite close to it. You could hide there until the heat dies down."

"We'll see. Did you see any one when you were hunting?" Caleb asked trying to change the subject. He needed time to think about her little plan.

"No, you better wake him, he needs to eat and dinner is about ready."

Caleb seethed. She was so bossy, but he had no choice but to take it, he needed her help. So he woke Seth as Kena took the meat from the fire and cut sections for everyone. He ate his portion in complete silence. A silence Seth filled by babbling to Kena about anything and everything. He wanted to tell him to shut up, but he just didn't have the energy. Instead he finished his meal, quickly laid down, turned away from the noise and went to sleep.

Seth seethed at his brother's attitude. Kena was nice and friendly. She listened to him and answered all his questions, and no matter what his brother thought he knew he was a good judge of character. "I'm sorry about him Kena. I will probably be apologizing for him quite a bit in the days that come. Just know I am nothing like him."

Kena smiled at the younger boy, "Oh, don't worry about it. My brothers didn't exactly treat me well. I can handle anything Caleb can throw at me. Besides I think he's just scared and he's covering it with bravado."

Seth wasn't sure he agreed, but unlike his brother he was too polite to argue. So instead he asked her about her home and by the time they settled for the night Seth had decided he was staying with Kena whether Caleb did or not.

Kena woke them early. She handed each of them a portion of the remaining pig she had left heating by the fire all night. Then Kena started them down the river at as fast of pace as they could manage. At noon they stopped for a short rest and a drink. Seth chatted companionably with Kena. The two of them seemed to be getting close which only made Caleb angrier.

As soon as they were back moving, Kena matched her pace to his. "I'm going to double back and look for followers. If you and Seth keep going this way you will run into the waterfall. We'll stop there for the night. We'll have to cut into the woods to go around it, it's way too steep to climb safely."

Caleb nodded not trusting himself not to snap back with a nasty comment. Kena took his accent and disappeared once again. He was getting a little sick of her ability to do that.

It felt so good to be on the wing again. She found a thermal and used it to soar high above the trees. She reveled in the feel of the wind in her feathers and the freedom the open air all around her. She flew along the river looking for any sign someone was following. When she reached the trail the boys had left escaping she followed along it as well. Her worst fears were realized when she found the three overseers following the boys trail. She watched them for a while. They weren't much better in the woods than Caleb and Seth and they certainly weren't moving very fast. She watched until they made the river wanting to see what they would do. Any hope she had they would turn the wrong way were dashed when they came to the right conclusion the escapees would try to avoid populated areas. She had to get back to the brothers and warn them.

Kena was relieved when she found Seth and Caleb waiting at the base of the waterfall. "We have to move on after all tonight, we are being tracked."

"Who?" Caleb wanted to know.

"The three overseers, the mean ones." Kena answered honestly without thinking.

Part of Caleb wanted to ask how she knew who the mean overseers were, but she didn't give him a chance moving off into the woods. "Follow as closely as you can. Try to move without disturbing anything, put your footsteps in mine." Caleb and Seth did what she asked as they tracked deeper into the woods trying to find a place to climb the steep hill of the water fall.

Coler pushed his brothers hard. He was going to string that boy up when he found him but not until he made him watch while he tortured his brother. He stumbled over the remains of the campfire. "They were here, see I told you. He was smarter than he looked, but not smart enough. We'll catch him and when we do, he's a dead man."

Kena kept them moving until way past dark. A couple of torches made it possible, but it soon became clear they were not going to be able to go much farther. "We'll stop here. Escaping does no good if we die doing it. Caleb, can you use your torch to start a fire? I'm going to try to find something for us to eat." ,

Caleb nodded, too tired to argue. Seth dropped where he stood, and Caleb handed him the torch, "Hold this for me while I gather some wood together." Seth nodded and took the torch. Caleb quickly gathered what wood he could easily find and by the time Kena returned with a pack full of berries, water cress, and wild carrots, Caleb had a cheerful little fire going.

"It's not much, but I don't dare leave you long enough to hunt." She handed each of them a share of her gleanings as well as a small piece of smoked meat. "It's going to be a hungry morning, but we'll live. I'll stand watch as long as I can. When I can't stay awake anymore, I'll wake you Caleb. Seth, you get as much sleep as you can we need you rested, it's going to be another long day for you I'm afraid." Seth nodded, fear he was trying hard to hide was clearly visible in his eyes. Kena moved to comfort the younger boy. She was driven to do so by her empathy and her genuine fondness for him. He lay his head down in her lap and she stroked his head just like she was the older sister comforting her young brother. Caleb watched and fumed.

Once Kena was sure Caleb was asleep she shifted Seth off of her. Seth groaned but was too tired to wake. She waited to see if Caleb would wake from the noise. When he didn't she changed, hopped a little way away from the fire and took to the air. She wanted to know where the trackers were. From the air they weren't hard to spot. She was shocked and dismayed by how far up the river they had gotten. She was going to have to slow them down or they would catch them tomorrow. She flew back to camp to wait for morning. As soon as she saw the first orange and reds of the rising sun she woke Caleb. "Hey you've got to get moving. I'm going to back track and try to slow down the trackers, you and Seth keep moving as fast as you can along the river."

"Kena," Caleb asked concerned, "how are you going to slow them down?"

Kena shook her head. "I don't know yet. I'll kill them if I have to." She ran off to the woods changing not even making sure Caleb couldn't see her do it. She was in the air before Caleb had even been able to bend to wake Seth. She circled the waterfall watching as the men broke camp. She landed on a boulder in the center of the river at the top of the waterfall and watched the men debate the next course of action. She could clearly hear the argument and she shook her head at how dumb the three of them really were. It made her job easier when they decided to split up. Coler was climbing the waterfall, Bleck and Kemp headed off into the woods.

Kena waited a moment longer before she left her perch circling the water fall as Coler climbed. He was an easy target splayed on the wet cliff. Kena waited patiently until Coler had reached a point high enough that a fall would kill him. She circled one last time casting a shadow he never even noticed before she dove striking at him with strong sharp talons. Coler didn't stand a chance he looked up just in time to see Kena's talons as they sank into his eye. He screamed and fell backward hard against the rocks bouncing twice before he fell in the rapidly flowing river. Kena followed his body until it washed up on the shore a significant way down the river. She glided over the body while calling fire. She circled and watched as he burned past the point of recognition before she called fire back and left the remains to the scavengers.

She easily found the other two by the noise they were making. She landed in a tree a few yards ahead of their path. She watched them for a moment. There was no convenient cliff to drop them down, a more hands, or perhaps talons on, approach was going to be needed. She considered trying to scare them away with a little judicious use of her empathy, but she knew that once they were out of range they would just come back. Her only option to keep Caleb and Seth safe was to kill both of them here and now. She waited for the trailing man to walk under her perch before dropping on him easily crushing his skull in her talons. His yells brought his companion running back. He tried to grab her but instead of fists of feathers he got ravenous enraged fire. He screamed as flames burned up his arms igniting his torso, face, and head. He tried to run but there was no running from the blaze. He fell before he got two steps never to rise again. Kena forced fire back under control letting it feed on the final body before she extinguished it.

Kena flew away from the smoldering bodies. As soon as she could no longer smell burning flesh she landed changed fell to her knees and vomited. Spasms racked her body as she expelled what little she had in her stomach. She couldn't believe she had killed not once, but three times. She cried as dry heaves shook her body. Her mind told her she had only done what she had to, but even through her shields she felt the terror in each man as he realized he was going to die. When her stomach stilled she fell back pulling her legs tight against her chest. She had to get herself under control before she returned to the brothers. She concentrated on her shields making sure they were whole and strong. Fire had fed well this day, but it was always hungry; she couldn't take the chance it would escape. As soon as she was sure that wouldn't happen she rose changed and leapt into the air flying hard to catch up with the boys.

By nightfall they were only a few hours walk from the cavern. By the time camp was made and food hunted and cooked, full dark was on them. Kena heard Tam fly over, but neither Seth nor Caleb acted like they did.

Eagle Bennett
You can sleep freely little one, I will keep watch over all of you this night. Welcome home little one, you have been missed.

It took all of her control not to burst into tears at his words. What she had done this day was still weighing on her mind. For safety's sake she added a couple of layers to her shield but with Tam in the air above she slept soundly.

Little one it is time for you to awaken. I must get back to the cavern before dawn, and tell all of your coming. Your grandmother misses you nearly as badly as I.

Kena let thoughts of thanks and love hang in her mind for just a moment before she rose. As much as she wanted to be back on the trail home, they had to wait until first light or chance an injury or worse. She stirred up the fire and placed the remains of a squirrel over it. Warm meat would go down better this morning. She sat turning the meat and watching the flames just thinking. Three days of trekking and Caleb hadn't warmed to her at all. She was not at all sure how living with him was going to work. Her only hope was that once he heard the story and learned what he was his attitude would improve, but she didn't put much hope in that, not after the warnings Seth had given her. Well, she had dealt with far worse than Caleb, and at least he wasn't a threat physically. Besides he had a hard life, it was bound to make him a little bitter. It wasn't like she couldn't fly out of the cavern any time if being around him got to be too much.

As soon as she could see light she woke Caleb and Seth. "Time to wake up, as soon as you are ready we will be leaving. We'll make the cave I was telling you about by midmorning. The sooner the better, once we get there we will all be safe from discovery even if we are followed by more than the three I killed yesterday."

Caleb shuddered at the reminder that Kena had killed the three brothers. He raged inside at the thought, but there was nothing he could do. He was powerless to help save himself or his brother. If Kena hadn't come along when she did they would be dead, either from Coler, Kemp, and Bleck or from the elements. He wanted to be grateful but the best he could come up with was contempt.

Kena was right and with the pace she set they made the little path along her pond earlier than she thought they would. She didn't even speak when she turned away from the river to follow the path from it. Caleb didn't try to make conversation he was lost in his own thoughts. The path turned away from the pond and up towards a huge mountain, a mountain that seemed oddly out of place. Caleb had never seen mountains, but it seemed like there should be more than just one out in the middle of nowhere, but here it stood all by itself on flat land. It was by no means a huge mountain or even really all that tall, but surrounded as it was by marshy flat land it felt large and vastly out of place.

Kena practically ran up the path to her home. She couldn't wait to be inside and safe. She wasn't sure what was driving her, but she was sure it came from within herself since she had strengthened her shields as soon as she starting feeling the drive. She had thought perhaps the living murals were projecting their feelings onto her, but with her shields at full strength with absolutely no cracks or openings and many layers, that could not be the case. The only conclusion was it was something inside her, some instinct, which was driving her on. Thankfully she could see the entrance to the cave. She glanced behind her and found Caleb and Seth not far behind. She hurried to the entrance and only then did she stop.

Caleb was about ready to call for a stop to rest, when he saw the entrance to a cave. Kena had stopped at the entrance and was doing something with a long stick. It wasn't until the stick burst into flames that Caleb figured out Kena was making a torch. He had little time to try to puzzle out how she had done that, as soon as they were within reach Kena handed Caleb the torch. "It's as dark as a pit in there. I know the way, but you don't. There are no dangers inside but I thought it would be better with this. Come on, try to stay close." Kena moved inside and Caleb gave Seth a little shove. He wanted his little brother in front of him so he didn't fall behind.

Kena slackened her pace a little now that they were all safely concealed. At the entrance to the cavern she stopped to scoop up some water from the clay bucket placed there to catch the dripping water. She took a long drink from the primitive clay cup that sat near the bucket then got more and handed it to Seth as the boys caught up. Seth drank some and handed the rest to his brother. Caleb followed suit. Caleb was a little surprised by the clean clear taste. It had a slightly mineral taste to it but it was incredibly cold and refreshing. As soon as he was done he handed the mug back to Kena who set it back down next to the bucket. "Up ahead is the entrance to the cavern I told you about. It's my home and it is safe. No matter what you see up ahead please trust me that there is nothing that will hurt you in there and as long as you are in here you are safe from anything that would hurt you out there." Kena didn't wait for a reply simply turned and starting running toward where she had pointed.

Seth didn't hesitate either as he starting running behind her, so Caleb was forced to swallow his pride and follow. Kena hadn't paused at the entrance, but Seth did, so Caleb hurried to catch up. He was shocked and scared by what he saw. Inside was the largest chamber Caleb had ever seen. The inside area was larger than the holding barns at the plantation. He had never in his life seen an area enclosed that was so big. But the size of the cavern wasn't what had sent chills up and down his spine. Inside was the largest thing he had every laid eyes on. It was the size of a house. It's head as large as the largest draft horses and even though he couldn't see them he was sure it probably had huge teeth in that huge head. The only thing that stopped him from running back the way they had come was what the thing was doing. Caleb shook his head, but there was no doubt the thing was hugging, yes hugging was the only way to describe it, hugging Kena. Kena stood with her face buried in its chest circled by its strong forearms. By the way Kena's body shook Caleb knew she was weeping and wondered at the weakness and what she could possibly have to cry about.

The beast lifted its head and looked straight at them. "Come and be welcome. You are safe here. I mean you no harm."

Caleb nearly dropped on the spot, a beast that could talk. Seth wasn't afraid at all though and walked into the chamber looking up and down and around. Caleb

Eagle Bennett followed, but he never took his eyes off of the beast and Kena.

Kena forced control on her self and checked her shields. She took a deep breath and turned to Seth and Caleb, "This is my friend Tamaloc. He's a Dragon and I promise he is no threat to you."

Chapter 14 Tamaloc

While Tam told the boys his story and the story of the cavern, Kena went to her grandmother and her comfortable bed of fur and soft warm sand. As she reached the wall where her grandmother stood she reached out and touched the mural, relishing the warmth of the touch. She turned and put her back on the cave wall next to the mural and slid down until she was sitting on her furs next to her grandmother. She listened to Tam with half her mind and the other half she thought about what had happened and the men whose death she was responsible for. The thoughts were dark and her grandmother must have felt some of her pain even through her shields because she trilled a quiet comforting warble and radiated unconditional love. Kena wanted to tell her grandmother all about what had happened, but she didn't want to interrupt Tam and the story of why this place existed, so instead she threw her grandmother a smile and added a layer to her shields so as not to disturb her grandmother or any of the other murals. She could deal with this on her own, there was no need to trouble anyone else with her inner torment. Tam was just coming to the part where he told the boys they were in fact children of the ancients and Kena wanted to see how the boys reacted to that tidbit of news. So far the brothers had taken everything in stride, but that could be because Tam or one of the murals was calming them. Seth seemed the more relaxed, but he was trusting and easy going by nature. She smiled at the boy. She had developed a true fondness for him on their trek. Unlike Caleb, she knew he was smart, capable, and mature well beyond his years. Caleb only saw what he wanted to see, not necessarily the truth.

"So one of them, one of the living murals, is your ancestor and it is up to you to find which one. Only you and they will know which one. Go children, see the murals find your grandparents find your true selves."

It was Caleb who caught the plural. He and Seth were brothers wouldn't they share the same ancestors like they shared parents. Before he could voice the thought Tam heard it and answered it. "It has been many, many generations since we have walked among your kind. Since then our blood has been spread far and wide, but two different bloods will not mix. If your father carried the blood of one ancient and your mother a second you will inherit only the connection of one."

Kena's interest was piqued by that thought. "I was under the impression that there were few of us that shared the blood of the ancients, how likely is it that both their parents shared blood?"

Tam looked at her not at all surprised by her question. Kena was always curious and her questions were always answered to the best of his abilities. "Because, as you well know, blood calls to blood so it is common for our children to seek each other out even when they are unaware they are. Ancient blood always breeds true, even when the parents are incapable of accessing their true nature and gifts. Now, boys, go see the murals."

Caleb was still a little hesitant, but Seth had no such reservations. He also seemed to know right where he was going and made a bee line for the mural of the Dragon. His eyes lit up as the mural welcomed the child with opened wings and groans that Kena knew from Tam were of joy. Kena was surprised by that. Of all the ancients she thought the boys might share blood with, Dragon was not one of them. Of course she hadn't realized they may not share the same blood and she was going more on Caleb's personality, but still, a Dragon. When she looked at Tam he was nodding his head like he knew this was the case and a quick glance at her grandmother showed she also was not surprised. Caleb moved more circumspectly around the cavern looking at each mural but not approaching any. Kena had not moved, she knew, though she didn't quite understand how, that Caleb was not a Phoenix. Caleb knew it too, since he never even hesitated in front of her. It seemed by his actions that he was torn between the Gryphon and the Gryphel. This was not a surprise. Kena had gotten to know the ancients and their personalities and this choice fit. Caleb acted without thinking and he had little control over his anger. Kena watched as Caleb approached the Gryphon. He was welcomed with a purr, a strange sound coming from the beak of an eagle, but clearly a welcome all the same. Caleb reached out and touched the painting closing his eyes as he did so. Kena could never know what was said between grandparent and grandchild, but it must have been exactly what Caleb needed to hear. He sighed and leaned against the painting. Kena felt her grandmothers warmth encircle her and she knew Caleb

Eagle Bennett
was getting the same kind of comfort and love from his grandparent.

Tam sat in the middle of the cavern for a long while. It was imperative that the bond be strong, but he wasn't nearly as worried about the boys and their bonds as he was worried about Kena. He had read her thoughts and knew all that had happened even what she hadn't shared with him. He also knew that she wasn't dealing with what had happened and she must. She had closed that part of her off and she needed to open it up. Tam was sure beyond a shadow of a doubt this would not be the last men Kena would have to kill to survive. If she didn't deal with these deaths she might hesitate the next time and that could get her killed. It wouldn't be long before she would have to return to the world of the pests looking for more of her kind putting herself back in the path of danger. He was not surprised when he felt a poke of emotions and he turned to find Kena staring at him. He reached into her mind to grab the thought. *Tam I have to go out and check to see if we were followed and I need to hunt, but I dare not change here in front of the boys it will scare them I think. I have no wish to frighten them.*

Tam pondered the problem for a moment. *There is no need to hide your abilities. The boys will learn to do the same soon, and while they are in the cavern we can calm them if it scares them.*

Kena sighed, and moved away from the cavern wall. While she changed the magic of the cavern opened the ceiling just enough for her to fly out before closing again. She didn't linger but sprang in to the air with a powerful down stroke of her great wings. Within a few wing strokes she was free of the cavern and flying high in the bright sun. Once again she savored the feeling of flight, the delight of the wind blowing through her feathers, the freedom of the open sky. Kena began to relax just a little as she soared high on the thermals. For just a moment she let all the worries of the past days and all the concerns for the future drain away. She couldn't allow herself much time for this, but the few moments she took were necessary for her sanity. As soon as Kena was once again feeling balanced and in control of her thoughts and feelings, she tilted her wings back the way she and the boys had come. She needed to see if they were followed by anyone else. She flew down the river many miles never once spotting anyone. She even circled for a while just to be sure. The cavern was wonderful and she could supply all the daily requirements the boys would need, but they would grow bored if they had to stay inside all the time. Now, as sure as she could be that they were not followed this far, they all could relax. She also needed to find meat and plenty of it as well as any edible greens she could get before night fall. With two more mouths to feed she was going to be busy for a while, or at least until Caleb mastered changing.

Caleb hadn't felt this safe since he had been taken by the tax collector and sold into slavery. He wouldn't have believed any of this if he hadn't seen it himself. But Tam was real and so was the Gryphon. How he understood the Gryphon he didn't know, but he did understand him as clearly as he understood Tam or Kena.

You are safe here grandson, both you and your brother are safer here than you have ever been in your life. You are also loved and appreciated. While love is not a foreign emotion for you, appreciation is. In the days and weeks that follow you will learn much about us and about yourself. No matter what happens though remember you will always have me as your champion.

Caleb reached out a hand to the Gryphon in gratitude, but his inner thoughts were troubled. How could a painting on a wall, no matter how alive, protect him?

We may be paintings on a wall but do not think us helpless. We have magic of our own. Our gifts still function and we have complete control of them.

Caleb jumped back a little. "How did you know what I was thinking?" He spoke to the wall.

It is one of our gifts to read thoughts and you were thinking rather loudly.

"So everything I think you can hear?" Caleb gasped.

Yes and no. Yes, I can hear. No, I won't be listening to everything. Of course, I will teach you how to do this as well and how to shield your thoughts from me and any other thought sensors you will come into contact with.

"I'll be able to read minds?" Caleb asked, thinking that it would be a useful skill.

Yes, but you will also be taught ethics of doing so. For instance, you don't want to read the thoughts of Kena without her permission. There will be times you will need to read her thoughts as she cannot communicate mind to mind, but without permission it would be an invasion of her privacy to do so. Caleb nodded, he understood what he was being told. *Your brother however, he is Dragon and can mind speak. Actually, Dragons are the strongest of the mind speakers and can reach much farther than any other ancient. You and he will be able to communicate, even far apart, once he grows into his full power.*

"What do you mean? Why wouldn't he have full power now? You imply that I do."

Seth is not as yet full grown. He is only as powerful as a fledgling Dragon would be and certainly not as powerful as he will be. When he changes, he will not even have the strength to fly as yet. A few more years, I would, think before he comes into his full power.

"Wait...when he changes? What are you talking about changing? Changing how?"

I believe Kena is about to show you exactly what I mean, watch.

Caleb did watch. He had almost forgotten that Kena was even in the cavern with him. She had gone over to a giant flaming bird picture and stayed there. Caleb hadn't even thought about her until now. He looked over to see her rise and reach back to touch the painting then move swiftly to the center of the cavern, but not too near the big black bulk that was Tam. He heard and felt a slight rumble and glanced up to see the ceiling moving. His first thought was that the ceiling was collapsing and he was preparing to run.

Easy little one, his grandfather interrupted his thoughts, *it is just one of the little magics of this place and is no more a danger to you than the lighting in the cavern. Watch Kena carefully now.*

Caleb turned his attention back to Kena just in time. One second he was watching the girl he knew as Kena the next he was looking at a giant red, orange and brown feathered bird. She was huge, as big as a full grown man. He found himself afraid of her and what that beak and long sharp talons could do to him. In the next breath she was out the hole in the top of the cavern and gone from site as the gap closed as quickly as it opened.

Fear not grandson, Kena is the same whether she is phoenix or pest. Her nature remains the same, her thoughts are still good. She only goes to hunt and make sure you were not followed. It will be faster and easier for her to do that in her phoenix form.

Caleb thought about the Gryphon's words. He instinctively trusted him and he didn't know why. After all, his so called grandfather was a picture on a wall, a moving talking picture but just the same a picture on the wall none the less.

You trust me because blood calls to blood. We share a kinship you have felt with none other than Seth. It is also the reason you trusted Kena even when all of your instincts said to trust no one. I and the others also offer you something I am not sure you have ever truly had, safety and security. I will also teach you things that will make it impossible for others to abuse you ever again. You are free to leave of course if you wish but I do not think you wish to?

No, Caleb thought at the wall he had no wish to leave. This was as good as place as any to hide, and if he could learn things… A thought suddenly came to his mind as he was able to digest what he had seen Kena do and what his grandfather had just told him, "Will you teach me to change like that?"

Yes, only you will change into a Gryphon. We are fierce, are we not?

Caleb had to agree with that. For one thing they were huge. Not as big as a Dragon, but huge nonetheless. They were easily the biggest of the pictures other than the Dragon. The Gryphel were slightly smaller, not in height but in mass. Their beaks were sharp and Caleb had little doubt the front talons could render any enemy limb from limb.

I should also warn you we tend to fight first think and ask questions later. Tam was right, it was us the Gryphons and our cousins the Gryphel that started the war with the pests. It was our mistakes that ended the reign of the ancients over our world.

Caleb looked hard at the picture. He could hear the regret in its mind tone. "You did what you felt you had to do. I certainly can understand you wanting to protect those you care about."

That is because you to are a Gryphon, if at the moment in a weird small little package.

Caleb sighed and slid down the wall to the ground catching his brother's attention for just a second. Seth quickly turned his thoughts back to his grandmother. *He is fine little one, only just beginning to realize what he is. He has little control over his anger and anxiety so his grandfather is calming him.*

Eagle Bennett
Are you doing that to me?

Not anymore. When you first entered the cavern the Gryphon calmed both of you to prevent you from bolting, but it quickly became clear you didn't need any outside influence. You knew you belonged here. You felt it. Just as you knew Kena was a friend, you knew we were as well.

Seth nodded and leaned against the wall completely at ease with his surroundings feeling safe for possibly the first time in his life.

Chapter 15 Kena

Kena sighed and hunched her feathered shoulders. She was perched at the same waterfall where she had sent Coler to his death. The thought of that made her queasy. She forced the thought away she just didn't have time right now to dwell on anything but keeping the four of them fed. The sound of the waterfall was calming. It had been a week since she had brought the boys back to the cavern. They had settled in well, but they couldn't change or hunt. Tam spent all his time with Seth and hadn't left the cavern even to hunt since his arrival, adding to her feeding burden. It's all she did from the time the sun rose until it was too dark for her to see prey was hunt. Caleb was trying to help. He did all the cleaning and skinning as well as cooking. He had also cleared a plot of land and planted herbs and edible plants. Kena could see the wisdom in this, it would be nice to have these plants close at hand, but it didn't help with the immediate problems. Kena sighed again, she was so tired, and she couldn't be in the cavern at all anymore without the loneliness of the murals wearing on her even through her shields. She needed to be out searching but she couldn't until Caleb could hunt for all of them. She couldn't even get any reserves stock piled. Seth ate like he had a hollow leg, and Caleb wasn't far behind him. She knew Seth was growing and Caleb was rebuilding fat reserves but it meant she had no time for anything else. She didn't even have the energy to talk to her grandmother anymore. Tam was so focused on Seth he didn't even notice her. Her relationship with Caleb was confusing to say the least. He always seemed grateful, but his snide remarks cut like knives. Between his taciturn attitude and the pain of the murals she had no choice but to build up shields so thick nothing got in or out. She had never felt more alone or lost. It was good she could not cry as Phoenix or the river below would be just that much fuller. Kena dropped her head to her chest with another sigh only then noticing the dried blood on her talons and chest. She longed to plunge into the cool river, but that would require hours of drying time, time she just didn't have. With one final sigh she returned to the skies winging east, hoping for easy prey.

Caleb threw the entrails of the stag he had just gutted over the cliff. After working with his grandfather all morning on controlling his mind sensing and speech he welcomed the physical activity of cleaning the meat Kena brought in. He glanced over at Seth weeding the garden. He was proud of his brother. In many ways Seth was having an easier time mastering his gifts than he was. He turned back to the hanging stag. He had to concentrate on what he was doing. The only knives they had were falling apart and had been sharpened so many times the metal was paper thin. They were going to have to get a new knife soon. Kena chose that moment to drop two rabbits at his feat. "Thanks, but we need to replace this knife if you want me to keep skinning these things." He wasn't even sure she heard him as she jumped back into the air. You're going to have get over your pouting and do more than just hunt soon." He yelled at her quickly disappearing form.

"Caleb you could be more understanding. Kena hunts all the time because if she doesn't we'll starve. I mean we aren't being much help. Also, if you took the time to listen, you'd hear the other murals groaning over her not leaving to find more of us, but if she leaves now we'll die of hunger. She's being pulled in so many directions I think it's killing her. Do you really think you should add to it?"

"What are you talking about?" Caleb snarled.

"Did you think she was just miraculously there where we needed her when we needed her to help us escape? Do you think the plantation fire that covered our escape just started all on its own? Do you think the overseers just gave up on us? Come on Caleb you're smarter than that. The murals, they sent her after us. Well not us precisely, but others of our kind, other Changers. She started the fire and she killed Coler, Kemp and Bleck to protect us. I think she's earned a little kindness from you."

Caleb was dumbstruck. He should have known, but he hadn't had time to think about it. He also knew he should be grateful, but all it did was make him angry. "What difference does it make even if it is true?" He rounded on his brother.

"Nothing, forget it. I need to get back to Tam and Grandmother. The weeds are beaten back for another day." Seth answered, "Just think about cutting Kena some slack that's all. I'll see you later." Seth beat a hasty retreat. He knew better than to bother talking to Caleb when he was in one of these moods. He tended to go from talking to fighting without warning.

Caleb scoffed at his brother. Maybe his brother should be a little less understanding. It wasn't like he failed to help anyway he could. He was working all the time, all she was doing was flying around pouncing on things. He turned and took his anger out on the hide of the stag finding himself wishing it was Seth or better yet Kena he was skinning.

Chapter 16 Sami and Kena

Kena circled the small village high up so as not to be clearly seen. Her new target lived here she could feel the blood calling to her. It had taken three weeks before she had dared leave the cavern to search again, but now Caleb could change so he felt more comfortable going out to check the fish traps. Tam was hunting at night again, so she had little worry that they would starve while she was away. Caleb was working at hunting as the Gryphon, but he was not doing well so far. At least now he knew hunting wasn't the simple task he believed it was. It was becoming imperative that they start a small herd of goats or sheep soon or they might all starve and freeze this winter. Well, there was no reason she couldn't walk into this village and look for trade. She hadn't brought much with her of course, not being sure where she would be heading, but this village wasn't more than a few hours flight from the cavern certainly close enough to return here whenever she chose. She banked back to her left being bored with circling to the right. She had not caught sight of her target yet, but if her target was an adolescent he or she would be hard at work and not necessarily that easy to spot from the air. Kena was careful not to fly too low. This was not a plantation of slaves afraid to look up. Those in the village could and had looked up at her from time to time since she started her circling vigil, but from this height she looked like no more than a rather large eagle or hawk certainly nothing to be afraid of. All the weeks of endless hunting had made her strong and given her stamina, she could circle all day and half the night but that would not serve her purpose or help her find the target. Kena could almost taste her frustration it was weighing on her so deeply. *Well, all this circling is getting me no where* she thought to herself, and banking hard to the right she reversed her flight angle to retreat back into the deep woods. Making sure no one was around she landed in the top of a tree not far from the main trade road. She actually remembered this village from her days with her traveling clan and knew having strangers looking for trade would not be anything new or surprising. Hopping from branch to branch she carefully made her way to the ground changing as she dropped from the bottom branch. Well nothing to it now but to walk into the village center and see if there was a market for her furs, no reason she couldn't kill two birds with one dive.

Sami smiled at the smith when he came into her father's shop, but she was careful to keep the spinning wheel going. Her father certainly wouldn't mind her taking a small break, but this wool needed to be spun into thread for a large order. Her father was still insistent on closing the shop. He hated that all Sami's time was spent at the wheel, "Sami this shop should not be your life. You are adventurous and daring you should be out there not trapped in this dark hole." Sami smiled, rather tired of him telling her this, but there was no choice. They needed the income of the shop to survive. Her father had been frugal and saved, but they didn't have enough to live on for long.

Back at the counter in the back of the shop she heard her father trading several spools of bright thread as well as a few folds of the silk fabric for some metal work. Almost all of their business was in trade. Cash money usually went to the tax collectors, merchants and crafters were taxed based on the money they took in not trade goods. Perhaps it was wrong, but the tax levies were so high it was their only choice if they wanted to eat. The king sure didn't care if his people starved. Sami knew they had no use for the metal pots and pans the smith was offering, but they were always good trade items. The farmers were always willing to trade food items for good copper pots and pans, and the traveling clans that came through here often were willing to pay good gold and silver coins for such items as well as for the thread and fabric they had to offer providing the money they needed for the tax collector. She heard her father finishing the deal with the big smith promising to deliver the trade items by end of day tomorrow as he turned to leave. He stopped long enough to smile at Sami and give her an encouraging pat on the back. Sami couldn't see her father, but she knew he would be refolding the fabrics he had opened to show the smith.

Sami let her thoughts wander as she worked the spinning wheel and as usual they wandered to her mother and brother. Their deaths were still so fresh in her mind even though it had been months since the accident. No matter how hard she tried her thoughts always settled on Ty or the accident. She and Ty had their lives all planned out, but that life ended the night of the accident. Somehow her father survived, but it was as a cripple. She had no choice anymore, she had to stay and take care of him. Sami used her shoulder to quickly wipe a tear from her eye and forced her thoughts to something happy, she wouldn't let her father see her cry.

She glanced out the window the spinning wheel was placed in front of to capture as much light as possible. Something caught her eye in the sky. She was surprised to see such a large bird circling the village. There were few enough large birds still living in the woods. They seldom ventured out over the village. She watched the bird for quite some time marveling at its pretty colors. It was definitely red, orange and brown, not the typical bird colors. Her first thought was it looked so much like the fire bird in her father's old tales. Oh how she missed those stories of dragons, fairies, tiguras, and pegasi. When she was a child she used to dream of having a Pegasus come and carry her away on some fanciful adventure. That was a child's dream, and this was reality and the bird was just a bird and there, it had seen there was no easy prey here and it was moving on. Sami felt a little sadness as she watched the bird heading out of sight. Well, she had work to do and little enough time to do it.

Tobias looked over at his daughter working away on the wheel. This was not the life he had wanted for her. She deserved to be out there somewhere not stuck in here taking care of her crippled father. She had flatly refused to accept the offered apprenticeship with the rangers even when they had offered to return in a year, and there was nothing he could do to change her mind. He realized she was watching something out the window and followed her gaze to the remarkable bird. It was quite striking, and he wondered if Sami was wishing she could fly away like the bird. He was so close to being able to close up this shop. Soon, very soon, he would have enough to survive on. He would have to soon enough, he had refused to tie Sami to this shop. Out there was her life, not trapped in here. This was his and his wife's life. They had always known neither of their children were meant for this, but how to get Sami to understand. The healers had warned him then as they warned him now more than his arms had taken injury in the crash. He really shouldn't have survived, but his continued survival was measured in months not years. He was certain as were the healers he would not see the snow fly again. The fact that he had survived as long as he had was pure stubbornness on his part. He had been making arrangements for Sami's continued care. The supply of fabrics and threads would be a nice dowry, but he knew what Sami never said. She had no attraction for men. He and his wife had both known. He just wanted Sami to be happy. One way or another he was not going to have her continue on here. He was just contemplating how he was going to get past her arguments and make her understand all this when a young woman no older than Sami walked into the shop. She stopped and spoke to Sami with a confused look on her face. Sami pointed to the back of the shop and the youngster went were she was pointed reluctantly, seeming to find it hard to take her eyes of off Sami.

Sami looked up at the most striking person she had ever seen. She had never felt this strong of attraction for anyone before. She wasn't sure she believed in love at first sight, but she was beginning to believe. It was with a monumental effort she turned her attention off the strange girl and back to the job at hand.

Kena was shocked when she had walked right into her target. She could tell the call was close, but it was the draw of thread and fabrics that had pulled her to this particular shop. To make matters worse one look at the girl and her mouth had gone dry and her heart had nearly jumped out of her chest. It took control she didn't even know she had to ask who she could speak with about a possible trade. It certainly didn't help that the girl seemed as tongue tied as she and could do no more than point. Kena smiled, nodded and moved to the back of the shop where she was directed. "Excuse me sir," she politely asked when she got near him grateful she seemed to be back in control of both her tongue and emotions, "I am sorry to disturb you sir, but I was hoping to discuss the possibility of trading with you."

Tobias smiled at the child. If he gauged her age right she couldn't be more than a half a year younger than Sami. "Traveler, are you child?" He asked. She had the look of traveler about her, dark eyes, dark weathered skin, lean muscular build, though her confidence belied that upbringing.

"I was sir. My clan was going to force me to into an underage marriage pact, so I left the clan. Now I have a small place northeast of here."

"That's a hard choice child, I'm sorry you had to make it. I have traded with travelers my whole life and I never understood their treatment of women. I respect your bravery and judging by the look of you, you're doing all right for yourself."

Kena smiled at this man. He was nice and she felt at ease in his presence something she wasn't with most people of any kind. It certainly helped her to regain her composure. "Thank you sir, unfortunately while I have been able to supply myself with the basics of survival I have no way to make or get fabrics and thread and as you can see I am badly in need of these." Kena dropped her eyes to the floor embarrassed by her appearance in this neatly kept shop.

Tobias recognized her shame and put a stop to it quickly enough. He reached out and raised her head back up so she was looking him in the eyes again. She had such beautiful eyes, deep dark brown with hints of red throughout. "You have such beautiful eyes child you should always hold your head in a way to show them off. I certainly am willing to discuss a trade. What is it you have to trade?" He asked her smiling.

Kena couldn't believe her luck, the first shop she had stepped into she had found her target and a kind man willing to trade. Unfortunately this was also her worst fear. The girl at the wheel was clearly his daughter, and he was kind and considerate. There was no way her target was going to leave this man to live in the wilderness. This was not some underappreciated girl, or a slave. Well, she would have to work that out. First thing she needed thread and fabric. Kena reached into her bag and pulled out the small black squirrel fur she had brought with her. "I don't have much with me, but I have many furs back at my place. This is a small sample of what I have. I have countless hare, tree hare and rabbit fur, many more squirrel in black, gray and brown. I also have dear and antelope hide. All are dried and ready for use. I can retrieve whatever you think you may like in a day or two."

Tobias took the small fur from the child. "What did you say your name was child?" He asked as he looked over the hide for problems.

"It's Kena, sir." She replied wondering if she should have used her real name, but what were the chances her clan would come through this man's shop and strike up conversation?

"Well, Kena, this is fine work and this is a fine fur. If the others you have to trade with are this nice I will certainly be more than willing to trade. Fur and hide are in high demand around here. I think I can supply your thread and fabric needs. I also may be able to supply some of your other needs as well. I trade for many things I can never use and I may be able to save you trips to other shops and take advantage of your hunting skill at the same time. I have needles and pins here as well as pots, pans, mugs, plates. I even have a few sets of eating utensils. I can get spices and herbs and have them here by the time you return. If there is something else you can think of you may need I can certainly try to trade for it if I don't all ready have it." Tobias had to swallow a laugh when he saw the expression on the youngsters face. "Have no fear child. I know what you left your clan with, or not with. I understand that you will have many needs, but the fact that you still survive is a tribute to your determination and intelligence, and the gold I can get for your furs will be more than worth the trouble."

Kena had to get herself back under control. She had been so shocked by this man and his offer she had even lost part of her shields. She mentally brought them back to full strength, but not before confirming that he was indeed feeling what he claimed and something else, he felt content like he had seen an answer to a problem. Well maybe they needed these furs. She knew he could probably sell them for far more than he was trading for, but she had plenty and if this helped this man and his daughter then she was happy to help. "Thank you sir, your offer is very much accepted. It will save me immeasurable time to be able to trade with just one person. I would ask for leather stripping if it's possible to get as well. I have plenty of hide and I'm a good enough carver to get the soles, but I can't seem to get the stripping I need to make shoes. I could also use a new skinning knife and maybe a carving knife." She added remembering Caleb's request.

Tobias thought on the request. "I can get you all that, I think. I may even have some in the back, but I also have a heavy duty thread that may work better and I will throw that into the bargain as well. It's made from a sturdy plant and twisted and braided together. It's more pliable and easier to use than leather strips, and it lasts just as long. The knives I know I have here."

Kena smiled. "I think I know what you mean, sir, my clan used to use it. I thank you for thinking of it. I will leave right away to get the furs. I should be back in a couple of days." Kena replied trying to make sure she carefully spaced her visits so he didn't question how she was going to travel so quickly.

"Well that's fine Kena, but it's nearly dark. While I am sure you can take care of yourself, even in the dead of night, I don't see why there is huge reason for haste. Unless you need to return to your home quickly?"

Kena thought about the answer to the question carefully. Neither Tam nor the boys would be expecting her for several days at least, so no there was no need for haste. A little break from Caleb's antagonism would also be nice. "No sir, there is nothing that needs my immediate attention."

"Good then," Tobias answered, "You can spend the evening with Sami and myself and leave in the morning, first light if you wish. I'm sure you wouldn't mind a meal you don't have to cook yourself and I am fair cook if I do say so myself." He smiled at Kena and she couldn't help but smile back. Through their whole conversation Sami had worked her wheel with no indication she had even heard anything that was said. Tobias called to his daughter then, getting her attention, "Sami, we have a guest this evening. It's quitting time and the thread will wait until morning. Why don't you take young Kena back to the house while I close up and I'll see you both at home."

Sami's had lost herself in the strangers eyes. She had never seen eyes so beautiful. It had taken every bit of her control to point the girl in the direction of her father. She kept her wheel going but still listened intently. When her father had made the offer for this Kena to stay Sami found herself hoping Kena would answer in the affirmative. She didn't even realize she had been holding her breath until her father called her name. Sami nodded at her father, "Of course, I would be happy to." Sami replied as casually as she could muster. "Hi Kena, it's nice to meet you. I'm Sami, come on we don't live far." She grabbed Kena's hand

and practically dragged her out the door. Trying hard not to notice the warm feeling she got holding Kena's hand and working hard to keep her nerves in check.

Tobias hadn't missed Sami's reaction to Kena though she covered it well. If Kena and Sami could become friends then maybe Kena would be willing to take Sami with her. Sami would be free of this shop and this village. In a few years when the grief wasn't so fresh she could decide what she wanted, but she wouldn't be alone trying to deal with his death and this shop. Yes this was the answer he was looking for. He had always been a good judge of character and this Kena was clearly what she claimed. She didn't even try to hide who she was or what she wanted, and she was clearly a good hunter if that squirrel hide was any indication. Black squirrels never left the highest limbs. Hunting them took the greatest skill with strong bows. If she could hunt black squirrels, hunting rabbits, hare and bigger game would be no problem. Yes, this was the answer. He would see that she had everything she needed and he would make sure she returned often. If she was only a few days' travel away it should be no hardship. Yes, yes he would encourage this friendship, it would be good for both girls. After all, it couldn't be good for Kena to live alone out in the middle of nowhere. With the first bit of happiness he had felt in a long time, he locked the shop early turning the sign that said he would return in the morning and headed to the herb shop to make arrangements to get the supplies he had promised and maybe a few more he hadn't mentioned.

Sami couldn't have been happier with her father's suggestion that Kena spend the night with them. She couldn't wait to learn about Kena's life and hunting and exploring and, well, everything. For the first time in months her thoughts were on something other than Ty and his death. "Come on, we live down this alley now. We used to have a small homestead just outside of town, but father sold it after my mom and brother died and moved us here, closer to the shop. We have to buy the raw wool now, but it's easier with just the two of us. The house also has an indoor pump and fireplace in the kitchen that the old house didn't have. Sure makes it a lot easier to heat water for a bath. You could have one if you want? Do you really live alone? Did you really leave your clan rather than marry?" Sami knew she was babbling but she had so much nervous energy she just couldn't seem to stop. It wasn't like her at all and she was afraid of the first impression she was making.

Kena smiled at Sami. It was so nice to be around someone who was friendly and wanted nothing but friendship from her. Kena was surprised by the warm, loving feelings she found bubbling up but a quick layer on her shields put her back in control. Kena quickly decided to avoid the subject of her home for right now and landed on the question that no longer hurt her to answer. "I'm sorry. I lost my mother and sister not too long ago too. It's why my father was going to force me into a marriage pact in exchange for a wife of his own. There were no women suitable in our clan and no man in the clan goes long without a wife."

Sami seemed to ponder that for a moment. "Father taught me about the clans. He never liked the way they treated women. He told me that women were little more than property with no rights of their own. So your own father would trade you like he was trading goods?"

Kena sighed, "Yes, to the clans females are no more than goods to be dispensed with as the men saw fit. Once you're married you have no hope for any other sort of life so as soon as I could I ran away with little more than the clothes on my back. That was this spring. I got lucky and found a nice cave to live in with a pond and river nearby. I had watched my cousins and learned how to hunt a little, but if it wasn't for the fish traps I made I would have starved long before I mastered the ability to hunt. I lived alone until just a few weeks ago. I stumbled onto a young runaway slave and his brother. I'm letting them stay with me for now. My life was hard in the clan but nothing like theirs as slaves." Kena was surprised how at ease she felt around Sami. Yes blood calls to blood, but she certainly never felt like this around Caleb and Seth was like a younger brother to be cared for.

Kena and Sami had identical shudders as they thought of the life of a slave. "I'm sure you're right. There are no slaves in the village and surrounding homesteads, but I know from the traders who visit the plantations how bad it is there. The tax collector offered to take my brother and me in lieu of the gold or silver for the taxes, but my father threw the money at him. Father told him he would sell himself into slavery before he allowed my brother or me to become slaves. It's very nice of you to help them. I can't imagine they are much help?" Sami was surprised how jealous she was of these escaped slaves living with Kena.

Sami seemed to be echoing Kena's thoughts. "No, they can't do much, but they are learning." Kena smiled, Sami was all over the place. She had never seen anyone with this much energy.

Sami laughed. Her nerves were getting the better of her again. She was vibrating being this close to Kena. "I know how it is. I'm glad you came to our shop. Father will treat you fairly and any time you come to town you'll have a place to stay. Father and I aren't rich, but we do ok so you won't have to worry about going hungry while you're here either. Here we are, this is our house." Sami said unlocking the door and opening it for Kena.

Kena, with just a little hesitation, went through the open door. The sun was starting to set but there was still enough light to see by streaming in from the open windows. Kena couldn't believe her eyes. She had spent all her life living out of a wagon or now a cave and what she saw before her seemed like the lap of luxury. The floor was wood not dirt and even had some sort of fabric covering the wood. Kena jumped off the fabric feeling a little self conscious about having stepped onto it to begin with.

"Oh, don't worry, you won't hurt that old rug." Sami told her when she noticed her move off the rug. Kena smiled, grateful that Sami hadn't laughed at her. Let me show you around. It's nice to have a friend again."

Kena beamed the biggest smile anyone but Tam and her Grandmother had ever seen. "I've never really had a friend before Sami, thanks."

Sami felt warm and knew she was blushing fully aware she for one would do anything to have a relationship built on more than friendship. She changed the subject quickly, "Well this is the living room. This is where we spend most of our time. In here is the kitchen and right through this door is where we keep the tub so we can bathe in privacy. You can have a bath later if you want, I'd be happy to help you get the water. Up here are the sleeping rooms," Sami darted up the stairs. Kena followed more slowly, she had never climbed more than a couple steps into the wagon, but Sami waited patiently at the top ignoring her new friend's nervousness. "The room at the end of the hall is my father's room. This one is mine," Sami said as she pointed to both doors, "and this is the one you'll use when you're here." Sami opened the door and motioned her inside. Kena entered, then stopped, staring. She couldn't help herself, she walked over to the bed and pushed down. It gave way under the pressure and came right back up. It was nothing like the beds in the wagon which were straw filled mattresses placed in boxes. She pushed again and once again it bounced. She must have been a vision of confusion.

Sami politely pretended like she didn't notice. "You'll find some books over in the corner too. This is where father stores them, but you should feel free to read them if you want. Most are legends about the ancients. Father loved those stories. He still tells me stories about them when I get sad. It always makes me feel better to hear stories about fairies and fire birds and stuff." Sami told her as she sat down next to her on the bed. Kena almost choked when Sami said this. She let her shield slip just a little to see if she could sense anything from Sami, and was pleased to feel nothing more than joy, with a touch of longing.

Kena decided maybe she should change the subject, "So, what do you usually do in the evenings after work?"

Sami looked to be thinking hard, "Well normally, to be honest, I lie in my bed and wait for father to call me for dinner and just think. Not much fun I know."

Kena shook her head. "No I understand. I like to just sit and think too. What do you think about if you don't mind my asking?"

"Oh, I don't mind, really. I remember my brother Ty and the accident. I miss him so much sometimes, but most of the time I think about father and how to keep the shop going."

Kena's heart went out to her new friend. She had noticed Tobias crippled hands. She had politely ignored them, but she understood what Sami meant. There was no way Tobias could do the work of spinning and weaving anymore. "Have you come up with a plan in all your thinking?"

"To be honest no, and I'm not sure why I'm telling you this, but I'm not sure I want to keep it going." Sami replied her eyes growing wet with her sadness.

Kena opened her shields and projected understanding and calm. It was a trick she had just recently mastered, but she was very glad she had. "You don't like spinning? You looked like you were really good at it."

Sami felt an odd comfort come over her, a sense of warming that dried the tears forming in her eyes. "Oh, I'm good enough at spinning and my weaving is adequate, but I hate doing it. I hate being trapped inside all day, I hate how the wool rubs my hands raw, I even hate the way the dyes smell, but what can I do?

Without the shop we have no income and I can't leave my dad. I'm a pretty good hunter. I'm a good shot with my bow and sling, I'm a decent trapper and fisherman. I can cook and sew and I could survive on my own like you, but I can't leave my father. I think my father wants me to find some nice boy and marry and live happily ever after, but I don't want to get married. I don't know exactly what I want, but I know I don't want to get married. I don't really like most men. I'm not sure why I'm telling you all this, it's just been so long since I had anyone I could tell this to, not since my brother died, and to be honest it feels good to be able to say it out loud." Sami couldn't hold the tears back any more and she buried her face in her hands and wept.

Kena put her arm around Sami's shoulder and hugged her close to her. She may be a few months younger than Sami, yet she felt so much older and wiser right now. "I can't make it better for you Sami, but I can listen. I have a feeling I'm going to be in and out of the village a lot before winter, so I'll be around for you to talk to. I know what it's like needing someone or something to listen to you. I am happy to be that for you, after all like you said, we're friends now." Kena carefully added acceptance to the emotions she was projecting all the while forcing her own feelings back behind her carefully built walls.

They were interrupted by the door down stairs closing and Tobias calling for them. "Sami, Kena, are you here?"

Sami quickly answered, "We're up here Father!"

"Well, come down, I have a surprise for you both." He called back.

Sami dried her eyes, and thanked Kena with a smile that could melt the heart of a harder person than Kena, grabbed Kena's hand and giggling like little girls they ran down the stairs.

Kena lay on her back in the very comfortable bed. Her arms were folded behind her head and her eyes closed. It was pitch black in the room but she didn't mind. Tobias had offered her a lantern for the night, but Kena declined, she had no fear of the dark. Besides if she needed to see she could always change. Her night vision as a Phoenix was superb, not that she had told Tobias that. Kena couldn't believe how happy she was here. It would be so easy to stay here forever. Tobias had told her she was welcome to stay if she wanted to. Part of her wanted to accept that offer so badly it hurt. She had never known a man could be this kind, gentle and thoughtful and being around Sami brought a strange joy and a weird fire she had never felt, even around Tam or her grandmother.

On his way home, Tobias had stopped at the bakeshop and got the girls a pastry each that he let them eat while he cooked a wonderful dinner of lamb and tubers. Kena had never eaten so well. Tobias had even insisted she take one of the fresh red fruits up to the room with her. "I know how hungry younglings can get in the middle of the night, so you take that up there with you, then you don't have to come all the way back down here." Oh how she would like to stay, forget all about the cavern, hunting and fishing, keeping the boys alive, and suffering Caleb's snide mean remarks but then she remembered her Grandmother, Seth and Tam. She couldn't leave them, not ever. They were her family, but that didn't mean she couldn't have this once in awhile for herself. There was no reason Sami couldn't live here and come to the cavern. Once she learned to change she could make the trip in a few hours if she turned out to be a winged ancient or instantly if she shared blood with the unicorn. Sami already believed in the old legends, she probably wouldn't even be afraid of Tam. No this was going to work out. She could come here to trade and this could be her little sanctuary when things got too much. Her new friendship with Sami was an unexpected bonus. At least she wouldn't have to take care of Sami. She was capable of taking care of herself. Well, first thing in the morning she would head back to the cavern. If she hunted on the way she could rest in the afternoon and return the next morning with the furs. She was going to have to make several trips back and forth over several weeks to get all furs here and all the supplies home. Tobias wanted her to come to the shop and take the needed knives, thread, fabric and needles back with her, "No sense in you making a trip empty handed. It's going to be a lot of walking back and forth as it is. I trust you to bring what you promised back." Kena had felt proud that she had Tobias' trust and she had no intention of doing anything to harm that. Somehow with all these thoughts running through her head, in the dark room she fell asleep into the most wonderful dreams she had ever had.

Morning light and a larks call woke Kena the next morning. She was disoriented by the feel of the soft bed under her, until she remembered where she was. She stretched and threw the soft blanket off. She folded it and placed it back on the bed. She grabbed up the clean clothes Tobias and Sami had insisted she take last night. Thankfully she and Sami were near enough the same size that the clothing fit well. She shoved her old stuff in her bag put on her worn old shoes and headed down the stairs. Sami was up and in the kitchen when she entered it.

"Good morning, Father said you would sleep in a little since this was probably your first time in a soft bed, so he asked me to wait and make sure you ate then bring you back to the shop before you headed home. Father went in early to pack up a load of stuff for you. Kena, did you mean it when you said I could come back with you sometime?" Sami asked like a child that was afraid of losing a sweet.

"I meant it, any time you are free you are welcome. I look forward to showing you my home and repaying some of the kindness you have shown me. There have been few enough people in my life showing kindness."

Sami smiled and felt the now familiar warmth spread through her body and quickly set two bowls of porridge down on the table as a distraction. "I waited to eat with you this morning. I didn't think you'd mind."

"Of course not," Kena replied with a grin sitting down at the table in front of the porridge.

Sami brought over two small pitchers and a small bowl with a spoon before she brought over two mugs full of dark black tea giving one of the mugs to Kena and keeping one. Sami pointed to one of the pitchers. "Extra tea in that one, goats milk for your tea and cereal in the other and, of course, sugar if you use it in either." She explained while she poured milk into her porridge and tea, then scooped several heaping spoonfuls onto her cereal. Kena never had much sugar growing up and she sure hadn't had any since she had left the clan so this was quite a treat. She scooped a couple small spoonfuls in to her cereal with just a touch of milk and sprinkled just a little into her tea. She was pleased to find the tea at just the right temperature to drink and she swallowed it down quickly. She ate more slowly enjoying the taste of the sweetened porridge. "There's more if you want" Sami told her getting up to get it.

Kena would have loved to have had more, but she had a long flight ahead of her and one thing she couldn't do was fly on an overly full stomach. "No thank you Sami, I have a long fligh...er, walk ahead of me."

Sami didn't seem to notice Kena's slip. "Okay, let me just clean up real quick, then we can head to the shop. I want to get that order of thread done faster than ever now."

Tobias had carefully laid out a strong square piece of linen on the counter and he was carefully putting several folds of fabric in the square. Bearing in mind what Kena had told him about the two slave boys living with her he made sure to include some colors that would appeal to them as well. That done he put in several spools of different threads in different colors and thicknesses. He piled several packages of pins and different size needles on top and for good measure threw in a spool of the heavy thread that should work well for shoes. Then he wrapped the linen around the pile and tied it closed. He carefully whip stitched a strap of leather about finger length wide on the makeshift pack. That done he stood back and admired his handiwork. Yes, this should be easy to carry. He placed three knives in their sheaths next to the pack and smiled contently. He couldn't believe how well the two girls were getting along. They acted more like sisters than two girls who had met not a day before. Tobias had little doubt that his plan was going to work. Just this morning Sami had asked for permission to return with Kena to her home sometime when she didn't have so much work that needed done. Well he could certainly make sure that there was no more work after what Sami was working on right now. The furs Kena had promised to bring would supply him with more than enough gold to survive on. Just then the door swung open and both girls jogged in giggling and chatting. "Well, it is always good to see such beauties this early in the morning." Tobias smiled as Sami, used to his compliments, shushed him, but Kena blushed obviously not used to compliments of any kind. "Kena, I have a pack of stuff ready for you whenever you are ready to head out," Tobias told her motioning to the pack.

"I'm as ready as I am ever going to be sir. Thank you very much for everything. I'll be back in two days with as many furs and hides as I can carry. Is there anything in particular you would like first?"

"No, no Kena whatever you bring will be fine. You are quite welcome and you are welcome any time and you can stay as long as you like. We look forward to your return."

Kena didn't know what to say so she settled for nod and took up the pack slinging the strap over her head and shoulder so that the pack rested nicely on her hip, she hung the three sheathes on her battered belt and quickly turned and headed for the door, but Sami

Eagle Bennett
grabbed her hand. "I'll walk you to the end of the village."

"That's okay Sami, stay get to spinning. The sooner you're done the sooner you can travel with me." Sami looked disappointed but didn't press. Kena quickly exited the shop and ran as fast as she could out of the village before she changed her mind and never left.

The flight back was fast and uneventful. She noticed many new places full of prey to hunt, but she didn't dare try to dive with the added weight of the pack. The pack did slow her down some, but she still made the cavern by midmorning. She circled once waiting for the top to open far enough for her to slip inside. One day she would understand how the magic worked that opened the cavern, but for now she was just grateful that it did it saved the long walk through the tunnel. She gently dove into the cavern back winging hard to land on the soft sand. The landing was a bit harder than she was used to, but this was the first time she had landed with such weight. She quickly changed just before Seth ran to her hugging her.

"Kena I've missed you. You should see what I can do know. Look!" Seth skipped back away from her, scrunched his face into a vision of concentration and changed into a small adolescent dragon. Kena was surprised that he was blue, a very dark midnight blue. He quickly changed back. "I can't seem to hold it for long, but Tam says practice will help."

Kena smiled at the youngster, she couldn't have imagined a better greeting and she was happy to have been missed. It made leaving her new friend a little easier, "Tam's right. I had a hard time holding my shape when I first starting changing too. You keep trying and you'll get it. Where's Caleb?" Kena asked surprised by the fact that she had missed him.

It was Tam that answered from the back of the cavern, "He has gone to check the fish traps. He has learned fast and well and will fly tonight for the first time outside the cavern."

Kena dropped the pack as she acknowledged Tam's words. "I am sorry I have returned without my target, but getting her here is not going to be as easy as I would have hoped. I did however strike a bargain to get us much needed supplies." Kena opened the pack to show Seth what she had. "With this stuff we can make clothes and shoes. As soon as I can pack up enough furs and hides I'm taking them back to trade for more supplies we just can't make here."

"If you could maybe get us a new knife, the one we have is next to useless." Caleb replied from the entrance of the cavern without a welcome or a hello.

Kena gave him a cold glance, and resisted the urge to toss one of the knives at him. Instead she dropped the two skinning knives onto the pack deciding to keep the little dagger before she went on with her story. "I have to get as many furs and hides back as I can. I am working on my target and I will try to get her to come back with me, but she loves her father very much and I don't think even the prospect of changing is going to get her to stay. I do believe she will be willing to return, but she won't stay." Tam nodded and the murals all made understanding noises and sent understanding feelings. At least they were not mad at her for her failure. "It will take me longer to return burdened with the weight I will be carrying. I don't think I will be able to fly." Kena told them trying to buy some more time with Sami.

Tam shook his head, "There is no reason you have to carry the whole burden. I will help you this evening fly the furs and hides to just outside the village and I will return the following evening to get the supplies. Caleb can accompany me, it will be good for him to stretch his wings, though he will not be able to carry any weight."

I would appreciate the help Tam, but I can't guarantee I will be ready by nightfall. In fact I am certain Sami, that's the target, and her father won't let me leave at night."

"So you leave during the day, camp and wait until nightfall. I will check every night for you so there is no reason for you to hurry. You can spend as much time as you need working on this new target. Will that suit your needs, little one?"

Kena thought about it, "Yes Tam that would be great. I would like to spend some time with Sami. See if I can't get her to come for a visit at least." Kena was surprised how badly she couldn't wait to get back to her friend. A burning in her heart at the mere thought of Sami surprised her, but before anyone could notice she added a quick layer to her shields.

Seth glared at Caleb. *Caleb you got what you wanted, you could at least say thanks.* Seth sent to his brother. He was still new at mind speaking but his anger was giving him power he didn't know he had.

Caleb jumped a little, it was the first time someone other than his grandfather or Tam had mind spoke him and he was surprised how forceful Seth's voice was. *Oh I should thank her for getting us something we needed to survive and that I am the only one using since I am the only one skinning. Okay, fine!* "Hey Kena thanks for getting us the new knives and the other stuff, it's not like we needed any of it to survive or anything." *There are you happy?* Caleb sent to his brother as he took the knives and stormed out through the tunnel.

Seth just shook his head, the entire time Kena was gone Caleb was almost nice. It frustrated Seth that Caleb seemed to save all his nastiness for Kena or him when he defended her. "I'm sorry about him, Kena, I don't understand why he acts like that."

Kena couldn't help how much Caleb's attitude hurt. A different kind of fire burned in her, but there was nothing she could do about it so she added a layer to her shields for safety and ignored it. "It's okay Seth, Caleb is the child of a Gryphon. He is who he is. I can handle it, I promise. So, anything else happen while I was gone?"

Kena had found a safe and hidden camp not far from the main road. They had brought no more than Kena could carry and walk the remaining distance to the village, but it was still an impressive pile of furs. It was clear that as much as she wanted to, Kena couldn't go into the village first thing this morning. She had no way to explain her two day's journey was accomplished in one. Unfortunately, this left way too much time for thinking and that was exactly what Kena was doing. Kena sat on the ground with her back against a tree.

Eagle Bennett

She would have been much more comfortable in the tree, but she had to guard the hides so for now she was earthbound. She didn't even dare a fire, for one thing someone may see the smoke and come investigate for another it had been a hot dry summer and a single spark could easily start a forest fire. Even with the control over fire she had Kena knew no one could stop a hungry fire in dry brush. So fireless and earthbound, all Kena could do was wait and think.

She tried to direct her thoughts, but they kept coming back to Sami. She was surprised by how much she missed her. She had never been more relaxed with anyone before. Just thinking about her brought a smile to her face. Kena moaned, angry with the way her emotions were leaking out from behind her shields. She had to get her feelings for Sami under control, but she had never felt like this for anyone before. Just thinking about her made her heart burn. Kena shook her head and forced her thoughts to something else. Somehow she wasn't surprised when they landed on Caleb. He was always so angry and well, mean was the only word she could come up with for him. Well he was still learning to control the Gryphon part of himself. She could deal with him until he did. She found herself wondering what ancient Sami shared blood with and trying hard to figure it out. Her strongest quality seemed to be her loyalty and she was a good crafter. Maybe she was a Dokul, somehow that didn't seem right. Loyalty may be a strong quality but Kena wasn't sure it was the deciding one. Somehow Kena thought her most defining qualities may be hidden behind her need to help her father.
"Grahhhggh" Kena yelled into the air. Why couldn't she get her mind of off Sami? There were so many things she needed to think about but every thought

came back to her. One thing was sure, she had to deal with whatever these emotions were before she made her way back to the village or she risked scorching the whole place.

By early evening Kena judged it safe to enter the village. The last thing she was going to do was sleep on the cold ground when she had a friend and a soft warm bed waiting for her. The walk in was actually shorter than she anticipated. She was not at all surprised to find both Sami and her father hard at work in the shop. Sami saw Kena as she made her way down the street and ran to meet her. Sami gave Kena a rough, exuberant hug and Kena returned it, a little more reserved, carefully making sure the inner fire Sami elicited stayed put behind the carefully constructed shields she had spent most of the afternoon building and layering. Still Kena couldn't believe how happy she was to see Sami.

Sami held the hug a little longer than was customary or necessary, but Kena didn't seem to mind. "Kena! Father said you would be here tonight. He was right as always. Here let me help with those, you've carried them far enough. Father and I were just waiting for you to quit for the night. We can take these to the shop, then we can go home to get some dinner. The furs will wait until morning." Sami rambled as they made their way down the street. "I finished the last bit of work and Father says that was it for a while."

Kena smiled and nodded happy to be back with her friend. She checked her shields and relaxed a little more when she found it was holding. Sami's easy going friendship was exactly what she needed. "That sounds like a good idea to me, I'm starving." Sami laughed and hurried her to the shop.

Dinner was a filling affair of a lamb stew Tobias had started earlier in the day and left to simmer over a low fire. It was full of big chunks of lamb and potatoes as well as carrots, turnips, and cabbage with a think heavily spiced broth. There were also fresh baked rolls from the baker and a special surprise for after dinner. It was a wonderful dinner and Kena ate more than she should, but since she wouldn't be flying or even walking anywhere but to a bed there was no reason not to. After dinner Tobias encouraged Sami and Kena to retire to the comfortable seating in the living room. The couch was placed to catch as much heat from the fireplace as possible, of course there was no fire now in the heat of summer, but it was still the best place to sit. Sami propped herself up placing her back against the arm of the couch and pulled her legs up hugging her knees. Kena took the other end of the couch sitting on one of her legs while the other one dangled. They chatted amiably about nothing in particular, completely comfortable with each other.

Tobias eavesdropped on the girls while he cleaned up the kitchen. He was pleased by the way their friendship was going. He knew for Sami it was more than that. Kena was a little harder to read, she was so in control, but he felt the feelings whether Kena realized it or not were mutual. As soon as he had cleaned up the kitchen Tobias joined them taking the oversized chair facing the couch. "Well children that was certainly a fine meal with very good company. Now what would you like to do since the evening is still young?"

Eagle Bennett

Sami and Kena looked at each other and smiled almost in unison they replied, "Tell us a story?"

Tobias looked at them, playing along since he had known quite well they would want a story. Sami hadn't asked for one since the accident and it was a good sign that she wanted one now. "A story? Well, I don't know… What kind of story would you like to hear?"

It was Sami that answered "Please Father, please tell us about the ancients!"

Tobias smiled "I think I remember a legend or two about them, but Kena is our guest. Would you like to hear a story about an ancient?"

Kena smiled a smile that actually made her look her true age instead of the adult she had been forced to be by family and circumstance. "Do you know any stories about the Phoenix sir? I would love to hear a story about her?" Tobias looked at the ceiling while he thought. "The fire bird huh? Hmm, not the usual request. Most of the time I get Dragons and Gryphons. Hmm, let me see. Why, yes, I believe I know a story about a Phoenix, it goes something like this."

"Plentia was a bird, a very large bird. She hunted almost anything she wanted and she soared high above the clouds. She was free and happy. She shared the sky with many others but she didn't mind, she was not on their menu and they left her to fly in peace. Flying was her greatest joy, and she did it as much as she could even when there was no reason for her to do so. That was why she was in the sky this day. She loved to dive hard and fast then at the last minute soar high reveling in the freedom of the skies. She also loved to wing through the clouds, watching how her wing beats moved the puffy white air. She avoided dark clouds though, she had no love of rain, and she hated how her feathers smelled when they were wet. She winged out of a puffy white cloud and saw something strange she had never seen before. There was a dark gray and black cloud ahead of her, but it was streaming up from the forest below. Clouds flew the sky like her, and they seldom dropped to the earth. When they did it was only in the peak of a storm when lightning attacked at its most fierce. She had seen this from afar a few times, but never over an area where the sun shown brightly. Her curiosity was peaked, what was this cloud that came from earth? She circled the column of gray cloud following it down to its origin. She landed neatly in the trees transfixed by what she had found. Everywhere she looked a bright orange and red being seemed to have taken over the trees and underbrush. The being danced with what she could only assume was joy over its victory. It was then the being seemed to notice her for the first time. It stopped its dancing in front of her and her head was filled with a voice. The voice was smooth yet it crackled and was different than any voice she had heard before. *Why do you not fly away in fear like your brethren who used to abide here?* She cocked her head at the being before she answered, "I am not as weak and fearful as the tasty things that live here." *Do you not realize I could kill you easily?* She smirked back at the being, "I am not easy to kill." The being danced again at her feet laughing at her answers to its questions. *Not easy to kill? Oh, that is funny, brave flier of the sky. I am fire. I can kill anything with a thought. When I am hungry I can destroy whole swaths of land. Nothing can stand before me, certainly not a mere flier.* She was angry now, a mere flier! She screamed at the being as she spread her wings preparing to fight. *Peace flier, I meant no disrespect. Perhaps we can work together. I do have one weakness. I cannot go where I wish, I am limited to where the wind and others take me. I am sick of being a slave to others, I wish for an equal partner. You will give me what I need, mobility, and I will give you an even greater gift, the gift of fire and all the gifts that come with that.* She stared at the being dancing all around her. Now for the first time she could feel the heat nipping at her wings and feet and she was afraid but she would not be anyone or anything's slave. "What do I get from such a gift? Death is preferable to answering to another for the rest of my life." *You misunderstand me brave one. You will not be my slave we will be partners. I will help you as you help me. I can make you invincible. Do you accept the bargain brave one?* She looked at the dancing being. "If I refuse, will you kill me?" *No brave one. I would not kill one such as you, you are free to fly away. If you see me again though, stay away or I will kill you. Do not make a hasty decision, my gift to you will be great, greater than you can even imagine.* She cocked her head to one side then the other considering her options. She could fly away and never make the same mistake again, but the gifts it promised her did seem to be great. "I accept your bargain being. I will be your partner." She had cause to regret her words as soon as they left her mouth. Fire surged all around her. She felt the fire licking at her feathers. She spread her wings and screamed at the fire. "What is this? What are you doing…" She barely had the words out when her feathers caught fire. She felt the fire eating away at her, the pain was nearly unendurable. She felt like she would be nothing but ash in moments. "Why have you done this?" She cried at the fire. *Patience brave one, we are nearly one.* It was only with these words she realized it was only her feathers that burned not flesh. Her talons were hot, but they did not burn. She opened her eyes and lost herself in the fire. She was taken by the beauty, by the hypnotic rhythm of the dancing flames. She looked at her spread wings a light with fire. She was fascinated how the fire moved when she moved her wings. She was not so much consumed by the fire but part of it. *We are one now brave one forever. You can call on me whenever you wish and I will answer. You are born again, born anew. You are no longer Plentia, from this moment forth you are Phoenix.* The Phoenix flew the sky for many years keeping her promise to spread fire. The fire was true to his word and the gifts he granted her were far greater than she could have imagined, but greatest of all fire extended the partnership to her offspring so the Phoenix could continue to fly the sky for generations to come."

The girls were silent for a moment. Sami was the first to respond. "That was great Father. I don't remember ever hearing it before." Kena was quick to add her agreement.

"You know, Kena, it is customary for a well told story to be rewarded by a story of one's own?" Tobias replied.

Kena thought for a moment, "Well I do know one story about the ancients perhaps you would like to hear it?" Sami was quick to agree. Kena was by no means the story teller Tobias was but she seemed to hold both Sami and Tobias' attention as she related Tam's story of the ancients.

When she finished Tobias' face held a smile, "I have not heard that story before. You did well Kena, you are a natural story teller." Kena blushed and dropped her head not being used to praise of any kind.

"Sir," Kena asked quietly, "You and Sami seem like you are not afraid of the ancients?"

Tobias looked at her surprised by the question, "No Kena I am not afraid of the legends after all they are just stories."

"If they were more than stories, sir, would you be afraid then?" Kena asked with a little more force. Something in her needed to know the answer. Something in her needed them to understand, both of them, not just Sami. She wasn't at all sure what she was doing but it seemed right somehow.

"No, Kena I would not. I have heard stories of the ancients my whole life. My grandfather even claimed to have sheltered an ancient once when he was young, of course he was going senile at the time and no one believed his story as more than that. But he swore it was nothing but the truth and was even able to describe the cat like beast in great detail. I wanted to believe him as a child, unfortunately like all children I grew up and I now know the truth."

Kena smiled at Tobias. He had given her the opening she desperately needed. "What if I told you he could have been right, that he was in fact telling the truth? What if I could prove to you the ancients do, in fact, still live." Kena forced the fear back behind her shields. If this went wrong, if she had misread the situation…

Sami's interest was piqued, "How Kena, how can you prove it?"

"If you promise not to be afraid, I can prove it right now right here!" Sami nodded Tobias looked dubious but nodded as well. "I'm sorry, but I really need you to swear it out loud please?" They quickly swore their words that no matter what Kena showed them they would not be afraid. Kena nodded and looked down at her feet. She would have to be very careful to control her emotions, not a wisp of fire could escape during this change, so she strengthened her shields to be safe. She closed her eyes as she changed, one instant Tobias and Sami were watching their friend, the next instant they were looking at a man sized red bird with a wickedly sharp beak and talons that could kill a steer let alone a man. Kena was not quite finished she wanted them to know unquestioningly that she was indeed a Phoenix, so carefully she called fire. She was ever so careful to keep it to only on her head and shoulders. Fire was angry, wanting more, but it obeyed readily enough and after Tobias' story she better understood the reason why. She allowed fire free reign for seconds only before she ordered it away and her head and shoulders returned to nothing more than feathers. It was only then that she dared open her eyes and look at her friends. She was deathly certain, even after swearing, that she was going to see terror reflected there, but there was no fear. She opened her shields ever so slightly and felt not fear or even dread, but admiration and wonder and surprisingly relief, longing and love. She quickly changed back and waited for either of them to speak.

It was Sami that spoke almost immediately, "It was you a saw flying the other day wasn't it?"

"A moment daughter," Tobias interrupted, "I am sure Kena will answer your question, but please let her sit back down she looks as if she is going to fall down if you don't."

Sami noticed Kena had gone quite pale and her curiosity was overcome by concern. Tobias helped Kena back to her place on the comfortable couch.

"Is this the reaction every time you do that?" Tobias asked concerned.

Kena shook her head at Tobias' question. It wasn't changing that had affected her, but their reaction to it. She still couldn't quite find the words to describe the relief she felt. Sami had ran off to the kitchen and quickly returned with a cup of tea that Kena took with shaky hands. After a few sips she was again composed and ready to answer their questions.

"Feeling a little better, Kena?" Tobias asked with all the concern of a loving father.

"Yes thank you. I was just so surprised by how you took my changing, I didn't expect such a reaction."

Tobias nodded, "When you are ready, would you be willing to answer some questions?"

Kena nodded more than willing to answer anything at this point. Sami started to rattle off questions and Tobias shushed her with a look.

"After such a performance, am I to believe your story was no story at all but a recitation of facts?" Kena

Eagle Bennett nodded knowing that was not the real question. "Then the lads, the slaves, you took in are they like you?"

This was a question that required an answer. "Yes and no sir. Yes they are children of the ancients like I am, but they carry Dragon and Gryphon blood while I am obviously a Phoenix. If your question is can they change, yes they can though Seth is having a bit of a hard time." Kena knew she was babbling a little but relief was making her giddy.

"Now, tell me true child, did they come to you or did you go to them."

Kena had no intention of lying for one thing she was terrible at it, for another she saw no reason to even try Tobias was headed somewhere with these question and Kena felt she had no choice but to follow his lead since she had no idea where he was going. "Yes sir, I was sent for them. I can feel others and follow that feeling to wherever they are. The ability to call fire is not my only gift. I am an empath as well. A gift I can use to find others."

Tobias nodded as if he had expected that exact answer, "Then it is not by chance that you stumbled into my shop?"

"No sir, it was no accident. I felt Sami's blood calling to me. She is like me too." Kena figured this pronouncement was sure to get her thrown out at the very least, but she was nearly washed away by the wave of relief that swamped her even through her shields causing her to add more layers to the shields.

Tobias eyes welled with tears as he took Kena into a

hug so fierce she was sure he would crush her, "Kena you are the answer to my every hope. Now, I will never again have to worry about my daughter."

It took several hours before Tobias' entire story was relayed to the two girls. Sami for her part took the news that her father was dying very well, almost like she was somehow aware even if he had not told her. Kena felt she probably was somehow subconsciously aware. It was hard to keep secrets from those you loved. Sami however hated her father's plan almost as much as Kena liked it. "Enough Sami," Tobias quieted another argument from his daughter. "I am leaving. You have your own life to lead now. You have much to learn, the last thing you need to do is take care of your dying father while you try to build your own life. I have always wanted to travel but the opportunity never presented itself. Now it seems the perfect answer. I have a buyer for the shop space and the house. You will take everything you need with you. I will sell the rest to my buyer, he is a good lad that I am sure will be happy to accept trade from you. Neither he nor the village need to know anything other than you have found a place to live and learn a trade that suits your temperament better. It is not really a secret in town that I am dying, but I am grateful the gossips never whispered it near you. Anyway, the sale of the house and shop will give me enough money to travel comfortably and see that you and Kena have some gold and silver to spend as well. Eventually the tax collectors will hear of your little place and come knocking and this will ensure you have something to give them."

Kena smirked at the notion but Tobias missed the look. Sami however was not finished with her arguments, "I could travel with you, Father. Kena can wait a few months."

Tobias ended that argument quickly enough, "Oh, so you can watch me die. NO SAMI, I will not allow that. What would you do if we are in a far away foreign land when I do die hmm? No this is something I must do alone and you have things you must now do." Tobias then took the sting out of his words by hugging his daughter, "I always knew you were special, you and Ty both. I knew you were meant to do important things. I understood why you couldn't go with the rangers and now you will have something all your own without the sting of Ty's memory." His words brought tears to Sami's eyes. "I will write to you daughter. The smith can collect my letters and you can pick them up from him. There are always traders willing to take a letter or two."

"Many of the travelers will carry a letter or package or two for a little consideration and almost all the travelers pass this way. Not all the travelers are as bad as my clan" Sami looked at her and nodded. "I have one other thing I would ask of you please Tobias?" When he nodded Kena continued, "Spread word to others like Sami and I. Trust your instincts, I believe you can tell who they will be. Many will discount you, but some will believe, send them to us, so they too can realize who they really are. In return we can supply you with furs as trade goods. I have plenty and if we are going to eat, plenty more to come. It should keep you in ready cash while you travel. "

Tobias seemed to think hard about the request, "If I do this word is going to eventually leak out of the existence of your little haven, bad people, and there are plenty of bad people in this world as you well know, will come as well."

Kena scoffed at the idea, "Then perhaps the surprise will be on them?"

Chapter 17 Pieces of Four

Sami was as awestruck by the cavern as Kena could have hoped. As expected, she showed no outward sign of fear when she met Tam for the first time, but Kena could feel her fear even through her shields. It surprised her a little especially when she found no cracks or leaks, so she strengthened them and added a layer. Sami's fear turned to joy when she was bid to join the murals.

Caleb's approach broke into Kena's joy at seeing her friend happy. "I bet Unicorn, she seems too princess-like to be anything else."

Kena wanted to say you don't know anything about her, but what she did say was nothing. She just shook her head and moved away deciding to avoid a fight.

Sami walked along the cavern looking at each mural. She privately hoped as she approached the Phoenix that she would like Kena share blood with her, but it was clear as she approached she did not. With a little regret she moved on. It was the next mural where she found her match. Sami gasped at the feeling that rushed into her heart, as she reached out to touch the mural. Sami searched her memories for what this ancient was. Try as she might she couldn't remember a story of a winged cat-like ancient.

Eagle Bennett

That is because of our gift, Granddaughter. We are Tiskin. Our gift disguises us, makes us invisible. We are the unknown of the ancients, but we prefer it like that. It is in our nature. Sami sighed as she slid down the wall to the soft sand. She heard the soft purr of contentment from her grandmother that perfectly mirrored her own feelings. *I am so pleased to finally meet you Sami.*

Please tell me more about Tiskins and our gifts. Sami asked.

The mural sank farther down the wall to be next to Sami. *We are the spies of the ancients, Sami. We can disappear into any landscape. Our greatest gift is a mind speech that makes the being seeing us see what we wish them to see, and when that fails we really can become invisible. That part of our gift can be dangerous, so we use it as a last resort.*

So we don't actually become what is being seen?

No Granddaughter, you are still what you are but anyone who sees you sees what you want them to see even those who know your gift.

Why is invisibility dangerous?

Ah, that is harder to explain but I shall try. Unlike mind speech, invisibility is real magic. Mind speech, empathy, the Unicorn's ability to jump, all of these are tied to who we are. Like breathing, they are instinctual, and like breathing we can control them but we can't stop them. The thought simply becomes the deed, but invisibility is true magic. True magic requires concentration and energy. The danger in true magic is the sourcing of that energy. If its source is your own energy, you could be drained before you realize you're in danger.

Sami considered what her grandmother was saying to her. *I think I understand, so is there a source outside yourself you could use to power your magic?*

Yes child, but sometimes they are not easily accessible. Energy is all around us, in the plants and the water, in the sun, even the moon has energy, but that does not mean we have access. The energy in fire, for instance, can only be channeled by a Phoenix, fire is far too dangerous for anyone not immune to it to dare touch.

So what energy can a Tiskin channel?

A Tiskin channels the energy of life. When you are fully trained and have come fully into your gifts you will be able to draw on the energy stored in the life that sprouts all around you. As long as the object is living you can direct its energy, but to do so from a sentient being would be wrong without their permission.

I understand that Grandmother and I would never do that.

It is imperative, Granddaughter, that you learn what I can teach you and quickly. It is unsafe for Kena to continue her missions alone and you are the clear choice to accompany her. You will be able to insinuate yourself places she is unable.

Sami couldn't help it, the thought of being alone with Kena made her breath catch and her heart rate rise.

Eagle Bennett

I think perhaps shielding will be our first lesson. Sami if your feelings are apparent to me, they will be doubly so to Kena and her empathy. Kena is the strongest empath I have ever known, stronger than her grandmother or any phoenix. Sami, loving an empath can be wonderful, but it can be fraught with obstacles. To truly love one such as Kena you will need patience, sympathy, and understanding. She will not be easy to love or to convince she is loved, but if you succeed the love she will return will be deep and pure, steadfast and unwavering. As an empath, to cause you hurt or pain is to inflict the same upon herself. Only you can decide if it is worth the risk.

Sami groaned, the warning came a little late. She was already in love with Kena. Well, patience was something she had plenty of, she could wait. Sami knew no matter how hard it may be, having Kena's love would be worth it. *Thank you for the warning Grandmother, but I think I will take my chances. So can we start now, I think learning to shield might be a good thing. The sooner I can help Kena the better.*

Chapter 18 Beginnings

Seth's frustration with his brother had reached an all time high. Two years they had lived here and Caleb was still just as cruel as ever. In fact it seemed to him the more Changers that came to live in the valley the worse he treated Kena. He had tried to have several conversations with him about his attitude, but all he ever got was defensiveness and accusations. Somehow, he always turned the conversation around on him, or worse, Kena. No matter what was said or what happened it was always Kena's fault. Conversations with Kena could be just as bad sometimes worse. Kena was burying her feelings and killing herself with work and she refused to see it. It was why he was in the sky this early in the morning. This was the only time Sami could meet him outside the cavern and the two of them needed to talk about Kena.

Seth tilted his wings back and climbed. He was early for his meeting and flying always calmed him. No reason he couldn't fly an early patrol. He circled north to the edge of the land the Changers had claimed. Sami and Kena had proved to be a great team when it came to bringing in others, and Sami's father was amazing. Now they had nearly two hundred Changers living here in what they called the valley. With so many to feed they had, out of necessity, extended their borders. They now claimed from the cliff in the east to the river in the west and from the snowy wastes in the north to the waterfall in the south. It was a huge area to patrol, but thanks to Kena and her organizational skills it was all getting done.

Seth adjusted his patrol avoiding the village. Thanks to the influx of Dokuls, everyone had shelter, if they wanted, in the new village. That's what Dokuls do, they build. They were really only happy when they were building, it was not just their nature but also their gift. There was nothing a Dokul couldn't build. After all it was the ancient Dokuls that built the cavern. The Dokuls had not only built shelter but forges, smoking and food storage sheds, roads, and a hundred other things that made living in the valley easier and better. They were even looking to build a commons building where everyone would go for meals consolidating hunting and cooking efforts. They were just waiting for approval from Kena to get started on it.

Seth made one last flight adjustment heading to the waterfall that marked the edge of their territory. It was the one spot that was guarded day and night. The river was the only way to get easy access into the valley. They had built a ford at the river making crossing easier and posted signs warning all to cross the river here. So far they had been lucky and everyone coming this way had crossed, respecting their land rights. He had volunteered for this mornings' guard so he and Sami could talk somewhere without any chance Kena would hear.

Seth was careful about where he landed. His bulk was enough to collapse the carefully built boulder overlook at the waterfall. It wasn't really big enough for him, but it was certainly warm enough even this early in the morning that the parts of him that rested in the water actually felt good. The Pegasi that had been on watch called a greeting and departed just as Seth saw Sami's sleek gray form winging in to land. She came to rest on his shoulder as the only place left for her to do so.

Sami didn't mind using Seth's Dragon shoulder as her landing point. Actually, it was far more comfortable than the boulders she normally sat on to keep watch. She pulled more than her share of watch. She enjoyed the quiet time. She had never been happier or more frustrated in her entire life. "So, little brother, I'm here what is so urgent that we are here so blasted early in the morning on the only day I have off?" Sami asked without preamble.

"Kena." Seth answered hearing, the groan and sigh from Sami.

Sami took a deep breath and quieted the nerves she always seemed to get anytime the subject of Kena came up. "Okay Seth, what do we need to talk about that concerns Kena?" Sami answered even if Kena was the last subject she wanted to talk about.

"Oh, don't tell me you don't see it Sami, 'cause I know you do. She's working herself to death. She does twice the work anyone else does. She's the one making all the decisions even on stupid little things. I mean, is it really necessary for her to decide who flies patrols when? It's the job of the Gryphons, Tiguras, and Gryphels to fly the patrols, why can't they decide for themselves who flies patrols and who hunts? I mean, you decide all that for the Tiskins. Why can't the other races elect a leader to make these kinds of decisions? Qwint certainly knows better which of his people are better suited to what job, and I have no doubt Caleb, Frandin and Dalis are better suited to decide patrols. For other things we could form a council like our ancestors had. Let all of us take on some of the responsibility of the valley and village. I think it would take some of the strain off of Kena. Maybe she could actually get some sleep and enjoy life, at least a little."

Sami sat quietly for a moment to consider what Seth was saying and how it would affect Kena. "I see your point Seth, but Kena is not going to take it well. She is going to see it as a personal attack, and she may even think we are siding with Caleb."

"I know, I all ready tried to talk to her about it. She shut me down, then took off."

"That's what she's been doing every time I try to have a serious conversation about anything with her. She will talk to me about inconsequentials, but anything of any importance she just shuts me out. Sometimes it's like talking to a rock. She's right in front of me, but she's gone. I know she's not hearing a word I say. Her mind is completely gone. I think that's worse than when she actually leaves." Sami choked back a sob.

"I know Sami. I know what she's doing, she's strengthening her shields, but I don't know why. Ancients know not even a wisp of a thought is getting through them. It's not just us. She doesn't really share with anyone. She's just going through the motions. Sami I'm afraid she's looking for an escape. If we don't do something soon I'm afraid she might find that escape."

Sami considered Seth's words carefully. "Unless there's a crisis, then she's her old self, working through all the problems and seeing everything that could be a problem. That's the answer, we need a crisis."

"Okay Sami, you're sounding like Caleb. 'Lets attack and kill everybody before the king can attack us.' I don't think we should manufacture a crisis just to get Kena to talk to us."

"Seth, I wasn't talking about starting a war, but last night I got word from my father of a possible Changer in the capital city. I was going to send Brent and Lenk, but why don't Kena and I go. I think I can convince her, and once we are out of the valley maybe I can get her to talk me. Maybe even get her to open up to me. We used to talk all the time when we were questing."

"Do you think you can get her to agree to leave? She hasn't been out of the valley in months, not since you and the other Tiskins took over the searching."

"I can if I can convince her that it's too dangerous for one of the Tiskins to go." Sami said brightening to the idea. Anytime she could get Kena alone was a good thing.

"Well it's certainly worth a try. If she wavers remind her I can mind speak her or you anywhere. If anything happens here I'll get in touch." Seth sounded hopeful, but he doubted Sami would ever be able to convince Kena to go.

Sami changed as she approached the fire. She had managed to convince Kena to leave the valley astounding Seth. It wasn't that hard to do Kena hating putting others in danger, but was more than willing to take on danger herself. There were times when she and Kena were searching out new Changers that the risks Kena took bordered on suicide. So, Sami just played up the danger a little, telling Kena she was taking Lenk's place on the mission. Kena put a stop to that insisting she go with Sami not Brent. She claimed it was because she was protecting Brent, but Sami hoped it was her Kena was trying to protect.

Kena was so close to the fire she might as well be in it drawing strength from it. Kena was deep in trance trying to find the blood call buried in thousands of emotions. Sami was careful not to disturb her, breaking the trance could be dangerous for Kena.

Eagle Bennett

Sami watched Kena from the other side of the fire looking for any sign that Kena was coming out of her trance. While she waited she cooked a tree hare she had caught unawares while out on her scouting flight and picked out the nuts from a few pine cones to keep her hands busy. She had even found enough edible greens to keep Kena happy. With nothing in particular happening and no dangers threatening Sami let her mind wander while she waited. The last few months had been a whirl of activity as more and more changers arrived in the valley. Sami glanced back up at Kena who was still deep in trance. So much had changed since it was just the four of them. Now the cavern was always full of Changers learning how to change, shield and control their gifts. The problem was the more Changers that arrived the more Kena pulled away. She was still involved in all matters of the Changers and the rapidly expanding society now living in the valley, but on a personal level she was just never really there anymore, completely unreachable even when she was standing right next to you.

"I hope there's enough for two I'm starving and it smells wonderful." Kena smiled at her as she pushed herself back from the fire and stretched her legs, startling Sami.

Sami's whole body warmed at the sight of that smile. A smile she saw all too little of lately and only when they were out of the valley. "Like I would let you starve. I know how hungry trancing makes you. There's plenty for both of us." Sami handed Kena her share of the greens and a handful of pine nuts before she took the tree hare off the fire. "Any luck finding the target?" Sami asked as she broke a piece of meat off and handed the spit to Kena.

Eagle Bennett

"No, I need to get closer to pin point exactly who we're looking for. I'm open to ideas. I'm not looking forward to walking into the capital blind, but I'm not seeing any other choice."

"We'll be fine." Sami had missed this. Outside the valley Sami caught glimpses of the Kena only she knew. This was the Kena she had spent nearly every waking moment with for over a year as they searched out more and more Changers. It wasn't until the first major influx of Changers from her father arrived that she and Kena had been forced to stop questing as other work took priority. Now Sami assigned one of the many Tiskin to the task, but there were times Sami would give just about anything to be able to go back to those simple days. "I've never been to a city this big before, but I have been to cities. Pests are always coming and going in and out, a couple of strangers visiting will make no difference. We have enough money with us to get a room at one of the inns. We can play at looking for work to search the city for the target."

"I think I can narrow it down to a general area of the city if that will help." Kena added thinking about Sami's plan.

"Yeah, that would help we will know where to start looking. I think we should be sisters. We look enough alike for it to be believable. If we're asked we tell them we're orphans, use my family's story to keep it simple. Once we have the target I can prowl at night as a street cat to get close. You can catch up on your sleep. Ancients know you need to. Between searching out targets and building the valley it's been months since you have had a good night's sleep." Sami was really concerned about that. It seemed nothing could be decided without checking in with Kena first. Granted Kena was the de facto ruler right now, a job Sami knew Kena hated, but others should be able to make some decisions. Even today Kena had to endure an hour long conversation long distance with Seth, and conversing mind to mind when you weren't a mind speaker was exhausting. The whole conversation centered on building corn silos and which fields should be plowed and which should be left open for grazing herds. Sami was so irritated, all of it could have waited the week or so until they got back, or someone else could have made the decision, it wasn't like it was a crisis.

"Come back to me Sami, you're a million miles away." Kena joked reaching over and touching Sami's knee.

Sami felt her heart skip and she quickly made sure she wasn't leaking her feelings. If Kena felt anything coming from her she would close herself off and it was so rare to get her to talk anymore Sami didn't want to do anything that might end the mood. "I was just thinking about the valley. Kena we need to do something."

Kena was shocked by the turn of the conversation, "Okay we will, about what?"

Sami had been trying to get Kena to talk about this problem for weeks. Seth had broached the subject as well, but every time they tried Kena either changed the subject or left. If anyone was going to be able to get through to Kena it was her. Kena was friendly with everyone, but she made friends with no one. Sami knew she and Seth were the only friends she allowed herself to have. She knew this could drive Kena away, but she had to try. "Kena, the valley is getting bigger and with more and more Changers coming in every day we need to do something about leadership. We always rely on you, which is fine, except it's slowly wearing you down. I'm afraid for you, Kena. If we don't do something you're going to work yourself into an early grave."

Kena scowled at Sami trying to figure out where Sami was going with this. Unlike Caleb at least with Sami, she knew she had her best interest at heart. "Okay. I give, I can't figure out what you are thinking. Care to fill me in?"

It was the opening she needed and Sami took a chance and jumped in head first. "Why not build a leadership council like the ancients used to have, one representative from each race of Changers. There are Changers from each race living in the valley now. Let them elect a leader and the leader sits on the council and will take responsibility for their race. Let the council make the decisions and give you a break from it." Sami braced for Kena's reaction, sometimes it was impossible to gage which way she would jump.

Kena stared at the fire for a moment, it always calmed her to watch the dancing flames. She was surprised how hurt she was by the suggestion. Did Sami think she wasn't doing a good job? She felt her inner fire burn and she quickly strengthened her shields before the flames could escape. Even still she felt the fire so near the surface she was afraid it would burst out any second. "I need to stretch my wings." Kena jumped up, changed and leapt into the air, flying fast enough Sami would have no chance to catch her if she tried.

Sami didn't even get a word out before Kena was gone. She growled at the situation. This had been happening more and more. Every time anything at all emotional came up, Kena disappeared. Sami threw another couple of logs on the fire. She hadn't brought up her and Seth's idea to hurt Kena or drive her away. She brought it up because she was afraid Kena was being stretched far too thin, pushing herself too hard. Sami hissed as she jumped to her feet in frustration pacing circles around the fire. She always thought better when she was in motion and she needed to think with a clear head. Her grandmother had warned her about loving an empath, but it was way too late for that, ancients it was too late when her grandmother warned her.

Sami kicked a rock out of her path. She tried to remember when all this hiding had started with Kena. Kena hadn't been like this when they met or when she had accompanied Kena back to the cavern. In the beginning Kena had been supportive and helpful with her training. They had become even closer when they started questing together. It was possibly the happiest year of her life. For sure it was the happiest she had been since her mother and brother had died. Of course Kena had always kept her at arms length, never letting the friendship blossom any further than just friends, but she always let her in as a friend.

So, when? When did Kena start pulling away from her? Another hiss escaped, all unwittingly, as Sami paced. The influx of new Changers had been a shock. Her father had done his job a little too well. They had been hard pressed to keep everyone fed and under shelter at first. Kena had dealt with all that. She kept every one organized, directing hunting, cooking, building, and dealing with every crisis that came up. It wasn't until the crisis had passed and the valley and residents had settled that Kena had started pulling away. The more Changers that came or were brought in by Tiskins, the more Kena pulled away from everyone. Part of Sami knew that wasn't the entire story. There was something else. The influx of Changers invading the valley was part of the problem and Caleb's attitude was part of it as well, but still something was missing. It didn't help that everyone looked to Kena to have all the answers all the time, and usually Kena did have the answer. Kena was good at solving problems, making do, forming plans that worked and it wasn't like Sami wanted her to stop doing that. She just felt that with as big as the valley was getting some of the responsibility and problems could be spread out to others leaving Kena to solve the bigger problems that only she could solve. Unfortunately Kena always disappeared before she could explain her thoughts fully. Sami sat back down at the fire, all pacing was doing was making her tired it wasn't helping her find the answer and she desperately needed an answer. So when had Kena started pulling away from them and why?

Kena winged hard and fast away from Sami and the fire. She needed to get away from Sami before she lost control and the fire went free. She hated to leave Sami like that she was her friend. She knew Sami wasn't trying to hurt her. Really, if she faced the truth, Sami was trying to help her. She had been sort of overwhelmed lately. She had been thinking much the same thing, so why did it hurt so much, why did she let it get to her? Part of her knew it was because it came from Sami, the only person she truly trusted, but the bigger part of her knew it was because of what Caleb

Eagle Bennett
had been saying. He argued with everything she did. He questioned every decision. She couldn't count the times she wanted to tell him if he was so sure he could do it better then do it. Now Sami was questioning her leadership. Had Caleb changed Sami's opinion? Kena ground her beak in frustration. I all honesty she didn't want to be the leader anyway. She never wanted to be the leader, but it was always her everyone came to for decisions what was she supposed to do?

Kena dipped her wings turning back to Sami. She needed to go back and apologize. She also needed to admit Sami was right. A council was exactly what they needed. Kena hated to admit it, but she was spread to thin and it was time to let some of the others start figuring things out. If Caleb wanted to find fault with every choice she made let him make the choices. In all honesty if it wasn't for Sami and Seth she probably would have left the valley a long time ago. Ancients, if she thought for a moment she could convince Sami to leave with her she would wing away and never look back. Maybe with a leadership council she would be able to do just that. It was the reason she had let Sami manipulate her into coming with her on this quest to escape the valley and the press of Changers all around her. She was well aware Brent and Lenk could handle any extraction needed. It didn't take long for Kena to return to Sami and the fire. Kena tried to gage Sami's mood by her body language since she was too afraid fire might escape to open her shields at all. Unfortunately by the look of things she might just be in trouble. "I'm sorry I took off like that. I shouldn't have. You were just trying to help."

Sami stared at the fire. She didn't trust herself to speak just yet. She knew not answering was hurtful, but gushing love could be worse and probably would drive Kena away again. Sami carefully chose her words when she did feel under control and safe to speak. "Kena, Seth and I are just worried that you are working too hard. Between building, hunting, dealing with the forge fires, clearing fields, helping with the plowing... Kena you are involved with every aspect of life in the valley. Every thought, every decision, every plan, every choice has to come from you. It would be too much for anyone. When was the last time you had any time for yourself? When was the last time you flew just to fly, or talked just to talk?"

"I have responsibilities Sami, I can't just slough them off on someone else." Kena fought the urge to leave again.

Sami grabbed Kena's shoulder preventing her from running again if that was on her mind hoping Kena cared enough about her not to scorch her hand or worse scorch her. "In the past, not long ago, yes there were things you had to do because you were the only one to do them, but Kena there are close to two hundred Changers living in the valley now with more coming every day, more than enough to take some of the workload off you. You don't have to do it all anymore. Let us shoulder some of the responsibility for a change. Why not let us take the minor things leaving you for the bigger ones, the ones only you can handle?"

Kena sighed, she was so tired. She couldn't remember when the last time she had actually slept for more than a couple of hours. She knew Sami was right. She could let some of the others take over now. She didn't have to do it all anymore and she hadn't really had to for a while. Kena sighed, "A council is a good idea. It

Eagle Bennett worked for our ancestors, I don't see why it wouldn't work for us. Each race has a leader and the leaders work together, no single leader taking too much power with the council making all the choices for the valley as a group. It would be good to have a break from making all the decisions. It would be good to have some time to myself."

Sami wasn't sure Kena really liked the idea, she just sounded defeated. For some reason this scared Sami more than she could say, but there was nothing she could think to say to make it better without hurting her more. She released Kena's shoulder quickly changing the subject. Nothing could be done about it now, better to focus on what had to be done now. Kena never went back on her word. As soon as they got back Kena would form a council. "Still some food left if you're hungry, going to need your strength to find this target tomorrow."

Kena let out deep breath, grateful as always for Sami's willingness to forgive and forget and she was certainly more than willing to move on to the more pressing matter of their target and a city full of pests.

Chapter 19 Adoration

Caleb loved the idea of a leadership council, but he was surprised when it was Kena that offered up the suggestion. I mean, yes she was spread a little thin, but certainly nothing she couldn't handle. Caleb landed in the field next to the river where all the Gryphons had been asked to report. He had little doubt he would be elected leader but he did understand the need for it to be the choice of everyone. It wasn't long until all the Gryphons had assembled. All over the valley the races of Changers were doing this very thing, electing a representative for the council. In the morning all those elected would meet in the cavern. Kena and Seth being the only representatives of their races were setting up a council area where they could meet without disturbing the murals or the training that was always going on in the cavern.

Caleb did a quick count, confirming all had arrived before he spoke. "You all know we are making some changes to how the valley will be led. Starting tomorrow, all matters concerning the valley and the disposition of work will be decided by a leadership council made up of one representative from each race voted on by the members of the race. We are here to choose that representative. Does anyone have any questions?" When it was clear no one did he went on, "So does anyone have any suggestions on how we should do this?"

Caleb was quickly elected the Gryphon leader. He wasn't surprised, but he did try to be as humble as he could be. He was getting ready to head for home when he noticed the most beautiful creature he had ever seen. He grabbed Blake by the shoulder stopping him in his tracks. "Blake, who's that?" Caleb asked indicating the woman.

Blake smirked at Caleb. "That's Marta, she was just released from training."

Caleb couldn't tear his eyes away from her. Beautiful wasn't a significant enough word to describe her. "She's amazing."

"Oh she is that," Blake admitted. "If you're interested, better stake your claim quickly, every unattached man and, gotta say quite a few women, are sniffing around her hoping to catch her eye." Blake laughed as he walked away enjoying the sight of their new, rather cocky, leader gob smacked.

Caleb's mouth went dry and his stomach was doing loops, but he had to meet her, he had to speak to her.

Marta laughed at the joke Haili had just told her. She had never been so comfortable anywhere before. She had only been in the valley a few weeks and she knew this was home. It wasn't like her life before had been horrible. She was just never truly happy. She worked in a small inn on the outskirts of the city of Nigorna. She had been working in some form or other her entire life. Her parents were poor, but they made sure she was cared for. She never went hungry even if the food was simple. She never lacked for hugs and affection from her parents, and she certainly never lacked for suitors. The problem was she always wanted more. She knew she was taking a chance when she had struck out on her own at seventeen, but she was desperate for something different. She tried to explain it to her parents. They were so hurt when she told them she was leaving. She was just so restless. She had to see what else was out there. Unfortunately, her carefully hoarded money ran out after only a few weeks on the road. She had been lucky to find the job cleaning and serving at the inn. The pay was terrible, but it came with room and board and the owner was friendly enough. As much as she hated it she had come to the conclusion this was the best she was going to do with her life. That had all changed the first time she met Rykle and Darisai. From the moment she met them she

Eagle Bennett

felt this need to be close to them. She now knew it was her ancient blood responding to theirs, but when it happened she had just been lost in that need. It wasn't at all hard for Rykle to convince her to leave the inn and her boring comfortable life for the adventure of building this new society. She hadn't even been afraid the first time she saw them change. Two days later she was on the back of a unicorn jumping to a new life and her friends Rykle and Darisai were on their way in search of others like her.

That day had started a whirl wind of activity that had ended just this morning when her newly found grandfather had pronounced her training sufficient to join the other Gryphons. She had been assigned to Haili as mentor to finish her training and help her acclimate to life here in the valley. Her grandfather need not worry. She loved the valley and got along well with all the Changers she had met so far. There was a part of her, the restless part, the part that had driven her from the safety of her parents and put her feet on the road to begin with that just knew she was home. "So, now what?" Marta asked her new friend Haili.

"Well I guess that will be up to Caleb and the new council. My guess is the Gryphons will be doing the hunting and patrolling, it is what we're good at. I lead a patrol, if you want you could join mine."

"That would be great. I want to help any way I can…" She was interrupted by the approach of who she now knew was Caleb and she was shocked by the animal attraction she instantly felt for him.

Eagle Bennett

Caleb gave Marta a shy smile before addressing Haili. "Haili, would your patrol take the early flight tomorrow since I will have to be at the meeting of the new council? Until I learn differently we will continue to patrol." Haili nodded and Caleb continued. "Are you going to introduce me to your new friend?"

Haili wasn't fooled for an instant. She knew exactly why Caleb was here. He wasn't the only Changer throwing their hat in the ring over Marta. Ancients, if Marta had showed more interest in women she would have jumped in too. "This is Marta, she's the newest member of my patrol."

Caleb couldn't pull his eyes away from Marta's bright blue eyes and engaging smile, "Hi I'm Caleb." He knew he sounded like an idiot, but he just couldn't seem to stop. Marta cocked her head shyly to the side, somewhere to his left he heard Haili chuckle and beat a hasty retreat.

"I think I knew that since I just voted for you." Marta joked at him with a laugh.

"Yeah thanks for that. So you've joined Haili's patrol? She's a really good leader, you'll like her. You wouldn't want to have dinner or something with me?" The last came out in such a rush that he doubted she could even understand what he said. "I mean I'm a passable cook if you…"

"That would be great Caleb," She interrupted him. "I'm staying with Haili while I wait for a place to be built and I haven't exactly had a chance to hunt or anything. So if you wouldn't mind hosting me."

Eagle Bennett

"Please, I mean yes I would be honored. Um, it's only a short flight." Marta had changed while he was finishing his thought and Caleb was astounded by her coloring. While most Gryphon's feathers where brown or golden hers were white gradually turning to a dark silver on her wingtips. Even the lion half of her was different instead of being tawny it was more cream colored. When she raised her crest feathers questioningly at him they were as white as new fallen snow. The colors were strikingly beautiful.

"I know, Grandfather says I might be the last of the desert Gryphon clan. It seems we didn't as a rule play well with others even other ancients so not much of our blood spread around to the pests, but your forest Gryphon clan just loved to love making up for the rest of us."

"Your coloring is stunning, Marta." Caleb told her while he changed and took to his wings. She quickly followed with a grace he seldom saw in those so new to their form. He changed to mind speech once they were in the air. *My place is in the center of the village I'll lead the way. I knew there were several clans of Gryphons when the ancients ruled our world, I didn't know they differed so drastically in color.*

It seems, according to Tam, that forest Gryphons were the most common, but there were several other clans and each had their own unique coloring and appearance. He said there was even one Gryphon clan that called the jungle home. They had orange and white feathers and orange and white striped fur, sort of cross between a Tigura and Phoenix. I would love to see one in person, Tam gave me a picture, but second hand pictures are never quite the same as real life. Marta new she was babbling but she was too nervous to stop and Caleb seemed interested.

Caleb grimaced at the reminder of Kena but quickly forced the thought out of his head. He wasn't about to let his anger and mistrust of Kena get in the way with this possible new friendship. *I think I would like to see one too, I am certainly glad at least one of your clan still lives.* He felt himself blush and hoped she didn't notice the sudden pinkness to his nares. *My place is right here.*

They landed almost in unison on the road in front of his place and changed. "Right this way." He motioned her up the path. Now that he had seen her Gryphon half he understood the extraordinary silvery white coloring of her shoulder length curly hair. It was common for some of the aspects of the ancient form to show through to the pest form. The grace she showed in the air as a Gryphon was continued in her true form. He was infatuated and ancients help him in complete and total love with this woman.

Marta chatted amiably with him while he put together a meal of grilled venison steaks, tossed greens, and slices of melon. She was suitably impressed by his cooking ability and she showed no signs of disgust when she learned he acquired the skill as a slave. After dinner she helped him clean up then instead of taking her leave she encouraged him to join her in the living area of his home. He was thrilled to do so and quickly joined her. He was looking forward to talking more to her, but she had other things in mind.

Marta didn't know what exactly she was feeling she just knew Caleb was special and she felt this insatiable need to be closer to him. She took his hand and led him to the bed in the corner of the room. His eyes were wide with shock when she kissed him. A few quick caresses and he began to respond to her exactly as she had hoped. It became clear pretty quickly to her that she was his first so she gently led him and he, for his part, learned quickly. He was gentle and considerate matching her touch for touch and kiss for kiss. His awkwardness was quickly replaced by his growing need that perfectly harmonized with hers.

Marta slept, her naked body curled around Caleb's, her head on his chest. Caleb rubbed her head and nearly cried tears of joy. He couldn't believe how in love he found himself and how much he prayed she felt the same way. He felt her stir and he quickly loosened his grip in case she felt the need to bolt. That was the last thing on her mind.

"So, is there anything left here for breakfast? I think it's my turn to cook." She told him as she sat up kissing him soundly as she did. "I have an early patrol and you have a council meeting, but maybe tonight we could get together again?"

Caleb's heart was beating so hard he was sure it was going to beat right out of his chest. "You are welcome here anytime." He answered hoping she would take him up on the offer.

Caleb winged into the cavern his mind lost in thoughts of Marta. Over breakfast they had come to a sort of understanding. She may not be in love with him yet but she was well on her way. He had invited her to stay with him until her home was built and she had accepted. His mind was filled with how he could make it even more permanent. He shook his head he had to get his mind on business. He needed his wits about him if he was going to counter whatever Kena's agenda was.

Kena watched as Caleb took the seat designated for the Gryphon and she wasn't surprised. He was the first to arrive other than her and Seth. She swallowed her angst and greeted him.

"Thanks," Caleb answered, "I know not a big surprise, but at least I had to be elected unlike the two of you." Pleased by the reaction his words and tone had caused in both his little brother and Kena. If he could keep Seth off balance and defensive he may hesitate before siding with Kena.

Seth would have had quick retort if it wasn't for Kena's restraining hand on his leg. He pulled the thought out of her mind, *It's not worth it Seth, he is who he is.* Seth shot her a look, letting her know he didn't agree but would subside for her sake. Thankfully the next person to arrive was Sami representing the Tiskins. She took the chair next to Kena even though technically that was meant for the Pegasi. Her body language made it clear she wasn't moving so when Tameera, the new Pegasi representative, arrived she simply took the seat Sami should have been in flashing Sami a knowing smile.

Kena had intentionally put the Tiskin on the other side of the table knowing it would be Sami they elected. Lately being around Sami was hard. She couldn't be near her without the burning in her chest, and ancients forbid Sami touch her, it was everything she could do to stop the fire from exploding. She didn't understand it at all. Her shields were as strong as she could make them and yet the fire still burned. Between her anger with Caleb and whatever was going on with Sami the fire was never far from the surface and keeping it under control was becoming nearly impossible. Thankfully the rest of the newly elected council members had arrived and gave Kena a chance to concentrate on something else. No one surprised Kena, every race had voted exactly like she expected them to. The Dokuls had elected Qwint, one of the few Changers with training in politics, the Tiguras had elected Dalis and Gryphels had chosen Frandin. Both were Caleb's friends and allies and could prove to be an issue in the future. The Unicorns had elected Kimball. Kimball was the oldest of the Changers having reached his twentieth birthday before coming to the valley, and was as fair minded and easy going as Caleb was neither.

Kena waited for everyone to settle and tender greetings before she started. "Thank you all for coming. From this morning on it will be this council that makes all decisions regarding the Changers, the village and the valley. I think the first thing we have to do is decide how often we should meet?"

Everyone at the table began speaking at once and Kena found herself wishing Tam would have agreed to mediate, but he flatly refused to get involved in the politics of the new Changer society. His point was as guardian he needed to be approachable to all. Kena waited again until there was a lull, then cut in. "We will get nothing done if we are all talking at once. Tameera, you had a thought?" Kena replied trying to keep things on track completely missing the glare Caleb leveled at her for taking charge.

Eagle Bennett
Chapter 20 Departures

Kena burrowed deeper into her fur covered bed in the mural cavern. When a chill ran down her spine she reached down pulling a fur up over her shoulders and tried to go back to sleep. She knew it was still early, or really late depending on your point of view. She cracked her eyes a little and glanced around the sleeping area of the cavern. Only Sami and Seth lived in the cavern with her. Seth stayed to be with Tam and she stayed to be near the only other Phoenix, her grandmother, but she had no idea why Sami stayed. Unlike her, Sami was popular with the Tiskins and, well, all the changers. There were dozens of changers snooping around Sami in the hopes they would catch her eye, but Sami showed no interest in anyone. Kena stopped on that thought, surprised how happy it made her that Sami had shown no interest in a relationship. Her heart burned a little as an emotion tried to make its self known, Kena put an immediate stop to that by adding a layer to her shields before the fire could escape. She rolled a little and confirmed Sami was asleep next to her and Seth across from Sami. She sighed and closed her eyes willing sleep to come. She needed her sleep badly, there was a council meeting scheduled for the morning and she would need all her strength to keep her shields intact and the fire controlled. Sometimes she thought it might be better just to let the fire consume them all and let the rest start over with new leaders. Maybe they could actually get something done. A month of meeting four days a week and they had made one accomplishment. The new commons building was completed. That was it, everything else they argued over until someone shelved the idea. Mostly Caleb used the meetings to try to get a war with the pests started and Kena prevented it. The council split on everything with Frandin and Dalis siding with Caleb and Sami and Seth siding with her. Kimball, Tameera and Qwint seemed to agree more with her making Caleb seethe with anger. She had thought this council would be a good idea, but she was just as tired and frustrated as she ever was. The work that the council seemed unable to delegate still needed done, so most of it she was still doing. She just felt exhausted and defeated, and part of her wondered why she bothered. She was just starting to drift back to sleep when she heard the rock ceiling open and almost immediately close. Kena jumped out of her bed followed closely by Sami and Seth knowing something was wrong for a Changer to fly in at this hour.

A Tiskin landed fast and hard right in front of them changing as he landed. "Brent what's wrong?" Sami asked as she reached to steady him.

Brent took a deep breaths, trying hard to catch his breath so he could speak, it was clear he had flown hard to get here quickly. "Sami, I just got word your dad is in Gregora. He only has a couple of days left. He sent me with a message, but I thought you might want to go to him. I got back here as quick as I could."

Seth handed Brent some water and steered him to his bed of furs to lie down and rest leaving Sami and Kena alone. "Kena I've got to go. I've been given a chance to say goodbye. I never thought I would."

Kena reached out a restraining hand, "Of course you do. I'll come with you, you shouldn't be alone. The council can argue without us for a few days, but it will take us at least two days to fly there. Instead let's wake up Kimball, he can jump us, we'll be there in an hour.

Come on." Kena changed followed closely by Sami and flew out of the cavern. Kena carefully left a thought hanging for Seth to grab. *Thanks for taking care of Brent, Seth. We'll be back as soon as we can. Please tell the council. This is too important to Sami to wait.* Seth quickly returned his answer, *Don't worry, we'll be fine take your time coming back, you both could use the respite.*

Kena landed outside Kimball's home. Kimball was the first Unicorn to come to the valley as well as their representative and a friend. The Unicorn gift of jumping was exactly what they needed right now. Kena knocked on the door calling to him. Kimball's wife Rayon answered, not at all perturbed by the middle of the night disturbance. "Rayon, I'm sorry to wake you but we just heard Sami's father has taken a turn for the worse. Time is short and we need a jump to Gregora."

Rayon reached a comforting hand to Sami. "I was awake anyway, don't worry." Rayon quietly closed the door as she exited her home. "No need to wake Kimball, I'd be happy to jump you both there right now if you want. I know the area. I should be able to safely jump you pretty close."

Kena looked over at Sami's tear filled eyes, "Yes please, the sooner the better."

Rayon nodded moving up the path to a clear spot and changed. "Climb aboard, and hold on I'll have you there in seconds." Kena climbed on and grabbed a handful of mane, Sami settled behind her reaching her arms around Kena to steady herself. Rayon looked back, "All set?" At Kena's nod she jumped and they were surrounded by darkness. As soon as the dizziness of jumping had passed, Kena slid off Rayon's back followed closely by Sami. "If you need a jump back let Seth know and I will come a running err, jumping. Please take care, Sami. All of the changers grieve with you. We all owe your father a debt of gratitude we can never repay."

"Thanks Rayon, we will." Kena replied with a smile of deep appreciation.

Kena looked around at her surroundings. Rayon had taken a big chance and jumped them to the entrance of the village. "Come on Sami, we need to find the healers." Kena grabbed Sami's hand and pulled her with her into the village. Gregora was large enough to have street lamps so finding their way down the empty roads was easy. Kena knew what she was looking for and it took no time at all to spot the healers well lit and welcoming entrance.

Kena walked Sami right up to the entrance, "Do you want me to come in with you or would you rather be alone?" Kena looked over at Sami's white face and knew the answer before Sami answered.

"Please? I don't want to be alone right now."

Kena's heart went out to her friend and she squeezed her hand in support and answer.

The door was unlocked and as they entered they were greeted by an older woman. "Welcome children, how may I help you tonight?"

Kena didn't wait for Sami to answer as, true to her nature, Kena took charge. "We got a message that my friend's father was ill and here…"

"You're Sami and Kena?" the woman asked. Sami nodded and she went on. "Come in child, yes Tobias is here. I'm sorry he doesn't have much time left I'll take you to him. We're making him as comfortable as possible. He's right in here," She said as she opened the door and motioned them in before she entered. "His strength is nearly gone. He is bleeding internally, the medicine he has been taking to slow it is no longer working. He has survived far longer than anyone could have guessed. He's not in any pain and when it happens he will just go to sleep. Stay as long as you like, I'll have some food sent up when he wakes, try to get him to eat too. If you need anything else just let me know, I'm Wills by the way. I'll check on you in a little while."

Sami had taken the chair next to the bed and taken her father's hand into hers. Kena's heart nearly burst to see Sami so scared, only just realizing how much Sami was the rock in her life. "Thank you Wills, we appreciate all your help." Wills closed the door behind her as she left, and Kena pulled a chair up next to Sami's. She didn't speak she didn't need to she simply opened her shields a little and projected comfort to her friend as she laid a comforting hand on her shoulder. It scared her a little to see Sami like this. There were few times since they had met that Sami had been anything less than a strong. Her heart burned with compassion for her friend, scaring Kena into closing her shields. She would just have to support Sami in the old fashioned way.

Kena didn't remember falling asleep but she must have since when she opened her eyes there was sunlight coming in the window. She could tell by Sami's posture she too was asleep. She smiled at her and moved carefully so as not to wake her. Kena had a feeling she would need all the sleep she could get.

"You've been good for her," Tobias whispered.

"I hope so, but I think she has been better for me."

"Perhaps or perhaps you are good for each other, you are certainly better together." Tobias coughed a dry hacking lung shattering cough that woke Sami.

Sami cried as she laid her head on his chest. He rubbed her hair, "I didn't think I would ever see you again. I'm sorry we won't have a lot of time to catch up." Kena quietly exited giving them time alone to say goodbye.

Tobias held his daughter, grateful for the chance. He didn't expect to ever see her again and he was surprised by how much she had grown, no, matured. He held her until her tears slowed. "We have little time left Sami, perhaps we should save the tears?"

Sami raised her head and gave her father a weak smile. "I'll try. I just didn't think I would get the chance to… It doesn't matter, I do have the chance and Father there is something I have to tell you. I can't let you go without knowing."

"Sami you don't have to tell me, I know, I've always known. Your mother knew too and I could care less. All I have ever wanted is for you to be happy." Sami forced the tears back, her father was right she would cry later. "You and Kena are good together. I knew you would be from the moment she walked into our shop and you love her." It wasn't a question but a statement.

Sami nodded, "Yes but she doesn't love me." Choking back tears.

Tobias gently reached up to stroke his daughters hair. "She does, I can see it in her eyes when she looks at you. She just doesn't know how to love. I see the same things in her I saw in your mother when I pursued her. Sometimes patience is all that is required and sometimes a more hands on approach is needed. You will know what is best when the time comes. What matters most is you are better together and that is a partnership few are ever lucky enough to find. Don't give up on her Sami. Someday Kena will realize the gift you offer her. Someday she will listen to her heart and let you in and I promise all the waiting, all the hurt, it will all be worth it."

Tobias never got to see another sunrise, but he died happily with his daughter by his side. Kena arranged for Tobias's body to be burned and the ashes gathered for Sami to take with her. They started for home three days after they had arrived. They didn't fly long before Sami made for a clearing with a small pond Kena followed her down.

"Sami, are you okay?" Kena asked, surprised by the detour.

"Yeah I just... I'm not ready to go back yet. I just need some time. I'll be fine if you want to go."

The words may have said to go, but her eyes clearly said I want you to stay but I won't ask. "I'm not going anywhere, you need a friend right now. I may not be able to take away your grief but I can give you a shoulder to cry on and an ear to listen with." Sami broke down into tears then and Kena did what any good friend would do she took her into her arms and comforted her unconsciously fortifying her shields with several more layers.

They stayed by the pond the rest of the day. Sami decided to spread her father's ashes here rather than take them back to the valley. Her father had never been to the valley and some part of her needed to leave her life as a Changer separate from her life before she knew she was a Changer. Kena melted a rock into a marker so if Sami ever wanted to visit again she could easily find the spot. By nightfall Sami was ready to return to her life.

It was just after dark a day later when they made it back to the cavern. Sami was actually quite relieved to see Seth and Tam had left for their evening flights so she would have a little more time alone with Kena. Seth was right, Kena only opened up when there was a crisis, but Sami knew this time Kena didn't open up. She had been supportive and helpful, but she never once opened her shields to use her gift. She had to try to get Kena to see the danger of closing herself off. "Kena, I wanted to thank you for going with me to see my father. I'm not sure I could have done it alone."

"Sami, I know I haven't always been the friend you needed, but I am very glad this time I could be. Are you going to be okay?"

"Yes, it's time for me to get back to the life he wanted me to have. You know you're part of that life right? I mean you don't have to hide from me." Sami wasn't sure if an outpouring of love would work or not, but it was the only thing she had left. "You know I lo... care about you right?"

Kena smiled at her, "I know and I care about you, but I think we better get some sleep we have a council meeting in the morning and I know I will need all my energy to deal with Caleb." With that Kena retreated to her bed before the warm tingling in her stomach spread any further.

Sami withdrew too, but not to her bed. Her bed was a little too close to Kena's right now. Kena had shut down again, had shut her down again. She had reverted to form as soon as they had crossed over into the valley. So instead she retreated to one of the dark corners of the cavern as far away from Kena as she could get. Her grandmother found her quickly providing warm comfort and quiet conversation.

I am sorry Granddaughter. I wish I could say more, I wish I could make it better for you. I'm not sure it will ever be better. I am afraid Kena is spiraling into a dive she can't or won't pull out of and I think it may be our fault.

Sami was surprised, first that someone anyone else saw that Kena was in trouble besides her and Seth and second how could it be the murals fault. "What do you mean Grandmother? What is happening to Kena?"

Eagle Bennett

She is beginning to lock herself away from any connections in this world. It was slow at first not even her grandmother noticed, but now the only connection she still seems to have is with you. We had all hoped that you would be able to get through her self imposed isolation, but it appears not even your bright burning love can break the walls she has erected. She has begun to turn away from even you.

"I'm not giving up yet. She might not be willing to admit it, but she does love me and more than as a friend. I'm too stubborn to give up. I will get through to her some way, somehow. That doesn't explain why this is the murals fault."

Kena needed to learn to build strong shields to be able to search out more of our grandchildren. It was essential for her to survive out among the pests once her gifts had fully awakened for her shields to be impenetrable. Any holes in those shields could have driven her insane. Our mistake was how we taught her. We meant no harm, but we needed to train her fast so we cut corners. We taught her through emotional pain. We bombarded her with anguish, grief and longing anytime we noticed her shields failing. It worked she learned to surround herself in leak proof shields faster than any one could have thought. We were all so pleased with ourselves, but we forgot, even her grandmother forgot. All of the Phoenix gifts are tied to fire, especially their empathy. Emotions are all of our inner fire, with the Phoenix that inner fire powers all of their gifts. It is essential that a Phoenix control that inner fire or they would kill themselves or others. If they lose control even for a moment the fire could burn free. We taught Kena control, but we failed to teach her how to lose control. We failed to teach her that only through connections to others can she truly control her inner flame. Her answer is to not feel, to never let any emotion out or in, to not allow feeling at all. She withdraws from those who care about her more every day. I fear it's too late, we may never be able to save her.

Sami was struck dumb and it was a good thing her emotions weren't connected to fire or the cavern would have been in flames. "You know what else you didn't consider? Her childhood. Kena was forced to hide her feelings from her father her whole life. When her mother and sister died she was beaten for crying and when she cried from being beaten she was whipped. She wasn't allowed to show any emotion at all growing up. Here, where she was supposed to be safe and loved, you demand she do the same thing. You've made it so she thinks she's not allowed to feel anything good or bad, but instead of being beaten for feeling she'll kill everyone instead. It's no wonder she's hiding, afraid to love or be loved. So what do we do about it, how do we fix this? I mean you have known about this mistake, this problem, for how long and you haven't corrected the problem."

I'm sorry Sami, we don't know how to fix it. I wish we did. We realized our error almost immediately but it was too late for Kena. No one can get through her shields, they are too strong and she won't let anyone in. You were our only hope. We had so hoped you would be able to break through.

"It's why you tried to warn me away from her?" Sami didn't wait for an answer she didn't need one. "Well, I won't give up on her. You may have written her off but I won't." Sami pushed herself away and left through tunnel needing to be far away from the murals right now, but not wanting to disturb Kena by leaving.

Sami winged over the path. It was overgrown but still visible. She was thrilled beyond measure to find her and Ty's little hut still standing and in good repair. Inside was covered in dust, but dry and bug free. She dropped to the rug and cried. She cried for her mother and father. She cried for her brother whose loss even after all these years still cut her like a knife. Mostly she cried for Kena. She couldn't stop loving her anymore than she could forget her brother. Sami had no idea how long she had cried before the tears dried and she was able to think clearly again.

Sami rose and started cleaning up the hut. It helped to be busy. She hadn't even thought about the place since discovering she was a Changer and she certainly never planned on returning, but after the fight with her grandmother she had wanted to be alone where she could think and she found her flight path had taken her over the long unused path. She thought with all the memories of Ty it would be painful to be here, but it was just the opposite. She could almost feel his presence welcoming and comforting her. She went to work on cleaning the fireplace and let her mind settle on the problem at hand, Kena. By the time she had gotten the fireplace and kitchen area cleaned to her liking the sun was rising, and she had come to only one conclusion; everyone else might give up on Kena but she wouldn't no matter how bad it got. Her father was right. She needed Kena and Kena needed her even if she wasn't quite ready realize that yet. Well she certainly could help even without Kena letting her. She had to head back to the cavern for the council meeting, but before she did she pulled the bedding out of the storage chests and hung it up to air out. As soon as the meeting was over she would be back to finish cleaning and clear the path. She wouldn't leave Kena, but that didn't mean she couldn't have some place of her own to retreat to, someplace of her own to center her emotions and think.

Chapter 21 Trepidation

Kena sighed and stretched her wings, back and neck before settling once again on the boulder ledge. Kena looked down the waterfall cliff, from this vantage point she could see all of the forest below. Somewhere down there Sami hunted, not that Kena, even with her sharp Phoenix eyes, had any chance of seeing her. Even though they had wings Tiskins were ground hunters, they had no talons to grab food out of the air. It was the Tiskins that caught much of the smaller game that kept all the Changers living in the valley fed.

The valley was prospering. Everyone who came not only brought the gifts of their ancient blood with them, but also the talents of their training. Farmers, potters, metal workers, glass blowers, builders, weaver, spinners, miners, ranchers, they all lived here now. The village was thriving and growing. Dokuls were always building. New cabins seemed to go up every day, and not just shelters but other needed buildings as well. There were even a few small farms and several thriving herds of livestock. The livestock were essential to their survival. The valley still thrived with prey animals, but with the amount of mouths to feed now the valley would have been hunted dry in no time. Most Changers still hunted like Sami and Kena, but it was more for the pleasure of hunting than for the need of food. They still traded with Sami's home village and a few others for things they couldn't make, but those things were getting fewer all the time. A small ruckus in the field across the river drew Kena's attention. She turned her fiery red head toward the sound. This was a field taken over by the Unicorns to train. It was too dangerous for them to train anywhere closer to habitation; their horns were sharp and as deadly as any sword. The ruckus was no more than a few young stallions fighting a little too roughly. It was essential that all the Changers learn to fight. It was only a matter of time before they would need to defend the valley, but they certainly didn't want any injuries. Kimball would sort them out. Kena watched their training for a just a moment. No matter what Caleb thought she understood the danger the king and his army presented.

The noise from the Unicorn field was almost deafening and very distracting to Kena's thoughts. She growled in frustration, but there was nothing for it so she did her best to ignore the sound of horn meeting horn violently, and direct her thoughts to the myriad of other problems she had no answer for. Unfortunately another distraction was just winging in to land just above her on the cliff. Caleb back winged hard to prevent splatting himself on the cliff face and touched down gently. He turned in a circle a few times and dropped to the ground. He didn't bother to change. Kena spent most of her time trying to avoid Caleb. It was easier to avoid him than deal with his hurtful remarks.

"Anything happening?" Caleb asked confirming why he was here as day guard and her relief.

This marked the edge of the territory they claimed so far. There was a ford within easy sight of where they were now that was the last chance for anyone venturing this far to turn back. They had posted a warning that this land was claimed and that trespassers were unwelcome. So far the warning had worked and all that ventured this close had forded the river to continue on their journey, after all most people respected others properties. However, just in case, the path was watched day and night. "I haven't seen a soul." Kena answered not even looking up at him. "Sami is down in the thickest part of the forest hunting, if anything or anyone is around she'll have seen it. She'll check in here when she is done." Caleb nodded and settled himself down for a long turn at watching. "Are you training again tonight?" Kena asked trying to be sociable.

"Yes, someone has to be ready to defend this place." Kena shuddered, and Caleb took a perverse pleasure in seeing that his words had struck home. "Not all of us are afraid of a good fight." He added for good measure.

Kena did her best to ignore him, "Well, since you are here now, I should get to my other duties for the day." Kena didn't wait for a reply just fell from the cliff spreading her wings to catch the wind and soaring high over the cliff and back toward the village.

Kena felt her anger rise at Caleb's words. She turned away from the village as fire burst out of her chest. Kena slammed her shields up, angry at herself for letting Caleb get to her again. She wondered if he knew just how close he was coming to his own mortality every time he picked at her. She carefully added more layers onto her shields. She built her shields up until she could no longer feel the fire of anger. Only then did she feel safe to turn back to the village and the jobs that needed to be done today.

Kena had chosen to work in the skinning sheds. She found the act of skinning beasts to be sort of soothing. It wasn't a job most Changers enjoyed, but they still needed the furs and hides to trade. Most of their clothing was made out of skins and blankets out of furs, so it was an important job that needed to be done right. The meat from hunting helped the commons feed the ever growing population supplementing the meat that came from the herds, and hunting was still an enjoyable occupation for most Changers.

Kena hadn't been working long when Sami came in with her catch for the day startling her. "Hey, want some help? Looks like morning hunts went well for all the hunters today."

Kena nodded. Sami always seemed to show up whenever she needed help or Caleb was being particularly hurtful, if she didn't know better she might think she had a bit of empathy herself. More and more Kena found she was relying on Sami to be a buffer between her and Caleb. "I could use a little help or I'll be here all day and I would really like some flying time."

Sami smiled as she picked up a knife and hung the carcass of the hare in her hand, "Well let's get to it, want some company on your flight? I wouldn't mind stretching my wings."

Kena considered the offer. Part of her wanted to accept more than anything, but being around Changers, even Sami, sometimes especially Sami, had started to become so hard. "I appreciate the offer Sami, but I really just want some time alone. I hope you understand?" The last thing she wanted to do was hurt Sami.

Sami nodded, "Of course, no problem." Sami concentrated on the job in front of her. Ancients, her grandmother had been right, loving Kena was the hardest thing she would ever do, but someday she would break through, she had to. Sami had opportunities a plenty now to make a lasting relationship or just accept a little comfort and release but Kena was the only girl she had any interest in. Sami saw Kena flinch out of the corner of her eye and checked her shields, no cracks or gaps. She wasn't projecting, so what was Kena picking up on? "Kena are you okay?"

"Of course, just tired, I was on the early watch." Kena answered. She checked her shields they were as strong as ever so why was she picking up on Sami?

Sami couldn't take it. Kena looked like she was falling apart. "Look Kena, why don't you take the day off? Ancients, why don't you take several days off? I'll get a Tiskin or two to take over here and Seth can certainly take over the fire making duties. In fact I'm guessing he will enjoy it."

Kena considered the offer, she was tired. She had been going nonstop since, well, forever. The council that was supposed to help had only compounded her problems. She desperately need time alone, away from all the Changers so she could relax her shields and get a small break from the constant vigilance of keeping fire safely confined. There actually were plenty of Changers to do all the jobs if others did some double duty too. "Sami, if you're sure you don't mind?"

"Go have that flight, I'll just go find some willing hands. If you want I can show you a place where you can rest and have some time alone."

"No thanks, I just need to fly."

Sami schooled her expression. Years of unrequited love for Kena had taught her that skill well. "Okay, I'll see you tonight back home in the cavern. Kena you know you can always talk to me, right?" Kena nodded and smiled, then quickly left, leaving Sami alone in the shed. Her grandmother had warned her Sami thought as she turned back to the hare. Not that she could change it now. Not that she would change it even if she could. She loved Kena with every ounce of her being. Maybe if Kena had shown interest in someone anyone else she may have been able to move on, but Kena never had. Sami ground her teeth in frustration. Every day Kena slipped further away and no one, it seemed, was going to be able to reach her. Sami finished skinning the hare and threw the meat in the bin to be smoked. A quick glance at the pile of carcasses decided her, extra hands were going to be needed.

It didn't take Sami long to find and draft several Tiskins for the job of skinning and a quick talk with Dalis and Frandin the leaders of the Tiguras and Gryphels and hands were found for the next few days. "You know Sami, we should rotate these chores between each race. It seems we may have been shirking some of the dirty jobs that have to be done for us to survive. Don't worry about it Sami, I'll talk to the other leaders and we'll make it all permanent like at the next council meeting." Dalis told her with a hearty buffet to the back.

"I think it would be best coming from you Dalis, if I suggest it, Caleb will oppose it for that reason alone. He will be sure to argue that the only reason I'm doing it is to get out of work or some other nonsense about Kena putting me up to it so she can be lazy." Sami warned. If it was up to her she would skin Caleb like she did the hare and smoke the meat, but Kena always defended him. No matter what Caleb did, Kena made excuses for him, built up her shields, and then disappeared. When she reappeared it was like nothing had happened except she was just a little quieter, a little more shut down, a little harder to reach.

"No problem Sami, we'll take care of it and we'll take care of Caleb and his Gryphons." Frandin added "You just take care of yourself and Kena if she'll let you."

Sami smiled a thanks, surprised that Frandin had noticed Kena's distress and that decided her. Kena wasn't the only one that needed a little alone time. She changed and leaped hard into the air winging to her little refuge.

When Sami returned to the cavern in early evening she considerately brought food for Kena and Seth since neither had stopped into the commons for the evening meal. It was probably for the best since Caleb was there making an ass of himself per usual. As Sami landed and changed she called to Seth who was all too glad to join her. It took more effort to pull Kena from her furs near her grandmother's favorite wall spot. "Come on Kena you have to eat something."

Kena checked her shields before she joined them. She was surprised by how hungry she was. "Thanks for bringing some food Sami. I was hungry, I can't remember the last time I had a decent meal."

"Me too, Sami. Learning the magics of the cavern just drains me. I couldn't seem to find the energy leave tonight." Seth added.

"You're welcome. The commons was a great idea. Magiv does most of the cooking. She told me she loves it and she is overrun with helpers. Frandin and Dalis were good to their words and everyone is already chipping in, even the Gryphons. I think we were dividing ourselves into races a little too much, now with the commons were socializing together more and working together better." Sami babbled trying to get Kena to engage. Seth caught her eye and shook his head, it was a lost cause. Kena didn't even look up from her plate. Sami grabbed Kena's arm to get her attention, "Kena, are you with us?"

"Oh sorry, I was lost in thought I guess." Kena answered barely looking up. "Something I need to know?"

"Actually, no, not really, we'll cover it all at the council meeting in the morning." Seth told her putting a restraining hand on Sami before she could say something else.

"Oh yeah, I forgot about that. I'm going to get some sleep. I'll see you in the morning." Kena rose and taking what was left of her dinner with her went back to her furs.
"Sami don't. Until she's ready you're not going to be able to force her. Whatever is going on with her we

have to let her work it out or come to us." Seth warned his friend.

"Seth, she's killing herself, don't you see that? I can't just watch her commit slow suicide and not try to stop it."

"You have to Sami, that's your only choice. If you keep pushing you're going to push her away." Sami fought the tears in her eyes trying to hide them from Seth, but she wasn't hiding anything from him. He pulled her into a hug, "Sami I know it's hard to watch someone you love struggle, but she's not listening and until she is she's not going to hear anything we have to say."

Sami pulled out of Seth's supportive hug, "You may be right but I can't, I won't, stay here and watch her waste away and die." She changed and with a running leap flew out of the cavern.

Chapter 22 Fire

Kena winged hard over empty snow covered landscape. She'd had another run in with Caleb where she had once again nearly lost control. Oh, she had wanted to burn that triumphant look off his face, and she had immediately felt contrite, so instead she added a few more layers to her shield and fled before she could do something she knew she would regret. Flying had become her only escape. Who was she kidding? It wasn't escape, it was running. She was now running away from Caleb, from the village, from the Changers. She was even running from Sami and Seth now. Every night she felt Sami's worry, and every night she worked at building stronger shields. Somehow she needed to build them strong enough to quit letting the raw emotions of the others in and prevent hers from leaking out. Every day it felt like fire was right there at the surface ready to pounce.

Kena caught a thermal and used it to soar higher. She hadn't had much of an appetite lately in fact she couldn't remember her last meal. Most changers went to the commons for meals, but Kena hadn't been able to yet. She had tried once but Caleb had been there and it felt like everyone was staring at her, so she left. Usually she hunted for herself when her stomach unknotted enough for her to feel hungry. Of course the only time her stomach unknotted was when she was flying far away from the valley and far away from her fellow Changers. The last time she was able to leave the valley was three days ago and if memory served the last time she did actually eat anything. Well, she could certainly remedy that. She hadn't lost any of her hunting skills, and as she got farther away from the village and her problems she felt hunger gnawing at her. She dropped down to glide over the landscape. Even here this far north hunting could still be found if you knew what to look for and Kena knew exactly what she was looking for. Her shadow marked her passage clearly on the snow covered ground and it wasn't long until she found exactly what she was hungry for as a snow hare broke for cover. Kena dove, grabbed, and back winging, soared back into the sky the rabbit an easy catch. A quick thought and her talon holding the hare burst into flames consuming it totally. Kena flew on until the stench of burning hair turned to the pleasant smell of cooking meat. Landing, she made a quick meal of the rabbit leaving its remains for the scavengers to finish.

Eagle Bennett

She returned to her flight refreshed and feeling better than she had in days. It was with renewed energy that she soared once again into the cloudless cold sky. She had no destination in mind until she saw a weird mountain peak in the distance. Her curiosity drove her towards it. To her surprise when she got closer the peak was not a peak at all but a crater. Inside the crater was filled with bubbling lava. At a low side of the crater the hot lava flowed slowly out trailing down the lee side of the mountain. Kena circled the crater for a while riding the hot thermals the volcano created and admiring the green oasis the heat from the volcano allowed to flourish. It was like a miniature paradise. Eventually she landed on the edge of the crater.

Be welcome child.

Kena heard the voice very clearly in her head. She knew full well she had no ability to speak mind to mind so she was a little shocked.

I can speak to whomever I choose, but I choose few.

"Is it because I am a Phoenix that you have chosen to do so with me?" Kena knew she should be frightened, but she wasn't she just knew that no nothing here wished to harm her.

Yes little one, but more because like your ancestor we are partners. A pact she made with me then and a promise you have made to me now. Have you come to make good on your promise? Kena knew full well the promise it referred to. She couldn't help but consider the question. She would be at peace, free from the pain of this world. Free from Caleb's malicious remarks, and Seth and Sami's anxiety. Free from the crushing weight of all the emotions that constantly weighed on her and free from all the responsibility that consumed her. Would anyone really miss her?

Do you truly believe no one would miss you little one? Kena didn't know how or where it came from but a clear picture of Sami came into her head. *What of her, would she not miss you?*

Kena had to admit yes Sami would miss her and she would miss Sami. Pain hit her heart at the thought of leaving Sami and she instinctually strengthened her shields.

I will wait for you. I am eternal, as long as the world lives I live. I am nothing if not patient, you will know when it is time. Is there something else you need of me? If it is something in my power to give then you shall have it.

"I did not come seeking you. I stumbled onto this place I was really looking for a place to be alone."

Do you really believe that? Whether you were looking or not you are drawn to me and to this place. So tell me little one, what troubles you? I have been here since the dawn of time and I have seen and heard much. Nothing can surprise me anymore.

Kena changed sitting on the edge of the crater as she considered his offer. Was it possible here in the middle of nowhere she had found a friend who could truly understand her? She felt the emotions of that word hit her and she once again strengthened her shields.

Eagle Bennett

That is unnecessary and will do you no good here little one. We are part of each other you and me. Here you cannot lock away what you feel from me for am I not locked inside you as well, do I not give you the power? You can turn away from those who love you, but never me. So here, Daughter, you are free to be yourself.

"You call me daughter?"

Should I not Daughter? Who else should, could claim that role in your life. The easy burning fleshy person who sired you and forgot you or me who has always protected and cared for you and always will. I may not have sired you but I created you.

Kena had to admit he was right. It wasn't until she changed and touched fire for the first time that she had truly felt alive. It was only in fire that she truly felt free.

Most importantly daughter I care about you. I feel your pain, it burns as hot as lava, and like lava if you lock it away it will eventually explode.

For the first time in years Kena cried and she couldn't stop. Fire flared out of the volcano and encircled her, comforting her. She was surrounded by the burning flames of love and she relished the safety the flames evoked in her. Finally her tears ran dry and she opened her eyes onto a dark sky. She needed to get home.

That was long past due Daughter. Now you can return to your friends with a little lighter heart. Come back as often as you like little one, I welcome your company and I can help you as no one else can. There is much about your power you do not know and more you do not understand.

Kena returned to the cavern late, well after Tam had left for his nightly flight. She moved quietly to her own bed, being careful not to wake Sami and Seth. She didn't want to explain where she had been or to talk at all really. She spent a few moments in her nightly ritual of adding to her shields and she didn't even notice her grandmother's worried expression as she fell asleep.

Sami woke just in time to see Kena winging out of the cavern. Her heart ached for Kena. *I've changed my mind, we need to do something about her soon.* Seth sent and Sami needlessly agreed. Sami couldn't talk mind to mind so joining Seth was the easier thing to do. "I'm hungry. Let's go to the commons, we can eat and talk." She didn't wait for Seth to answer. Sami changed and leaped into the air winging out of the cavern. It took Seth a few minutes to join her since he had to wait for the cavern to open fully before he could get out but he was flying at her side by the time they reached the landing for the commons. As they entered the commons they were greeted by smiles and pleasant salutations. Sami returned some good natured joking by a few of her Tiskins, mostly about her love life or lack of it, as she retrieved her breakfast. It was early enough that there were plenty of seats where they could eat alone. Sami had no intentions of having her worries for Kena become the latest gossip fodder.

"So did she even speak to you last night when she came home?" Seth asked.

Sami shook her head, "No, I think I was asleep though since I don't remember her coming in."

"I wasn't, it was late, really late. She made straight for her bed, I'm pretty sure she didn't even speak to her grandmother, let alone me. She kept her head down making sure to avoid eye contact with us in case we were awake."

"She was off early this morning too. She didn't speak this morning either, just changed and left. Can you reach her, can you tell where she's going?" Sami asked, not really hiding her worry.

"I can't, when I reach for her all I get are her shields. I have never come up against shields like she has set. I can't even mind call her as strong as her shields are right now. But Sami I'm sure she is going off on her own. I know she's not meeting someone." Seth tried to ease the hurt in his friend's eyes.

"It would hurt Seth knowing she had found someone, but I think I would feel better if she was meeting someone else. At least then I would know she was letting someone in because Seth if she doesn't open up soon... Let's talk to Tam see what he says."

Tam was a black lump of scales when they returned to the cavern. He quickly awoke as they changed and settled next to him. "I know why you are here and of what you wish to talk about, but there is no answer. Kena is lost. She has locked herself behind her shields. None of us are at all sure how to fix the problem. Kena is not talking to any of us either. None of the murals have been able to penetrate her shields and we have all tried. This is a problem we could not completely foresee. Not since Plentia made her pact with fire has only one Phoenix flown the sky. If another of her kind had been found Kena would then have at least one other being she need not have to fear hurting if or when her fire escaped. I am afraid your initial instinct was right Seth. If we push her she will do one of two things; leave or join the fire. Neither of them a good choice for her, for you, or for the valley."

Seth held Sami's hand tight wondering if either of those things happened if they wouldn't just lose Sami to. "Tam we can't lose Kena, there has to be something we can do. There has to be some hope."

Tam took a deep breath, "I don't know if there is hope. Only time will tell. We will continue to try to come up with an answer, but the two of you, the two who are closest to her must be prepared for the worst."

"I won't give up on her Tam, I can't. We lose Kena, I'm going with her whatever her choice." Sami told him as she stalked off.

Seth watched her leave before he turned back to his mentor, "Better come up with something Tam, she means it. If we lose Kena, we will lose Sami too and I'm not sure the valley will survive losing both of them."

Kena circled the volcano a couple of times before landing. She had only left a few hours ago but it felt like an eternity. As she landed on the edge of the crater she felt the essence of fire fill her with love and acceptance.

Eagle Bennett
Welcome back Daughter. I did not expect to see you so soon.

"To be honest I shouldn't be here, I have things I should be doing but I couldn't seem to stay away."

While part of me is pleased that you have found comfort here, I am concerned as well.

"Why concerned?" Kena asked confused by the turn of his mood.

My concern is wholly for you Daughter. Why are you not with your friends? Why do you refuse the comfort they offer?"

Kena considered how to answer that question. "It's complicated. My heart wants desperately to be with my friends, to laugh and talk like we used to, but it's hard to be near them too."

Why Daughter, why is it hard? Connections are part of living. You cannot truly be living without connections. It is why I sought out your distant ancestor, even I needed connections."

"You of all things should understand. I want the connection but if I do, if I let myself love like that I could lose control of the fire, it will destroy those I care most about. It is the ones I love the most that I put in the most danger. I can't take that chance."

Fire wished he had a head to shake or lungs to sigh with. There was so much she didn't understand about her own power, and so much she needed to learn, even he wasn't sure he was up to the task. Well he could only try, and he had to try because if he did not, if he did nothing she would be keeping her promise to him very soon, as much as he longed for her company he knew the world needed her still, so try he would. *Oh Daughter, I do not know who did you this great disservice, but I will do my best to correct the mistake.*

Chapter 23 Revelations

Caleb moved closer to Marta's naked body. It was early, the sun just starting to light the sky and he had no interest in rising just yet. He had no immediate responsibilities to attend to and a little cuddling with the love of his life was certainly one of the best ways to start his day. Marta moaned a little in her sleep before she came awake at his gentle touches. "Good morning Love," He whispered in her ear just before he snuck a little nibble in.

"Hmm Caleb, stop. I can't, I volunteered to for the commons breakfast shift. I've got to get up and get moving."

Caleb groaned but desisted. "I don't know why you're doing that. In my opinion flying patrols and hunting should be enough. I don't get why we have to help with everything else."

Marta looked back at Caleb. She never quite got him when he got into these moods. She seldom saw this side of him, but she knew he was like this almost all the time with Seth and Kena. When she did see this side of him she wanted to kick him in the ass and tell him to get over himself, but that would just make it worse. However, this time she couldn't just ignore it, not when he was so wrong. "Caleb, why shouldn't we all help out? Yes, we're hunting and patrolling, so is everyone else."

"Sure the Tiguras and Gryphels help us patrol and hunt, but none of the other races do."

"The Tiskins hunt, they just bring in smaller game and who else should patrol? The Dokuls? When did patrolling become such hard work that it was all we could do? Between all of us, we have enough Changers the most we ever have to do is fly one patrol a day. That's what, two hours. We don't hunt every day, usually more like every third or fourth day and again that takes like two hours. How much free time does a Changer need?"

Caleb was shocked. Marta seldom argued with him. "I just think the other races should do more."

"More? More what? Patrolling? Hunting? Who else should patrol? The Pegasi? They can fly, but even they will admit they aren't exactly graceful at it."

"What about the Tiskins? They're as skilled in the air as any of us?" Caleb debated back warming up to the argument.

"Sure, they are and faster than us too. So are we going to take over the questing? On any given day a good half of the resident Tiskins are gone looking for more of us. If it wasn't for them most of the Changers that live here now wouldn't be here including me. It was a Tiskin questing team that found me. You think a Gryphon can mingle in with the pests, blend in get in get out without being seen? I, for one, don't want to try. When they are here they're not sitting on their tails doing nothing. They're out there helping in the commons, working in the skinning and smoking sheds, helping with the livestock, training and doing all the millions of other things that have to be done to keep the valley running."

Caleb hated it, but he had to admit she was right. The Tiskins were performing a valuable service, but he wasn't quite done with the argument yet. "Fine, I'll grant you the Tiskins are doing their share, but I don't think you can argue the same for all the races."

"Oh yes I can. Caleb, hunting and patrolling aren't the only important things. If it wasn't for the Dokuls we wouldn't have homes or any of the other conveniences of life. If it wasn't the Unicorns and Pegasi we wouldn't have fields of corn and grain. All of us, all the races, help serve in the way that best suits their skills and gifts and we all chip in where we can. Patrolling is no more important than building and hunting is no more important than tending the flocks and fields."

Caleb had one more point to make the point he was working up to the entire argument, "What about Kena, I never see her in the commons and she certainly could fly patrols and hunt."

"You're right, she doesn't work in the commons. On the other hand, she never eats in the commons either and she does hunt and she's the only one who patrols the northern wastes she just does it alone. She does everything alone. If it is a job that can be done alone Kena is probably the one doing it. It's like she's afraid to be around any of us."

Caleb sneered at the statement, "More like too good to be around anyone."

Marta shook her head, "I don't think that's it Caleb. I think there is something wrong. She just seems to be fading. I saw her the other day and she just seemed absent, like I was seeing a shell of Kena." Marta saw Caleb's clear denial and even though she wasn't trying she could clearly hear his denial and disgust in his thoughts. "Look, I have to get to the commons and I have an afternoon patrol, but just think about it, okay?" Marta gave him a long hug and kissed him soundly. "I'll see you tonight. I'll bring something home from the commons so we can be alone. I'll make it up to you this evening, I promise. Love you." Marta told him as she closed the door leaving him alone.

Caleb groaned as he rolled out of bed, and he grumbled to himself as he pulled on a pair of pants. He hated to admit it, but Marta had made some good points and he had to agree. He had been letting the Gryphons slide in the chore department. Well, he would fix that today when he assigned patrols. There was no reason the patrol leaders couldn't handle making sure the Gryphons did their fair share of the menial chores. Caleb smiled at his solution as he washed up in the tepid water in the wash basin wishing the water was colder to help clear the sleep from his head. He needed to be able to think clearly this morning. He heard his stomach growl and that decided him, he had to meet Frandin and Dalis this morning about a personal project but he should have time for a bite at the commons before he met up with them.

Kena winged in to land on the crater being careful not to drop her meal into the lava. She was basically living here these last two weeks. She had built a comfortable little shelter at the base of the volcano in the little oasis that thrived due to the warming the volcano provided. She told no one where she was going. Part of her felt guilt over this secret while another part yelled why feel guilty you are only conversing with a friend, but she knew that was a lie. Only here did fire converse with her. Here she had come to know fire as more than a friend. Here she had come to know fire as her father. It was here at this volcano that fire started. It was from here that all other fires set forth returned when they had fed. Even the fire that was part of her started here. As her ancestors before her, she was one with the flame and she felt that more here than anywhere else, and because of this it was here that she felt the most at ease. It was here and only here she could let someone in and not fear losing control so it was here that she had come to hide.

Kena heard the clink of her talons hitting the sheer rock of the cliff as she settled on the edge of the crater. She had no fear of falling if she did she would simply fly out, the lava held no more fear for her than water.

Good morning Daughter. How did you rest?

"Honestly, I didn't. I have a council meeting today and well thinking about returning to the valley... I'm thinking about skipping it. I'm not sure I can deal with it today or any day. It's not like we ever get anything done at these meetings. We bicker and argue, it's been months since we have even been able to make a decision about anything."

You worry too much Daughter, you have strength even you don't realize. You'll be fine and I will be here

Eagle Bennett

when it is done, I have been here since the dawn of time, I am always here.

Kena considered her father's words for a moment. Life was about doing what had to be done, not about doing what you wanted to do. "Thank you father I will be back as soon as it is done." Kena promised.

There is no hurry, perhaps staying at least long enough to converse with your friend, the Tiskin?

"Maybe?" Kena answered noncommittally, knowing full well she wouldn't. Of all the Changers, Sami was the hardest for her to keep control around. Whenever she got close to her she could feel the fire in her chest trying to explode no matter how many strong layers she built up. It was easier to keep control around Caleb. Who would have thought loathing would be easier to control than affection? Kena tossed her uneaten breakfast into the lava her stomach making it clear it wasn't interested in food and launched herself into the air hoping this council meeting was short so she could escape sooner.

Kena winged in through the cavern roof. She quickly realized she was the last to arrive and it was clear Caleb had already been spreading his vile. She tried to make eye contact with Sami as she changed but Sami quickly ducked her head confirming her worst fear, she had lost her last friend. Kena was surprised by how much it hurt and quickly pushed it all back behind her shields. She had pushed Sami away now, there was nothing holding her to this world. She forced herself to see and feel nothing just wanting this over.

Eagle Bennett

Sami seethed as she sat at the council table. Caleb had once again begun his daily targeting of Kena, causing unrest amongst the council. Her anger was near to exploding and she knew Seth felt the same way. Caleb never let any opportunity to attack Kena, either directly or behind her back, slip by. This time he was implying she was a coward and worse using her empathy immorally to make sure his ideas were quashed. Anybody who knew Kena knew nothing could be farther from the truth. In fact, just the opposite was true. Kena had built her shields so strong nothing got in or out. Sami tried to remember when Kena had started hiding behind her wall of shields. At first things were good. Caleb was snide and bitter, but that was just who he was, he was like that with everyone. As other Changers started to arrive and more Gryphons started looking to Caleb as a leader, his jibes took on a more pointed bent and were most often aimed at Kena. The thought made Sami fume a little more. It was always Kena that was the target, no one else. Kena wouldn't even defend herself, telling anyone that would listen that it was just Caleb's nature and Gryphon blood. Well, Sami might believe that if he would pick at someone else. She and Seth did what they could but it wasn't enough and they were slowly losing Kena. They went days without seeing her now, and when she did return at night she went straight to her bed and never said a word sometimes she wouldn't even bother to change. Sami couldn't remember the last time she had heard Kena speak. Out of desperation, Seth had tried to read her mind, but came up against the strongest shield he had ever felt. Nothing was getting past those shields. Tam had conferred with the Phoenix mural and now knew Kena wasn't talking or sharing with her either and she had been unable with her empathy to break through Kena's shields. Sami fought back tears thinking about what the mural had told Tam. *If we do not break through her self imposed isolation soon we will lose her. I fear she already seeks the fire.* Sami knew what the Phoenix had meant by seeks the fire, she had a death wish. Her biggest fear was the wish would turn into seeking. Sami would die before she let that happen, so killing Caleb was certainly an option. If he didn't shut up about Kena being a coward she would make sure his death was long and painful.

The cavern roof opened slightly then, grabbing Sami's attention as Kena flew in. She had lost weight and there was a dullness to her eyes and feathers that broke Sami's heart. *If he doesn't shut up I'm going to fry him I swear.* Seth sent to her mind. Sami didn't have time to respond as Kena was landing and changed as she approached the table. The changes in her as a Phoenix were all the more evident when she changed. Sami about burst into tears at the sight of her and only Seth's restraining hand on her leg kept her from going to support her. Sami choked back her feelings, Kena wouldn't welcome the help and knowing they worried would force her even more back into her shell. As Kena sat down next to her she didn't even acknowledge her, it was like Kena couldn't even see what was right in front of her. Sami watched her out of the corner of her eye. The beautiful red brown eyes she had fallen into and in love with were empty and lightless surrounded by dark circles. Her checks were sunken and it looked like it had been days since she had eaten. *We can do nothing for her yet Sami. You will hurt her more if she notices your concern.* Sami knew he was right, but it was so hard to watch and do nothing, so she ducked her head and avoided making eye contact.

Caleb started his usual diatribe about the nonexistent war. His allies, Frandin and Dalis, quickly joined his side. Everyone looked to Kena to lead the opposition, but she stayed mute staring at the dancing flame of one of the candles. In fact she seemed a thousand miles away her eyes unfocused, Sami wasn't even sure she was hearing what was said.

"So Kena, what have you to say to keep us hiding in our valley this time?" Caleb asked.
The others were quiet, some even looked concerned for Kena, finally seeing what she and Seth knew. Kena was slowly killing herself. Everyone waited to see if she would have an answer for him, but she didn't even seem to notice she had been addressed. She stared straight ahead.

Kena heard Caleb arguing once again about war, but she just didn't care anymore. All she could think of was getting out of this cavern and away from the Changers. It was time for her to keep her promise. Sami was the only thing keeping her here and now even Sami turned from her. Kena forced her feelings back behind her shields being careful not to project what she was thinking to any of the many thought sensors, not that she thought any of them would care or try to stop her. Caleb would probably be willing to help her. Either way she just had to get through this last council meeting.

Sami had seen enough though, "Look Caleb, talk all you want but until we see a reason, some sort of act of aggression, we will not be part of a war. It's that simple. Now, let's move on to what these meetings are supposed to be about." Caleb glared but said nothing just as Sami knew he would. She was too hard of target for his bullying, she fought back and she wasn't at all afraid of him. Sami glared right back waiting for Caleb to back down. Caleb dropped his eyes Sami smiled and continued, "Qwint, you had a piece of business you wished to discuss, something about needing additional forges."

As soon as the meeting was done Kena changed and launched herself into the air. The cavern roof barely had time to open a crack before she slid through. She had no interest in talking to anyone. She winged hard, flying fast out of the valley back towards the volcano. Part of her cried against what her heart wanted. Perhaps she could just disappear. No one knew about the volcano or where she was going when she left. It could well be years before she was discovered. Either way she was never going back to the valley and the emotional agony of being surrounded by Changers.

Fire could feel the turmoil of Kena's thoughts and knew exactly what she was thinking. *You can't do either of the things you are thinking of doing. You are needed on the council. Once my children flew the sky as numerous as the stars and as beautiful as well, but now I have yet to have sensed any but you. The council needs that wisdom or your society will not survive. Tell me of the meeting what has brought you to these conclusions.*

"It was not pleasant."

Tell me, perhaps I can be of help.

"There's nothing there for me anymore, even Sami avoids me now."

Fire hid his frustration with his daughter. In her current state of mind knowing how he felt may drive her even from him. Weeks of careful prodding had gotten him nowhere. Kena had reached rock bottom, but perhaps she was ready to listen. It was time to be a bit more straight forward. He had nothing to lose. She had already arrived at the worst case scenario she was ready to die where else could he push her. *You are right Sami does avoid you but not for the reason you think. You have locked yourself so far away from everything and everyone, Daughter, you are unable to feel what is clear. Sami avoids you because she cares for you and hates to see you in such pain. She fears if you see her worry, her concern, it will hurt you more and drive you even farther away. They do not know what to do to help you. In that they are not alone. Kena, if you do not address your feelings soon, the fire trapped inside will destroy you. I know part of you seeks that, part of you always will. That is why it is so important for you to have connections. Only with connections can you hope to fight the draw of the fire.*

Kena considered his words, she couldn't hide her feelings from him. He knew the reason it all hurt was because as much as she denied it she did care about the Changers and the valley and she did care for Sami she was her first, her only friend.

Then why hide from that love? Why hide from that friendship?

Kena had the answer for this. "If I let my feelings out, if I lose control, the fire will burn free. It will destroy and kill. I can't love Sami without killing her." Kena yelled, tears trailing down from her eyes, "So how can I love her? How can I claim to care for her and put her at such risk? How can I care for anyone and put them in such danger?"

There Kena had finally admitted her real fear and given him the opening he needed. *Kena you control the fire not the other way around, just as you control your emotions. You have been hiding from both and it's time to come out from behind your fears. Your shields are supposed to protect you, not hide you.*

Kena sat quietly for a moment considering what he said. She knew he was right, she was hiding. "It's not love but anger that drove me to hide. It was anger that caused the fire to burn so hot. I began losing control when I was mad, then I started losing control when I was happy. Now I lose control with just a wisp any feelings."

Anger shared is anger defeated. Only through connections do you have any hope of truly dealing with anger. You need to trust yourself. You are stronger than you give yourself credit for. You can control the fire without shielding yourself away. You have a choice to make Kena, you can keep your promise and join me or you can start letting others in because if you don't you'll be joining me very soon any way and bringing many others with you. Kena before you decide you should know they need you. I am eternal I have seen this before. If you walk away from this then all you have built will crumble, the war will come and destroy all. Like the ancients, the Changers will become extinct. Deny it all you want Daughter, but for the valley and the Changers to survive you must step up and lead. Your grandmother refused to do so when she was called and the price for her failure was death and destruction, your price could be even higher. The choice is yours to make.

Kena knew what her choice had to be. She had to go back, she had to return to the Changers. She had to learn to deal with her issues instead of hiding from them. She knew it wasn't going to be easy and she just didn't think she could do it alone.

You are not alone. Fire jumped on the thought as quick as he felt it. This was what he needed her to understand. This was what he had been trying to get her to understand this whole time. *If you open your heart you will know you have never been alone. She has waited for you. She waits for you still. She can be your anchor, your tie on to this world. She can be the friend you need and the partner you yearn for, you just have to let her in. You just have to let her help.*

Kena knew he meant Sami. She knew Sami loved her, part of her had always known Sami loved her. She carefully examined what she felt for Sami and knew without a doubt she loved her just as much. It was only her fear that kept her from responding from accepting the friendship Sami could give her. Her whole life she was forced to stand alone to be in complete control and to rely on no one. It was time she learned how to lean on someone else to allow herself to believe in someone else. She allowed her love to push forward out from behind the walls and found the fire burned but didn't escape.

Kena, Daughter, love is fire and fire is love, you cannot have love without the other, no one can, but for you the relationship is more intimate. That should be a benefit not an issue. Use your fire to fuel your love and find

Eagle Bennett

the friendship and support you need to be the leader you have to be.

Kena felt like she had been hit by a bolt of lightning as she finally got it, finally understanding what she had been striving to understand from the moment she had learned to change. Controlling the fire didn't mean containing it. Fire burned, fire needed to burn it was only in containing it that it became explosive. It was only when the lava was contained in the earth that it exploded and became destructive. When allowed to flow it burned powerfully yes but slowly. She had the power the strength to control fire, even in love even in anger she was the one in control not her gift and not her inner flame. Fire obeyed her, not the other way around. Fire was her partner not her master. She had been letting fire be her master, but not anymore. She was the master of her fate, no one else.

Now you're ready. Ready to love and ready to lead. Ready to be the leader they need you to be. Ready to be the leader you have to be for the Changers to survive.

Kena knew he was right and the first thing she needed to do was find Sami. She was just getting ready to say her goodbyes when fire interrupted her. Kena could clearly hear the urgency in his mind voice.

Wait, Kena, there is trouble at the ford.

"What? What trouble?"

I can't tell you what, there is no fire there. I am blind without fire but the beings that work the hot fires are running and shouting. They look for you. You are needed at the ford.

Kena didn't hesitate but leaped strongly into the air. As soon as she was clear she beat her wings down seeking air and speed. Fire helped blowing a hot thermal and granting her more lift quicker than she could achieve on her own. *Remember Daughter, you must be the leader they need. You control the fire it does not control you. I am always with you and together we are an invincible foe.* A tail wind abruptly blew up speeding her where she needed to be faster than she thought possible and stopped as soon as she arrived. Kena sent a mental thank you to fire as she landed next to Caleb and Frandin.

She quickly saw what the alarm was about. Along the river a traveling clan was approaching the ford. Kena forced the fear away. This was what she was meant to be, this was what she was born to do. She must be the leader the Changers needed. She would be the leader the Changers needed. She felt fires' power surge through her in answer. She was stronger than she had ever been and it was time Caleb found out just how strong she really was. "Caleb, do we have a Tiskin near them yet?"

Caleb was a little shocked to see Kena taking charge after her performance at the council meeting, but Frandin didn't hesitate to answer. "Yes, Sami wanted to go, but I told her to she was needed here as the Tiskin leader and suggested she send someone else. She sent Lenk and Marta is listening."

"Good, that's what I would have told her as well, where is everybody else?"

This time Caleb answered. "I made Seth stay in the cavern with Tam where he would be safe. Everyone else is near, ready and listening for orders. I can broadcast anything you wish to say."

Kena looked at him. Her father was right, she was the leader they needed, not Caleb, he was too angry too reckless. She had no choice now she really never had a choice. "What does Marta say they are saying?"

Caleb's eyes unfocused as he sought the mind that was Marta's. It wasn't hard, he knew Marta's mind better than anyone's. "They have yet to see the warning sign." He hated it but he knew Kena was the right person to take charge. He wasn't good at seeing all the possible outcomes or planning for all the contingencies, Kena was.

Kena nodded and opened her shields slightly. She blocked out all the emotions near her and concentrated on the feelings from the people approaching along the river. Something even this morning she would not have been able to do. It seemed her awakening had come just in time. She shook her head at the force of the feelings she felt. She knew without a doubt they were not going to cross the ford. She closed her shields so she could think clearly without other's emotions playing on her. "Caleb, they are not going to stop, we are going to have to stop them. Have the Dokuls get any Changer too young or not trained to fight into the safety of the cavern where the murals and the Dragons can protect them. I want you, Qwint, and Kimball down there to greet them. Change first. I want them to see Qwint for who he is. Please try to be tactful. If they fail to ford tell them of their error. We will give them the chance to correct their mistake. If they insist on fighting, we will make sure they regret it."

Caleb eyes closed as he concentrated on broadcasting Kena's words. Even those without mind speech he implanted the thoughts. A cheer rose from all around as Caleb leapt into the air to meet Qwint and Kimball. Mintell quickly took his place. She was a good choice since she was the strongest mind speaker and the weakest fighter. She was small in stature no matter what form she took, and while brave she would still make an easy target.

Kena nodded to her as she continued "Kimball, if all goes wrong I want you to get all three of you out of the way of the fighting. Sami, Dalis, I want the Tiskins and the Tiguras ready to ambush. Dalis, the Tiguras job is to take out the men and any women who choose to fight. If they fight, they forgo any hope of mercy. Sami, I want the Tiskins to separate any children too young to fight. They should be fearful enough of you that you can herd them away from the fighting just don't pick a form too scary or they may be too afraid to move. We will not kill children. We are not animals or barbarians. Any women who chose not to fight, herd away with the children. This is a traveling clan. The women may fight, they may not, I do not know. We will not kill any woman, child or man that does not bear arms against us." Mintell quickly relayed her words and Kena saw movement all around the ford as Tiskins and Tiguras melted into the landscape.

"What of us?" Frandin asked.

"The Gryphon and the Gryphels are our air force. You will come in from above. Dive on any you can without hurting the Tiguras or the Tiskins. I know you've been practicing that. Frandin, in Caleb's absence you are in charge of both Gryphels and Gryphons. Senna, in your brothers absence you will lead the Dokuls. The Dokuls will defend the village, if any one gets through kill them before they reach the village. Seth you and Tam protect the council tavern and the murals." *The murals can protect themselves thank you.* Kena was interrupted by the thought. She knew it was one of the murals that had interjected, but she didn't know which one but she guessed it was the Gryphon. She ignored the interruption and continued. Tameera, you will lead both the Pegasi and the Unicorns. I need you to work your way in behind the ... target." Kena couldn't quite bring herself to call them enemies. She could easily be related to some if not many of the people headed this way. She could also feel the blood lust coming from the Changers. They wanted this fight, they wanted to kill. "Tameera, let none escape, but only kill if you must." Mintell broadcast her orders, and Kena felt and saw everyone moving to obey.

Welcome back little one, you have been missed. It is as it was always meant to be. It was not coincidence that brought you to the mountain first, it was destiny. Perhaps it is time to accept fate for what it is.

Kena recognized Tams mind touch, but she chose for now to ignore the implication and the way it mirrored her father's thoughts. "I will be whereever I am needed." Mintell sunk a little after she broadcast the last. "Mint, I would like you to stay with the Dokuls in the village. If there is trouble there they will need a mind speaker." Mintell nodded and took to the air as the down draft from her powerful wings ruffled the feathers on Kena's head.

Kena shook her head and took to the air herself. She wanted to position herself close enough to the meeting place to hear anything that went on. She also had a plan to protect the trio if needed. She circled above for a few moments watching everyone move into the positions they were assigned. The Unicorns jumped with the Pegasi to a spot behind the travelers. The Tiguras and Tiskins were invisible in the forest and undergrowth around the ford. The Gryphons and Gryphels positioned themselves far enough back so as not to be seen until needed. Part of Kena hoped they would not be needed. Part of Kena still hoped the travelers would simply read the warning and cross the ford, but she knew, she could feel, they would not be crossing the ford. For whatever reason this clan had decided they would not deviate from their course this time. Perhaps they had a new leader, perhaps they had heard rumors and wished to confirm. Whatever the reason, Kena intended on sending a message to anyone else who decided to test their defenses, come this way if you wish to die. Kena landed in a huge tree just above where the warning was placed. From here she could see and hear everything that was about to happen.

The clan hesitated at the ford. Kena could hear clearly the discussion, a few of the men didn't see the profit in trespassing, but most didn't want to add the three days of travel that crossing would add. Kena shook her feathered head. She lowered her shields slightly and tried to project fear, knowing it probably wouldn't work. The clan leader had made his choice, "Mount up, we go forward." He called to the clan. Kena growled to herself, *idiots*. She saw the threesome of Qwint, Kimball and Caleb approach. Kena felt fear biting at her heart. She knew help surrounded them, but they were still unarmed and wearing no armor. Kena gathered fire to her, there was a chance she could protect all three of them for a few moments with fire, give them time to change and escape if they needed to.

It was Qwint that spoke first. "You are trespassing on our land and we ask that you cross the ford and leave peaceably."

Kena was thrilled that he had chosen phrasing that was diplomatic and that it was he that was speaking and not Caleb. Caleb was spoiling for a fight, and Kena was hoping they could still prevent that. Though the clan leader's next words made it clear that was not going to happen.

"Who are you to order us, who are you to prevent us from taking the trail we have taken for generations?"

Qwint was quick with his answer, "I am prince Qwint, youngest son of King Tarneon, and I do order and you will obey or you will face the consequences."

"Ha, if you are Qwint, which I doubt, then you know you have been stripped of your title and a rather large bounty placed on your head. Enough for us to pay our taxes for years. Perhaps I will take your head just in case you are the real Qwint." The leader made an almost imperceptible signal, and crossbows appeared in hands of the drivers of every wagon. They had been planning for a confrontation.

Kena saw the danger before the threesome did. She reached into herself into the anger and fear she felt and threw up a wall of fire between the arrows and her friends. She had never used her gift like this before, but she knew she could now. Now she controlled the fire not the other way around. The arrows burned to cinder long before they could come near their intended targets. Kena could not maintain control over the emotionally driven flames for long, but a moment was all they needed. Kena from her vantage point saw all three change. Caleb leaped into the air and Qwint threw himself over Kimball's back just as Kimball jumped out of harm's way taking Qwint with him. Kena called the flames back as Kimball jumped, already they were scorching the earth looking for food. The men of the clan were clearly confused by the loss of their targets, but targets oozed out of the forest in the form of the Tiguras. Women screamed as children too young to fight sought shelter under the wagons only to find themselves chased by fierce winged animals. The Tiskins proved to be experts at separating the non combatants from the fray. The Tiguras ambush was devastating. The men hardly had time to pull or reload weapons and the weapons they were able to put in hand were not much use against the claw and teeth of the Tiguras. Any chance the clan had of mounting a counter attack was ended when the Gryphons and Gryphels made their appearance dropping well placed projectiles or grabbing attackers with claws and talons. It was over very quickly, and when the dust cleared a half a dozen men stood were more than thirty once had. Kena took to her wings, screeching a halt both vocally and mentally, before landing in the middle of the fray and changing. She was joined quickly by Caleb.

"I am Kena, leader of the Changers and this is our land." Kena replied noticing Caleb wince at her words. "You have trespassed and attacked us and we exacted the price for your foolishness. Now I grant you leave to surrender and save your lives. Your leader is dead who will speak for the clan." Kena let the anger she felt leak as she spoke. She wanted not only the surviving members of the clan to feel it but also Caleb. She needed Caleb to clearly know she was back, ready to lead. For years she had waited for someone, anyone, else to prove they could be the one in charge, but still they looked to her every time there was a crisis. Well she was done waiting, she couldn't, she wouldn't take the chance her father was right.

A young man stepped forward. Kena was surprised by how young he was. "I am Gil and I will speak for the clan. We do surrender."

Kena needed more than that. "Why Gil, why did your clan decide this course of action was the best? Why force us to kill?"

Gil dropped his eyes, "It was Fend, the clan leader. He had been working everyone up for weeks, angry over not being able to enter the valley. I'm not sure why. He insisted we take this route, and insisted we ignore all the warnings to cross the river. It wasn't like him. When the trespassing signs first appeared many of the older men wanted to ignore them, but Fend always said we as a clan honored peoples land and rights."

Kena pushed back the suspicions that crept into her head. Why had a man changed so drastically, so quickly? She hoped she was wrong, but she was pretty sure Caleb may have had something to do with Fend's change in attitude. "Thank you, you may take your people and leave. I warn you do not return or we will be forced to kill everyone." The Tiskins had herded the non combatants back to the wagons once the fighting had stopped and it was safe. Kena changed and sprang into the air where she was joined wingtip to wingtip with Caleb. Kena let her orders hang as thoughts in her mind so Caleb could grab them. *Tell Dalis to stand guard with his Tiguras and have Frandin fly patrols over the clan until they are safely free from our land. Everyone else can stand down.* Kena saw Caleb nod in response and knew that her orders would be carried out. Kena winged north she needed some space to think before she confronted Caleb with her suspicions. She was not a Gryphon to react first and think later. The implications of her suspicions were serious. It certainly might not be Caleb, it may not be any of the Changers that had planted the idea in Fend's mind. It didn't matter unless someone admitted it, there was no way for her to prove it and the damage knowing could cause were beyond measure. She soared higher circling the village below. She watched as the fighters returned to their daily tasks, all but the Gryphels and Tiguras who, as ordered, were making sure the traveler clan got back on their way and off Changer land. The clan was gathering their dead and would be moving soon. Kena knew she had already removed the clan from her mind and concerns. The price of this little battle may be high but there was nothing she could do about that right now. She shifted her wing angle slightly when she saw the Tiskins making their way back into the village. The events of the last few hours did not change what she needed to do, only clearly proved her father's point. She was needed, but to do what she must she needed to let others in and the one Changer she wanted to let in most was Sami. Kena landed a little ways in front of the Tiskins and waited for Sami to notice her. Sami jumped over to her as soon as she saw her.

Kena trilled a welcome, for once not surprised or alarmed by her joy at seeing Sami. She welcomed the warming burn in her chest this time, it reminded her she could have feelings and still be in control. "Sami, do you have anything you need to do or could you spare some time for me today?"

Sami purred at Kena, "I can always find time for you. What do you need me to do? Did you need help with something? You know me I am always available if you need a favor."

Kena sighed, sorry she had locked herself away, but it was time now to pick back up the life she had nearly given up and Sami was a big part of that life. "I was wondering if we could talk anywhere quiet and private?" Kena followed her statement with a cocky smile.

Sami was shocked by the request. Kena had never in all the years Sami had known her asked to talk. There was something different about her. The light was back in her eyes and there was a confidence about her Sami had never seen before not even when they had first met. Even then she was reserved and almost shy. Sami knew crisis always brought out a different part of Kena, but this was different. Kena had smiled. It had been so long since she had seen her smile. Sami considered for just a moment about where they could go before nodding at Kena and taking the lead.

Sami sprang into the air, Kena was a breath behind her. Phoenix were the fastest fliers but Tiskins were anything but slow. Sami chose a westerly direction deliberately choosing a direction away from the way the clan would be heading. Sami seemed to have a location in mind and when only a few minutes into the flight she changed her flight angle to land Kena followed her lead. As soon as they were on land Kena changed and Sami followed suit. Sami took Kena's hand as soon as the change was done and led her off down a path. "I've been coming here lately when I want to be alone. It's close enough to the valley to be near if I'm needed, but far enough I'm not easily found. My brother and I had a fort in these woods, no one knew where, not even father. It was our special place. You said you needed somewhere quiet to talk where there was no chance we would be interrupted, figured this would fit the bill."

Sami never let go of Kena's hand and Kena couldn't believe how good it felt to have contact with a living being. She couldn't remember the last time she had allowed anyone close enough to touch her. The warmth that spread throughout her body was as different from the fire as ice was to flame. She couldn't help but smile. "Thanks Sami, you're right, I do need to talk and it would be best if I could get it all out without interruptions. Ancients know, interruptions are all we will get anywhere in the valley."

Sami led her a little ways down the path around a corner. It became clear why Sami had not flown straight to the little fort. It was so imbedded in the flora landing here would have been impossible, it was also invisible from the air, a fact Kena found oddly comforting. Sami opened the door and motioned Kena through, then followed.

The fort was more like a little hut complete with a small kitchen. Two small beds in the far corner of the room were the only furniture, but the soft carpet on the wooden floor would be as comfortable to sit on as the sandy floor of the cavern. There was even a sturdy little fire place in the kitchen. "Sami this is amazing. You built this?"

"With my brother when we were kids. As we got older we made improvements. We used it as a hunting lodge then. No one else knows it exists, or can find it. You can come here anytime you want. It can be our secret place if you want."

"Thank you, Sami. I have something important to talk to you about, but first I want to apologize for being absent these past few weeks... ok more like months maybe even years. Ancients, maybe I've never been completely in the here and now. I've been lost in my own fear and loneliness and instead of accepting help and friendship from you, or from anyone really, I disappeared into a wall of my own guilt, worry, and grief. I was so afraid I would lose control of the fire I decided it was better to be alone. I convinced myself I was protecting you and it was the right thing to do. I'm so sorry, Sami, to have put you through it." Kena couldn't hold back the tears, but Sami was ready. She took Kena into her arms and held her while she cried herself out.

Kena's eyes were red and sore by the time she got hold of her emotions. "Sorry Sami, I shouldn't have..."

"No, why, why are you sorry? That's what friends are for. Kena you keep all of your emotions locked up inside. You don't have to, I'm here for you. I will always be here for you. Please, I love you and I can help, I just need you to let me in." Sami rubbed a gentle hand on Kena's face wiping away the remnants of the tears and gently steered her to one of the little beds, the only furniture in the little hut coaxing her to sit hoping beyond hope that Kena wasn't going to bolt but mentally preparing if she did.

"I'm sorry Sami. It seems the more Changers' emotions that I have to block out the more I block my feelings in. There are days I miss you so badly I can't even think straight and you're right next to me. It's my fault. I just don't know how to open up any more. I don't know how to let down my shields and trust that I can control my inner flame, but if I don't learn it will kill me."

Sami laughed, "Any more? Kena, it's always been hard to get you to open up, from the day I met you. You keep everything personal closer to you than your feathers. I think plucking you would be easier sometimes."

"Try it and I will scorch your paws." Kena joked back.

"I'm serious, Kena, you're going to kill yourself if you don't let someone in. If it's not me, maybe Seth, or anyone? You just have to let someone in. We can't, I can't lose you."

Kena looked at her friend, her best friend. Sami had been with her from nearly the beginning. Sami who she had been taking for granted for years now. She always seemed to be right where she was needed whenever she needed her. She was more than a friend, she was her protector. Kena felt the unfamiliar warmth spread throughout her body again. She had missed what was right in front of her the whole time. Sami didn't just love her she was in love with her and Kena finally realized she was able to accept that. Kena looked into herself and knew if she wasn't hiding from it anymore, she loved Sami the same way and probably always had. She had wasted so much time in hiding. "I'm sorry Sami, I really am sorry. I don't deserve your forgiveness..." Kena didn't get to finish her thought.

Sami put a hand on Kena face and leaned over and kissed her. Kena was surprised not by the action but by how it made her feel. When Sami started to pull away afraid of Kena's reaction it was Kena who stopped her by kissing her. Kena's troubles seemed to melt away as her body warmed at Sami's touch. She matched Sami touch for touch, both experimenting with what felt good and right. Layers of her Shields melted away as Sami found a particularly sensitive spot with her tongue. She let go then, relaxed in the moment, relaxed in Sami's arms and gentle caresses, relaxed into the feeling of love and being loved the whole time knowing she had perfect control on the fire.

The sun had set and the little hut was dark. Kena lay happy and satisfied in Sami's arms, nearly asleep, when Sami spoke. "We should go back. They'll notice we are missing. They may wonder..."

Sami's voice sounded strained and Kena felt fear grip her heart. "Sami, are you sorry about what just happened, I mean..." Kena didn't know what she meant, all she knew was that their relationship had changed and she didn't want it to ever go back the way it was. She needed Sami in a way she would never have thought. Sami was the light at the end of a very dark tunnel she had lost herself in. Fear gripped her at the thought that she had been wrong and Sami didn't feel the same way. That this was just comfort and need and not love.

Sami was plainly surprised "Ancients, no. Kena I have been thinking about doing this with you since basically the day we met, but you never seemed interested in anything more than friendship. Of course, you never seemed to be interested in anyone else either so I had hope and I waited. Today felt right somehow. It felt like you wanted me, needed me, but I don't expect anything Kena. I don't have to have anything but friendship..."

Kena turned to face her love. "Sami, I can't, I won't be without you. I do need you and ancients know how badly I want you. I should have seen it long ago and would have if I had not been so unwilling to let myself feel. I can't tell you how grateful I am that you patiently waited. It's not going to be easy. In fact it may be the hardest thing I have ever done, but not having you is unthinkable. Not being part of your life is not an option. Sami I love you." Kena must have said something right because Sami responded in the way that proved to Kena she agreed and it was clear they weren't going anywhere this night.

The sun streaming in the window woke Kena. The initial surprise at her surroundings quickly gave over to the happy memory of last night. She was curled around Sami's naked body, warm and safe. Kena leaned in close nuzzling the back of Sami's neck, savoring her scent, reveling in the warmth and closeness, relishing the feeling of skin on skin. Kena was shocked, she, an empath, had totally missed Sami's feelings and in all honesty her feelings for Sami. If there was one thing she had learned in the past few years it was how to examine feelings, perhaps it was time to examine her own. She started with what she knew was love for

Sami, but it was more than that. The love she felt for Sami was tinged with need and want and there was no denying the lust that was attached to that love, but there was also a protectiveness that surprised Kena. Sami was proficient and capable and needed her protection about as much as a lion need to be protected from a calf. No, that part of her love she needed to not respond to, Sami would not thank her for it. Kena pushed what she was feeling for Sami to the back of her mind. If she was going to build on this relationship she had to figure out exactly what she felt for Caleb. It was a little like prodding a sore tooth. Her relationship with Caleb had always been confrontational, but lately it had taken on a hurtful bent. Kena forced those emotions out in the open where she could really feel them. Caleb had pushed her and instead of pushing back she withdrew, hiding just like her father had said. She felt tears form behind her eyes and a cold twisting in her guts. She wanted to stop, but to be able to love Sami, to give her everything she deserved, unrestrained complete and total, she had to figure this out. She had to be able to deal with Caleb without withdrawing into herself again. She had to be able to deal with Caleb without hiding. The simple fact was he may have started her down the path, but she stayed on it. That was the answer. Caleb was going to push, he was going to hurt, it was who he was, but she didn't have to let him get to her anymore. She had Sami, when she found herself walking that path again she just had to let Sami help lead her off it. She just had to let herself trust not only in Sami but in her own ability. She controlled the fire, the fire did not control her.

Sami stirred next to her. Last night Sami had been the initiate, she had started and led Kena, but not this morning. Kena moved from nuzzling to kissing her neck bringing Sami completely awake.

"Kena?" Sami seemed surprised.

"What, did you think I wouldn't be here this morning?" Kena answered between kisses.

"I wasn't sure. I wasn't sure it was real and not a dream and well…"

Kena wrapped her arms fully around her lover and pulled close to her reveling in the feel of Sami's skin against hers. "What Sami, please we have to be honest with each other completely, totally, hurtfully, if necessary, honest."

Kena felt Sami's body go limp in her arms. "I wasn't sure if you would still be here. We have all seen flashes of this before. When trouble happens you are right where you're needed doing whatever is needed, but as soon as the crisis is over you disappear. It's like there are two Kena's, the confident and capable leader and the fearful and isolated recluse. So, yes, I was afraid you were going to disappear again. Worse, I was afraid I may have pushed too hard and drove you away, maybe permanently."

Kena felt tears spring to her eyes, Sami was right, Every time feelings ran hot she ran away. It was easier to hide from everyone's emotions, especially her own, than it was to deal with them. "I know Sami, and I'm sorry, but that stops now, at least from you. I won't promise I won't hide from other changers. Sometimes their feelings are overwhelming, but not from you never again. I can't believe how much I love you and more, than that, need you. I can't believe it took me this long to figure it out. Sami, I am nothing without you. You are my rock, and you can be my anchor. I have changed and I plan to prove that and I plan to make up for all the lost time when I was too scared or too blind to see what was right in front of my face." Kena pulled Sami into her arms and kissed her, but Sami pulled back.

"We should get back, we will have been missed."

"Another hour isn't going to make any difference." Kena insisted, continuing her kissing assault undeterred and determined. Sami responded just as Kena hoped she would and everything else in the world disappeared for a least a moment.

Chapter 24 Enlightening

Kena admired Sami as they flew wing tip to wing tip back to the valley, and was surprised she had never noticed how beautiful Sami's coloring was in her Tiskin form. Her fur was a silvery gray fading to light gray and white on her wing tips, tail and belly. Her flying skill and power was all too evident to Kena's keen Phoenix eyes. The flight was all too short as far as Kena was concerned. She wasn't ready to deal with the consequences of yesterday's battle yet, but like it or not they were going to have to. Ancients, making some of her fellow council members see the reality of their situation was not going to be easy. Kena and Sami circled the cavern as they waited for the top to open enough for them to slip in. They both still lived in the cavern with Seth. Kena knew she had stayed to be close to her grandmother, but until last night she had no idea why Sami hadn't moved down into the village. Kena mentally kicked herself for not realizing it sooner.

"You need to stop that Kena." Sami told her as they landed near where they slept to change into clean clothes.

"Stop what?"

"Regretting, what is done is done. We can't change the past."

"How did you know? Tiskins don't have mind speech or empathy and I was shielded." Kena asked as she changed with Sami following suit.

"Kena it's not a gift, I have always known what you are thinking and feeling its part of being in love, in being devoted mind, heart and soul to someone."

Kena smiled and rubbed Sami's arm, then stopped forcing the need to touch Sami back but just for the present. Now she needed to concentrate and she couldn't do that if she was thinking about being with Sami and remembering the delight of last night.

"You're back! You're back! Where were you?" Seth all but bowled the two of them over in his youthful exuberance. He hadn't seen either of them after the battle. He may have known they were alive but it hadn't made waiting for them any easier.

Seth was so mature and composed most of the time it was easy to forget he was only sixteen. "Seth, we're fine we just needed some time alone to talk. Has anything happened? It's not like you couldn't have mind spoke one of us if you really needed us." Sami told him pulling her shirt over her head trying to be contrite but not really feeling sorry at all.

"No, nothing happened. Caleb has called for a council meeting in... well now. I was about ready to mind call you when I saw you. Are you both all right?"

"We're fine Seth." Sami answered not sure how much Kena would be comfortable telling him.

"Better than I have been in a long time, little brother, maybe better than I have ever been." Kena answered eliciting a smile and a gentle touch from Sami. Seth looked startled, but smartly said nothing. Kena knew Seth was picking up on more than their body language. She knew she was shielded but she hadn't added all the layers back and she wasn't trying to hide her thoughts of Sami. She didn't care who knew, especially not Seth, the one Changer she knew would support them no matter what. "So, we are dressed in clean attire and of sound mind and good heart, so let us to the council area where we will discuss war and blood and death for that is the path we started down yesterday and now we must follow it until it's inevitable end." Kena strode out of the sleeping area and into the open cavern followed closely by Sami and Seth.

They were the last to arrive and it was clear the discussion had already been heated. As soon as they spotted Kena, all fell quiet. No one knew what to expect. Kena had two sides, the competent and strong or hiding and unsure, and everyone wondered which Kena was going to show up today. Kena took her seat and felt Sami and Seth take the seats on either side of her. Kena opened a little door in her shield just large enough to draw strength from the burning hot beacon of love she felt coming from Sami. This support, this love, had always been there and she ignored it. Now though, she would not only acknowledge it, she knew how to use it. Now she understood no one could stand alone in this world. Kena smiled as she felt her inner fire rise and tapped in to it to give her strength. She was in complete control of both her emotions and the blaze that was her inner soul. Things were going to change as of right now. She was done with the bickering, fighting, and back biting. That was all they did every council; meeting argue about little inconsequential nonsense and nothing ever got done. If it wasn't for the individual leaders working with their races, the valley would have fallen or sunk into civil war. None of them wanted a monarchy, but a leadership council wasn't working either and if, in the heat of crisis, they were going to look to her to make all the decisions then so be it. They made their choice.

As soon as they were seated Caleb started with his war and death talk. "We shouldn't have let them go. We should have killed them all. They will just make more trouble. Letting them go was a mistake, but a mistake we can fix. My patrols have been watching them all night…"

Tameera, the Pegasi representative was clearly sickened by Caleb's statement, even his closest ally Frandin was looking a little green at the thought. There were dozens of women and children in the clan that were innocent. Kena had heard and seen enough. "Enough!" Kena warned with enough force to not only cut off Caleb but also stop any counter argument. Caleb looked shocked and stricken and Kena found a perverse joy in that. "Things have changed and are going to change further and I don't just mean about the battle. This doesn't work. We sit here hour after hour, day after day, fighting amongst ourselves. I'm done, we're done. None of us want or will stand for a monarchy here, but we need a leader, someone to stop the fighting and keep us on track. We spend hour after hour, meeting after meeting, arguing about minute details and minor issues and accomplish nothing. I, for one, am done." Blank faces and scared eyes turned to her. "So right now the first thing we are going to do is elect a leader."

It was not surprising that it was Caleb who found his voice first. "Are you suggesting disbanding the council Kena? It was your idea in the first place."

Kena smiled. "Absolutely not. The council will still be essential. Each and every race of ancient must continue to have someone to speak for them. It will be the council that will elect the leader, and it will be the council who can at anytime choose a new leader if the majority feels the leader is not making the right choices. It will be for each race of ancients to choose their council representative just as they have done so far, but it will be an annual election. Anyone have anything to add, anyone have any dissent?" Kena wasn't sure what to expect. She knew Sami and Seth would back her giving her the support of three votes of the nine. She needed to sway at least two more Changers or this was all dead in the water and they would go back to bickering and getting nothing done.

Everyone was silent for a moment and Kena felt her guts tying in knots. She knew this was the right course and somehow she had to convince them. Her father's warning was weighing heavily on her mind. It was

Caleb who found his voice first. "I suppose you think you are the obvious choice for the new leader?"

"Actually Caleb, if I could quit the council I would in a heartbeat and you know it. You find another Phoenix out there and I will gladly step aside, until then my voice is as important as yours even if I choose not to speak without thought at the top of my lungs or in a way meant to hurt and demean. I say this because we know this is the right course. Look at what happened yesterday. We didn't have time to gather the council, decisions had to be made quickly and on the spot. I did what had to be done yesterday and I'm still doing what has to be done. No matter what you think Caleb, I am doing what's best for our society. So, until you have something to add that isn't sarcastic and hurtful, you can keep quiet. Does anyone have anything constructive to say? I am open to any ideas." Kena glared at Caleb. She knew her attitude was scaring everyone, she didn't care she was doing what she knew was right even if she had to channel her inner Caleb to make it happen.

Sami and Seth were awe struck by Kena's new attitude and couldn't seem to find their tongues, and the rest of the council seemed to have been smacked in the back of the head with a log. If the situation weren't so serious she would have laughed at their expressions. Everyone just stared at Kena not sure what to do or say mouths hanging open. Caleb glared his eyes filled with anger and hate.

It was Qwint who finally found his voice and decided to diffuse things before they went any further. "I think Kena has made some valid points and being disparaging of her and her idea is below us. We need a frank and honest discussion, and I would like to start. I think she is right. I think we do need one person to be the leader with us as advisors. I like the idea that we can, as a whole, decide to change the leader if it becomes needed. I will vote for the election of a leader and I would add who ever the leader we select they should be someone who always keeps the greater good of all the Changers firmly in mind and has the ability to think clearly in any crisis. In my mind, there is only one choice, Kena. So I move that not only do we accept this new leader policy as Kena has suggested but that we quickly elect Kena as that leader so we can get on with what else has to be dealt with and there is a magnitude of things we need to deal with."

Caleb scowled at Qwint, but as Qwint spoke Kena could see his reservations melting away. Caleb was argumentative and confrontational, but he wasn't stupid and he was open to listening to other opinions as long as they didn't come from Kena. He also knew when he was on the losing side of an argument. Kena was surprised when it was he who seconded the movement. When it did go to a vote it was unanimous.

"Now, for the first time we are building our own society and not a refugee village. We need to work together to make that happen. Okay, we have avoided the conversation long enough. We have to talk about the battle and the consequences of that event." The council exploded, but Kena put a quick stop to it. "Enough, yelling at each other isn't helping and isn't solving anything. It doesn't matter how we got here, we're here now and we have to deal with it. This was, like it or not, the opening volley in a war we knew was going to come eventually. There is nothing we can do to change what happened yesterday. First, I am sure we have some time to prepare. Yes, in a couple of days that traveler clan will meet up with another clan and they are going to talk. And let's face it, travelers travel, it won't be long and the story of that battle will be all over the globe. Remember how quickly the story we existed at all was spread after Sami's father started the rumor? That was one man, but it will take some time. Many who hear the story just won't believe it, but some will and those are the ones we have to prepare for first, curiosity seekers and bounty hunters for sure and they too will spread stories. Eventually even the most ardent doubters will believe and then we will have all out war. We need to prepare now. Our worst disadvantage is the same disadvantage our ancestors faced, pure and simple, we are outnumbered." Kena looked around to see what the reaction to her statement would be.

"Good sound tactics and taking advantage of our gifts will solve that." Caleb replied with way to much confidence for Kena's peace of mind.

"You think so Caleb, I don't and history backs me up." Kena pointed at the murals who had smartly moved as far away from the council area as possible. "They're here because they thought their gifts would keep them safe. Yes, you are right. Good tactics will help, which is why I am putting you in charge of our defenses. You are by far our best tactician, but the key word there is defense, not offense. For right now we will stay defensive. That may change but we are not ready now to take an offensive position." Kena felt Caleb gather himself for another argument but he quickly subsided. Kena suspected he may have gotten a few words mind to mind from one of his allies. Kena was grateful to which ever mind speaker it was. She really didn't want to fight with Caleb, but she also could no longer back down. "While we get ready Caleb I trust you to keep us all safe and continue the training, getting everyone equipped for when we are ready. We still need to address the lack of our numbers. Right now we have what? 500 Changers and not all of us are capable of fighting. I believe there are more out there, more Changers who either couldn't or wouldn't make their way here. We slowed searching when so many started just showing up, but we need to go find them. The more fighters we have the better our chances and there may even be lost Changers out there with combat training. Sami, I need the Tiskins to do what they're best at, what they were born to do. I need them to infiltrate society and find those Changers and get them back here. We will force no one to come. That is not our way, but I want all to have the option. The more we can get back here and trained the better our army will be. I will leave it up to you as the chosen leader of the Tiskins to decide how to do it. Remember, all of us are here to help with any necessary extractions."

Sami nodded already thinking on how best to make this happen. "I think Kimball and his Unicorns will be invaluable with their ability to jump."

Kena glanced at Kimball, who nodded his assent. "If other help is needed, go to Caleb. He will know who the best choice for the job will be." Caleb nodded as well but for once didn't speak. "Caleb, draft any help you need and I'm sure Frandin and Dalis will help you in any way they can. Qwint, we need more shelter, clothing, and food storage built as fast as possible. Tameera, Kimball, Sami, any one not engaged in another activity should work with Qwint and the Dokuls. We need to plan for an influx of Changers and they can't live in the cavern. All the space in the cavern will be needed for training." Sami at first looked startled, but that expression was quickly replaced with joy. "Except for you Seth, if you want to stay with Tam, as the guardian he has to stay here."

Seth smiled, "No, I think it's time I found my own way in our new world. It's not like I won't see him whenever I want. I'm old enough now to be out on my own and I can certainly continue my training as guardian without actually living in the cavern."

Kena pushed the sudden burst of pride in the boy she considered her little brother back down, now wasn't the time. He had truly grown into a remarkable young man. Kena knew that was the next friendship she desperately needed to rebuild. "Dalis, Frandin, Caleb, when you're not training we need the Tiguras, Gryphons, and Gryphels to hunt and the hunts are going to have to take place farther from the valley then any of us would like. We can't completely deplete our land of game, but we need more meat reserves without depleting the livestock herds. Seth and I will help with that as well as using our fire to smoke and dry the meat. Kimball, Tameera, we need more land cleared and crops planted. We can expand north, there's nothing there but space. Draft anyone willing to turn their hands to holding a plow. We need full silos of corn and grain. When this war comes, unlike our enemies, we won't be able to keep the farms going. Everyone will be needed in the fight. Our only hope not to starve is to have it already in storage. To be safe we need at least a few months of food and supplies in reserve."

"I will have my metal workers on building plows immediately, we should have a few for you in a day or so, that should give you time to scout where you want the first fields. I will get my carpenters and masons working on additional food storage first, then housing. With the number of trained Dokuls and all the additional help, the building should go quickly, after all that is our gift; build and build fast." Qwint informed the council.

Kena nodded at Qwint. "Can anyone think of anything I may have forgotten?" When no one spoke, Kena went on. "Okay, I know there are things that are going to come up, so we will have a standing council meeting every other day first thing in the morning. If you can't make it please choose a second to attend in your place. Until then I think we have plenty to do." With that Kena stood and grabbed both Sami and Seth pulling them away toward their sleeping area. No one tried to stop them. As soon as they were out of earshot Kena spoke quietly mostly to Seth. "Seth, I know you read that Sami and I are together."

Seth smiled a smile that lit the cavern. He may not know what had brought about this change in Kena, but he welcomed it with open arms and heart. "Yes, and I couldn't be happier." He said as he hugged both of them. "I had begun to give up hope you would ever open your eyes to the clearly obvious Kena."

"Tell me about it." Sami replied under her breath but clearly audible.

Kena smiled at Sami's remark. She deserved it and by no means minded the gentle teasing. "Thanks Seth. The reason I'm telling you this is we have a little place about a fifteen minute flight from here, that's where we will be living. If you need us when we are there you can mind call us, I just ask that you don't share where we are with anyone else. We need that place where we can be truly alone."

"I can understand that, I won't tell anyone."

"Thanks." Kena turned to Sami and kissed her soundly. "I know you are going to be busy the rest of the day. You have to organize your Tiskins, but I will be home when you're done." Kena pulled Sami into a hug and whispered in her ear "I love you."

Sami smiled, happy tears in her eyes, before she turned away, changed and sprang into the air winging quickly out of the cavern. As soon as she was out of sight, Kena turned back to Seth. "So, any idea where you're going to live?"

"Actually, yeah, there's an open cabin not too far from Caleb's."

"Seth, Sami is not the only Changer I need to make amends with. I owe you not only a huge apology but also a big thank you. First, I'm sorry for all I have put you through. Second, thank you not only for standing by me, but for being the friend Sami needed. I couldn't be there for her like she needed, like she deserved. I should have been, but I just couldn't, but you were. You helped her survive and made today possible. I owe you everything for that." Kena got it all out in a rush.

"Kena, we're family, you, me, and Sami, and that is what families do. I owe you my life and my freedom. I would do anything for you and Sami. So, let's forget about the past and any mistakes that have been made. Do you want some help getting this stuff wherever your little hideaway is?" Seth asked wanting to move the subject along still a little afraid to push Kena away.

"You really are the best, Seth, and I will love you forever little brother." Kena told him, and then surprised him even more by pulling him into an embrace.

Seth smiled, he had no idea what had brought this change on Kena, but he was thrilled with it. If he had to beat his brother to a bloody Gryphon pulp to stop him from hurting Kena anymore, he would. Ancients knew he deserved it.

Chapter 25 Insight

Sami forced all thoughts of Kena out of her head. She needed to concentrate on what she needed to do now. As soon as she was clear of the cavern she dove for the village flying just above the tops of the building and chirped a call to all Tiskins to come to the meeting place. She circled the village three times repeating her message then flew off to the clearing by the river where the Tiskins held all their meetings. She was the first to arrive, but she knew all of her race would arrive soon. She took her customary place on top of a smooth boulder. She used the time before the others arrived to try and form her thoughts into cohesive words. She didn't have much time to think before the others started to arrive. She acknowledged each arrival but waited until everyone was in attendance before she started. She knew her mind was wandering, but she just couldn't seem to stop it. The events of yesterday had changed things, both good and bad, in ways she would never have thought possible. Sami smiled at the memory of the night before. It was all she had ever hoped for with Kena. Another Tiskin winged in, landing just in front of her. Sami easily recognized Brent. He was the only Tiskin so far with tawny fur. She nodded at him but she didn't let him distract her from her thoughts. As good as it was with Kena, this second part of her couldn't shake the feeling it could be temporary. There had been other times Kena had come out of herself imposed isolation before and quickly returned to hiding behind her shields. Sami shivered a little despite the warm sun shining down on her. They perhaps should have spent a little more time talking last night, perhaps some of the nagging questions would have been answered. The question that was nagging her most was what brought about this change in Kena. If she knew that perhaps she could believe it would last, on the other hand did it matter? Did she really need to know the how and why and if she didn't want her new relationship with Kena to be temporary, then she would just have to make sure it wasn't. Relationships took work and she was more than willing to put the work in to keep Kena. She smiled as several ideas on how to make that happen popped into her head, then quickly wiped the smile off her face. There were some very somber problems they needed to solve, seeing her smile would not be good. Sami growled pulling her thoughts off of Kena and back to the here and now. A quick count and she knew all of the Tiskins had arrived and it was time to deal with yet another change caused by the events of the day before.

"Thank you all for dropping what you were doing and meeting here. We have a lot to discuss and some decisions to be made. First, there is no denying we are at war. Yesterday we killed 36 men and by men I am including boys no older than twelve or thirteen, there will be retaliation and we must prepare for that. The council has taken steps to prepare for the coming war. The first step and, in my opinion the most necessary, the council this morning elected a new leader."

"Better be Kena, if it's Caleb...," Zeran interrupted

"It's not Caleb," Sami cut him off before he could say something he could not take back. "I think it will come as no surprise Kena was elected and elected is the right word we all voted and the council can hold another election any time if we feel the current leader is not doing the job they were elected to do." Sami wasn't really surprised to see everyone seemed happy or at least content with the arrangement. "Now, one of the decisions we need to make as a race is who will represent us on the council." There was an uproar at the suggestion anyone else should lead the Tiskins but her. "Wait, before you decide you need to know about something else that happened that has nothing to do with the coming war. Last night Kena and I came to an understanding and we are now together and I hope it's for a long time." Whatever Sami might have been thinking was going to happen this was not it. There was an uproar but it was all positive, everyone was nothing less than happy and a few of her closer friends bordered on ecstatic. She thought she had hidden her feelings for Kena pretty well, but it looked like she was wrong. "You all knew that I cared for Kena. That I was in love with her?"

Again it was Zeran that spoke up, "Sami I think the only one who didn't know how you felt about Kena was Kena."

Sami was truly relived and gratified by their reaction. "Ok so I guess I stay your leader, if you ever have any doubts I am always willing to hold an election and let someone else have a shot." She paused letting that sink in. There were some very good leaders among the Tiskins and she wanted them to know they could have a chance if they wanted it. "Well, with Kena as leader the council was finally able to cut through the bickering and get something done." Sami explained all the preparations that were happening and the clearly outlined what part the Tiskins would be doing.

"Makes good sense," Zeran added when she was done. "We are the best choice to go out among the pests. I can't find any fault with that reasoning."

Sami looked for and got agreement from everybody, "Not all of us will be needed to search and, let's be honest, not all of us are suited to be part of the search. Those of us that are not searching will be assigned to the myriad of other jobs that will need to be done. What I would like to do is elect two seconds. One will be in charge of the searchers and other in charge of distributing help where it is needed. Does anyone have any ideas?"

It was quickly ascertained that Zeran and Rykle were the choices of the group. Sami considered both. Zeran was young and a natural leader. He had uncommonly great control of his gift and extensive hand to hand fight training. Rykle was a little older and the better organizer of the two. "Okay, Zeran, I'm putting you in charge of the searchers. Rykle, you will be in charge of the group staying here and you will sit on the council if I ever can't. The council is meeting every other day." That solution seemed to please everyone. "Choose where you can be the most helpful, but be honest with yourself about your skill set. I know you are all brave, but the searchers are going to be in real danger. If you have any question about your ability to control your gift searching may not be the right thing for you. Don't worry, the jobs you will be doing here in the valley are just as important. Anyone who wishes to stay please meet with Rykle, everyone joining the search meet here with me and Zeran.

Brent stopped her before they could disperse, "Sami, has anyone considered that when this war does start we could act as spies and taking into account the moral ambiguity of it, we could also serve as assassins?"

Sami forced the revulsion of killing out of her mind, in war people died and if assassination ended the war sooner, shouldn't they at least consider it? "I will take your suggestion to Kena, or perhaps Caleb, since Kena has put him in charge of the defenses and tactics. I will see what he thinks. Anyone else, any more ideas" When no one spoke Sami continued, "If that changes please speak up, we need all the ideas we can get."

With a nod from Sami, the Tiskins started separating into two groups. Sami made mental note on who went where, preparing to adjust the groups if necessary. She was happy to see that everyone made what she considered the correct assessment of their abilities. Sami waited for everyone to settle again. A quick glance and she knew Rykle had his group completely under control. Turning her attention back on the group that was going to be searching she said "Okay Zeran, I need to talk to Kena, but I think there may be a way for us to pin point some targets for you. No one goes out alone, pick teams of twos and threes. Seth is going to be checking with all the teams and Kimball and his Unicorns will be available to jump the teams to and from location as well as retrieving targets and teams if necessary, but you will still be on your own most of the time. While I work on locating you some targets, Zeran, I would like you to work on hand to hand combat training. I know most of you have been through the training before but a refresher course will not hurt. We have to assume you will need to fight. I would prefer you hide over fight, but I can't shake the feeling that you're right Brent, and we are going to have to resort to a more hands on approach before this is all over. Zeran, as soon as I have some targets I will let you know. Until then they're all yours, check in with me first thing in the morning." When Zeran gave her an odd look Sami changed her mind, "Okay, maybe mid-morning, I don't plan on getting much sleep tonight, might need to sleep in a little." Her statement was met with laughs and good natured teasing all around.

Caleb watched the threesome leaving the council area. He had dropped his opposition to Kena when he saw she was backed by the majority of the council. Even his own conspirators had backed her. He knew he couldn't win, not right now, but he could bide his time. Kena was right about one thing, time was on their side. She was wrong however about tactics overcoming superior numbers. He was surprised Kena had put him in charge of the defenses and training. He might not be able to launch an all out offensive like he wanted, but at least he would be the one preparing for it. Well, watching Kena, Seth and Sami talk wasn't getting anything done.

He easily found the majority of the Gryphons near the empty field they had commandeered for training. He sent a couple of his fastest flyers to round up the missing. Within moments, Caleb was standing in front of the entire complement of Gryphons. They agreed with what the council had decided with just a little grumbling. Like him, they wanted to start an offensive.

Caleb waited for the grumbling to die down. "Okay, now training and hunting take precedence. We need to stockpile meat, so that's our job. Starting tomorrow we'll divide into two groups. Blake you'll lead the first group, Haili you'll lead the second. When one group is training the other will be hunting. The hunters will be flying farther out to find game which means they can scout while they hunt. I may not agree with Kena on everything, but she is right about stock piling food." Everyone had to agree with that. "The Dokuls are setting up a bigger smoke house and will be assigning Changers to do the skinning as well as other countless jobs that need done. Anyone with free time should see Qwint or whoever he puts in charge to help out. Any questions? Okay, Blake, Haili, pick your groups. You know the abilities of your fellow Gryphons as well as I do. I need to confer with Frandin and Dalis. We will be training, hunting and scouting with both the Gryphels and the Tiguras. I will check in with both of you later." He was about to change when he saw Marta walking towards him. His heart skipped a beat as a smile that was for her alone spread on his face.

"I just wanted to make sure you were okay? I heard rumors you and Kena exchanged words."

Caleb pulled her into an embrace enjoying the feeling of her warm body next to his and needing to just feel her love. "We did, but she wasn't completely wrong, so I let it go. When the time is right the council will side with me. I just need a new angle since after yesterday everyone knows Kena is not a coward."

"Caleb I love you, you know that, but I'm not sure your right about this. Sometimes I think you have blinders on when it comes to Kena. It's like the Tiskin gift, you only see what you want to see and forget to look for the reality behind the fog. Just keep that in mind when you deal with Kena. Any way, Haili's making me a patrol leader so I better go find out who my new minions are. I'll see you tonight." She kissed him soundly and jogged toward her group, changing as went.

Caleb watched Marta for a few seconds considering her words. He scoffed at the idea that he failed to see Kena as she really was. Yes, he was surprised yesterday when she took charge, not that he didn't approve. She did have this unusual ability to see the entire problem and plan accordingly. He wouldn't have thought of separating the children or blocking their retreat. Even he had to admit Kena saved his, Qwint's and Kimball's hides with that wall of fire. Caleb ground his teeth, he had no idea Kena could use fire like that. It was an incredible weapon. He was sure this new take charge attitude wouldn't last much past the engagement, then she shows up at the council meeting gets elected leader and comes up with even more plans he wouldn't have thought of. Just thinking about Kena made his blood run hot and his anger simmer. He couldn't figure out why he was the only one that could truly see what she was really like. No he didn't have blinders when it came to Kena, everyone else did, but they would see it eventually.

Sami circled the village and outlying areas, she needed to find Rykle and see how things were proceeding. She had a feeling Kena was going to ask as soon as she saw her. She got lucky when she saw him in a clearing not far from the village center. As she landed, she heard a Dokul talking about building a smoke house here, and what Rykle's Tiskins could do to help. Sami waited for Rykle to be done not wanting to interrupt, but eager to finish this last chore before she could search out Kena. She had always felt a need to be near Kena. From the moment she had met her she'd felt a connection to her. Now, well anytime she wasn't with her, touching her, she felt a little lost and the longing was almost unbearable.

Rykle noticed Sami and excused himself from the conversation. "No one can talk quite like a Dokul. I didn't expect to see you until morning, is everything all right?"

Sami's smile didn't alleviate his fears, "Yes, Rykle, everything is good. I just got so busy with the searchers I didn't get a chance to see how your group was progressing."

"Great actually, first thing in the morning most of us will be helping here with the new larger smoke house. We have smaller groups assigned to projects all over the valley depending on their likes and skills and everyone is doing time in the skinning shed preparing meat the hunters will start to bring in soon. Qwint has made his sister his second and Senna has a schedule all worked out so everything is divided fairly and no one race gets stuck with all the dirty jobs. I have hunters scheduled to go out in groups every morning and every night. While they're hunting they can patrol the woods. I know Caleb has the Gryphons, Gryphels, and Tiguras hunting and patrolling but he tends to forget us Tiskins and we are the best choice to keep an eye on the woods. We can get places and see things the bigger Changers just can't. I think I got everything covered and everyone where they can do the most good."

"I have no doubts at all Rykle. You're right about hunting. Small game will be just as valuable as the big game in the long run and no race is better at patrolling in the deep woods than us. We will be able to spot any intrusion into the woods. I can't shake the feeling winning this war will hinge on more subtle tactics than head to head battle. One other thing, remember every one needs some time off to unwind and relax. We need to push to get ready but wearing ourselves out won't help either. I will report back to Kena that we are set."

"I will find you tomorrow if I have anything, otherwise I think were set for now. I know the searchers are going to need more of your time right now, and Sami don't forget to take your own advice for Kena's sake as well as your own."

"Thanks Rykle, I intend on it. If you need me, Seth can call me and he is anything but hard to find. I'll see you tomorrow."

Rykle smirked. "Enjoy your evening." he teased.

Sami slapped Rykle on the back, "Oh, I definitely intend on doing that!" changed and sprang into the air winging hard toward the little hut hoping she would find Kena was done for the day as well.

Sami landed and jogged up the path. She was shocked when she found a small clearing just big enough for the smaller changers to land about twenty feet from the little hut. Only Seth could have taken trees of that size out roots and all like she would pull weeds in a garden.

It was easy to figure out why being able to land right at your door step would be easier and quicker. Kena had also picked a good location for the clearing the hut was still obscured from the air. As Sami turned back toward the hut she saw smoke coming from the chimney and she felt her heart warm, Kena had to be inside. She didn't hesitate a moment more.

Kena sensed Sami on the path and knew she had stopped at the clearing. She hoped she wouldn't be mad, but if there was an emergency they needed to be back as fast as possible and Kena refused to give up this little refuge. She heard Sami open the door, but before she could speak Sami had her in her arms and was soundly kissing her. Kena felt the fire she had been fighting to keep at bay all day rise up as she responded to Sami's need matching it with her own. Before she lost all her senses she snuffed the fire out in the little stove so their dinner didn't burn.

Sami couldn't resist, she saw Kena and she had to touch her, she had to kiss her. She needed to reassure herself that Kena hadn't changed her mind, but Kena responded with need of her own that easily matched Sami's. Sami let her need take over, she was stripping Kena of the cumbersome clothes before they tumbled to the rug covered floor. The clumsy sweetness of last night was consumed by the fire both of them were feeling. It was hard and sweaty, fueled by need and lust and when the moment hit, Sami felt for just a minute what it was like to be consumed by fire from the inside out.

Kena and Sami lay where they had fallen both trying to catch their breaths. "Hmm, it's nice to see you too Sami." Kena panted. "You are free to come home like that any time you want." Kena would have been happy to lay here forever curled in Sami's strong embrace, safe from the worries of the world, but she knew that wasn't to be.

"I will if you will greet me like that." Sami snuck a kiss in before continuing, "I see you saved our dinner, I don't know about you but I'm starving." Sami got up and offered a hand to Kena helping her up and pulling her into an embrace. "By the way, I love you too." She whispered in her ear stealing a quick nibble before pulling away.

As Kena relit the fire with a thought and got dinner cooking again, Sami got a chance to really look around the little hut. All of their stuff from the cavern was there, as well as some stuff from storage like table and chairs, cookware, dishes, water barrel, all the things that made a shelter a home. "Wow!" was all Sami could muster to say.

"Thanks, I did such a good job delegating this morning I didn't really have anything to do, and neither did Seth, so he helped me clear our stuff out of the cavern and move it here, then I helped him with his stuff. He's moved into a small place not too far from Caleb in the center of the village. It means he has to land outside the village since there isn't a clearing big enough for a Dragon to land and walk home, but he says he doesn't mind. He didn't say anything, but I think he's a little worried about how much time he spends as a Dragon. Any way, after we got everything moved in we pulled some stuff from stores to make life a little better. I was able to clear the air and make my amends to Seth while we worked, all and all a productive day. I did a quick hunt for dinner and waited for you to come home. Oh,

Eagle Bennett and I had Seth clear a few trees to make flying in easier, hope you don't mind."

"Are you kidding? It's great. Seth needed to know where the hut is and he won't tell anyone else. I've wanted a clearing here for a while but it's not like I could do it on my own. Dragons can be kind of handy. Thanks for cooking, I know you hate it."

Kena smiled at her love as she set dishes down on the table. "I do, but I don't mind cooking for you. I love doing anything for you." Kena reached over to squeeze Sami's hand before changing the subject to her day and how things stood with her Tiskin corp.

Chapter 26 Truth

Seth was pleased with his new home. He missed Kena and Sami, but he was far too happy for them to wish it any other way. He had been able to really talk to Kena today for the first time in a very long time. She didn't hide or run, she was totally open with him. He wasn't completely sure what had prompted her changes, but he really didn't care. If Kena needed him to know she'd tell him. Kena was alive and happy, something he never thought he would see and that was all he cared about.

He sipped at a cup of tea as he sat on his new little porch watching as Changers made their way through the village back to their homes. He got calls and waves from everyone who saw him. The little cabin he had commandeered was really only big enough for one. It was one of the first shelters built in the village and didn't even have a kitchen, just a simple fire with cook stove. It had been vacant for a while since no one really wanted it, but it was perfect for him. He would be spending most of his time in the cavern and he always ate at the commons anyway so he didn't need much room. The overly large porch more than made up for lack of space inside. He was lost in thought when he was jarred out of them by Caleb's approach. Seth had been hoping Caleb would stop by. He needed to share a few thoughts with his brother.

"Well, brother, it is good to see you out of the cavern, but I am a bit surprised I figured you and Kena and Sami would find someplace together. Are you going to be all right all by your lonesome without your mommies to take care of you?"

"I think I will manage, but I will miss my friends." Seth responded, refusing to rise to the bait. "Listen, Caleb, I have to tell you something and I'm not sure how you're going to take it, but you should hear it from me and not from the rumor mill that's already churning up thanks to Sami telling her Tiskins, you know how they talk."

"What are you talking about Seth, what do I need to know? I'm really tired, I miss Marta and I have to be up early so if this can wait…"

"It really can't. Kena finally saw what was right in front of her. She and Sami are together now."

"Together? Oh you mean 'together'. Kena and Sami? I mean I knew they were close, like sisters close, but I didn't think Sami loved her like… that." Caleb mocked. "Sami has every eligible Changer, male and female, in the valley vying for her attentions, and she settles for Kena? I gotta say I didn't see that coming."

Seth growled at his tone and the implications. "Then you were the only Changer besides Kena that didn't see how Sami felt." Caleb gave his brother a calculating grin causing anger to rise in Seth's guts. "I swear on my grandfather Caleb if you make trouble, if you even try to make trouble I will burn you to the black cinder I think your heart has become. Oh and one more thing brother, I know you planted thoughts into the mind of the traveling clan's leader. I know you wanted him to provoke an attack. I know Kena knows it too, but for whatever reason she has chosen to drop it. Unlike you, I trust her so I won't question her decision. I am serious don't push me, don't push Kena or Sami and don't make trouble for the two of them. This is not another way, a new way, for you to attack Kena. This is not your new angle to cause her pain and misery. This is not another way to drive her away or to her death."

Caleb looked at his brother and knew he meant every word he said. Somehow, some time, his baby brother ceased to be a child and had become a man. "Do you think I hate Kena so much I would seek to hurt her like that?" Caleb answered defensively.

"Caleb, you hurt her like that every chance you get. You hurt me every chance you get, you try to hurt Sami but she is too tough let your bullying get to her like you can Kena and me. Caleb, I know it's easy to attack your family, to take life out on them, and if you want to keep picking at me, feel free, I can take it. I am not the sickly little idiot kid you seem to think I am and I won't let you pick at Kena anymore. I mean it, I will kill you, and then I'll comfort Kena as she grieves. You are blind to how close we came to losing her. You failed to see how far you pushed her and how close she came to joining the fire. Somehow she found her way back and I won't let it happen again. So figure out what ever your problem is and deal with it, or I swear, Caleb, I will kill you." Seth having said his piece went inside, leaving his brother to mull over what he had just heard.

Caleb watched his brother until he shut the door in his face. He had no doubt Seth meant every word he said. He knew he had been pushing Kena, trying to provoke a reaction, but it seemed the more he pushed the less reaction he got. If he thought back on the last few months Kena had noticeably changed. She had stopped disagreeing with him at all. She didn't argue or defend herself. In fact she seldom even spoke to him. Other than at council meetings he never even saw her. As much as he hated to admit it, Kena wasn't looking very good the last few times he did see her. She had lost weight and the fire was gone from her eyes. Had he went too far, had he crossed from pushing to intentionally hurting? Did he enjoy causing Kena pain? Caleb let the thoughts sit there as he walked back down the walkway to the main street. He mulled them over and over. He didn't hurt Kena. He teased her certainly, but he always had. He tried to undermine her leadership but that was for the good of the Changers, not to hurt her. He turned and headed for home, but stopped. He didn't want to bring these thoughts home. They were weighing on him and he didn't want to take these feelings out on Marta. The thought hit him like a punch to the gut. He protected Marta from his moods. He never teased her or picked on her, in fact he went out of his way to never hurt her. He stopped, trying to catch his breath. Was he trying to hurt Kena? Had he driven her to the point of suicide? Was that what he intended, was that what he wanted? What was he doing? He needed to think, he needed Tam. He changed and launched himself into the air. Tam would be able to tell him what he needed to know. Tam would be able to help sort through these thoughts and feelings.

He landed himself next to the huge black lump that was the old guardian of the cavern. It was pretty much assumed Seth would take over as guardian when Tam died, but thankfully Tam was still vigorous for his age.

"Your thoughts are troubled, child of the Gryphon, what brings you to this state in this time and place?" Tam asked easily reading Caleb's thoughts.

"I'm sorry to disturb you, it was a short conversation I had with my brother that troubles my thoughts."

"A conversation with which brother? Your brother you share parents with or the brothers you share blood with?"

"I don't understand the question, it was Seth, of course. He is my only brother."

"Is he? Because it seems to me it is your fellow Gryphons you see as your real family not Seth. Seth you see as a responsibility. Someone you have to protect even though he no longer needs it. Someone you have to take care of and wish you didn't."

"I love Seth. I saved Seth. He would have died on that plantation if it wasn't for me. I got him out, I could have left him behind. Isn't that proof enough I care about him?"

"Did you or did Kena?"

"We both did." Caleb growled back, feeling his anger rise and not caring.

"Yes, you grabbed your brother and ran, but it was Kena who killed to save you. It was Kena who left the encounter with blood on her hands. It was Kena who exacted your revenge."

Caleb gasped as he realized where Tam was leading him. "Is that why... I mean, Tam am I mean to Kena? If I am, is that why?"

"I only read your thoughts, little brother, it is the Phoenix that reads feelings and only you can decide why you act and more importantly, react, to those you claim to love."

"I do care about them. Seth, Kena, Sami. I never realized... until Seth... Tam what have I done, what have I been doing? Please, I don't know what's happening to me!"

"Caleb, your Gryphon blood boils all the time and you have not been in control of it. The ancients weren't perfect, we all had flaws. Take the Phoenix for example. They are bombarded by others feelings all the time. They build strong shields to keep those feelings out, but they forget to let any feelings in or out. It becomes easier to withdraw from others, to hide behind those same shields until they burn out, the fire consuming them totally from within. The Gryphons have the opposite problem. Their blood runs hot, they react first think later, but Caleb you don't have to be like that. It is a choice, little brother. Kena, she chooses to build stronger shields to hide within and you choose to inflict as much hurt as you can on those you love most, Seth and Kena."

"And Sami."

"Kena is your target, Sami just steps in front of the arrows. If she didn't, chances are your and Kena's choice would already have killed her. Caleb, your choice is going to kill you as well."

Caleb's stomach knotted and his breath caught in his throat. He hadn't really believed Seth. Kena was strong and independent. How could... but if he took off the blinders like Marta said, ancients like everyone had tried to tell him, he knew he had. If he thought back over the past few years and especially the past few months Kena had been in a slow decline. The more she showed weakness the harder he had pushed, the more he had attacked her, the quicker she deteriorated the happier he was. He had pushed Kena too far and he hadn't cared. In truth he had rejoiced in her deterioration. "How do I stop when I don't even realize what I'm doing? When I don't even know why I act like this towards Kena."

"Caleb, I think some part of you is still angry with Kena. I think it goes all the way back to your first meeting."

"Seth and I wouldn't have survived if she hadn't helped. I know that, I am grateful to her."

"You are grateful to her for helping to save you, but I think you blame her for exacting the revenge you, as a Gryphon, feel it is your due to collect."

Caleb gasped. Tam's words were like a barbed arrow hitting a target. Part of him, the Gryphon part, hated Kena for doing what he felt he should have done. She killed Coler, Bleck and Kemp. It should have been him. It was he who had suffered at their hands, not her. "By the ancients, Tam I think you're right. How do I stop, how do I make it better?"

"Stopping is as simple as awareness and will. You now have the awareness of what you have been doing. Do you have the will to stop doing it?"

"If that's the case, why didn't you tell me? Why didn't Kena tell me? Why didn't Seth or Sami?"

"Would you have listened? Would you have believed any of us? Kena did what was unfortunately in her nature to do, withdraw. As to fixing it, stopping is a good start, apologizing is a better second step. I speak now as your friend and not the Guardian of the cavern, Caleb. The Changers you have hurt the most are the ones that love you the most. Kena and Seth, they will forgive and forget everything, love does that. Sami, however, may forgive but she will never forget. Fair warning, son of the Gryphon, if you continue to hurt Kena it is not the Dragon you need fear, but the Tiskin. Seth may hesitate, Sami will not."

"Thank you Guardian, you have given me much to consider. I think I should sleep on it and Marta will be expecting me." Caleb bowed his head and was surprised to see tears dripping onto the sand below. Tears that were too long in coming drained from his eyes as he changed and jumped into the air winging towards home.

Eagle Bennett

Caleb was grateful to find Marta still awake and waiting for him. He had tried to get his inner turmoil under control before he got home, but the harder he tried the worse it got. He gave up as he entered his home and fell weeping into Marta's arms.

Marta held him until Caleb's sobs ceased. This was the Caleb he allowed only her to see. Caleb could be egotistical, condescending, and downright arrogant, but he was also fiercely protective and loving. Ancients knew she loved him, but that didn't mean she didn't see all his faults. She could easily read his thoughts since his shields had failed the moment he entered their home. The awakening she hoped would come had been forced on him. She had heard about Kena and Sami at dinner and like everyone else was thrilled. Somehow she knew Caleb wasn't going to see it the same way. Ancients knew she understood how it felt when your Gryphon blood was boiling, but it always seemed worse for Caleb. She felt him shudder and knew he had cried himself out and was back under control. "So, love, do you want to talk about it?"

Caleb raised his head from his beloved's shoulder. "I know my shields are down so I know you know... Marta, am I evil?"

"Oh love, no, you're not evil, just misguided and maybe a bit spiteful when it comes to Kena."

"You see it too! Everyone else seems to have seen it but me. How come no one told me, why didn't you tell me?"

"Caleb, sweetie, I did. Many, many times, but you heard what you wanted to hear. Frandin and Dalis they have tried to talk to you about it. Ancients know Seth and Sami have tried to get through to you, but until you were ready to listen... It's not too late. Caleb you can fix this if you want to."

Caleb just lay still for a moment trying hard to get some control and a grasp on everything. He knew everyone was right, and he knew what he had to do but knowing it and doing something about it were two very different things. He wasn't even sure Kena would talk to him. Maybe he should start with changing his habits, prove he was changed then apologize. He knew it was the coward's way out, but right this moment it seemed like the best answer. "I just need sleep before I can decide anything."

"I agree my love. Come, I think I can help you get to sleep." Marta took his hand and gently led him to their bed.

Chapter 27 Regrets

Kena laid awake just watching Sami sleep. She was so lucky Sami had waited for her. She could easily have given up and moved on. Kena felt hot tears building, she had wasted so much time locked up in herself. Sami had found the key. She owed her so much and she would have the rest of her life to make it up to her.

Sami stirred a little and Kena held her tighter. Sami opened her eyes warm and safe. "I could get used to this you know, waking up in your arms."

Kena kissed Sami's cheek. "Well get used to it, I intend on it being a regular occurrence. You want some breakfast? I think we have some food I can throw together."

"No, I think we should make a point of eating most of our meals in the commons. We need to be approachable, especially now."

"I guess you're right," Kena answered her extricating herself from the bed and reaching for her shirt.

Sami was caught off guard by her tone. It was devoid of feeling, completely monotone. Kena was withdrawing into herself again, into that place that no one could reach. She could almost feel her adding layers to her shields. "Stop that." Sami scolded breaking into Kena's concentration.

"Stop what?" Kena asked surprised.

"Stop hiding your thoughts and feelings from me. I know you are our leader, I know you have to be strong out there. In here Kena, this place this is the one place you don't have to do that, and I am the one person you don't have to hide from. You can't make me stop loving you, you've tried for years and here I am. There is nothing you can do or say that can make that happen."

Kena knew she was right. She had to stop withdrawing, at least with Sami. She had to find the balance between when she shielded to protect herself and when she did it to hide. Now she was definitely hiding. "I just, I'm scared Sami. I haven't been scared since I learned to change, but this scares me more than anything."

"What scares you?" Sami asked confused by the turn in the conversation. Kena may withdraw into herself but her courage was never in question.

"This," Kena said rising and pacing around the hut. "This. I've never been happier in my life and I'm scared it's all going to be taken away from me. That somehow I am going to lose you. That someone is going to convince you of the truth, that I don't deserve you. That I am using you or, I don't know, something. Sami I'm not sure I can survive that, I'm not sure I want to." Kena cried, tears streaming down her face.

Sami grabbed Kena in her arms comforting her through the worst of her tears. "It will never happen Kena, I won't let it happen. No one is ever going to come between us. Nothing will ever come between us. We will fight and disagree, that's life, but fighting doesn't mean love stops. You talk and listen and compromise and make it better. If you have ever trusted me, trust me now. There is nothing that will ever make me stop loving you."

"But what happens when the others find out. What will they do? What will they say?"

"Relax Kena, I told the Tiskins yesterday. You know what they said? 'About time.' I promise Kena. No one thinks it's wrong for you to have someone you love. Why are you worried about that?" Sami was truly baffled by Kena's anxiety.

Kena stopped pacing and dropped onto the bed next to Sami. "I think… I think because I feel I'm not allowed to be happy. Every time I feel happy, or even content, something horrible happens. I think that's why it was...is so easy for me to hide behind my shields. It just feels more natural to be miserable."

Sami reached up and wiped the tears from Kena's face. "Of course it feels more natural to you to be miserable. It's all you have ever known."

"It's more than that. Sami, I can't... I was so close... I'm not sure what I'm trying to say."

"Brutally honest, hurtfully honest, remember?" Sami pointed out as she took Kena into her arms. "Just tell me. I promise, no matter what, I will always love you."

Kena forced herself to relax in Sami's warm embrace, drawing strength from the love she felt even through her shields. "Sami, I'm not sure you know how close I was to leaving, how close I was to joining the fire." Sami nodded fully aware of how close it was but not wanting to interrupt. "I let Caleb's words and attitudes convince me that everyone felt the same way he did. I convinced myself the Changers would be better off without me. I started running away. I wasn't just withdrawing, I was physically running. I told myself I was protecting everyone, that being around me when I was so close to losing control was dangerous, but really it was just running. Deep down I knew I had perfect control over the fire." Kena hesitated for a moment gathering her thoughts before continuing, "You know, to me, a being born of fire, fire has always been more than an object? To me it's sentient, a living being. I mean it never talked to me in words, but in feelings."

Sami was shocked by the turn in conversation, but she knew Kena was going somewhere with this and it was clearly something Kena needed her to know. "Of course, emotions are our inner fire, so that would be the way it would communicate with you."

Kena sighed, relieved that Sami could accept the concept so easily. "Yes, until I discovered him. When I discovered the source of all fire, I learned that fire can talk to me in words. Through fire I learned more about who I was, I mean the Phoenix side of me." Sami nodded and Kena took a deep breath before she continued, "More than that he made me understand that without connections, without love, I was going to kill myself. Even more he made me realize that I was needed. I had to be the leader the Changers needed, or I risk losing everything we built. That's what led me here to you and that's why I'm scared. Sami you're my anchor, my rock, the connection I need to keep myself centered and in control. I love you, but more than that, if I lose you…"

Sami stopped her, "You won't Kena. There is nothing any Changer, any pest can do or say to make me stop loving you. I loved you the very first time a looked into your eyes and I will love you until the day I die. I will do my best to be anything you need, rock, anchor, friend, lover." Sami kissed her trying to convey all the love and devotion she felt in that one simple action. "Besides, any one bothers you, Seth has promised to fire blast them."

Kena couldn't help but chuckle. Seth loved to fire blast, he didn't need much encouragement to do it. "That's better," Sami added smiling and lovingly wiping away the remaining tears trailing down Kena's cheek. "Kena I mean it, this is your safe place. You can tell me anything. You have to stop bottling up your feelings, fire's right, it's going to kill you, and I'm pretty sure I couldn't survive without you either." Sami held Kena for one more moment before letting her go. "So what are your plans for the day?"

Kena beamed at her love and allowed herself to feel reassured. "I'm meeting with the murals, Tam and Seth trying to see if we can't point your Tiskins in the right direction. If you're free I would like you there."

"Of course, I can always find time for you. Let's go get some breakfast, I'm starving."

Caleb winged into the clearing. The Gryphons, Gryphels, and Tiguras were already on the field practicing. He just wanted to see how his new seconds were doing with their respective units and working with their Tigura and Gryphel counter parts. He saw no problems and relaxed a little. He felt the breeze of a down draft and knew Frandin had landed behind him followed quickly by Dalis.

It was Dalis that spoke first, "They look good considering they have only had a day of practice working together. We'll be ready when it's time, don't worry. I've just been to see Qwint and they are working on an armor that will help protect us from arrows but still be light enough for us to fly in. He thinks a combination of leather and metal might just work. I promised test subjects when he was ready."

Caleb looked over at the Tigura, "I assume you mean to test if it flies versus test if its arrow proof."

"Well, if he needs subjects to shoot arrows at, we'll make sure to send him Gryphons." Frandin joked walking up beside them.

"That's not funny Frandin." Caleb growled.

"Wow! Over react much, what's gotten into you today?" Frandin asked shocked by Caleb's reaction to his joke.

"Nothing, I just didn't sleep well. Seth and I kind of exchanged words yesterday and I can't seem to stop thinking about what he said."

Dalis and Frandin exchanged a knowing look but it was Frandin that braved the question, "So what did he say that has you so worked up?"

"Well, let me ask you this, did you know Sami and Kena were together?"

"Heard last night at dinner, Kimball told me. You know how Unicorns talk. Said he heard it from a Unicorn, who heard it from a Dokul, who heard it from Rykle the Tiskin, who heard it direct from Sami. Why?"

"It certainly explains Kena's reemergence as leader with Sami egging her on. You're not surprised or troubled by this little glitch? You're not worried about the influence Sami will have on her?"

Frandin was genuinely surprised by Caleb's attitude, "What glitch? No I'm not surprised. Sami didn't hide her feelings for Kena. Besides, Kena needs someone she can lean on. She's stood alone for too long. She carries us, all of us. She lets this place wear her down, or hadn't you noticed? Sami will be the support she needs, the support she won't accept from any of us. Don't you see Caleb? Kena's relationship with Sami will make her an even better leader. Caleb, we need Kena to be that leader, even you agreed to that yesterday."

"Yes, but that was before I knew she and Sami had…"

"Why shouldn't Kena have a partner, someone to love? We all have been able to find willing companions, why should it bother you so much that Kena and Sami now have as well?"

"I don't know. You don't think she will favor the Tiskins?" Caleb asked, grasping at any excuse.

Dalis couldn't stop himself he broke into laughter and he just couldn't stop. "By the ancients Caleb," he gasped holding his sides, "listen to yourself, you're whining. Be a grownup already. No, no one is worried that Kena will favor the Tiskins. Even if she would, Sami wouldn't let her. If anything, Sami will work her Tiskins even harder to prevent anyone from even thinking that thought in Kena's direction. Think about it, who has the most dangerous job right now; the Gryphons out there playing war games, hunting, doing high flight scouting over empty lands or the Tiskins who are out there searching for more of us in the middle of the pests? Caleb whatever your problem is, get over it, go apologize to your brother, Kena and Sami, not necessarily in that order, and get back to being friends. We, the three of us, got our war and if we are fighting amongst ourselves we're never going to win."

"And without Kena's leadership we can't win." Frandin added, wanting to make it clear to Caleb.

Caleb knew they were right, "Okay, you're right. You're right! Can you two handle this today? I have some things I'm thinking I should take care of as soon as possible."

"Yeah, we got it, we'll mind call you if we need you but we won't. Solving this problem is more important than anything else you may have to do. Oh, and Caleb? Try not to be a Unicorn's ass when you talk to Kena for once. She deserves better than that, especially from you." Dalis responded, waving Caleb away.

Caleb growled as he sprang into the air, intentionally stirring up as much dust as possible with his down sweep.

Seth awoke early from a fretful night. His anger had only grown as the night wore on, and he had no convenient friends to talk out his troubled mind with. Kena was always good at listening, it was with sharing that she had trouble. Seth couldn't just sit here anymore he needed to do something. He threw the blankets off himself, and dressed quickly. He walked purposefully out of his new little cabin picking up his pace until he was running down the street to the clearing where he could safely change. Sometimes being a Dragon was troublesome. He changed in full run stretched his wings and lumbered into the air. The air around him seemed to groan with the strain of his passing. Once he was in the air he flew lightly. He chose to follow the river, if he was lucky perhaps a stag would wander down to drink. He wasn't in the least bit hungry and when he was he would go to the commons not relishing in the least raw meat, but he was sure Tam would like some fresh meat. The sun was just breaching the horizon shining orange and red light on his black blue scales. It felt good to be on the wing and luck was with him as his flight took him over a herd of deer headed for their morning drink. Seth, as was custom and common sense, was selective of which deer he chose. He singled out the oldest male in the group and with a quick dive he seized the stag soaring back into the lightening sky. The kill was so fast the rest of the herd hadn't even scattered. Seth dipped his left wing circling back toward the cavern.

Tam looked up just as Seth dropped the stag at his feet. "Hmm....so one brother keeps me up late the other wakes me early? Is this a plot to kill me by lack of sleep? Are you really in that big of hurry to become guardian?" Tam joked as he seized the stag and swallowed it whole. "A tad early, but a nice way to start the day none the less. So why are you here with the sun today, Seth, or can I assume this has something to do with the conversation I had with your brother last night."

Seth was shocked. "Caleb was here? Last night?"

"Yes, little one, he was. He had questions he needed help answering, and that is part of my job as guardian, someday it will be yours."

"I hope not soon. I'm not good at that sort of thing, witness my lovely conversation with my brother."

"Fear not. I grow older, but hibernating has extended my life greatly, I am in no danger of expiring anytime soon. However I find fault with that logic. Your conversation forced your brother to face certain realities he refused to see before, now he does. What he chooses to do now that his sight has cleared is up to him, but I think in his heart he wants to do the right thing."

"He better Tam, I meant what I said. Kena and Sami are more important to me than anything, including him. They are my family, more than he has ever been. If he insists on staying on this path I will kill him rather than allow him to hurt them anymore."

Tam said nothing, there was nothing to say. He just hoped Caleb did what needed to be done so that Seth would never have to keep his threat. He knew Seth would do it, he just wasn't sure Seth could live with himself afterward.

Caleb opened his mind as he circled the village. Frandin and Dalis were right he had apologies to make and if his apologies to Seth and Sami were going to be as sincere as he intended he needed to make amends with Kena first. He knew he wouldn't feel her mind through her shields, the wall she kept around herself would prevent that. Kena's was the only mind he couldn't touch. Seth was the only one who could mind call Kena. Of all the mind speakers, he was the only one she allowed a key to her shields. Caleb was shocked when he felt resentful. He pushed the emotion back, he had no right to feel that way. After all, he had caused this, and by the ancients for once he wasn't going to shift blame away from where it belonged. He had caused this problem, him not Kena. As he circled above the commons he found what he had been searching for. In among all the minds he felt the blankness that was Kena's shields. He sighed. He had hoped to find her alone.

Kena was astounded, Sami was right. No one, not one Changer, seemed to care about her and Sami. No one glared, there were no nasty comments. In fact, those who did have anything to say were supportive and seemed happy for them both. Kena had always sort of held herself apart from most of the Changers. She had always believed that was best. She was the only Changer with empathy and few knew how dangerous her gift could be if her shields were to fail and not just to her. Only those closest to her ever got to see the real Kena, well the Kena she allowed them to see and only Sami and Seth ever got inside her shields. It appeared Sami was right, she wasn't protecting the others. She was hiding from them. They were willing to be, if not friends, at least friendly. Well she could change and she would. As long as Sami was by her side she would be fine.

Sami led them to a round table that sat about eight. A couple of changers Kena knew were tiskins were all ready seated and by the empty plates just finishing up. "Good morning Sami, Kena. Hunting must have been good yesterday, it's nice to have fresh meat with breakfast don't you think?" One of the Tiskins Kena didn't recognize replied as they welcomed them to the table. Before Sami could respond a couple more Changers, plates full of fried tubers and meat, sat down. Kena didn't recognize them either but apparently Sami did.

"It is indeed, Andicin. Kena this is Andicin and Cort, they're part of my Tiskin corp, and that's Serge and Pierta. You all know this is my girlfriend, Kena." Sami replied eliciting a smile from Kena as she took a seat.

"Yeah, like we don't know who she is." Serge joked sarcastically but in great good humor. "Hey Kena, nice to meet you in person and all. And we're not Tiskins, thank the ancients. I'm a Pegasi, Pierta's a Unicorn. Don't want to be lumped in with that lot."

"Yeah, can't have you two giving Tiskins a bad name. We all know Pegasi are the worst gossips." Cort joked back.

Kena smiled at her table mates. She had never taken her meals in the commons. Most of the time she hunted and cooked her own food on her own or Sami would bring something back to the cavern for the two of them to share. As Andicin, Cort, Serge, and Pierta continued their good natured bantering Kena found herself not just smiling but laughing, something she could barely remember how to do.

Sami smiled at her love. Kena was relaxing, smiling, laughing, it felt so right and so good to see her finally just a little happy. A movement at the door caught her eye. She fought down her anger before Kena could sense it. If Caleb thought he was going to get anywhere near Kena he was sadly mistaken. Caleb closed the door and had taken about four steps toward Kena's table when Zeran stood up and blocked his path.

"Hey Caleb," Zeran kept his voice calm and friendly even though all he really wanted to do was punch him, "I'm not sure it's a good idea for you to be here now.

Maybe I could grab you a plate and bring it to you outside?"

"I'm not here to cause trouble. I just need to see Kena."

Zeran leaned in close, "Believe me, that is not going to happen." There was no friendly left in Zeran's voice.

Caleb was shocked, "Hey, I just need to talk to her."

"Save it for the council meetings then. We are not going to let you cause trouble for her and Sami. We are done with your superior, condescending attitude toward Kena. So I think it's best if you just leave and come back later." Others at the table rose at Zeran's threat, making clear Caleb had no allies here.

Caleb wasn't sure what to do. He certainly didn't mean to start a fight especially not with Zeran, a Changer trained to kill and gifted with invisibility. He looked around the commons to see hard looks directed at him, some from friends and fellow Gryphons and Gryphels. If he had any doubts how badly he had treated Kena in the past they were all erased. He looked around trying to find a way, without fighting, to get out of this when Kena put a stop to it for him.

"Stop, please, you have no idea how much it means to me that you all care. I really am beyond grateful and I'm not really sure what I did to deserve it, but we can't fight amongst ourselves, not now. If there are problems between any of us we need to deal with them now. Caleb, you needed to see me?"

Zeran glared at Caleb one last time before he returned to his seat and his breakfast making it clear what would happen if he did cause trouble. Caleb swallowed hard and turned his attention Kena. "I was wondering if we could talk someplace alone?"

Kena nodded and made a move to follow him out of the commons, but Sami grabbed her arm. "That is not going to happen."

"Sami, I'm fine. Caleb won't hurt me." When Sami sneered, Kena adjusted her wording. "I mean, Caleb can't hurt me, not anymore, not ever again." The words did nothing to end Sami's resolve. Kena was not going to be alone with Caleb, not now, maybe not ever.

"It's okay Kena," Caleb jumped in before anyone interpreted this as trouble. One look at Sami and he knew she was never going to let Kena be alone with him, not that he blamed her. "Sami deserves to hear what I have to say, it will just save me some time finding her later."

Kena nodded, and this time Sami let her follow Caleb out following closely behind. "Is there someplace we can go where we won't be disturbed or over heard?" Caleb asked. If he was going to open his heart and soul he didn't want to be interrupted in the middle of it or have it be the new subject of the gossips.

Kena nodded. "I know a place, north of here about an hour's flight no one else knows about it. Will that work?"

Caleb nodded, changed and waited for Kena to take the lead, followed closely by Sami.

Eagle Bennett

Kena landed at the base of the volcano in the clearing she had made near her little shelter. The shelter wasn't big enough for all of them, but they could certainly talk here in the clearing. Sami was the first to speak. "Where are we Kena? How did you find this place?"

"I found it when I was hun… well, let's call it what it was. I found it when I was hiding from…"

"Me," Caleb finished for her.

"Yeah, and Sami and Seth and everyone else. I come here to escape the crush, to be able to relax my shields and to talk to him."

"Him?" Caleb asked.

"Fire, my father, the creator of my ancestor. He, it, helped me accept that I was killing myself and…"

"I get it" Sami said, stopping her, gently laying a hand on her shoulder. "You don't need to say anymore." Sami didn't trust Caleb not to use anything he heard against Kena in the future and she really didn't want Caleb to see how much pain she was still in. It was a window into Kena that Caleb might choose to exploit in the near future.

"I get it too Kena." Caleb added as he sat down on the lush grass. Kena and Sami followed suit, Sami taking Kena's hand in an obvious sign of support. Caleb noticed and realized it hurt that Sami felt Kena needed support to protect her from him. "I'm an idiot."

"No arguments here." Sami scoffed.

"Sami, please." Kena begged, and Sami subsided out of respect for Kena but not without a glare for Caleb.

Caleb easily interpreted the look, and Tam's warning about Sami was loud and clear in his head as a shiver ran down his spine. "No Kena, she has the right. I mean, I've been an idiot. You know it, she knows it, Seth knows it. It seems everyone knows it but me. And no matter how many Changers told me I was being an idiot, I wouldn't hear it. I was sure I was right. I always believed I was right."

"It's the Gryphon in you…"

"Kena, no matter what I do, no matter how badly I treated you, you still supported me. You still defended me. I spent so much energy doing anything I could do to hurt you. I wanted you to suffer, the only time I seemed to be happy was when I knew you were hurting, whether I caused it or not. I reveled in the fact that you were in pain. Then I would feel guilty that I felt that way and I'd blame you for that too. Ancients help anyone who had the courage and caring to stand with you. They became my targets too, and I made excuses. Blamed my blood, blamed them, but mostly I blamed you Kena. Anything bad in my life, no matter what it was, I blamed you. It didn't matter what you thought on any subject, I made sure to stand against you. Even when I agreed with you, I would disagree and rally anyone who would listen to my side. I tried to turn everyone away from you. I didn't stop to think about any of it. I didn't stop to think about the why, the why didn't matter, not to me, not then. It does now. It took Seth actually threatening to kill me and meaning it to make me realize maybe it wasn't you that had the problem, maybe it was me. After a long conversation with Tam, then Marta and spending most of the night soul searching, I finally got it." Caleb paused for just a moment to look into Kena's eyes. For just a moment he saw what Sami had always seen, the beauty and depth. "I was blaming you, but not for something you did, for something I failed to do. You saved Seth. You killed Coler and his brothers. I was supposed to do those things, not you. I loved you for what you did and I hated you for what you did. The only reason I'm alive, the only reason my brother is alive, is because of you. It all just grew from there and I never let myself realize what I was doing or that I was wrong. So I'm an idiot, and I'm so sorry. Kena please believe me, I am sorry. I'm not saying I will never disagree with you but it will be because I actually disagree and not because I just want to be disagreeable. I'm not saying I won't still be inconsiderate and say things that hurt you, but I promise it will be because I'm dense, not vengeful. I can't change the past, but I am going to try to make it up to you, both of you, and Seth. Starting with you two have my full support. I am truly happy for both of you. Everyone needs a partner to love and lean on. You both deserve to be happy and finding happiness together just makes it that much sweeter."

Kena couldn't stop the tears. She knew in the way only an empath could that Caleb meant everything he said. "Thank you, Caleb. I do forgive you."

"Wait, there's one more thing I have to tell you before you forgive me. I was so certain you were wrong that you were just being a coward. I wanted so badly to hurt you, that I did something really stupid."

"I know, I figured it out right away. You, and I'm guessing Dalis and maybe Frandin, since it would take a concerted effort by more than just one mind speaker, antagonized the traveling clan leader into attacking us. Am I right?" Sami gasped, Kena had never gotten around to telling her and unlike Seth she had no mind reading or speaking ability to hear the thought.

"Yes, but to be clear, I talked them into it. They were against it, but I convinced them. They believed me. They thought it was the right course of action. They did the wrong thing for the right reason. I did it to hurt you. I thought I was forcing your hand, but I think now I was just trying to cause you as much pain as possible."

"It doesn't matter Caleb. No one can know what you three did, no matter why you did it. Caleb you started a war, Changers are going to die. All of us may die. Knowing it was you that started it and not the pests could, probably would, be our downfall. Caleb, what I said in the council meeting is still all true. I need you to plan this war. I don't know strategy and tactics it's not part of my nature, it is yours. I need the Changers to follow you. So please never tell anyone about this for the sake of all the Changers."

Caleb nodded his understanding. It was essential if they were to survive they must be united. Once again he had failed to see past his petty wants to the consequences. He failed to see the big picture. "I may be able to be your martial leader, Kena, but I'm very bad at the big picture."

Sami had heard enough. "No, but if you will actually listen to her, Kena is. Caleb, you can apologize all you want and Kena may forgive you, but those are just words. I'll be waiting for you to prove it. One more thing Caleb, you ever hurt her again, Seth will be the least of your worries. You'll never see the knife that slits your throat."

Caleb nodded, "I won't. If I do I deserve it, but I won't. You're right Sami, this is all just words, but words are all I can give you right now. My future actions will be the real proof." He gave Kena one last look trying to express one last time how sorry he was, changed and took to his wings, leaving Kena and Sami alone.

"You forgave him too easily in my opinion, if you want my opinion." Sami replied trying to get her anger under control.

"Of course I want your opinion. I have always wanted your opinion. I was always listening I just failed to make it clear I was hearing. I might not agree, but I will always listen." Kena pulled Sami into an embrace. "Sami, Caleb isn't the only one who needs to apologize. You have been my best friend. You have always supported me, protected me, been there for me and I looked past you. I took you for granted. Part of me always knew you would be there so I didn't put any real work into the relationship and relationships take work. I can't believe how lucky I was that you persisted. That you didn't just decide to give up and move on. I wanted you to know it wasn't because I didn't love you. It was because I didn't think it was safe for me to love anyone. Caleb wasn't the only one fighting his blood and his past life."

"It doesn't matter Kena, let's make a deal with each other. Let's agree to forget about past mistakes. You aren't the only one who made them. Ancients know I made my share. We can regret the past all we want, but that doesn't change anything and certainly doesn't help the future. Let's just decide to enjoy the present and let the past stay in the past, no more regrets, no more apologies for the past."

"And if I lose control?" Kena asked still fighting that fear.

"Well, then we burn, but at least we will burn together."

Kena wisely answered her the only way she could letting their love burn through them.

Sami tossed Kena her shirt, "I'm guessing we should be getting back. I need to check in with my seconds and we need to see if you can find me some targets to go get."

"Yeah we do, but I need you to meet someone first. It's important and it won't take but a second, I promise. Do you trust me?"

"With my life, you know I do."

Kena turned and where she looked a small fire sprang merrily to life. Kena approached it and as she did it grew and took the form of a Phoenix in full flame. "Thank you for coming, Father."

I told you I would answer your call anywhere anytime. I am always available to you daughter.

Eagle Bennett

Sami forced her natural fear of fire down. Kena would never put her in danger she knew that, but her head wasn't exactly listening to her heart right now.

Kena placed her hand on the shoulder of the fire bird. "Sami, this is my father, the creator of the first Phoenix. Father, this is my beloved, Sami." Sami couldn't move her eyes were locked on the flames.

Approach little Tiskin, you have nothing to fear from me. You love her little Tiskin, you have always loved her. It was your love that saved her and for that I am eternally grateful. Your love for her burns in you white hot like the hottest fire. Your courage is shadowed only by your loyalty. You are special little Tiskin, special enough for her. You would gladly burn to protect her. So this I give you little Tiskin, as long as the love burns in you, you will not. No flame can harm you. No fire can burn you. Safety in the midst of the inferno is yours, as it is for her. Love brought you together and together in love you will always be safe.

It felt like a hot poker had skewered her but as fast as it came the pain disappeared and she was filled with a loving warmth, a presence deadly yet protective. Before she realized what was happening the fire Kena had started was gone, but not the fire she now had burning in her. Somewhere meant only for her ears she heard the voice of fire, *Call on me if you or she should ever need my help. As I answer her so I to now answer you, little Tiskin, beloved of my only daughter.* Sami let out a breath she only just realized she was holding trying to understand all she had just heard. "Wow, and I thought my father was special." Kena hugged her and the warmth in her heart spread through her entire body.

Eagle Bennett
Chapter 28 Laments

Caleb winged in over and past the village. A quick mind check with Frandin and he knew he was still not needed so he had time to find Seth and he knew right where he would be. As he approached the cavern, the little magics that protected it sensed him and opened the top. He dove through and heard the rock closing behind him. He knew Seth would be here. Someday Seth would take over guardianship of the mural cavern and he spent most of his time here with Tam learning how to feed the magics that kept the cavern safe and working. The magics that kept the cavern hidden from non-Changers was allowed to drain, but the magical protections and the magics that ran the roof still needed to be fed and maintained and only the guardian knew exactly how this was all accomplished.

Caleb easily spotted the two dragons huddled with the murals of the Phoenix, Dragon and Tiskin. Oh, this was going to be fun he thought to himself as he landed and changed. He was finding he could more easily control the Gryphon side of himself if he was Caleb. His anger and frustration with Kena started long before he learned to change, but changing, tapping in to that side of him, had certainly intensified it. As he walked over toward the group Seth craned his long neck around to see who approached. Seth's expressions as the Dragon were often comical, but this morning there was no joy in the glare he leveled at his brother, and Caleb shrunk back wondering if he was about to be fire blasted. Caleb halted far enough away so as not to hear what was being discussed. If they were discussing Sami and Kena, he didn't want any knowledge of it.

Tam noticed Caleb just as Seth pointed him out. "Ah, Caleb, we were just discussing ideas for the searchers. We are not sure how well targeting is going to work and until Kena arrives we won't be able to try. So we are trying to think of some other ideas to find those who share our blood. The Tiskins can certainly feel the draw, but only when they are near a target. The problem seems to be getting them near enough to the target to feel the call without wasting time on wandering all over. It seems only Kena has the ability to feel the call from so far away and none of us have yet to figure out how she is doing it or how dangerous doing it is going to be."

"I'm sure Kena and Sami will be along shortly. They just needed a little time to themselves after our talk. I am sorry to disturb, you but I was wondering if we could talk alone for a moment Seth?"

Seth was shocked by the conciliatory tone of Caleb's words. *Close your mouth and open your mind grandson. If Kena can change so too can Caleb, give him a chance to prove it.* Seth cast an eye at the Dragon mural before he changed and walked toward his brother. "I can spare you a moment Caleb. Let's go into the council area, it's empty and quiet."

"I have spent most of the morning apologizing to Kena and Sami and now I come to you to beg for forgiveness. I've been an idiot Seth. I've been terrible to you and horrid to Kena and Sami. Everything you said was true. Kena has forgiven me and I hope you will too."

"Has Sami forgiven you?" Seth scoffed despite his grandfather's advice fresh in his mind.

Caleb completely understood his brother's attitude and skepticism, "She's sort of in a circling pattern. I think she's willing to, but she's waiting to see if I hold to my word."

"Smart of her." Seth growled

"Look Seth, I promise, I am going to change. I want to rebuild my relationship with my family and that includes you. All I'm asking for is a chance to prove it."

Seth was surprised by the sincerity behind the words. "I think you should add me to Sami's circling pattern. I'm willing to give you a chance, but Caleb if you ever hurt either one of them again I won't hesitate to follow through with my threat."

"Yeah, good luck beating Sami to it, you might have to settle for fire blasting my dead body." Caleb said in all seriousness.

As many questions as Sami had for Kena about what just happened, she had no choice but to wait, asking questions while on the wing without mind speaking just wasn't possible. They also had to meet up with Seth and Tam, trying to focus their gifts in an effort to locate more changers still living in among the pests. Sami understood why Kena was so insistent on finding the lost. When this war started they needed all the help they could get, even if they didn't want to join they should be aware of who and what they were.

Kena landed first and didn't change so Sami followed her lead. Kena hopped skipped over to Tam and Seth using her wings to balance, Sami followed a few steps behind. Her gifts would be of no help she was strictly here in an observing role. *You're here for another reason Sami,* Tam imparted to her, *for this to work Kena is going to have to lower most if not all the layers of her shields. It is dangerous for her. She will need someone to anchor her to this here and this now.* Sami pushed down the fear, it was the last thing Kena needed right now.

"Sorry we're late, there were a few things we needed to take care of this morning and they took longer than I expected." Kena told the Dragons and murals as they approached. "So how does this work?"

It was Tam that answered her, "You, Kena, will lower your shields, carefully, then you will reach out with you gift searching for the call of common blood. You know the feel well enough to know what you're looking for. Seth will be hitchhiking on your gift with his. When you find a target he will read their minds looking for any information he can read and relay that to me. Sami is here to anchor you. Sami, your part is easy. Just concentrate on how much you love Kena. Kena's gift connects only with feelings, the stronger the better this time. She will need to be able to feel your love through all the noise of other feelings."

Kena nodded. It seemed so simple but she knew it wasn't. "Truth Tam, Sami is here as the only person who has a chance to keep me sane when my shields are down and I get assailed by everyone in the worlds' emotions. You're hoping her love will be able to weed through the din to me to bring me back from what is sure insanity and prevent me from burning us all in a torrent of fire."

"I think that's what I said only with fewer words and less pessimism. It is very dangerous, are you sure you want to do this? We can find another way, we don't even know how effective this is going be."

"A few days ago, there is no way I would try it, but I know no matter how many emotions weigh me down I will be able to find the fire of Sami's love, so let's just get this done."

"Then make yourself comfortable. Sami stay close to Kena, physical contact will help. Seth, are you ready?"

Seth nodded and Kena settled on the warm sand. Sami sat down next to her wrapping her tail around Kena's claws. Kena reached into herself finding the thick layered box that was her shield. She had lowered no more than a few layers or opened a small door since she learned how to put her shield in place and feed it energy through the fire of her emotions. She was hoping she would be able to leave at least some layers in place, but she was prepared to dismantle the whole thing if she needed to. As soon as she lowered the first few layers she felt a few stray feelings from those around her. It wasn't bad yet, all Changers learned to shield so there wasn't much to feel here. It wouldn't be until she cast her gift out into the world of the pests that things would get bad. Kena carefully lowered another couple layers and allowed her gift, her essence to fly out over the green fields deep into the word of the pests. Misery, pain, and anguish struck at her from every angle. Life here was horrible. The king seemed to revel in the misery of his people. The more wretched his subjects' lives were, the happier he was. She funneled those feelings away they only got in the way of what she was looking for. Once she felt able she

Eagle Bennett lowered one of the last two layers of her shield. She fought back the clawing of the emotions of those her essence soared over. She was searching for something different, more a need than an emotion. As breathing was to life so was this to need. It was instinctual and not controllable, not even by those who knew it existed. She scoured the land to the west, flying over the terrain in a predictable pattern. Time had no meaning to her now. She had no ability to feel tired or hungry. All she could feel were the emotions of those she flew over. Kena was about ready to concede the final layer of shield to the cause when she felt it, just a twinge. She raced toward that twinge and made sure Seth knew who the target was before she moved on with her pattern.

Sami watched the face of her lover, watching for signs that she was in trouble. Kena appeared as calm as she always did, but Sami didn't relax her vigilance. This could go bad fast. She focused on Kena's eyes. The eyes she had fallen into and in love with now stared blankly into space. Sami forced her mind back on Kena it was essential her thoughts didn't wander right now. Sami hated this, the waiting, the wondering. She knew it had to be done but she didn't have to like it. Sami had actually lost track of how long they had been working when Tam brought her back to the here and now.

"Sami, we have to bring them back now or they will burn through too much energy and not be able to come back. I will bring Seth out, you bring Kena. Just think of her and how much you love her, how much you need her, how devoted you are to her."

Sami did exactly that. It was the easiest thing she had ever been asked to do. It wasn't long before she saw the light return to Kena's eyes and Sami knew she was back in her body, safe. A quick glance at Seth told her he too was back. Sami breathed a sigh of relief, both were safe.

Tam seemed to droop a little with relief, "Sami, take Kena home, feed her and make sure she rests, both physically and emotionally. In the morning, return and I will share with you the targets we have located so your Tiskins know where to look."

Sami nodded, it was too late in the day to send anyone out anyway, and by the way Kena and Seth looked it was more important to take care of them right now. Morning would be soon enough. Sami supported Kena until she had enough strength left to make the short flight to their hut.

As soon as they landed in the new clearing Sami changed, just in time to catch Kena from falling after she changed, "No, none of that love, you don't want to collapse here. There is a nice soft bed just a few steps away to do that in."

Kena leaned on Sami hard for the few steps to the hut and up to the bed where she fell in like the dead. "We can't do this more than every few days if it's going to hit me like this and from what I'm feeling from Seth he isn't any better."

"Do you remember, was it worth it? I mean how many did you find."

"I can't say if Seth found out anything from them, but I found three."

"Just three, is this worth it?"

"I don't know, it might get easier with practice, most things do, but yes, that's three in a relatively small area that we searched." Kena yawned.

"Get some rest Kena, I'm going to find Zeran, fill him in, and check in with Rykle, make sure he doesn't need anything. Are you going to be all right?"

Kena answered with another yawn and a nod already mostly asleep.

Sami leaned down and kissed Kena on the cheek, "I'll bring food back with me. I'll swing by the commons to get it so it's edible. See you in a few hours, get some rest. Sami tore herself away from the bed. She wanted to sit there and watch Kena sleep just to make sure she was okay, but it was a pointless gesture and she had things to do. She changed as soon as she was out the door, springing into the air as soon as she was clear of the trees.

Kena didn't remember falling asleep, but she must have because the next thing she did remember was Sami returning with food and feeling quite rested. Conversation was light during the meal, but Kena knew it was only a matter of time before Sami brought the conversation around to the events of the morning. So when it happened while they were cleaning up Kena was ready with her answer.

"Kena, was that really your father today, I mean, the fire, did it really talk to me?"

Eagle Bennett

"Yeah, fire has always been sentient to me, but it didn't use words to speak just some pictures, but mostly feelings. Emotions can communicate far better than words sometimes. I have always known fire was part of me, like our blood calls to blood, fire always called to me. It feels the same, like white noise only in my heart. My grandmother warned me it could and would seduce me, I had to be stronger than it, force it to be my partner, not my master. When I set the fire to rescue Seth and Caleb, I nearly joined it then. I got lost in it. I longed for its embrace. It scared me. I built stronger shields and I locked the fire out."

"And locked all of us out in the process."

"Not at first, but yes. I was afraid of what would happen if fire ever got loose, if my emotions ever got loose. Sometimes I could feel the fire so close to escaping… It just became easier to hide from what everyone else was feeling like I was hiding from the allure of the fire. I didn't even realize I was doing it. The more Changers that came the more I locked their feelings out and mine in. A few weeks ago I was escaping a particularly nasty run in with Caleb and found the volcano. I couldn't lock the call out. It was fierce, I tried to turn away but I couldn't. It was then he spoke to me. I learned more about what I was and the partnership he had formed with my ancestors. It was he who finished the training my grandmother had been unable to do. It was he who made me aware I was committing a slow suicide. If there is one thing the ancients and the pest had in common it was the need for closeness. Like food and water we have to have it to survive. He helped me to peel away the layer of shields around my own heart, and when he did I found you. He

Eagle Bennett encouraged me to accept what I felt, to quit hiding and to allow myself to love."

"Then I owe him more than I can ever repay."

"Sami, you owe him for more than that. Don't you realize what he did today?" Sami looked confused and shook her head. "He gave you this." Kena grabbed her hand, at the same time she turned her own hand to fire.

Sami jumped expecting pain, but there was no pain. The flame wasn't burning her at all. "Kena, is this what he meant?"

"I can't hurt you. I can love you freely with no fear of my fire hurting you even if I lose control. As long as you love me, fire can't hurt you." Kena confirmed as she let her hand go and extinguished her fire.

Sami looked down at her unharmed hand still lost in the wonder of it. She looked at Kena who was clearly worried about what her reaction would be. Sami smiled at Kena and pulled her into her arms. "Then I will be safe from fire for as long as I breathe."

Kena buried her head in Sami's shoulder not even trying to hide the tears of joy streaming down her face. Her father was right, connecting with others, loving others was the only way to survive in this world.

Chapter 29 Revelations

Caleb watched his forces, proud of what he saw. They were as ready as they could be. The Dokuls had out done themselves. Not only did they have armor that they could fly in to protect them from arrows, but weapons they could use from the sky as well, projectiles that flew straight and true and exploded on impact. The Unicorns had armor as well and had proven to be great ground warriors, working well with the Dokuls who would make up the majority of the ground forces. The Tiskins, masters of hiding, would be spies and assassins. A strike at a commander could end a battle with less bloodshed, and Caleb had been amazed at how good the Tiskins were at that. It wasn't just the army that was ready. Hunters had out done themselves and smoked, salted, and dried meat enough to last a year now filled the storage facility. Silos of corn and grain, even apples and tubers, everything they needed to stay alive for at least a year had been preserved and stored. The Tiskins, with Kena and Seth's help, had brought in over a hundred new Changers, swelling their numbers. When the war came, they were as ready as they could be to defend their home. Caleb had accepted Kena was right about an offensive attack. The king had thousands of highly trained pests at his disposal and even more untrained he could conscript. They had no chance fighting a war on his terms. Their best bet was to defend their home where they knew the territory. He could sense Kena had an ultimate plan but not even a wisp of it was escaping. If Sami knew the plan she was keeping it locked deep behind her shields. A patrol of scouts coming in grabbed his attention.

"Caleb, a small army wearing the king's colors camp near Geroug village in the south."

"Any signs they are here to attack us?"

"No sir, but the force is too large for anything else we have seen."

"We need information, time to see how good our spies really are. Get some food and rest, I'll need you to fly another patrol tonight."

Caleb reached with his mind until he found the mind that was Sami's. *Little sister we may have trouble and I need the special skills of your Tiskins, do you have a moment to meet me?* Caleb listened for her response. She couldn't send an answer he would have to read it from her mind so she kept it simple for him, *Yes, where? When?* Caleb thought for just a moment, the cavern would be bad he didn't want the murals involved. *Kena's volcano as soon as you can get there, bring Kena if you can.* He sent to her mind. He signaled his seconds, "We've done enough for today call them in. Get some food and rest." They acknowledged him and, as Caleb launched himself into the sky, he heard the horns calling for a halt. As he flew he mind called to Frandin and Dalis. *We may have trouble, can you two call in all the scouts and hunters and see about getting a council meeting set for the morning? I should have more information by then. I'll make sure Kena knows what's going on.* Their answer came quickly. *We'll round everyone up, no problem, let us know if you need anything else.*

Sami beat him to the volcano clearing, not really a surprise since she was a much faster flier than him, and she had brought Kena with her. He landed next to them and changed. His relationship with the two of them over the last year had certainly improved. He and Kena proved to be a potent team when he worked with her instead of against her. Oh, he still said stupid inconsiderate things, but now one of them would clock him in the head, usually Sami who seemed to get a perverse pleasure out of it. Even preparing for war the three of them and Seth had managed to find time to have some fun and grow as friends. The fact was other than the looming threat of war this had been the best year of his life. His relationship with Marta had even improved and he didn't think that was possible, but once he stopped hating loving became easier. He completely understood Sami's devotion to Kena, he felt the same way about Marta. Well when this war was over they would all be able to pursue a normal life. "I'll get right to it. The scouts found what may be an army mustering. We need more information. I've asked for a council meeting in the morning, I would like to bring more than speculation to the meeting, do you have anyone you can send in?"

Sami thought hard for a second. Most of her Tiskins trained for this were out either on other spying missions or bringing in new changers. "I'll do it. I'm still the best at getting in and getting out."

Caleb expected Kena to argue this was possibly the most dangerous missions the Tiskins had done, but she just nodded at her lover and turned her attention back to him. "They're massing at Geroug village." Caleb finished.

Kena smiled, "Perfect, that's surrounded by heavy woods, it will be easy for me to hide."

"What!? Wait, Kena, we can't take the chance that something could happen to you. You're our leader, we lose you…" Caleb countered concerned.

"And you will lead, I'm just a cog in the machine and I am replaceable. Besides, you know full well I can take care of myself. Pests do burn rather easily." The crooked confident smile she had developed recently accompanied the words. "I may not like to kill but I have and I will again if they make me. So I will be Sami's back up, we need to be in place as quickly as possible, Caleb call Kimball. We need a Unicorn to jump us closer." Kena turned her attention back to Sami, "So how do you want to play this, you're the spy master?"

"There are always dogs and cats hanging around a camp that will be the easiest. I'm betting they know nothing about us, so they won't be looking for us, not that they would see me anyway."

"I agree, but don't assume that. It has been generations since the ancients walked the world, but legends still exist. The pests may know a counter to your gift, after all the Tiskins were hunted to extinction with the rest of the ancients."

"I know, I doubt it, but I know which is why I'm the one going, besides worse comes to worst, you'll give me a convenient fire to jump in."

"Kimball will be here in a moment, he will jump both of you as close as he can safely, and he will stay close so he can jump you back. Kena what do you want me to do while we wait?"

"We need more scouts out. Do you have enough units to have constant flights? We need to know if more units are coming in and from where." Caleb nodded. "We also need to post perimeter guards; Pegasi, Dokuls and Unicorns can take those so you're not spreading the aerial forces too thin. You agree?"

"Yes, I'll assign a mind speaker to each of the ground units as well. I can use some of the newbies, I'm not comfortable with them in the fight just yet, some of them are pretty young and unsure of their changing and gifts."

"Yeah, young like we were when this all started." Kena answered just as Kimball made his appearance.

"So it starts. Well, I for one was sick of waiting. Are you two ready?" Kimball was all business, he didn't even comment on his surroundings.

Kena looked over to Sami who nodded and pulled herself onto Kimball's back and reached a hand down to help Kena. Kena didn't really need the help, but she knew it was more about the contact than the help. Sami was brave, but Kena was an empath and knew how scared she was too. As soon as they were safely settled, Kimball jumped. Jumping with a Unicorn was a unique experience. One second you were one place the next you were someplace else, usually followed by a wave of dizziness and nausea that thankfully passed quickly. Kena slid down off Kimball's back followed quickly by Sami. "The village is just through those trees there. I'll wait here, I need a little more cover than you do Kena. If you need me send me a signal."

"Thanks Kimball, we'll try to come to you, if something happens I'll send up a signal fire."

"I'm hoping I can get the information quickly, if I get into any trouble I know how to signal Kena." She and Kena had been practicing with the second gift fire had granted her and she could now call fire at will.

Certainly not the size and strength of fire Kena could, but enough to signal her if she needed help and possibly one big enough to hide in until help arrived.

"And I will come in, fires blasting. Okay Sami, let's get this done." Kena and Sami changed. Kena took flight heading for a tree to take cover in where she could keep an eye on Sami, Sami bounded off.

Kena kept a close eye on her beloved, she wasn't at all happy with Sami going in alone, but she understood this was something Sami had to do. Besides she couldn't protect Sami from everything any more than Sami could protect her. She had accepted that fact, but she didn't have to like it. Kena knew what to watch for and yet she still lost Sami as she entered the encampment. Kena waited a bit then sprang into the air to find a better vantage point closer to Sami if she needed rescue. Kena had refused to kill since she had done so saving Caleb and Seth, but if she had to, to save Sami, she would annihilate the entire encampment. Kena shuddered a little at that thought, but she knew beyond a shadow of a doubt that she would not hesitate, and thanks to her father she could do just that and Sami would walk out of the fire unharmed. Kena also had no doubt that was exactly what her father had in mind when he gave Sami the gift. She found a good perch and settled in for a long, lonely, worrisome wait.

Sami melted into the brush, when she exited it she looked like a village cat. A lucky catch of a mouse made the look complete, no one would even look twice at her. She wormed her way around several of the tents, looking for one that was different or a command tent of some kind. She dropped the mouse, she just couldn't take the taste anymore. She licked a paw trying to get the awful taste out of her mouth. She sensed rather than saw Kena settle onto a perch within easy striking distance. Well, that was kind of a relief.

Sami made one last quick lick then she was off stalking again. She needed to find someone in charge so she could follow and eavesdrop on what this army was here for. Everyone she saw wore the same uniform. She needed someone in a finer uniform. She circled around the camp some more making her way slowly into the center. All of the pests around her were too busy doing things to talk to each other. Sometimes gossip among the pests was more informative than anything else. If worse came to worst she could wait until the meal, everyone talked over meals. Sami kept meandering through camp making sure her movements had no discernible pattern. Kena was sure the pests would have studied the old legends so they would know what the changers were capable of. Sami wasn't sure she agreed, the pest leadership was overconfident, not likely to doubt their superiority, but she would take precautions anyway. After what seemed like hours, but was probably more like minutes of pacing through camp Sami finally found what she was looking for, the command tent.

There was no way to sneak inside, but Sami didn't need to, not with Tiskin hearing. She found a nice spot in the sun, after all, cats liked a nap in the sun. She pressed her body up against the canvas of the tent and listened.

"Have the scouts returned?"

"Yes General, but as ordered they did not go north."

"No reason to alert the freaks to our presence. We still have several days before the entirety of the army with Prince Malcal and Prince Adan arrives. We are to hold until then. Did they see anything?"

"No sir, nothing unusual. Are we sure the stories are true? They do seem pretty farfetched. I mean these beasts of legends still being alive."

"No Lieutenant, we are not sure, and the king doesn't care. Anyone, anything, that builds an army is guilty of treason and they are to be arrested or exterminated and I prefer exterminated."

"Yes Sir."

"I want the scouts out everyday no excuses. We need to map the area, when the battle begins I want to be the one picking the ground we fight on."

Sami had heard enough, she stood stretched and with tail swishing paced her way as quickly out of the camp as she safely could.

Kena watched looking for any signs of Sami. It was with huge relief she saw the gray striped cat she knew was Sami heading out of camp. Sami made one quick glance up at her and Kena knew exactly what she wanted. Kena took to her wings and within moments was back to the clearing where Kimball was waiting. She changed as she landed. "Kimball Sami's on her way back. We will want to jump as soon as she's here."

Kimball motioned with his horn, "Well get on then already. I'm sure ready to be out of here."

Just then Sami broke through the cover, covering ground fast. She didn't bother to change just launched herself at Kena. Kena caught her and Kimball jumped before she was completely settled. "Good jump Kimball, I think I was followed, but I'm not sure. I could have just been paranoid." Sami hopped off and Kena followed suit.

"Well I hope you got some information to make it worthwhile." Kimball said as he changed. I'm for a good meal a hot bath, and some quiet time with my wife and I suggest you two do the same. This might be the last quiet night we get for a good long while. I will see you both at the council meeting in the morning."

Kena and Sami thanked him before they took to their wings, headed for the serenity of their little hut.

"I'm for a quick bath to wash the smell of pests off me. If you want, I will throw some food together after."

Kena smiled this last year had been beyond any happiness she deserved. "Sounds fine, since you know if I cook it won't be edible."

Sami laughed, it wasn't entirely true, Kena was an okay cook but she hated it so much she would rather starve. Sami stripped as she made her way to the back of the hut and the bath. As soon as the water had filled to a level Sami was happy with, she called to Kena. Cold baths were a thing of the past, an advantage of having a Phoenix for a girlfriend. Sami watched as the water

Eagle Bennett
burst into flames and burned merrily on for a few minutes then extinguished. She crawled in with a sigh of relief. She would love to lounge about for a bit in the hot water, but she was hungry and she had some other ideas of how she wanted to spend her evening. She reached for the sponge and soap only to encounter Kena's hand already on it. Surprise turned quickly to pleasure as she submitted to Kena's gentle ministrations.

Chapter 30 War

Sami's news to the council did not come as a surprise. They had been preparing for this war for a year. Their numbers had swelled as Zeran and his Tiskin searchers had found and sent new Changers back. Their training was rushed but they were ready as well. All that was left was the planning.

Kena waited patiently as the others spoke their piece, surprisingly Caleb remained quiet as well. He had changed so much over the past year. Kena trusted him completely. She caught him looking at her and she opened her mind and shields to him. *We need to end this Kena, I'm about to revert to form don't worry it's just to cut through the arguments so we can actually get something done.* Kena let her thoughts sit in her mind for him to grab, *Warn Sami and Seth too if you haven't already, I would hate to see you become Dragon fodder.* Kena watched Sami out of the corner of her eye for a sign she had gotten the warning. Sami had become very protective of her lately, a problem she was going to have to deal with soon.

Eagle Bennett

"Enough!" Caleb roared. "I've heard enough talk. They are here to destroy us. I will not stand by talking and arguing while they marshal their forces. I say we attack now! I say we fly over there and kill everyone and destroy the village so they can't use it again."

It took everything in Kena not to break her somber expression when Caleb added for her mind only *Ancients, that was fun, sometimes a bad reputation can be handy. Okay Kena I think they might be ready to listen to an actual plan now. I'll keep playing the foil if I need to.*

"Caleb, while I appreciate the sentiment, I'm not sure that is the best course of action. First we need to remain calm. Caleb did your morning scouts see how far away the rest of the army is? How many fighters did they see?" Kena asked a glimmer of an idea starting to form in her mind.

"Four maybe five days, but they won't be fit for battle for at least a few days after that. The scouts counted about five thousand."

"Sami, how many do they have right now do you think?"

Sami managed just barely to keep from smiling when she answered Kena's question since Kena was well aware of the answer. They had compared notes on what they had seen in between this and that and she had helped Kena form the plan she was about to put in play. "I didn't exactly count, I was focused on staying hidden. I would say somewhere about three thousand."

Eagle Bennett

"Thank you Sami that lines up with what I saw. I did have time to count while I watched Sami's back. We need to end this war before the second force gets here, we may be able to defeat that size of army but I would rather not find out. Tameera, a little localized flooding should slow them down." Tameera smiled, her Pegasi could call water at will and this task would be fun. "Don't engage." Kena warned when she saw the smile. The prospect of battle seemed to have boiled everyone's blood. "Sami, where is Zeran right now?"

Sami was ready with the answer, "He was sent to the city of Mulikin."

Kena nodded, "He has back up with him doesn't he?" When Sami nodded Kena continued, "Seth we need to get a message to Zeran. I need him to break off his target and get to the capital. Mulikin is no more than a hard day's flight from Tornion City. His new task is to kill the king and queen."

Kena heard the gasps from around the table, even Caleb seemed shocked. "I'm done living my life under the threat of war. Our whole existence is dictated by war and it always has been. We defeat this army and what happens? They send another and another and we wait and prepare and put our lives on hold while we wait for another attack. The king won't stop until we are gone, as long as he is on the throne we will always be targets. When he is dead we put someone on the throne sympathetic to our cause."

Everyone at the table looked at Qwint who had gone white as what Kena was saying hit him. "Kena? Me, king?"

Eagle Bennett
"Yes. It's the only way to forge a lasting peace with the pests."

Qwint sat quietly for a while, pondering. "Okay Kena. I agree he won't stop until either we are or he is dead, but I have two surviving brothers."

Kena nodded, "Your brothers are leading the reinforcement army, Sami will choose a team of Tiskins with Tigura backup to take care of that problem." Kena looked at Sami, but before Sami could choose to do the job Kena stopped her, "Assign anyone but yourself, we need you here." Sami nodded, but the fire in her eyes told Kena there was a good chance she would hear about it later but she respected her too much to argue in public.

Qwint nodded, "Okay I'll do it, but only until I can get a leadership council elected and a council leader in place."

"Qwint, what you do once you are king will be totally up to you as long as you keep peace." Kena told him. Qwint nodded, accepting what Kena was telling him. He was not a Changer puppet. He would be free to make the right choices for his people without interference from the Changer council. Kena trusted and respected him to do the right thing for both his people.

"Well that just leaves the army at our door step. We could attack them where they camp, but doing so will do damage to a village that we have traded with and has never threatened us in any way. Many of us have friends in that village. I'm all for killing our enemies, but if we kill and destroy innocent pests not only are we no better than king Tornion, but we will turn all the pests against us. We need to convince the army to attack us on a field of our choosing."

It was Caleb who saw where she was going with this plan. "We plant the idea, let them think they're choosing but actually we are."

"Yes, Caleb, I need you and Frandin to scout and find us the kind of battle field that will suit us. Head to head in open ground is their strength. We're ambush fighters. We need someplace that suits us. Caleb once you find the perfect place, start working on convincing their leaders what we want them to believe. Dalis, we'll need you for that since Tiguras plant the clearest picture. Seth, Sami, call in all the Tiskins still searching have them get to a place safe for the unicorns to jump them home we need them. Can anyone think of anything I have forgotten?"

Qwint cleared his throat, "What about us, what can the Dokuls do?"

"Keep training with Kimball and the Unicorns. I'm hoping we can win this with mostly aerial and ambush attacks, but if they get too close we'll need infantry and that's where the Dokuls and Unicorns come in."

Qwint and Kimball shared a look and nodded at Kena, knowing full well if it came down to sword to horn they were in deep trouble.

Kena had one more thing to say before she ended the meeting. "This is war. We knew it was coming, we've known it was coming for a long time and we are ready.

Eagle Bennett
Everyone keep in contact with Seth. Caleb, if it's okay, I would like to come with you and Frandin today."

Frandin nodded as Caleb answered, "Of course, I just need to assign the patrols first. I'll meet you at the river ford in, say, two hours?"

Caleb did a quick circle around the river ford. Frandin was searching southwest he and Kena would be searching southeast. Kena had not arrived yet, so he had some time to think. It always scared him a little when she went into fix it mode. She had this incredible ability to just know what to do and get everyone to do it. She may claim she didn't know tactics, but he would beg to differ. Her ideas were spot on this time too. She never seemed to be wrong.

"Oh, I'm wrong more than you think, just ask Sami. She'll be happy to fill you in. I mean did you see the daggers she was shooting at me during the meeting." Kena laughingly told him as she landed next to him.

"Adding mind reading to your gifts?"

"No thank you! I have enough problems with the empathy. No, I read your feelings, not hard to figure out what you were thinking from those. We need to get this done. The sooner done, the sooner we get this war over."

Caleb nodded and they both took to their wings.

Kena let a thought she needed Caleb to hear hang in her mind *You know this is going to come to face to face battle eventually. There is really no way to avoid it.*

Caleb thought about that carefully before he answered. *I know, and not to sound like my old self, but I don't think it's going to be as bad as everyone seems to think.*

Caleb war means death, there is no way around that. I want to make sure you don't let your confidence affect your planning. This isn't a traveling clan full of cowed women and children, this is a trained and well armed fighting force that outnumbers us six to one and the odds get worse if we can't slow or stop the reinforcements. All our planning and tactics are going to do is even the playing field a little, it is still going to be bloody and hard and Changers are going to die. Kena needed Caleb to know the cold hard facts. His certainty of an easy victory could cause problems when the worst happened and Kena unquestionably knew the worst was going to happen.

Caleb considered Kena's words, but it was a little more than he wanted to think about right this moment. Right now he just wanted to finish this mission and get back to Marta and Caleb had little doubt he was not who Kena wanted to be with right now either. *I'll keep that in mind Kena I promise, but let's get back to the mission at hand. As much as I might like flying around with you all night, it is not what I had in mind for my evening. You know, there probably isn't going to be a perfect location just sitting there waiting for us.*

Kena knew there would be no perfect location they would have to make one. They had to find an open area with a heavily wooded area surrounding it. That described a great many places in this area. Geroug was really the last village close to the valley and it was an hour's flight straight south, several hours on the ground away.

Eagle Bennett

We may need to create the perfect location Kena. Caleb sent to her mind echoing her thought.

I know but the less work the better. I can clear brush and the like quickly enough but clearing large swaths of trees would require a fire bigger than I can safely control.

That's why you don't just burn the army isn't it?

Yes. I control the fire by sheer power of emotion. I don't have the power to control the size of fire it would take to destroy the king's army. Perhaps if there were more Phoenix, but then again that may be exactly why there aren't more of us.

Kena if you control your gift of fire with emotions, what happens if you ever lose control?

Caleb's mind exploded with images of burning pain and death. He could almost feel the heat of the flames. For the first time he realized what he almost caused when he pushed Kena.

It's why I locked my feelings away. Pray to the ancients Caleb that it never happens, but if it does for the sake of all we hold dear kill me before it happens.

Chapter 31 Consequences

Kena circled the Changer village, all was ready. The general of the army had unwittingly fallen right into their plan. He had moved his army right where the Changers wanted them. Caleb had taken advantage of the armies march to pick off as many fighters as they could with moderate success. Kena was making sure the Dokuls and Unicorns were ready. They represented the entirety of the Changer infantry. The battle plan was simple the Tiskins and Tiguras had been harassing the army all night, exploding out of the cover of the trees, killing, and retreating back to the trees only to emerge in a different spot moments later. The damage they were doing was negligible, but it was keeping the army on the alert and getting no rest. At dawn the first of the aerial attacks began. Patrols of twenty Gryphons and Gryphels flew over, dropping exploding projectiles, but the army adapted quickly and the attacks were doing little damage. It was time to escalate the fight. Kena circled once more, assuring herself everyone was ready. Senna was leading the Dokuls, not Qwint. The second part of their plan required Qwint and they couldn't take the chance he would be hurt or killed in the coming battle. He would stay and lead those staying behind to defend the village. If the kings army made it to the village the war was lost and Qwint dying really wouldn't matter. Kena spotted Qwint and, back winging hard, she landed right next to him.

"I still hate this plan Kena, if Zeran fails..."

"If Zeran fails then we are all lost." Kena interrupted him, "but he was the best choice."

Qwint rounded on her, "That's not really true, Sami was the best choice. Her gift is the strongest. "

Qwint wasn't the first Changer to make the veiled accusation since they had decided to send in an assassin to kill the king and she had little doubt he wouldn't be the last. "Sami does have the strongest gift of hiding and invisibility, but the gift is only part of the equation.

Sami doesn't have the skill to kill Zeran does. He is our most gifted assassin."

Qwint recoiled from Kena, "You're right, I'm sorry, I just hate the waiting and worrying, it makes me edgy."

"I know. Remember, if the worst happens you can always retreat into the mural cavern. Tam and Seth have renewed the magic, only Changers can see it again."

"I know, we already moved the children and enough adults to care and defend them into the cavern. I'm guessing it's nearly time. Be careful Kena, I will see you when this day is done."

Kena nodded and returned to the air to wait for Caleb's call. She didn't have long to wait. *It's time.* Rang in her head and she dove for Kimball and Senna calling so all knew to be prepared. Kena hardly checked her momentum as she hit the ground next to Kimball extended her wing so she was touching him and felt the black of jumping encircle her.

A split second later Kena opened her eyes on the rear of the Kings army, the Dokuls howling a challenge as they charged. Pegasi swooped in from the right and left flanks and Gryphons, Gryphels, and Tiguras hit the army head on. Tiskins, led by Sami swarmed from the underbrush. Kena took to her wings she was useless in head to head battle but she could do some damage from the air.

Kena flew low chancing arrows and hated what she saw. Death was everywhere on both sides. Senna had fallen in the initial charge, Kimball just after trying to protect her. The Pegasi armor was not as effective against swords as it was against arrows and they rode right into a slaughter. All the Changers were taking heavy losses, but not nearly as heavy as the army. Bodies piled up where the dropped, killed by claw, talon and teeth. Kena burned all she saw, Changers and pests, ashes together. She had to continually add layers to her shields to keep from going insane and losing control with all the pain. If it wasn't for Sami she may just have let her control go and ended this all right here.

By nightfall both armies had fallen back to lick their wounds. Kena was the last to return to the relative protection of the village. She had stayed burning bodies until she couldn't anymore. As soon as the village was in sight she shed a few layers of shield to locate Sami. She hadn't seen Sami during the battle. She knew she was fine, because even through her shields she always felt the burning of Sami's love in her heart. It had been that burning that had helped her endure this day.

Kena quickly located Sami perched on the tallest building watching for her. As soon as Sami saw the unmistakable form of Kena in the air she quickly took to her own wings joining her in the air. As much as she wanted to take Kena back to their hidden safe little hut they were needed here. Jointly they landed at the commons and changed. Sami put a restraining hand on Kena preventing her from entering the building. "Wait Kena you need to know…"

"I do know. Senna, Kimball, Mintell, Serge, Anacidin, Partia… too many more to name. I sent them to ash today."

"Marta too."

Kena gasped. She hadn't realized, she hadn't seen her body. "Oh ancients, Caleb?"

"Not surprisingly, taking it hard. He won't talk to anyone, sends anyone who approaches him away, sometimes violently. I think he needs us more than they do." Sami told her indicating the Changers in the commons.

"I'll go, but you need to see to the Tiskins, I know how many we lost today. They will need to see you."

Tears sprang to Sami's eyes as she thought about her friends she would see no more. She felt love, comfort and understanding encircle her heart just as Kena encircled her in a loving hug. She had to stop, she would grieve for her friends after the war, right now more pressing matters took precedence. "The way he is Kena, I don't think you being alone with Caleb is a good idea."

"He won't hurt me, he can't hurt me."

"Not physically, but…"

Kena grabbed Sami's hand and placed it on her heart. "As long as I have you, as long as your love burns in my heart, no one can hurt me again. Please, go be with the others, they need to see you, to grieve with you, just let me know when Seth hears from Zeran when the job is done."

Sami nodded tears in her eyes, "I will always love you," Sami kissed her reinforcing her statement and

Eagle Bennett
left to do what she could for grieving hearts including her own.

Kena concentrated, looking for Caleb. His pain hit her like a load of bricks and she knew right where to find him.

Chapter 32 Mortality

Caleb was sitting alone at the top of the waterfall, staring at the fire, lost in his thoughts when Kena approached him. She could feel his pain calling out even through her shields and she needed to try to help. "Caleb, may I join you?" Kena asked sitting beside him by the fire.

"I'm not fit company for anyone tonight. " Caleb nearly sobbed, biting back tears.

"You shouldn't be alone right now Caleb."

"Dear Kena, always there for me, even after what I put you through. I don't deserve a friend like you. I don't deserve friends at all."

"You're right of course, but you're stuck with me and them none the less. "

Caleb knew he could scare the others away, but not Kena. She, of all the Changers, would understand his pain. She was right, he shouldn't be alone right now. He could feel the anger simmering in his blood. All he could think about was vengeance. He pulled himself back away from the thought and addressed what was really bothering him. "Kena I'm not sure I can come out the other side of this. I loved Marta so much and her death, all the deaths, they're all my fault. I started this. I brought this all on us."

"Well I can't argue with you, you did precipitate this war, but Caleb you know full well this war was coming. Did you bring it on us earlier than we may have wanted, yes. On the other hand if you hadn't we may not have gotten ready for it until it was too late. We wouldn't have been preparing and looking for trouble the way we needed to. If they had taken us by surprise we would all be dead. Caleb there is no fault here. I wish I could take away your pain, I know what you are feeling. I can't make it go away, but I can share it with you if you will let me."

Caleb broke into tears, collapsing into Kena's arms, "I just don't think I can survive without her. I don't think I want to survive without her. It should have been me not her!"

Kena could do nothing but hold him. She understood his feelings all too well. How could she tell him he could and would come out the other side of this when she knew she had no intentions of living without Sami? She had to try though. She loved him too much not to try. "Time, Caleb. That's all I can tell you. Nothing will make the pain go away, but in time and distance it will ease and you will be able to remember the good times and your love without the heart wrenching pain. Marta will always be part of you. She will always hold a special part of your heart.

"Do we have time? I have to be fit to fight tomorrow, to lead more Changers into battle and to their deaths." Caleb looked into Kena's eyes to find them filled with compassion but also a hardness he had never seen before. "Just deal with all the loved ones we have lost after we win the war right?"

"Unfortunately, yes. Caleb I'm sorry. That is war, that is what happens, loved ones die. I have burned so many bodies today that I'm numb." Kena knew her words were not comforting, but they were necessary. She stroked his hair, streaked with mud and blood. "I know that seems callous and unfeeling."

"I do understand Kena, I may not have before. I was so sure we could just, I don't know, overwhelm them with our size and gifts. I didn't think they would be able to hurt us let alone kill us." Caleb stopped he knew going down that path again wasn't a good idea. "Kena you should be with Sami. Hold her, tell her how much you love her, because, trust me, you might not get another chance and you don't want to live with that regret."

Kena could have said I tried to tell you, she could have pointed out the pests exterminated their ancestors, wasn't that proof enough. Caleb knew all this. He didn't need to hear it again. "Right now, right this minute, I want to be with my brother who needs a shoulder to cry on and someone to hold him and remind him he is loved and cared for. Caleb I can't make the pain go away. I can't bring back all the Changers that have died, I can't bring back Marta. I would if I could. I can promise you Caleb one way or another we end this war tomorrow. Zeran is in place, tonight he will assassinate the king. We attack in the morning, either our plan will work or they will annihilate us. Either way it will be over. "

Caleb sighed, not sure which outcome he wanted right now. Zeran could very well be on a suicide mission and everyone including Zeran knew it. So many friends and loved ones gone, not just Marta. Kimball was dead along with better than half of his Unicorns, nearly a third of the Tiguras. The Gryphons and Gryphels that once numbered nearly two hundred were now down to a third that number. Sami's Tiskins had been decimated they made the easiest targets and the Pegasi were down to just a few survivors. Three quarters of the Changers living in the valley when this started were now gone to ash. "One final push. one final fight. If we fail we are doomed." Caleb didn't even realize he had spoken that out loud until Kena answered him.

"Except we are not going to lose brother, I won't let that happen. I will do what needs to be done." Kena didn't tell him what she was willing to do, but after all the bodies she burned today she would if she had to fire the entire army and deal with the resulting uncontrollable inferno after they were dead.

Caleb allowed himself to be reassured. He wanted this war over more than he ever wanted anything in his life, more than he wanted freedom as a slave, more than he had
wanted Marta to love him, more than he wanted this war to start. He had been so stupid so self assured and self involved. Kena had tried to warn him. He deserved his fate, he deserved the pain. He didn't deserve Kena, but he couldn't seem to push her away. Besides he didn't think he could. He tried to push her away from the moment they met and she was still here, still by his side. She still loved him. She had forgiven him for all the pain. Sami and Seth, they still had reservations, but

not Kena. He had always seen Kena's kindness and compassion as weakness, but now he knew it wasn't weakness but strength. It was because of her compassion that she was the leader she was. The leader they needed to survive the war. He also knew that he lacked the internal fortitude to ever do all that Kena had done and would do. He felt the warmth of her love and knew she was projecting, helping him cope. He knew she shouldn't waste her energy on him. She was going to need all she could get in the morning if they were going to pull off her plan, but he couldn't seem to ask her to stop. All he could do was lie in her arms and cry.

Kena didn't remember falling asleep but the sun was just starting to rise as she opened her eyes and the fire was nothing but ash and coals. At some point while she slept Sami had joined her and Caleb and was now curled around her back warming her with body heat and the fire that was her love. She lay still not wanting to disturb either of them, there were a few more minutes before they would be needed. She studied the dying coals of the fire lost for just a moment in its glow. *Fear not daughter I am with you today as I am with you every day. I will come when you ask.* Kena sent thanks back. It helped to know he was with her. She sighed and shifted just a little. Sami jumped awake as Kena moved and that woke Caleb.

"Sorry, didn't mean to wake you." Sami apologized as Caleb and Kena rose, stretching limbs and loosening sore muscles. "I came to tell you Seth heard from Zeran, the deed is done, the king and queen are dead. The capital is in chaos. I didn't want to wake you when I found you asleep and it wasn't like there was anything either of you were needed for until morning." Sami finished.

"Zeran, Tillin, and Brax, are they okay?" Caleb asked hoping for some little bit of good news.

"Yes, they used the chaos to escape the city and Rayon jumped them back. I was able to meet with the three of them before I found you." Sami told him with a smile.

"Good, with all our losses we need them." Kena placed a comforting hand on Caleb's shoulder. "It's time. Are you ready? We could do this without you if you want."

Caleb rose and dusted himself off. "No you can't, both of my seconds are dead and I haven't had time to promote someone else. I'm not even sure there is anyone left I could promote. I need to finish this. I'm ready. I'll have your back up where it's needed when you need it. Today it ends, today we have peace one way or another. However this ends, whatever the outcome, I want, no need, you both to know how much I love you and appreciate everything."

Sami hugged him and whispered in his ear, "If I don't survive this promise me you will take care of her."

Caleb nodded, he would gladly make that promise, but he knew in his heart if Sami died Kena would follow her into death. Sami was Kena's world, the one thing she could not live without, her anchor on reality. Caleb released Sami with a kiss to the check, hugged Kena, gave her a nod and a smile, changed and leapt into the air. He had to get his forces ready for the final push.

Sami kissed Kena soundly then hugged her so hard it took Kena's breath away. "Be careful, don't make too much of a target of yourself."

"You too, I need you to come back to me."

Sami nodded, "Always beloved," and following Caleb's lead changed and sprang into the air, winging hard to rejoin what was left of her Tiskins.

Kena watched her for a moment and sent a quiet plea to her ancestors to keep her safe before changing and joining the rest in the air. She had to meet Qwint. He had the hardest job to do today, and it was her job to protect him. She was pleased to see he was right where he was supposed to be surrounded by his body guards of Dokuls. Kena landed next to him, but didn't change. She had more power in her Phoenix form, better able to protect him with. "Are you ready Qwint?"

"As ready as I'll ever be. I heard it's done, my parents, the king and queen, are dead?" Kena nodded and Qwint went on fighting back his tears, "Well then let's hope this works, I owe Senna this much."

Tameera appeared with the last of her Pegasi just then landing without a word. She had taken every loss to heart and Kena knew if she survived she would bear scars physically and mentally for the rest of her life. Qwint reached up to rub her neck. "Thank you Tameera."

Tameera nodded in response as Qwint mounted followed by his body guards. "Let's make an impressive entrance don't you think Kena?"

"I think I can arrange that, your highness." Kena replied as she sprang into the air letting her fire consume her completely as soon as she was flying clear. Tameera and her Pegasi followed as closely as they safely could with the heat coming off Kena.

As soon as she was in sight of the kings army, Kena dove. Arrows flew at her but they passed harmlessly through her flames coming out the other side nothing more than ash. Kena let sparks drop from her wing tips and tail feathers. It was an impressive display followed closely by Qwint and the rest.

Kena dove towards the general in charge. "We seek a truce. Will you meet with us to talk terms?"

The general nodded. He had little choice, his forces once numbered in the thousands now numbered in the hundreds. His reinforcements were stuck in the mud with no leadership surviving and he had just learned the king had joined his sons in death. There was no reason to continue the fight. "Order our forces to stand down. We will talk terms."
He watched as the beasts landed in a place exactly center between his lines and theirs. When this had all started his forces far outnumbered the enemy. It should have been a quick and easy victory. His army was disciplined and well trained. They should not be here now talking terms they should be burning the last of the beasts' bodies. He hated surrender but he had no choice. His army was demolished, their numbers nearly equal to the beasts now. They had no chance of winning, continuing to fight would simply mean all their deaths. They would have to make peace with the beasts. He would have gladly courted death if the king still lived, his fear of him far greater than dying, but a messenger had brought the news not an hour past that the king was dead, the queen with him. Their throats slit by an assassin that got in and back out without any

of the kings highly trained guards even seeing who the perpetrator was. The general growled, he just couldn't shake the feeling that the beasts had been holding back for some reason. The assassination of the king proved that. He waited for the signal horns to cease then nodded at his lieutenants indicating they should follow him. He rode forward to where the beasts stood. His horse balked and would have bucked but he administered a hard spur to its side. He glared at the flame beast, the fire bird. His horse was afraid of fire, he wasn't. "Dim your flame, or the horses will bolt."

"Then you will dismount from your beast before you approach. My body guard will not lower her defenses."

The general glared again, this time at the mounted dog like thing next to the fire bird. It was a ploy to make him look weak. The beast stayed mounted on its winged steed looking superior while he stood on the ground. He considered turning around, riding back and ordering the attack. He looked back over his shoulder at his bedraggled army and thought better of it. They had him at a disadvantage and they knew it. He dismounted, but waved his lieutenants to stay mounted. He paced forward the last bit of distance between himself and the beasts.

Qwint watched the general carefully, and Tameera listened. *He knows the king is dead. He also knows he is defeated. Now would be a good time for Kena's little demonstration.* Qwint nodded at Kena, it was purely for show Tameera was communicating the same things to both of them.

Kena stepped forward and let her fire burn brighter if not hotter. It was all show as was the bluff they were

about to tell. She concentrated on a large empty area and large showy red orange flames appeared blanketing the entire area in front of the enemy army.
"You are finished General, we can fry the rest of your army while we walk among the flame completely unhurt." The bluff was more than just that. If their ploy worked and they ended this war here and now Kena wanted the rumors of the Changers to be greatly exaggerated.

It was Sami's turn to add to the bluff. She stalked out into the open. She was making herself look larger and colored much like a white Tigura with beautiful gray ghost stripes. Kena forced her concentration back to the fire and the general and off her love. Sami leaped into the flames her white fur remained clearly visible. She stayed in the flames for a moment before exiting. She had wanted to exit on the army side of the flames, but Kena nixed that. When she was in the flames she was safe, Kena could prevent anyone or anything from getting to her, but once she was outside the flame her protection ceased and she was way too big of a target. She continued her stalking until she stood at Kena's side, close enough that the fire should be burning her fur and sat wrapping her tail around Kena, its tip continuing to twitch as she leveled a steely gaze at the general.

The general growled, he had been right they had more weapons. "Why have you not used this weapon of yours before?" He snarled at the dog-man.

Tameera bobbed her head up and down much like a real horse sick of standing for too long when in actuality it was a sign for Caleb to bring in the next bluff. *He*

Eagle Bennett
believes you have been holding back and you just confirmed it. Caleb's forces will cement that belief.

Qwint waited to answer him, watching him bristle at the perceived slight, until he saw the shadows of Caleb's forces in the sky. They were a carefully selected mix of Gryphons, Gryphels, and Tiguras. Their job was simple implant the thoughts and pictures of the army burning and writhing in pain. They had to make it as believable as possible. The army had to feel like they were on fire. "We didn't use this weapon because not everyone over there deserves to die a horrible, painful death." It was a complete bluff. The reason Kena hadn't burned the entire army was simple. She didn't have that kind of power. She could certainly start the fire and yes, it probably would have destroyed the army, but there was no way she could control that size of fire. It would not only burn through the king's army but her army as well. Chances were it would burn through the valley making it unlivable for a long stretch of time, a chance no one was willing to take. The general however didn't know that and when Caleb and his force reinforced what the general already thought, the effect was impressive and horrifying.

The general grabbed his head, then looked at his hands. He was on fire, he saw it, he felt it, but he was perfectly fine. Judging by the screams of those behind him they had a similar experience. "Enough with your threats and your tricks! If we are to talk terms, let us talk terms."

This was what Qwint had been waiting for. He had the general completely off balance and the remaining pest army too scared to move. "Your army is defeated, continue to fight and we will kill you all. The terms are simple; the complete surrender of your army. They will drop all weapons where they stand, turn and leave this valley never to return. Intrusion into this valley will be punishable by death."

Tameera bobbed her head, *He is thinking a retreat is a good idea, he can make peace now, take over the country with the king and royal line dead and raise up another army. Maybe buy off a few Changers to fight with him. Doesn't know us very well, does he?*

Qwint motioned to Kena and the wall of flame dropped, "Your king and his sons are dead. The queen and all of her daughters are dead. Only one member of the royal line still lives and that is me." With that Qwint changed and still mounted on Tameera he was clearly visible to all. Qwint raised his voice to be heard by as many as possible, "You will acknowledge me, Prince Qwint, youngest son of king Tornion as your new ruler."

"I will never…" The general yelled only to be cut short by the knife in his throat. He made one short gurgling noise before he dropped to the ground unable to make a sound as he bled to death.

Qwint's arm snapped forward flinging his knife with perfect accuracy into the general's throat. "Then I pronounce you traitor and I sentence you to immediate death." Qwint looked at his lieutenants, "Do you accept the terms?"

They were all too quick to drop from their horses immediately to their knees. "All Hail king Qwint." the army responded in kind.

Eagle Bennett

Kena circled the retreating army. So far the retreat had been orderly and without incident, but Kena knew their luck may not hold. Not all of the army was happy with the retreat and she was sure someone was going to make trouble. Kena was trying to spot Sami and the Tiskins. They were down there somewhere supervising the retreat. Kena hated that Sami was in amongst the enemy. She wouldn't be able to relax until all of the Changers, but especial Sami, were out of danger. Clashing metal brought Kena up short. What she was afraid of was happening, a skirmish was breaking out between a small group of Unicorns and horse archers. Kena dove at the fighters just as Sami and Rykle interspersed themselves between the two opposing forces. They were supposed to be disarmed, where the arrow came from was unimportant. What was important was that Sami had no chance of avoiding being hit at that range. Sami looked down at the arrow that seemed to grow out of her chest, then dropped like a stone. It had been a perfect hit to the heart, death was nearly instant. Kena screamed into the air as she felt Sami's touch fade away. She hit the ground hard next to her beloved. "No no no no. Sami, no, you can't do this, you can't leave me!" Kena knew it was too late, the red hot touch that was Sami's love was gone, she was gone. "NO!"

Caleb saw what was happening and dropped like a stone from the sky. He heard and felt Kena's anguished cry. He knew Kena had lost control, he knew her shields were failing, as her pain washed over him in waves. He knew what was coming next. The presence of others would make no difference, in her grief Kena was as lost as Sami and now all he could do was save those he could. "Get back if you want to live. Kena has lost control." He dove as close to the melee as he could.   Rykle and the Unicorns responded instantly, the unicorns jumping to safety while Rykle leaped into the air clawing at the sky as he tried to gain distance from the tragedy they all knew was about to happen. The horse archers never had a chance. The only mercy they were granted was their deaths were quick, as flame so hot it scorched the air erupted all around them. Caleb found himself tumbling backward through the burning air before he could stop himself. Gryphons couldn't cry, but his heart wept as he watched the circle of the inferno spread. Part of him considered diving into the flames and joining them in death, until he saw the anguished Rykle and knew his job here was not yet done. With Kena and Sami gone he was needed more than ever. He wouldn't let all that Kena had built die with her. Their losses were extensive but they could and would rebuild. He would see it rebuilt and repopulated and then he would join Marta, Sami and Kena.

Kena didn't care how many pests she killed, she didn't care if the inferno she had just started spread and destroyed the land. Nothing mattered any more Sami was dead. She cried into the fire, begging it to consume her to take her and her beloved together. *No daughter it is not time, your job is not done.*

Kena turned her hurt and anger on her father. *I will not live without her, she was my everything, my reason for living.*

You misunderstand me daughter, it is not time for either of you, fire kills but it also renews, it destroys but it also restores. You are fire daughter. You have destroyed and killed, but you can revive. It is your final gift daughter, my greatest gift to the first and my greatest gift to all who came after her. Like fire, love is eternal the one thing death cannot touch if your love is strong enough. Combine your love with your fire daughter and bring back what matters most to you. Kena looked down at the limp body of her beloved held in her arms the damned arrow gone to ash its mission complete. She knew what fire wanted her to do, but how could it work. *You must believe daughter for it to work. If you have ever trusted me, trust me now, your love for each other is stronger than death. Believe and bring back your beloved.* Kena believed, truly believed. She reached out with her gift extending her love into the fire mixing it and directing it to consume her and Sami. She felt it burn and she welcomed the pain reveled in the searing hurt as her skin burned. She embraced the pain of the fire as far less agony than the grief in her heart. She was sure her final moments were near when she felt the white hot fire that was Sami's love. It was back burning strong in her heart. Her skin was whole and healed, the pain gone like smoke in the wind. Kena felt Sami stir in her arms, and she didn't even try to stop her tears as they dropped from her face turning to steam before they hit the ground. Sami opened her eyes and looked around the fire, "Remind me never to do that again." Kena pulled her tight as time lost all meaning to Kena lost in the fire with her beloved.

Caleb circled the fire. It had burned for hours but it had not spread past the initial circle. If Kena was dead it should be out of control. His only conclusion was even though he could not sense her Kena, for some reason, still lived. They had dumped bucket after bucket of water onto the inferno but they had no effect. Caleb had called a halt whatever was going on with this fire all they could do was wait it out. As long as it burned he would keep vigil, he owed Kena and Sami at least that much. Others had joined his vigil including Seth and Tam who looked like Dragon statues as they watched the flames burn, the reflections dancing in their eyes. Every surviving and uninjured Tiskin that remained grieved at the fire. Sami was a very popular leader. Gryphons, Gryphels, and Tiguras flew honor patrols over the flames just high enough to keep from burning themselves. The quiet of the valley seemed oddly out of place, no one seemed ready to move on. The war was over, the enemy withdrawn past their borders limping back toward the capital lead by Qwint, but it all seemed for naught. They had lost so many friends and loved ones, but losing Kena and Sami seemed to be the final strike. Right now for all the Changers it seemed like all hope was lost when that arrow hit Sami ending her life and Kena's in one quick shot. It was all so needless, all so wrong and Caleb knew, no matter what Kena had told him, it was his fault, he had wanted this war and look what he got. The love of his life and his two best friends were gone to ash. He screeched his grief into the night to be answered by a chorus of grief from the rest of the waiting Changers.

Caleb had no idea how long they had been there but the sun was setting and many of the Changers had given up their vigil and hobbled back to their homes to lick their wounds and mourn their dead. Seth still maintained his watch, even though Tam had returned to the Cavern. The Tiskins also stubbornly refused to leave. Caleb was beginning to think perhaps the fire would burn forever when it started to change. He felt it before he saw it. The heat from the fire was dissipating noticeably. He dove for the ground near his brother, landing just as the fire ended. One minute it burned the next it was nothing more than scorched earth and smoke and standing in the middle of it all was Kena and by the grace of the ancients Sami, weak but alive.

Epilogue

Kena and Sami flew wing tip to wing tip over the scorched earth where thirty two pests lost their lives to Kena's flame. Now that Sami was strong enough to fly Kena needed to see it to make peace with what she had done. She had learned a valuable lesson about hiding her emotions and she would not repeat mistakes of the past. She circled the area twice before she landed, Sami right next to her, both changing.

Sami grabbed Kena's hand, "You were trying to save my life Kena." Kena had told her the story complete, start to finish, and in true Sami nature she had taken her own death completely in stride.

"No Sami, I wasn't. You were gone. I knew you were gone. I didn't care what or who was around me, I wanted me, them, it, everything to burn. I lost all control, my greatest fear."

Sami shook her head, "Kena look at the circle. It didn't spread. You did maintain control. Your power fueled by pain and rage could easily have destroyed everything. You didn't, it didn't. Don't you see, in the worst moment of your life, completely consumed by grief, you did maintain control. If that didn't cause you to lose it, nothing will." Kena didn't even try to stop the tears of joy as they dripped down her face onto the scorched earth. Sami pulled her into her arms. "I love you Kena, I will always love you." It was all that needed to be said.

Eagle Bennett

Caleb waited in the clearing near Kena's volcano. He had been here for hours trying to get a handle on his emotions and thoughts. He knew what he had to do, but it wasn't going to be easy. This had been the only place he had ever felt was home. A shadow passed over right before Sami landed next to him and changed. She looked surprisingly good for someone who was dead just four days ago. He hugged her, grateful she was alive.

"You're going to squeeze the life out of me Caleb!" Sami squeaked just as Kena landed. "How many times do you think Kena can bring me back?"

"Sorry little sister, it's just so good to have you still alive. I have heard the story and I still don't understand it but I don't care. I am just grateful that you and Kena are both here, alive and well."

"Tell me about it," Kena said as she hugged him only a little gentler than he had hugged Sami. "So big brother, why are we here? You could have reassured yourself of Sami's recovery at any time by visiting our hut."

"Yeah sorry about not coming to see you both, I figured you could use the time alone and I just needed a few days to think things out. Now I know what I'm going to do and I want you, my family to know it first. I'm stepping down from the council. I'm not sure what I'm going to do, but I can't be part of the council anymore not after the war, not after my part in starting the war." As far as he knew Kena, Sami, Seth, Frandin, and Dalis were still the only Changers that knew it was his idea to trick the travelers into attacking, but it didn't matter. He knew and that was what counted.

Eagle Bennett

Kena smiled at him, "We know Caleb, you've been broadcasting your feelings to me for days. It wasn't hard to interpret where they were leading. We understand. We are all different people than when this started. None of us can go back to the way things were. The pain is too fresh, the scars too new, the grief too recent. Each of us will have to deal with the scars in our own way, but Sami and I have come to the same conclusion. We are stepping down as well."

"Wait, Kena, you're not just on the council, you're the council leader and the only Phoenix. You can't step down."

"Someone else will step up as council leader. Right now, right this moment I don't have the energy left to lead. I can't deal with any more crises. I just want peace Caleb, no more fighting, no more killing, no more death. I wasted so much time hiding from love. I just want be with Sami. I came so close to losing her, losing us. I don't want to have any more regrets."

"I know, I get that, but who will represent the Phoenix race if you step down?"

"I'm it Caleb. I'm the last. There may never be another one. The Phoenix will go the way of the fairies to live only in memories and legends. Perhaps someday fire will find another worthy to carry the flame, but until then... Once I accepted that I realized there was no need for representation. The council will do fine without me."

Sami put a supportive hand on Kena's shoulder. It still hurt knowing she was probably the last of her kind.

Eagle Bennett
"Rykle is taking over my seat. Tameera is staying with Qwint in Qwint city, with a handful of other Changers so he will have support and protection. Dalis, Frandin, Rykle, Seth and Tam will handle things while each race of Changers elects their representative."

Caleb acknowledged what Sami wasn't saying, "Some of the races didn't have many left to choose from."

"Yes, but they will rebuild and repopulate. Zeran wants to keep searching he's gotten really good at it. We know there are more Changers out there and more being born everyday. He doesn't want to leave them not knowing about their blood and what they are capable of. Some at least will want to come here."

"That's a good idea, maybe that's something I could do? I know I can't stay here. Everywhere I look I see Marta. I know I need time, but I think I also need distance. I need to look at something, anything that doesn't remind me of her and what I've lost."

"Well, since you brought it up," Kena smiled at him, "Sami and I are leaving the valley too. If we stay the new leader, whoever it is, will never truly be seen as the leader. They will always look to me to make the decisions. We all need a fresh start, so we're going to do some traveling and search for other Changers, and, well, we want you to come with us. Seth can call us if we're needed. A Unicorn can jump us from anywhere, but I don't think we'll be needed. We built this place for them, the three of us, but it's time we leave it to the Changers we built it for. It's time for others to do the work, to take on the duty and for us to get some much earned rest and maybe just a little peace. "

"Speaking of Seth, what about him?" Caleb asked part of him all ready aware of the answer.

"He's ready to be on his own. I don't think he will truly come into his own until we are gone. He will make a fine guardian when Tam's time is up. So what do you say, brother? Do the three of us look for new adventures together?" Kena asked.

Caleb nodded, happier than he could think possible after all he had been through.